PRAISE FOR *LOVE LOVE*

"You will love *Love Love*. Like Kevin on the tennis court, Sung J. Woo marries brute force with clever misdirection; brilliant flourishes with measured restraint; craft with strategy. The result is a gem of a novel, by turns poignant, heartbreaking and wickedly funny. The only dangling thread: when's the film adaptation coming out?"

—JON WERTHEIM,
Sports Illustrated executive editor and author of
Strokes of Genius: Federer, Nadal, and the Greatest Match Ever Played

"With antic humor and boundless sympathy, Sung J. Woo gives his broken characters something to reach for. *Love Love* is an ace."

—ED PARK,
author of *Personal Days*

"*Love Love* is sad and funny and full of absolutely brilliant writing."

—STEWART O'NAN,
bestselling author of *West of Sunset* and *The Odds*

"Sung J. Woo's *Love Love* is a wonderful read—funny, tender, touching, and true. This is the novel about tennis, porn, art, and family that the world has been waiting for."

—ALIX OHLIN,
author of *Signs and Wonders and Inside*

"Sung J. Woo has written a surprising, moving novel that powerfully explores notions of family, creativity, skill, and—yes—love."

—LOUISA THOMAS,
staff writer at *Grantland* and author of *Conscience: Two Soldiers, Two Pacifists, One Family—a Test of Will and Faith in World War*

"This tale of unconventional love in unconventional families is funny, knowing, and always surprising. *Love Love* has got it all: tennis, of course, but also organized crime, pornography, a venomous snake, and more twists than a bag of Rold Golds. Give it half a chance and it will charm the terry-cloth headband off you."

—J. ROBERT LENNON,
author of *Familiar* and *See You in Paradise*

"Full of wit, humor and heart, the book succinctly captures the struggle of an immigrant child trying to fit into American society—and in his own dysfunctional family."

—*Chicago Sun-Times*

"A novel that both delights and instructs."

—*Kirkus*, starred review

"There's a certain genius inherent in choosing a strip mall as a 1980s period setting, and Woo makes the most of it, filling the book with the way customers' and neighboring storeowners' lives touch—sometimes only glancingly—on the three Kims' first year in America. . . . Woo has cleverly constructed a central narrative that runs like a Venn diagram through the tour of Peddlers Town."

—*Christian Science Monitor*

LOVE

A NOVEL

SUNG J. WOO

SOFT SKULL PRESS • AN IMPRINT OF COUNTERPOINT • BERKELEY

LIBRARY OF CONGRESS CATALOGING-IN-PUBLICATION DATA
Woo, Sung J.
Love love : a novel / Sung J. Woo.
pages cm
ISBN 978-1-59376-617-7 (alk. paper)
1. Single women—Fiction. 2. Single men—Fiction. 3. Adopted children—
Fiction. 4. Brothers and sisters—Fiction. 5. Koreans—Fiction.
I. Title.
PS3623.O6225L68 2015
813'.6—dc23
2015009333

Jacket design by Jennifer Heuer
Interior design by Neuwirth & Associates

Soft Skull Press
An Imprint of COUNTERPOINT
2560 Ninth Street, Suite 318
Berkeley, CA 94710
www.softskull.com

Printed in the United States of America
Distributed by Publishers Group West

10 9 8 7 6 5 4 3 2 1

for Dawn

"Love is something eternal—the aspect may change, but not the essence."

—Vincent van Gogh

"Love is nothing in tennis, but in life, it's everything."

—Anonymous

PART I

•

A WEEK IN SEPTEMBER

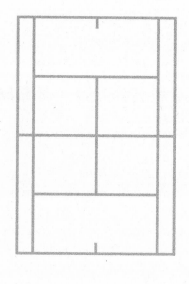

1

The best part about being a temp was what Judy Lee had decided to do an hour ago: leave for lunch and never come back. She counted the number of the daily *Far Side* calendar sheets pinned on the gray wall of her cubicle, twenty-five in all. She rose from her chair and plucked away her favorite, the one where the fat boy with glasses was pushing with all his might to open the door. The joke was that the kid trying to enter the building, Midvale School for the Gifted, wasn't smart enough to follow the sign on the door that read PULL. At some point in her life, she'd owned a shirt with the same cartoon, the silk screen in full color unlike this grayscale image. She'd bought it because she felt sorry for him. She'd done stupid things like that all her life, and she wasn't even a genius, not even close.

At her job, she served this vast corporate machine by comparing the tiny rows of numbers printed on wide white and green computer paper, the kind with holes on the sides, to the even tinier rows of numbers on the Excel spreadsheet glowing on her computer screen. She had to match up the corresponding rows and input the third column on paper into the second column on screen, line after line, page after page. After doing this for a whole day, Judy was sure that her job would qualify as an effective method of torture. By three o'clock, the slight pain behind her eyeballs would swell into a full-blown migraine, as if a gremlin had climbed inside her skull and placed a chisel against her forehead, whacking away with his mallet.

The only thing that would save her at this point would be a cigarette, or at least that's what her nicotine craving whispered to her. For the first week, she was able to stave off her need, but that was all the resistance she had in reserve. Granted, she'd gone cold turkey for only a month, but in a life of few tangible accomplishments, Judy had considered it a major victory.

Her phone rang, the display on the LCD panel flashing extension 3095, Nakamura, R. Which was strange, because Roger had never called her before.

"Hey," she said.

"Hi. Just wondering if you're going out for your noontime smoke."

"Yeah . . . ?"

"I'll meet you there."

Judy slid back her chair too far and bumped into the wall of her cubicle. From the other side, she heard the falling of small plastic objects, the collection of Happy Meal toys that her neighbor Harry had carefully lined up on the edge of his shelf. Luckily, Harry was not at his desk, though she'd have to deal with his muttered curses when he returned. *Screw him*, she thought. *Screw this whole place, I'm outta here.*

The only spot where smoking was allowed was by the loading dock, which offered the lovely view of the back parking lot with its cracked asphalt and a row of Dumpsters against the rusting chain-link fence. It wasn't exactly raining outside, but it was misty and cool, the kind of weather that spoke of summer's end. It was already the first week in September, and as Judy leaned against the damp brick wall and lit up a cigarette, she tried to account for the last nine months of her life. So far, it had been a year of taming her vices—drinking only on the weekends, ramping down to three cigarettes a day, eating no processed sugars like chocolate or candy or anything that actually tasted good. Everyone else she knew was doing productive things like buying bigger houses, raising smart kids, getting promotions. And here she was, a temp at age thirty-eight, with no husband, no house, no job, nothing. She knew she should be concerned, and to some degree she was, but whenever she fully recognized her utter lack of everything, the sheer emptiness of her life filled her up, leaving no room in her heart to even feel scared.

A flock of Canada geese flew by, honking down to her as they crossed the sky. How did they know to get into that V formation? Every time she'd noticed this natural phenomenon she'd asked herself this very question, but not once had she actually taken the initiative to find the answer. Well, damn it, she would. Go to the library this weekend and look it up on Wikipedia. Here at the office, they didn't allow Internet access to drones like her.

Start out small. That's what her mother used to tell her years ago, when she was still around, when Judy was still young enough to believe in her words. Set up small goals, be patient, try again.

The door swung open and Roger walked out. "Couldn't wait, huh?"

"Nope."

She watched Roger flick his lighter six times until she handed hers to him. He raised his lighter against the sky to see the level of the butane in the clear orange plastic. He tossed it into the trash can. "All gone."

She'd lose a lighter way before that would ever happen. Like pens—she'd never once had to stop writing because the ink had run out. She thought about mentioning this to Roger, but she was tired of Roger. She was tired of his vague displays of attraction to her. He was one of these men content to admire from afar, and in the beginning that had been fine. She'd enjoyed the attention he paid her, however disguised or indirect—like complimenting a new haircut when nobody else noticed. But when she realized that Roger would never actually *do* anything, she felt robbed, like he was trying to get something for nothing.

But he had called her today, to make sure she would be here for their smoke break. Roger didn't wear a wedding band, and the only picture on his desk was that of a cat, a Siamese, its little brown and tan face and bright blue eyes in a tiny round frame. He wasn't a bad-looking guy, either, probably in his late thirties like Judy, jet-black hair with a touch of gray on his short sideburns. Not handsome, at least not in a pretty-boy kind of way, but there was something attractive about his lean frame, the way he stood up as straight as a lamppost. When he held his cigarette like a pencil and took a deep drag with his eyes squinted, he looked a bit like an Asian Clint Eastwood. She wondered if he'd practiced this pose, and it made her smile.

"So," he said.

"So." Judy knew he was about to say something, but she was feeling playful, wanting to torture him a little, so she spoke before he could continue. "Why do geese fly in a V?"

"What?"

She happily repeated the question, but her joy at perplexing him was short-lived when she saw how she'd completely flummoxed him. It was a stupid move on her part; she wished she'd kept quiet, but of course she hadn't. "Never mind."

"Oh," he said.

Because she'd started smoking before him, he was only halfway through his cigarette when she was done. Feeling naked without one between her fingers, she tapped the last one out of her box and lit up. "So I'm gone after today."

"I know."

"What do you mean, you know?"

He looked down at his feet. "I overheard you on the phone. Sorry."

She'd called Beverly, her contact at the temp agency, in the morning, grateful that she could leave a message and avoid her bitching. Had she been talking loudly enough for it to be heard? It was possible, and now that she thought back to it, she did remember hearing Roger's voice in the vicinity at the time of her call.

Judy tracked darker clouds rolling in from the east, obscuring the already overcast sky like a heavy curtain slowly being pulled. She took a super-big drag at the end of her cigarette to get right down to the filter. The back of her throat burned, but it was fine. This was good, cathartic pain, what she wanted right now. She held the hot smoke inside her lungs, then exhaled through her nostrils, smelling and tasting every last hint of the burnt tobacco. Judy pushed herself off the wall and poked the butt into the round ashtray of sand on top of the trash can, adding her lipstick-tinted cylinder to the vast arrangement of stumps that stuck up like tombstones. According to the information printed on the back of her empty pack, she'd just experienced the full richness of the finest Turkish tobacco, but what was left in her mouth tasted like old leather. She crushed the box and chucked it into the trash can.

She should've known that this was all Roger wanted, to share a final smoke, the most vague yet in his continuing repertoire of vagueness. The unexpected phone call had given her more hope than she'd thought. When was she going to learn?

"Well," Judy said, "see ya."

Roger flicked his spent cigarette onto the parking lot, the ember diffusing instantly as it struck the wet sheen on the ground. "It was great working with you."

"We never worked together."

Roger nodded, smiled, looked away. "You know what I mean. It was nice seeing you here."

"No," Judy said, "I don't know what you mean." And before he could say anything else, she walked back through the building.

Back in her cube, she closed up shop. There were only two personal items on her desk, a miniature cactus shaped like a doorknob and a framed photograph of her family when she was seven, her brother nine, and her mother in her early thirties, taken out on the deck of their old house. Her father was there, too, though Judy would've liked to have cut him out of the picture altogether with one swift snap of a scissors, but he had placed his hands on the shoulders of his children. Even so, she liked that photo, the sky above them cloudless and forever, the trees in the background lush with blurred green leaves, everything and everyone so alive.

Her phone rang, but this one had no internal identifier.

"Judy?"

All he'd uttered was her name, but she could tell there was something wrong with her brother, Kevin.

"Yeah. You okay?"

"I don't know," he said. His cell phone was cutting out too often for her to make sense of what he was saying.

"You're breaking up," she said. "Is it about Dad?"

"Yes. Kind of. You're at work?"

"I was just leaving."

"For lunch?"

"For good."

A pause on the line. "I thought this was a six-month assignment. You're not just quitting?"

Judy leaned into her chair and sighed. "Don't change the subject, okay? Do you want to tell me what's going on?"

They agreed to meet at her place at half past one. It was almost a two-hour drive from his house in rural northwestern New Jersey, but he said he was on the road anyway and didn't mind.

In their early twenties, they'd lived in Montclair, five minutes away from each other, dropping by, dropping in. Those easy days were gone now. Everything required more distance, more time, more effort. God. Sometimes life just exhausted the hell out of her.

2

Kevin made the mistake of getting to Judy's apartment on time. How could he forget that his sister, at her very best, ran half an hour late? Usually he was smarter than this, but he was a little out of it. The phone call from Dr. Elias had done a job on him.

"Kevin, I'm sorry," he'd said, "but you're not a match."

The blood type couldn't be the problem—Kevin knew he was the universal donor.

"Yes, you're O negative, so that's not the issue," Dr. Elias said. "It's the crossmatching that failed. Simply put, with the current set of drugs available, there's no way we can fool your dad's body into thinking that your kidney is his own. If we drop yours in there, it'll likely fail in a short amount of time."

The silence that followed led Kevin to think there was something else Dr. Elias wanted to mention. At the kidney transplant orientation a week ago, the doctor had told a story of how one potential donor, through the rigorous prescreening tests, was made aware of some deadly disease which would have surely killed him otherwise.

"I thought—I thought you said this was like a routine thing, right? That within family, the matching is guaranteed?"

"Well, usually, but I'm still wondering."

Dr. Elias cleared his throat, and Kevin, who'd been on his feet while talking on the telephone, leaned against the edge of his desk for support. This back corner of the pro shop was the closest thing to an office at the tennis club, where he had a small wooden desk, a matching chair, and the upright racquet stringer. Kevin stared at the machine, its metallic knobs and quick-release clamps, the piano black finish of its star-shaped base.

"Do you remember when we talked about human leukocyte antigens? It was in the tissue-typing portion of the presentation."

"Yes," Kevin said, more out of fear than actual recollection. He flashed back to classrooms, teachers calling on him for answers he didn't know.

Dr. Elias summarized the information for him anyway. Everyone has six unique antigens that are inherited from their parents: three from the father and three from the mother. So if a child is donating a kidney for his parent, there is a guarantee of at least three matches. The ideal donor matched all six, but even a half match wasn't bad.

"So if I'm an O and I matched three with my dad, how come it won't take?"

"Well, that's the thing," Dr. Elias said. "You don't match at all."

"No match?"

"Not one."

"I don't understand."

Then Dr. Elias said the words that Kevin kept hearing in his head on his way over to Judy's: "What it means is that your father is not your biological father."

My father, not my biological, Kevin thought. *I almost failed biology in high school. Maybe if I had done better, this wouldn't have happened. Maybe if . . .*

Dr. Elias asked if he was still on the line.

"I'm here. I'm just . . . okay. All right."

"I'm terribly sorry to be the one to tell you this, Kevin, I really am. Information of this nature should've come from your parents, but I figured you deserved to know."

He'd thanked Dr. Elias and hung up as fast as he could. He was grateful that a boy came in to have his racquet restrung, glad to perform a familiar physical act to bring himself into some sort of equilibrium. Babolat co-poly on the mains, the strings that ran vertically, forty-nine pounds per square inch; Wilson synthetic gut on the crosses at fifty-seven pounds. After he'd strung three more racquets from the backlog, he felt calm enough to dial Judy, and now here he was, waiting at his sister's apartment in Asbury Park, still dazed.

Sitting on the stoop, he watched car after car on her street, tires cutting waves through the heavy rain. He could still remember when this part of Main Street was a simple neighborhood street, no double yellow lines down the middle, kids playing street hockey even around rush hour. It was a sport he'd played himself, though always as the goalie, the solitary sentry. Even in team sports, he always found a way to be alone. Was this a trait passed down to him from his unknown father? It felt as if his life so far had been someone else's.

At two o'clock, Kevin decided he had watched enough of the falling rain. To pass the time, he climbed over the railing to straighten up his sister's patio. Unlike her neighbor's, hers was a mess, so much so that he had a hard time figuring where to start. To gain some room, Kevin picked up little piles of newspapers and magazines off the ground; one issue of *People* dated back a couple years, the cover story featuring two Britney Spearses, one fat, one thin. Once he had them all stacked against the brick wall, he felt more in control, not only of the immediate surroundings but of his own life. So his father was somebody else, and his parents didn't want him to know. It was big, but he could handle it. He'd just ask his dad about it, and his dad would apologize and tell Kevin the real story. Simple as that, no big deal, life goes on.

After sweeping up the floor, he went to work on the green plastic table and the two plastic Adirondack chairs. In the corner next to the rusted charcoal grill, Kevin found a sun-faded box of trash bags, so he plucked one out and filled it up with empty beer bottles, sticky plastic cups, and almost-empty bags of soggy potato chips that were crowding the tabletop. On one chair were more magazines and newspapers while the other supported a Jenga-inspired tower of pizza boxes. The last time Kevin saw a disaster like this was back in college, when he'd shared an apartment with three other guys, though he had to admit, Judy trumped even the combined entropy of three male nineteen-year-olds. When he was through, he had filled two trash bags to the top, barely able to tie the knots to keep the contents from spilling out.

She hadn't bothered to draw her vertical blinds, so he cupped his hands and leaned against the balcony window. Not surprisingly, the chaos wasn't limited to the patio. It was actually worse inside, her clothes lying twisted and crumpled everywhere—on the carpeted floor, off the armchair—a sleeve of a shirt desperately clinging onto the finial of a lamp. By the shapes and locations of her discarded clothing, he could guess the actions that precipitated their final repose. Next to the torch lamp was a pair of shorts she had simply dropped and stepped out of, the two holes for her legs looking back at him with fuzzy brown carpet eyes. Skin-colored pantyhose, peeled away after a tiring day of brain-dead temp work, hung limply off the back of her loveseat. Food-encrusted dishes competed for real estate on her coffee table, and an open pizza box with two slices remaining was balanced on top of the television set.

This is how his sister lived, and Kevin felt sorry for her, which was how he felt whenever he visited. A coverless pillow and a frayed blanket were haphazardly piled and pushed against one corner of the sofa, which meant she was still sleeping on the couch. She started doing that when Brian moved out, but that was more than a year ago. As far as he was concerned, Judy was about six months behind in breaking out of her funk. An ex-husband could no longer be an excuse for her to just let things go like this. He knew this better than anyone; when Alice left their house, the hardest part for him was getting used to sleeping alone, accepting her vacancy as the new normal. He would wake up in the middle of night, his hands scrabbling for her body and finding nothing, like a tongue probing at the hollow of a pulled tooth.

It was now a quarter past two. Kevin sat down in one of the chairs and took in the parking lot of the apartment and the row of tall evergreens blocking the view of the strip mall beyond. Rain fell, the soaking kind that came down all day long, the beat of the raindrops so steady that it faded into the background.

What it means is that your father is not your biological father.

Not a big deal? Who the fuck was he fooling? This was the single most devastating news he'd heard in his life. Not the most difficult— that honor would go to the doctor who announced with sociopathic dispassion that his mother had advanced colon cancer and would at best last a year. How Kevin had wanted to choke him so he'd never be able to speak again.

Kevin had trouble even thinking about his recent unpleasant discovery for any length of time. Every time he recalled Dr. Elias's words, other thoughts pushed them out and took their place, like his mother's death or the state of his sister's living room or the sad dissolution of his own marriage. A time like this was when you most needed the support and guidance of your partner, but Alice was no longer a part of his life. Like Judy's Brian, she, too, would forever be referred to with the *ex* prefix. Both he and his sister became single again within just months of each other—how the hell did something like that happen?

He heard Judy's car before he saw it, the loud whine of the exhaust preceding the squeal of the brakes. There was a hole in her muffler, and although Kevin had referred her to his mechanic, even offered to pay for it, she hadn't done it. By the way the car jerked to a stop, Kevin knew she'd put it into park without stopping fully, a terrible habit he'd railed against for God only knew how long. Judy emerged from the driver's side door and sprinted in his direction without an umbrella, her footsteps splashing up rainwater, like a child running through a puddle.

3

"**A**re you laughing?"

She knew her brother was getting mad, but Judy couldn't help it. The more serious and pissed he got—sitting on one of the two chairs in the dining room, his hands slowly curling into fists—the funnier it seemed. Kevin got up so quickly that the chair almost fell over backward.

"Wait, no," Judy said, walking out of the kitchen. She grabbed his arm and turned him around. He'd played the protective part of the older brother on occasion, but surprises threw him. The grimace he now wore looked identical to the one she saw when he received the letter from USC saying he didn't receive the tennis scholarship he was certain he would get. That was more than twenty years ago, but it was strange how memory worked like that, picking out the scenes from the dusty archives of the brain and making them fresh.

The news he told of his phone call from Dr. Elias was funny, at least to her. Because the first thing that came to her mind was what her dad used to say to her whenever she screwed up:

Why you not like your brother?

The answer now was very simple, and it was fucking hilarious.

Kevin, after listening to her explanation, disagreed. "It's not funny at all," he said, and he sat back down hard, the feet of the chair scraping against the floor. "There's nothing even remotely funny about any of this."

Judy stood behind him and kneaded his tense shoulders until they loosened somewhat. His right was bigger than his left, years of cranking those super-fast tennis serves.

"Are you hungry?" she asked.

"What?"

"I don't know about you, but I'm starving. It's like almost three o'clock, isn't it?"

"I could eat. I guess."

She stepped back into the kitchen and announced she'd make a ham and cheese sandwich, but the contents of her refrigerator refused to comply with her plans. The ham was a month beyond the expiration date, and in the side compartment, all she had was spray cheese in a can. A jar of strawberry jelly sat at the bottommost shelf on the door, its mouth crusted with dried-up goo. She still had half a bag of whole wheat bread in the freezer, she knew that much for sure. Outside of a six-pack of beer and an open can of Beefaroni, there was nothing else edible in there.

Judy handed him a bottle of beer. "How about a nice PBJ instead?"

Kevin shrugged, twisted the bottle open, and chugged down a third of it with one swig. She placed another one on the table for him.

After rooting through her cabinets, Judy found no trace of peanut butter. Brian was the one who'd enjoyed the occasional PBJ, so after he left, she had neither the occasion nor the inclination to buy another.

"No PB, just J," she said.

"Whatever," he said. He was already on his second beer.

Judy pulled the bread out of the freezer and pried apart four frozen slices. If Kevin still had Alice in his life, he probably wouldn't even be here, but this was something, wasn't it? She, his little sister, was the person he wanted to talk to, not his best friend, Bill, and it made her feel good. This was what being family was all about. Maybe all those miserable Thanksgivings and Christmases she'd endured weren't in vain.

At the same time, she felt a little jealous. Nothing would make her happier than to find out that she had no blood relations to her father, but as usual, it was Kevin who was blessed with good fortune. She didn't mean to belittle his crisis here—after all, waking up one day to find out that your parents lied to you about something as significant as this would fuck up anybody, especially at age forty—but still, why couldn't it have been her?

The toaster dinged. She slathered on the gelatinous goop with a steak knife, the smell of preserved strawberries as strong as bubble gum. She brought the sandwiches out to the table and sat down next to him with her own bottle of beer.

"Remember how when we were kids, people used to say I looked like Dad while you looked like Mom?"

"Yeah. I never thought much of it."

"My bet is on Pastor Kim," Judy said.

"What?"

"If we're playing the 'Who's your daddy' game. Mom always had a thing for him."

"Wishful thinking on your part. I think it was you who had a thing for him."

"Every girl has her *Thorn Birds* fantasy."

Kevin bit into the sandwich. The extra jelly squeezed out from one end and plopped onto his dish. To compensate for the lack of peanut butter, she'd put on too much, but her brother didn't notice. "I don't think it was anything like that."

As much as Judy wanted to believe otherwise, he was probably right. Though if there was anybody who deserved to be cheated on, it was her father, who'd had the audacity to carry on an affair while his wife was dying.

"Nothing's changed, you know," Judy said. "You're still you."

"I don't know why they never told me."

"Are you going to ask him?"

He nodded vaguely, then snapped into focus. "You weren't there at the transplant orientation."

"I was busy," she said, trying not to sound defensive, but it still came out that way. She had never considered going in the first place, but she hadn't wanted to argue with Kevin, and she didn't want to argue now. "I called you, didn't I?"

Kevin shook his head. "I don't care about that. I've just been so scatterbrained that I forgot to tell you that I can't give him my kidney."

"You were going to donate your kidney?"

He looked at her as if she were the dumbest person in the world. "How the hell do you think I found out about all this? I was getting tested for compatibility."

"Well, you didn't tell me that."

"I didn't?"

"No."

Kevin put the sandwich down. "Shit, I'm sorry."

"It's all right," she said, and she genuinely felt for him. She might've hated her father, but at least she knew who he was. Maybe she wouldn't be so delighted if she were in her brother's shoes after all.

"So, are you going to get tested?" he asked.

"What do you mean?"

"Well, if I can't give him one of mine," he said, sounding less sure as he continued, "don't you think maybe you could?"

Judy stared at him evenly. "I'd sooner give my kidney to a stranger."

"Judy—"

She stepped into the power of her anger, embraced it, drew strength from it. "I'd carve it out myself and throw it into the river before he ever sees it."

"Come on—"

"He killed her!"

Then silence. She watched her brother's stare. He was having difficulty believing what he'd heard, and Judy wasn't entirely sure just how or when those three words had assembled themselves in the language department of her brain. It was almost as if the thought had come after she'd spoken. She'd always blamed her father for her mother's death, but Judy had never put it so bluntly, and the funny thing was, she hadn't even been thinking about her mother—at least not consciously. Her mother was never very far away, right below the surface of the mind. One little touch was all it took to disturb the illusive calm and reveal the fury that burned beneath.

"Okay," Kevin said. He drained the rest of his second beer and got up. "All right."

Judy sat down and couldn't think of anything to say, so she took a bite out of the sandwich. It was awful. The bread had an aftertaste of old ice cubes, and there was entirely too much jelly, the sweetness overpowering. She swallowed just to get it the hell away from her tongue.

"I'm gonna go," Kevin said.

"Yeah."

As he opened the door and was about to walk through it, he turned and said, "I think he did the best he could."

Wasn't good enough, she said to herself.

And yet something collapsed in her when the door closed and she heard the quiet click of the latch. She ran out to her patio and yelled after her brother, who was walking to his car, soaked by the rain that was now coming down hard. She would've given him her umbrella if she knew where it was.

"I'll! Call! You!"

"Okay!" Kevin yelled back, and she watched him go. *You're still you,* she'd told him. Easy for her to say. She wished she'd told him something smarter. As she watched his red lights fade into the dark afternoon, she heard the phone ringing in the apartment.

"Judy?"

"Yeah?" The voice was familiar but she couldn't place it.

"It's Roger."

"From the office."

"Yeah."

She sat down, sipped her beer, and waited for him to continue.

"Is this a good time to call? I mean you're not in the middle of anything?"

"I'm good," she said.

"The bird in the lead," Roger said in a distant, self-conscious voice that sounded as if he was reading from a textbook, "the one that's at the forward point of the V formation, is working the hardest by being the first to break through the air, which offers resistance to its flight. Just as a boat leaves a V-shaped wake of smoother water behind it, the lead bird leaves a V-shaped wake of smoother air behind it. The lead bird creates a trail of air turbulence that helps lift along the V-shaped direction, so it's easier for the other birds to fly in the wake of the lead bird. If you watch a V-formation carefully, you'll notice that the lead bird does not stay in that position for very long and will drop back into the formation, while another, not-as-tired bird takes the lead, breaking through the air first."

Judy smiled. "Thank you," she said.

"You're welcome."

"How did you get my number?"

"I know the guy at HR."

"You couldn't ask me for it?"

"No," he said, "I guess not."

Judy closed her eyes and bit her lower lip. She was doing it again, saying the wrong things. "That was a joke. I was only kidding."

"I'm beginning to understand that," Roger said, and it made her laugh. "Do you want to have dinner with me sometime?"

They agreed to meet the next evening at Gaetano's, an Italian restaurant in Red Bank they both knew.

After she hung up the phone, Judy finished her beer and opened another.

"Cheers," she said to the room, and she clinked her bottle with the three empty ones on the table, the last one with enough gusto to topple it over. It was Friday night, after all, and tomorrow she had a date. But then she remembered her brother turning around in the middle of her parking lot, his face wet with rain. The box she'd brought back from work was still inside her car, but she didn't need to see the framed photograph to remember it. She and Kevin were holding hands, squinting against the sun as they smiled for the camera, with hope and innocence only youth could justify.

4

Nothing impressed the beginners more than his serve, but like cars and computers and airplanes and anything else that seemed complicated, when broken down to its component parts, the magic was just good, fundamental execution. There was the toss, where Kevin held the fuzzy little ball with his fingertips, raising his arm straight as if he were a statue and letting the ball go at the apex of the lift with a touch of spin. For most amateur players, what they saw at this moment was a yellow, round object hanging momentarily in midair, but for Kevin, who'd tossed up a tennis ball like this since he was eleven years old, the open space above him was as closed and limited as the inside of a closet. When the ball reached the top right corner, he'd draw his feet together, pull his racquet from his arched backside with his thumb on the fifth strip of his grip, and spin and strike the ball on the unpainted hole inside the giant *P* printed on his racquet. During his college years, he would hit the exact same quadrant of squares on the grid of his strings, the joined corners accruing a bright green filigree that he'd happily pick out between points.

Being alone in the club's indoor tennis courts and listening to the hollow, vaguely metallic sound of the ball striking the concrete surface was as soothing as a regular beat of a drum. This was how Kevin started each working day, going over his schedule as he served to emptiness. Balls bounced and struck the canvas fence with a dull thud and rolled to a stop. He thought of the various personalities he'd have to slip into for today. Saturdays were jam-packed, with four one-hour individual sessions taking him to lunch, then the junior camp group from two to six.

Robert Weathers III would be his first, a silver-haired fifty-five-year-old CEO of a small but lucrative drug firm. Robert was a steady client of Kevin's, in here three times a week, and teaching and playing with people like him was what made Kevin feel more like a whore than a tennis instructor. From the first time they met, Robert made his terms clear.

"Kevin," he'd told him, "I'm going to win every time. Do you understand?"

"Sure," Kevin said. After doing this for almost a decade, nothing surprised him. At least Bob the Third was comfortable enough with himself to say what he wanted. Last year, there was a guy who was so angry at losing that he threw his racquet at Kevin, launched at his head like a warhead.

"I'm glad we can do business," Bob the Third said, offering his hand. Kevin took it, feeling the practiced solid squeeze of a veteran handshaker. "I think of this as a positive warm-up to my day."

"Everyone comes here for a different reason," Kevin said. "I'm here to give you the workout you want, Mr. Weathers."

"Call me Robert. And it won't be too terrible, Kevin. You won't have to hold back much, because I'm a very capable player."

This turned out to be the truth. Robert had a pinpoint forehand and a terrific slice backhand, so all Kevin had to do was not run as hard and flub a return here and there, which actually made him feel worse. A part of him wished it wasn't so easy to play this limp role.

After Robert came Hillary Rosenbaum, a dentist's wife who cared more about her tennis outfits than the game itself. She was a horrendous player, barely able to hit the ball back to him, but she didn't care. She was there so she could tell her friends at Sunday brunch that she was taking lessons with a pro.

His third, Roy McDougall, was a twelve-year-old blimp of a kid. His mother came with him and stayed for the duration, badgering her son from the bench. After their first lesson, Kevin had suggested that she perhaps take advantage of the numerous facilities of the club—swimming, aerobics, yoga, anything. She shook her head tightly and quickly, as if she were trying to get bugs out of her hair.

"You see how fat my son is?"

"Well, he's kinda big for his age, but what does—"

"If I'm not here to push him, you think he'll do better?"

Kevin wasn't about to disagree with this woman, but that was exactly what he'd thought.

"Okay," she said, smiling like a slasher-flick villain right before she disemboweled her victim. "Next time, he's all yours."

She disappeared after dropping Roy off for their second lesson. Without his mother, the boy moved like molasses under water. He was a turtle on downers, no matter how much Kevin pushed or even yelled. Unless the balls were hit directly to him, Roy would just let them go by, not even bothering to stretch for the ones that came close. When his mother came back and stayed for the third lesson, Kevin said nothing.

Ball hopper in hand, Kevin walked over to the other side of the court to pick up the sea of yellow balls he'd been serving for the last half hour. His final personal lesson of the day was with Alexa. With her there was no acting, just tennis, though lately it seemed as if her interest in the sport was waning. She'd just started her third year of high school, and instead of asking Kevin about softening her drop shot or putting extra spin on her twist serve as she used to, the topic of conversation between games had turned toward the stupidity of the boys she was dating.

Still, he would take twenty Alexas over his other clients any day. It took her a year, but she now possessed a devastating single-handed backhand that she whipped out like a rapier from its sheath. Contained inside those economic series of muscular movements were tens of thousands of their exchanges on this court, hours of hard work compressed into one perfect swing. Whenever he saw her use it, his chest filled up with a warmth that spread like a shot of whiskey, his pride so strong it almost hurt.

"Hey, Kev!"

Kevin waved to Bill Flanagan, who jogged around the curtained fence and slipped through the flap in the middle of the court.

"You're here kinda early," Bill said.

"You too."

Bill was the club's other head tennis instructor and Kevin's closest friend. They'd known each other since high school, which made it something like twenty-five years. They had gone to the same college on the same scholarship, made the same amount of money, and had both messed up their respective marriages.

Bill, in his yellow and blue jumpsuit, chugged his morning bottle of coconut water. "So how did it go at the doctor's? When are they gonna yank out your kidney?"

He hadn't meant to lie, but that's what came out. "It's being discussed," Kevin said. "No definite dates yet."

They had always been equals, and maybe that's why Kevin didn't tell him the truth, not wanting to be the lesser one. He would come clean later, when he knew more about the situation, when he was ready.

"Hey, how about we do breakfast? I'll buy," Kevin said.

"I gotta get to the court for Janice."

"First-name basis with the mayor of Clinton."

"Let's hope she can make my parking tickets disappear."

Bill finished his bottle and looped it high over Kevin's head at the trash can as if he were shooting a basketball, the bottle rotating on its axis so precisely that it looked as if it wasn't spinning at all. Like Kevin, Bill was also an excellent athlete, and as Kevin watched the empty plastic container swish into the mouth of the metal can, he wondered if they should both be more appreciative of their innate gifts.

Robert showed up promptly at eight, as he always did. He was wearing his usual uniform of a white golf shirt and brightly colored shorts, turquoise blue today. His backhand was erratic, so Kevin stayed mostly to his forehand. For the last ten minutes, he worked on Robert's net game, feeding shots to him from the baseline. The CEO of Weathers Pharmaceuticals happily punched ball after ball onto the blue concrete, making satisfactory grunts following each batted shot. His impeccable silver hair never moved as he pivoted quickly to cover the court, and Kevin watched Robert's face as it made its motions: eyebrows furrowed with anticipation, mouth set firm as he reached with his racquet, gleaming white teeth flashing when the ball caught the line. This was probably what he looked like in the boardroom, too, as he figured out ways to push that new drug out quicker, to put away his competition, to win his corporate game.

Time went quickly, even with Hillary Rosenbaum, who unfortunately decided to go Serena Williams on him with a skin-tight hot pink tube-and-shorts combo that made Kevin wish for temporary blindness. Hillary wasn't overweight, but unless you had the physique of a world-class athlete or a supermodel, wearing something as revealing as this was the wrong way to go. Every time she crouched or leaned, fat gathered in satiny pink rolls.

"How do I look?" she asked.

"Maria Sharapova," Kevin said, "eat your heart out."

But once they got playing, it wasn't too bad, mostly because Kevin suggested that they practice topspin baseline shots, which kept her as far away from him as possible. At the end of their session, he asked her if she felt comfortable in her suit.

"Just perfect," she said as she yanked down on her shorts for maybe the hundredth time, to keep them from riding up the crack of her ass.

Hearing her reply, he thought of Alice, who always wore white cotton panties with little printed flowers except on their last anniversary, when she wore a black silky thong small enough to be an eye patch. She'd also tortured herself with a pair of four-inch heels, not so much walking but tottering to their restaurant, clutching onto his arm for balance. Once they were seated, she squirmed every so often to keep the string of her exotic underwear from digging into her delicate parts.

"Comfy?"

"Oh yeah," she'd said. "Just like the little tag said, *All you feel is naked.*"

"Maybe you should've tried it on for a while, you know, before doing it for real."

Is that what he'd actually said? Did he not even thank her for her self-inflicted agony? Probably not, but it wasn't fair for him to take on all the blame. That was near the end, when nothing went right. No matter what he or Alice tried to do to make their relationship work, it turned into an argument. Goodness, those fights, they'd go on all night, the two of them lying in bed like two dry boards, waiting for something to save them, waiting for the words that neither of them were capable of uttering.

After Roy finished his lesson, Kevin called his father. He was usually up by ten in the morning, so he'd waited until eleven to be on the safe side.

Soo answered the phone on the first ring. "He sleeping."

"Is he okay?"

"Very tired. Hospital yesterday and very tired."

"I'll come by tonight," Kevin said.

"Dinner?"

He didn't want to, but it was already too late. Soo spoke rapidly with the giddiness of a teenager. "Daddy sick, I cook no salt, no pepper, boring. For you I cook! Eat very small lunch!"

He told her he wouldn't eat lunch at all, which was a joke, but she didn't get it. Soo wasn't exactly famous for her smarts, but she was a sweetheart, and Kevin was glad his father had company after his mother's passing. It was true his father and Soo had gotten close during his mother's sickness, but Kevin had learned to forgive. Their relationship was an unfortunate by-product of a husband and his wife's best friend taking care of a woman they both loved, their shared grief turning into something more. Kevin's sister, on the other hand, would always consider it another mark against their father, a weakness he'd given into. Judy's stubbornness was as strong and immovable as their father's, the two of them connected by blood, while Kevin stood on the outer edge of that sanguine circle.

"Kevin?"

He was sitting on the bench where Mrs. McDougall continually taunted her fat boy Roy, and when he looked up, he saw Alexa standing before him, her legs bronzed and her ponytail blond from the sun, her racquet resting on one shoulder, her smile curious.

"Hey," he said.

"Didn't you hear me walk in?"

"Guess not."

She sat down next to him and bounced her racquet face lightly against her knees. Her peachy perfume was as light as summer. "What's going on?"

"Nothing," he said.

The hurt of her expression was unmistakable. "You don't want to tell me?"

"No, it's not that, it's just . . ." He didn't know what to say. Silence divided them like a stranger squeezing into the middle seat.

Alexa looked down at her feet. She wore size 6 ½, sneakers he'd helped her pick out at the pro shop. "We're friends, aren't we, Kevin?"

As he heard her serious words and saw concern in her little face, the real reason he didn't want to tell Bill became as obvious as the calluses on his hands, and it worried him. Like an actor who wanted to keep his material fresh, he wanted his first and most emotional performance to be in front of Alexa.

When he was done recounting his story, she said nothing, just stared at him.

"That's *so* fucked up," she finally said; then anger flared into her voice. "But I mean it's so like parents to do something so stupid, isn't it?"

He agreed with her in mind but not in his heart. He wished he were sixteen again, because news like this deserved the unbridled, irrational rage of adolescence.

"All right," Kevin said, getting up. "Let's smash some balls."

Kevin cranked his forehands down both lines; Alexa returned his shots with bullets of her own. Her crosscourt backhands from the corners were lethal, but Kevin was ready for them, mixing up his returns with heavy topspins and off-speed slices. After half an hour, they were both completely out of breath and laughing. Near the end of their session, they were at the net, trading volleys with robotic rapidity until Alexa nailed him in the stomach. Kevin acted as if it were a gunshot, holding on to his stomach and falling to the surface of the court and lying flat on his back.

"You got me," he said, and he closed his eyes, loving every pump of his beating heart. He felt so completely real—and then a set of lips pressed onto his own, and he didn't care that they weren't a woman's but a girl's. Eyes still closed, he felt her lie on top of him, her body hard and soft, foreign in ways that were both thrilling and intimidating.

It seemed as if neither of them broke the kiss. It ceased on its own, a creature coming to the end of its natural lifespan. He opened his eyes and found her brown ones staring into his. Sweat dripped down from her nose and chin like tears, and Kevin turned away.

"Look at me," she said, and when he didn't, she said it again.

"I can't," he said, eyed clenched shut.

"If you don't, I'm going to cry."

So he looked. Her face was so young, her cheeks rosy and porcelain, her nostrils quivering. He felt like a monster, but then she smiled so genuinely that he momentarily forgot his shame.

Then she leaped up and retrieved her tennis bag and walked to the back door of the court.

"See you tomorrow," she said, but there was uncertainty in her voice.

He sat up. "Okay."

Kevin knew he should get going. His juniors were minutes away from invading four courts, but instead, his fingertips found their way to his lips. He traced the surface of the delicate skin, tried to feel his way to some sort of understanding—and failed. He remembered his first girlfriend, a shy redhead, Shirley, seventh grade. She was the first girl he'd kissed, at a pool party. She'd tasted like chlorinated water. He supposed he did, too. Before Kevin could fall any deeper into reverie, his kids arrived, racquets in hand, stomping toward him like an invading army.

5

By four o'clock, Judy could hardly move. She'd spent the whole day cleaning up her apartment, even dusting the top of the painting that hung on the living room wall, the one that depicted the back of a girl's head as she looked out through the half-open window and into the yard. It was her first effort using egg tempera, the view from her old bedroom, and it wasn't bad, especially the perspective and the use of shadows. At one point, Judy had thought it would be her calling, to be a painter of portraits and landscapes and whatever else. To the right of the painting was the door to her closet, and behind that door, languishing in darkness, was an easel, a palette, and half-squeezed tubes of paint in a wooden rack. All she had to do was get them out, set herself up, and start again. Maybe this weekend she'd do it. Probably not.

The last time the living room looked this nice was probably the week after she and Brian had moved in, three years ago. The last item she'd unwrapped from the last box was the white ceramic vase that had been handed down to her from three generations of her mother's side of the family. When Judy tried to give it back, her mother knew exactly what her daughter had been thinking.

"You won't break it."

"How do you know?"

"Because this has been through two world wars and it'll certainly outlast you."

It was the best housewarming gift she received. She bought a round wooden stand that fit the bottom lip of the vase, and it was Brian's idea to display the ensemble at the top of the entertainment center so they'd always see it whenever they turned on the television. How infinite and generous her life seemed then, to watch her husband delicately set down the vase. It was the beginning of their future together, and she felt as solid as a tank, her happiness indestructible.

The vase was plain and pedestrian, a foot high with a slender flaring neck and a thick globular bottom, something you could probably find at a discount store for twenty bucks. But this particular vase went back a hundred years to a little rustic village in Korea, where it had first sat in the corner of her great-grandmother's room. Later, when Judy's mother went into hospice care, the vase was one of the objects she'd requested, so it was placed on her nightstand, where it would be the last thing she saw before going to sleep and the first thing she saw when she awoke.

"Her husband," her mother had said, "that's your great-grandfather Min Ho, he would place a new sunflower in that vase every morning for his wife."

"That's great," Judy said. She didn't know what else to say to this woman, who no longer resembled her mother but a translucent, skeletal representation of her.

"Like you, Min Ho was a painter, so in wintertime, he painted her a new sunflower every day, every single day."

A month before her death, her mother had told her all sorts of strange stories like this, and Judy couldn't decide whether they were true or spurious effects of heavy painkillers, but in the end it didn't matter. Later she would wish she'd either copied the words down in a notebook or, better yet, recorded them on tape, but she ended up doing neither of those things. When it became inevitable that her mother was actually going to die, the last thing Judy wanted to do was have hard evidence of those days and nights. It was really something to see a person go this way, to watch her life force slowly ebb away, like the gradual dimming of a light bulb until it blinked out altogether. It made you want to take a knife to a beautiful flower and lop its head off, shove it into a garbage disposal and obliterate its existence.

Now, as Judy stared at the vase sitting on the middle shelf of her wall unit, the afternoon sun catching the faint blue glaze, she thought of all the misery this contiguous piece of ceramic had witnessed in its lifetime, all the sadness and hardship and death of her family over two centuries on two continents, the wails and whimpers sliding down its narrow throat and settling down its wide, hungry base. Her eyes moved from the vase to a single index card on the coffee table. On it were three sentences:

I miss you.
I'll always miss you.
Where are you now?

It was in blue ink and it was her handwriting, though Judy didn't remember writing it. She'd found it during her mass cleanup, the note stuck between the pages of an abandoned mystery novel. The piece of paper may have initially acted as a bookmark, but at some point during her reading, its purpose shifted from being a keeper of pages to a beholder of her psyche.

She picked it up and looked at it inches away from her eyes, reading the letters one at a time until they became words. She could have written them for her mother. They could've been for Brian. But Judy knew who these were for.

When the little oval on the pregnancy test stick had shown a pair of pink lines, she immediately opened another one and did it again. As she washed her hands in the bathroom sink, she looked at herself in the medicine cabinet mirror and accepted the inevitability that she'd be alone in whatever decision she would make. She and Brian had been together for just three months, and she couldn't fathom a scenario where this could go well. From the outside, he looked like a solid guy, standing six feet tall with a friendly paunch, but he was fragile inside, both mentally and physically. In his youth he'd spent a summer at a sanitarium for an attempted suicide, and under stress his stomach ulcers bled. Father material he was not, and she was no mother, either, which was why she'd been on the pill for her entire adult life. And yet somehow a statistical miracle occurred, and now she had to deal with it.

He was at work when she rang him, his sales job at Best Buy. Thursdays were his off days, but she'd forgotten he'd swapped with a coworker that week. She didn't want to tell him then, but he knew something was up, and the concern in his voice was unmistakable.

"I'm pregnant," Judy said.

She imagined him at that moment, his slouchy posture frozen in front of the grid of widescreen televisions, all broadcasting the same vivid animated feature, the screens dancing in perfect unison as Brian clutched his tiny phone in his hand. She listened to the background noise of the electronics megastore, beeps and dings interspersing a steady drone of a pop tune with its incessant beats.

"Really?" he said, so quietly that she almost didn't catch it.

"Yes," Judy said. He'd said only one word and said it so mysteriously that all she could do was repeat it. "Really."

"Wait for me," he said, and he hung up.

He rushed over, the underarms of his cobalt-blue polo shirt darkened with sweat. He hugged her. He cried. To Judy's utter astonishment, he got down on one knee and proposed to her, right then and there. He produced a gold ring, passed down from his grandmother, tiny diamonds encrusted in the shape of a heart.

"You know this wasn't supposed to happen, right?" Judy said. "It was an accident."

He closed his eyes and lowered his head, as if in prayer. He was balding early, the crown of his curly brown hair thinned to a delicate fuzz.

"I know," he said. "But an accident can also be a blessing, don't you think?"

She didn't know what to think, and even worse, what to feel. A bead of sweat rolled down from one armpit, chilling her. That was a bad sign, wasn't it? But then here he was, her Brian, staring up at her with such unguarded earnestness. That was a good sign. Right?

She got down on the floor and kissed him.

Judy knew she could count on her mother's and brother's support, and she steeled herself for her father's disapproval, but even here, the worst of it was a backhanded compliment.

"Good," he said. "Baby make you grow up."

For the first time, Judy felt as if there was a plan to her life, and the plan was a new place, a husband, and a child, in that order. She and Brian moved out of their studio apartments into a two-bedroom in Asbury Park. Judy stopped drinking and smoking, and instead of feeling restricted, she felt clarified. Brian's gourd-shaped bong disappeared and out came a pair of running shoes from the closet, and when a managerial position opened up at the store, he wore his freshly dry-cleaned business suit and took the interview. He'd never shown such initiative, such energy, and even more impressive was his positivity when he didn't get the promotion.

"There'll be others," he told her, and maybe the most amazing thing of all was that she believed him. Brian wasn't the only one changing. As the child grew inside her, Judy, too, became a sunnier person, someone she'd always hoped to be.

She took care of herself in a way she never had before, loved herself as she never had before. When she awoke in the morning, her hands traveled down to her belly and felt a warmth emanating from this beautiful secret of a person. Next to her was Brian, mouth ajar and snoring away, her husband-to-be, her mate in this great adventure they were about to undertake. This was her own family, nestled together right here in this bed.

At her twelfth-week checkup, her obstetrician told her in her kindest voice that Judy had suffered a delayed miscarriage.

"I don't understand," Judy said.

The baby was no longer registering a heartbeat. It was dead, and it was still inside her.

There was a scene, one that Judy would not be proud of later, calling the doctor a liar, screaming it, a nurse hurrying in to calm her down. Brian was there fifteen minutes later. Tests showed the baby had been dead for a week, possibly longer. The doctor assured her that death almost always occurred without the mother's knowledge, but Judy knew she'd failed. Any mother worth her salt would've sensed that she was carrying a corpse.

The doctor offered two choices, a surgical procedure called dilation and curettage, or a pill. Swallowing a pill felt too simple, too easy, but Brian convinced her to take the misoprostol to dilate the cervix and force-evacuate the embryo. It was a white tablet like any other, oblong in shape, innocent in the palm of her hand. The doctor drew a glass of water then left the room, and now it was just Judy and Brian.

She lay down on the table sideways, and her tears flowed from her eyes down to the stiff white paper beneath. On the wall was a poster flowcharting the stages of pregnancy, and she ping-ponged between fury and longing as she stared at the final illustration of the mother cradling her baby.

"We'll just try again," Brian said, holding her hands. Then he put on his best fake smile, and she loved him for it. "And again and again and again."

A month later they were married, in a small ceremony by the Jersey shore with a few friends and immediate family. Everyone seemed happy, or at least pretended to be, so Judy did likewise.

She and Brian kept trying, but as her period appeared with clock-like regularity, Judy couldn't shake the feeling that the reason they were attempting to get pregnant again wasn't so much to have a child but to recapture the romantic whirlwind of promises and possibilities.

But they kept at it, and after half a year of striking out, they consulted with a doctor who deemed Brian's sperm plentiful and active and put her on Clomid because, three years shy of forty, Judy was past her peak. She didn't feel like an old woman, but apparently in the world of fertility, she was past her prime.

Their final attempt at pregnancy involved a round of injectable hormone therapy that maxed out their credit cards, which they had to stop when Brian got fired from his job.

"We'll just take a break while we get back on our feet, right?" Judy said, secretly relieved.

"No, we can't give up now," Brian said, more determined than ever, but it turned out to be an empty threat. Three times a week became once a week, and then a month passed where they didn't have sex at all. And then it didn't take long for Brian's running shoes to retreat to the closet and the bong to take their place.

Just when Judy thought their lives were stabilizing, her mother was diagnosed with cancer. Through days and nights of heartache and misery, Brian stood by her side; if he showed any signs of distress, she missed them. They buried her mother in April. When Brian decided to fly out to Seattle to visit his brother in May, Judy thought it was a good thing for him to reconnect with his sibling and recharge his batteries.

He called the next evening to tell her he wasn't coming back.

"It's the coffee, right? Once you go black, you never go back," she joked.

But he wasn't joking.

"I didn't plan this," he said. "But here, away from you, I remember I can be happy. Please, Judy, can you just let me go?"

Let him go? What, had she kept him chained in a dungeon? Once the shock of his words wore off, Judy found herself getting furious. She shouted into the phone for him to act like an adult, to make some goddamn fucking sense, but she stopped when all she heard coming out of the telephone speaker was his crying. It was a terrible, primal noise, an animal with a mortal wound, and she saw him for who he really was, someone more broken than herself. The razor scars on his wrists had almost faded away, but they'd always be there.

"I just can't," he said. "Don't make me, Judy. Please. I just can't, not anymore."

"You asked me to marry you. You could've walked away when . . ."

And now it was her turn to cry. Judy sank into the couch and balled herself and held the phone so tight that she thought she might crush it.

"I waited as long as I could," he said. "It wasn't good for me, but I stayed."

"Until my mother died."

"It was the best I could do."

Judy listened to the hum on the line, the faint mechanical buzz of the vast distance between them.

"Why did we try so hard?" Judy asked.

Brian's answer was heartbreakingly simple. "I think we just wanted to be happy."

He'd begged her to let him go, so she finally did. She hung up the phone.

A week later, his brother came and packed up Brian's clothes and CDs. The hall closet still contained a mountain of his stuff, things she should give away or throw away, but that would require her to open the door and sift through the most painful part of her life. In moments like these, while in remembrance and reflection, Judy could feel the heat of those objects in there as if they were alive—Brian's snowshoes, a his-and-hers set of beach towels, a mixer they received as a wedding gift but never opened—pulsing like a heartbeat, waiting to be freed.

Their marriage had been formed on the foundation of an accident. Was it any wonder that it had failed so spectacularly?

Judy grabbed a pen and wrote the following sentence below the last one.

I don't know where you are, but I am here.

What had come out after she took the abortion pill was a bloody golf ball–sized clump of tissue that plunked into the toilet bowl. She'd suffered through eight hours of cramps before the embryo was expelled. There was so much blood, and floating inside that unfathomable crimson pool was their child who never was and would never be. They hadn't talked about names, but she had picked out one for each gender: Mason and Abigail. She'd save the other name for the next child, because she wanted a boy and a girl—that's what she dreamed in those brighter days.

Judy heaved herself up from the couch, marched herself to the bathroom, and stripped. She stepped into the shower and turned it on, the sudden coldness of the water at first excruciating, then liberating. As the water warmed up, she closed her eyes and lifted her face to the familiar rain. She had two hours to get ready for her date with Roger, two hours to sequester her shadows into a corner and look askance toward the light.

6

There was something wrong with his parents' mailbox, and it wasn't just the white paint that had faded to reveal the underlying gray of the sheet metal. The whole structure was standing askew like the Leaning Tower of Pisa. Later Kevin would need to fix this permanently, but for now, he was able to straighten the post by jamming a few stones into the crevice at its base.

Frankly, he was impressed it had lasted this long, considering the circumstances of the day he and his father had put it in. That morning, they drove to the houses of four of Judy's girlfriends where she could've possibly spent the night, and when she was still nowhere to be found, his dad asked Kevin where he thought she might be. Community Park South came to mind, where she'd watched him take tennis lessons with his first coach, but that was years ago. The fact was, he hadn't a clue of his sister's whereabouts; they lived in the same house, but as a senior and a sophomore at Princeton High, they lead entirely separate lives.

Still, they had no better ideas, so his dad gunned the car down Van Horne entirely too fast, almost twice the speed limit. They parked and walked over to the swimming pool, but it wasn't open yet and the tennis courts were deserted. His father leaned against the chain-link fence, his forehead grinding against the metal.

"*Mi-chin-nyun*," he whispered. Korean curse words, Kevin knew well. His dad had just called his sister a crazy bitch, but those harsh sounds carried more worry than malice.

They left the park and drove down Nassau, passing by the university's gates, a pair of eagles with dispassionate stares perched on stone pillars. They slowed down at Thomas Sweet, the ice cream shop, hoping to see Judy sleeping on the bench or sitting under the outdoor seating under the umbrellas.

His father made a sudden, violent turn onto Harrison and slammed the car to a stop at Ace Hardware.

"Why are we here?" Kevin asked.

"New mailbox," his father said. He commandeered a nearby shopping cart and almost rammed it into another customer exiting the store.

The night before, his father and his sister had argued about the length of her skirt (Kevin also thought it was a little too short), but it was different than their fights before. Having turned sixteen a week ago, there was a new boldness to Judy that had surprised everyone, their father, too. That's why their father was so flustered, because his daughter was no longer someone he could even pretend to control. Still, this was crazy, filling up their cart with a bag of Quikrete, a pre-fabbed post, and a shiny white mailbox. It was the sort of thing that Judy would do. Couldn't his father see how alike they were?

"We should be out looking for her," Kevin said.

His dad thrust his credit card to the cashier. "We look, can't find. Where we look, Kevin? Where?"

"I don't know, the bus stops?"

Laughing without mirth, his father signed the receipt hard enough to run a gash through the paper. "Your sister, riding bus? Funny. Even she don't hate me that much."

There was no arguing with his father when he was like this, and besides, Kevin was tired of being in the middle. Twenty-seven days was what was left of his time here at home, the end of his adolescent prison sentence. Penn State would be his reward for putting up with his family's inanity for all these years, though maybe he wasn't taking Judy's running away seriously enough. Kevin was certain she hadn't done anything too stupid. But a little stupid?

When they returned home, his mother took him aside.

"Just help him put it up, okay? It'll calm him down. I just got a call from Elise's mom."

"We were just there."

"Apparently Elise was hiding Judy in her closet. Her mother is mortified. I'll be back."

By the curb, his father swung the sledgehammer with all his fury, almost knocking out the rotting post with a single swing.

"She was at Elise's," Kevin said.

His father took another mighty chop, and this time, the L-shaped structure flew away and landed on the other side of their driveway with a thud.

"I don't care," he said.

Kevin could see his father was ashamed of what he'd uttered, so Kevin did what he could to make everything go faster. He poured the concrete into the mixing tub and added water, first not enough and then too much, but his father didn't mind. As his mother thought, the physical act of running the shovel with two hands back and forth through the mixture calmed his father. Watching his father's patient strokes, Kevin thought of the ferryman Charon on the River Styx in those myths he'd craved as a child (and still loved in a nostalgic sort of way), guiding the lost souls to their intended destinations.

In retrospect, it'd been a terrible idea to build something so permanent at such an awful time, as if they were raising a monument to commemorate the difficulties between his father and Judy. Almost a quarter of a century had passed since that day, but now, as Kevin stared at the line of rusted screws on the bottom of the mailbox, a row of teeth bleeding red, he wondered if the reason why his father so often got angry at Judy, why he always gave her such a tough time, was because she'd been his blood-born child while Kevin was not. He hated himself for even thinking along such juvenile lines, but he couldn't help what he was feeling.

"Hello!" Soo said at the door, drying her hands on her apron. The smell of tofu soup with red miso and scallion-oyster pancakes swirled around her. Kevin hoped she hadn't gone too far with her cooking endeavors. Even though he enjoyed some Korean cuisine, he found most of it too spicy, but he'd never had the heart to tell Soo.

The second Kevin took off his shoes, she grabbed his arm and pulled him through the foyer. "I cook morning, I cook afternoon, I cook! Fifteen minute, you eat, okay?"

"Okay!" Kevin said.

And with that she was gone. At the threshold of the living room, Kevin leaned against the wall and observed his father. After seven years of peritoneal dialysis, the process had lost its effectiveness. His father felt tired all the time now, spending most of his life on the La-Z-Boy, dozing in front of the television. Because his circulation had gone south, his hands and feet were always cold; even during last month's scorching summer heat, his father wore mittens and furry slippers at home. And lately he had trouble walking, his ankles turning a bruised shade of blue all by themselves, the bottoms of his feet too tender to properly support his weight. Every time Kevin saw his father, he was reminded of the easy frailty of the human body, how it could all fall apart. It wasn't that long ago that he would walk to Trader Joe's two miles away, come back with a shopping bag in each hand.

Even though he was in pain most of the time, his father never complained. He had always been a man of few words, and continuous suffering hadn't changed that. Kevin knew of his father's difficulties only through visual cues, noticing the way he'd favor one leg over the other, or how he'd sit gingerly on the couch, usually meaning his hemorrhoids had flared up again. In the communications department, his father was no different than Snaps, Kevin's German shepherd; they both conveyed their feelings and needs through physical hints and gestures.

His father was sitting in front of the fireplace in his armchair, underneath the gaggle of framed photographs on top of the mantel, his eyes closed. The pictures were organized chronologically from left to right, starting with baby pictures of Kevin and Judy and ending with an eight-by-ten of the family at Christmas three years ago, when everyone had been there, Alice at Kevin's side and Brian at Judy's, their parents in the middle. It'd been taken in this very room, during Judy's photography phase. She'd set up the tripod and clicked on the delayed shutter on the camera and ran back to her position beside Brian, smiling and breathing hard. The whistling sound between her teeth made everyone laugh.

Now both children were alone, and Kevin wondered if his father felt responsible for their failures at couplehood. Probably not, because it wasn't something his father would even think about. He was not someone who dwelled on the past, except now, he was going to have to, because there were questions that needed to be answered.

"Dad?" Kevin asked.

His father's eyelids fluttered. "Hello, son."

Kevin pulled up the matching recliner and sat at the edge of the seat. On the drive over, he'd thought about this very moment, the words he was going to say. He told himself that he needed to keep calm, but now that he sat in front of his father, what he felt more than anything else was sadness for his loss. He still hadn't recovered from losing his mother last year, and now he felt like an orphan.

"I got tested last week," Kevin said. "For compatibility."

His father shook his head. With his mother, who had worked as a translator in Princeton University's East Asian Studies, he'd always been picking up new words, improving his English, but now that he was living with Soo, his vocabulary was sliding backward. Kevin pointed to his kidneys and added a few words of Korean he sort of knew to get his dad to understand, and it was very obvious when he did because the anger in his voice was unmistakable.

"No," he said. "No, why? Why you do that? I say no, you stop."

There was fear behind his words. Maybe that's why he'd been so against Kevin getting tested, for fear of the truth coming out. Kevin turned away to compose himself. The last thing he wanted to do was yell, but that's where this was heading.

"Your kidney, *your* kidney," his father said. "You young, you need two. I am old man. I get old man kidney, dead man kidney."

Kevin had to say it, just blurt it out.

"Who is my real father? *Jin-cha ah-pa?*"

Kevin had looked up the words in his Korean dictionary, to make sure he was being clear. A number of emotions vied for space on his father's face: surprise, dismay, disgrace, rage. But the one that won out in the end was nothing at all.

"Me," his father said. "*Jin-cha.*"

"Dad," he said. "Come on."

"I grow you," he said quietly. "I grow you, I your father."

"Dinner!" Soo said, startling both of the men. "Sorry, sorry. Dinner."

To say Soo had gone all out was an understatement of an understatement. Kevin felt as if he'd stepped into a restaurant; little bowls of colorful Korean hors d'oeuvres (kimchi red, spinach green, fish cake beige) surrounded a trio of main dishes: a serious stack of scallion-oyster pancakes, a heaping pile of beef short ribs, and a still-bubbling red miso tofu soup in a stone bowl.

"Dig in!" Soo said.

Kevin did as he was told, using his chopsticks to pick up a few strips of soy-marinated eggplant, and although he wanted to continue to question his father, the food was a welcome distraction. He didn't think he was hungry, but once he started eating, he couldn't stop.

Everything was so delectable, even stuff he usually didn't care for, like the dried anchovies, which were lightly sautéed in sesame oil and crunchy and salty like tiny slivers of potato chips. With a dab of rice, the combination was heaven.

"*Mah-shee-suh-yo*," he told Soo, a Korean phrase he knew by heart: It's delicious. He'd said it often to his own mother, and she'd reply to his Korean with her own, "*Gahm-sah-hahm-nee-dah*," thank you.

"More, more!" Soo said, spearing the longest short rib with her chopsticks and dropping it on his plate.

Kevin glanced at his father, on the opposite side of the dining table, who sat in front of a kid-size rice bowl. Before he got sick, his father would take enormous, mouth-filling bites, a messy diner who took to piling small stacks of devoured ribs around his plate.

His father said something in Korean to Soo, and a rapid-fire exchange took place. Kevin caught the words *jin-cha ah-pa,* but that was all, and in the end, Soo looked at Kevin with understanding eyes. "*Ah-eeh-goo*," she said, another familiar Korean phrase: Too bad. And there was no surprise whatsoever in her demeanor, meaning she'd already known about this.

Kevin put his chopsticks down.

"I want his name," he said.

His father ignored him.

Kevin slammed his fist against the table, and the little dishes rattled like discordant chimes. Soo drew in her breath.

"Sorry," he told her. "I'm sorry." But he wasn't, the harshness in his voice betraying his words. Even when Alice left, there had been no screaming, just quiet melancholy. In his youth, Kevin had a terrible temper and would gladly display it, especially on the tennis court, carrying three racquets with him to every match because there was a good chance that he would break at least one against the hard court. He would eventually learn to control his anger and channel it to his game, but this was no game.

Soo uttered another few words in Korean, and now it was his father's turn to slam his fist down on the table. But Soo, expecting this one, wasn't fazed, and she rose.

"*Ahn-juh!*" his father yelled, commanding her to sit, but she was already gone.

For a moment their eyes met, and Kevin realized anger was more than just an emotion. It was also an unfortunate heirloom, a darkness passed down from parent to child, and Kevin flashed back to those nights when his father returned from his job as a railway mechanic, his fingernails grimed with grease and dirt, walking straight from the front door to the den without a word to anyone. He drank his scotch in that room, alone, not enough to brand him an obvious alcoholic but enough to methodically destroy his health. In Korea, he'd been a train engineer, driving a thirty-car freight that ran seven daily round trips between Seoul and Incheon, until two people stepped onto the tracks of his train.

His mother hadn't wanted to tell Kevin, but eventually she did, when he was old enough. His father had yanked on his horn and flashed his lights, over and over again, but the figures did not move. The impact wouldn't even be felt by him, no different than a bug splattering on the windshield of a car. Mother and daughter. That's what he saw as he drove toward them, the mother wrapped in a black shawl, the child in a red dress, couldn't have been more than three or four years old, barely tall enough to come up to the middle of her mother's thighs.

His fellow engineers told him that these things happened, it was a part of the job, but Kevin's father never recovered. The police told him the woman was insane, her daughter an unfortunate victim. His father had nightmares for months, probably still had them even now.

Soo returned with a manila envelope in one hand and a Korean-to-English dictionary in the other. She held out the envelope for Kevin.

"*Chaang-nyuh*," his father muttered.

Chaang-nyuh? That sounded like it could be a name. Inside was a letter-size piece of paper. It was glossy stock, and at one point it must've been white, but now it was yellowed with age. It was blank on both sides, and as Kevin fingered it, he noticed it was actually two sheets stuck together. At the bottom was a date, 3-14-1973.

"Is that his name? Chaang-nyuh?" Kevin asked as he peeled the sheets away from one another.

Soo shook her head and flipped the Korean dictionary to look for the word so she could show him its meaning.

They were actually three sheets connected to display one long pictorial. The first crease was below her naked breasts, and the second crease was above the shock of black pubic hair. It was a centerfold of an Asian woman.

The black and white pages of the Korean-American dictionary slowly invaded the field of Kevin's vision. Soo's fingers pointed to the entry, a noun, with two possibilities: whore and prostitute.

"*Jin-cha um-ma,*" his father said.

"Okay," Kevin said, though this was not okay. It was not okay that no one told him his father wasn't his father, and it was furthermore not okay that his birth mother was staring back at him without any clothes on.

Soo tapped the back of the centerfold, her finger poking the belly button. Kevin turned it around and recognized his mother's handwriting on a piece of tacked-on white paper. The old brown tape around the note fell away when he touched it.

Dear Kevin,

You're right here, sleeping on my lap, as I write this. It's the night of your dol, *your first birthday. In Korea, rice cakes are devoured, gifts are lavished, and many cups of* soju *are drunk in your honor. None of those things happened today because we're in America, so your father and I held our own small celebration instead. Our neighbor lent us his Polaroid, so years from now, you'll see yourself on this day as I saw you.*

Except a picture cannot tell the entire story. Looking at this centerfold in front of me, all I know is what I see. I don't know who she is, her name, her situation. This woman is your mother, Kevin. I'm sorry that it's not me. It is one of the greatest sorrows of my life.

I'm not able to have children of my own, which I found out about a week before I found out about you. A friend of a friend knew an ER nurse out west, and that's where she saw you. She knew how to make it happen for us. So I got you and brought you home. We were so unhappy, your father and I, and then you came and we were a family and it was as if a thousand anvils had lifted off our chests. We love you so much, every tiny centimeter of you.

Were we being smart about this? Of course not. We could've waited like normal people, gone through the proper channels, but this felt right to us. It felt like destiny, and all it took was a small chunk of our savings. You were worth the risk, Kevin. I'd do it all over again.

This is not an easy

Kevin turned the sheet, but there was nothing more. He showed the letter to his father.

"I don't know." He shrugged. "Your mother do all. I do nothing."

"She says here that she couldn't get pregnant." Kevin again went through gestures until his father understood.

"Doctor wrong and stupid. Judy, Miracle Baby, your mother say."

Kevin placed the letter behind the centerfold, as his mother must have done almost forty years ago before she slipped them into an envelope and sealed it. What had she been feeling at that moment? He wished he knew. He wished she were here, so he could ask.

7

What if he didn't show? What if he'd changed his mind? It wouldn't have been the first time Judy was stood up. It wouldn't have even been the tenth.

Just stay calm, she said to herself. *Just fucking calm down, okay?*

This was the reason why she didn't date anymore, why she'd given up this part of her life. It was hard. It was hard to put on mascara, hard to wear heels that jammed her toes, hard to sit here by herself in this restaurant, to wait for her man.

She took another sip of water. The waiter, lurking at his station in the back of the room, met her eyes and smiled, but when the smile wasn't returned, when the smile, in fact, was answered with venom, the waiter dropped his gaze and slunk away through the flapping double doors of the kitchen.

Great. Can't wait to taste all that spit in my food.

She stared at the only thing she could stare at without repercussion, the mural on the wall adjacent to her table, a scene of what she assumed was some place in Italy. She'd come to Gaetano's many times, but she had never had the occasion to study its mural this closely. The waves of the sea were three shades of blue, and where the color was the lightest, the beige stucco poked through.

This was the way it was, wasn't it? With everything. With everyone. From afar, people and things looked solid, but upon closer examination, faults revealed themselves. A perfect example of this was her own life. From afar, someone might consider her a brave soul who defied society's preconceptions and lived life on her own terms. A person of courage who didn't tie herself down to a meaningless career and was willing to sacrifice financial security for the pursuit of . . . of what, exactly? What was it that she was so passionate about that required her to give up so much?

"Are you doing okay, miss? Anything you need?"

Her mousy waiter had been replaced by a girl in a ponytail with a smile so wide it had to hurt her jaws. Had Judy been waiting so long that the first waiter's shift ended? She glanced at her wrist, but she wasn't wearing her watch. The frayed leather strap was one small yank away from ripping apart, so in an effort to appear as beautiful as possible, she'd dispensed with the need to tell time.

"Yes," Judy told the girl, "I'm doing fine."

"You're waiting for your party to arrive."

No. I just like to come to a restaurant and not eat.

The girl returned a moment later, but not for her. She delivered desserts for the table next to Judy's, tiramisu for the man and a fruit cup in a martini glass for the woman. This couple had ordered their meal at the same time Judy had been seated. She'd promised herself that if Roger did not show by the time they finished their meal, she'd leave.

Unfortunately for her, they took their time with their final course. The man sipped his coffee, the woman stirred her tea, and after eating half of their respective desserts, they switched plates to share in their gastronomical delights. Even though the restaurant was almost full, Judy caught enough of their conversation to know that they were husband and wife and that tonight was their anniversary, but there was something else there, an edge she felt as the man clinked his spoon against the martini glass in an attempt to extract the last piece of fruit.

This was where her imagination was supposed to supplant reality. In her last screenwriting class she took at the community college, her instructor, a man who always seemed as though he was on the verge of saying something important (but never did), stressed the importance of extending the limits of reality into the realm of fiction. He'd told the class that stories existed everywhere, but only portions, just the roots. It was up to the artist to nurture and grow these buds into flowers of creativity.

As exciting as it had sounded, when Judy thought about it later, his advice was no different than the songs crooned by other cut-rate teachers she'd taken over the years—Mary Jane the sculptor who baked oblong vases in her barn, Vladimir the photographer with his fetish for orchids, Yuri the poet who forced everyone to write in rhymes. Even in these sad little classes, there were people more talented than she was, or if not talented, just more driven. It was obvious in the ways they talked, the ways they held themselves, their voices high and strong, making Judy wish she'd stayed home.

Home. That's where she would be going, because the couple was done. The man signed the credit card bill, and they rose, and Judy's evening was thankfully over.

But here was Roger, hurrying toward her, not even letting her have this crumb of satisfaction.

"My car," he said. "It wouldn't start, AAA took forever, and I kept getting your voice mail?"

She'd forgotten that she'd silenced her cell earlier in the day to avoid the wrath of Beverly, the woman at the temp agency who'd been ringing her phone on the hour, as robotic and as inescapable as the Terminator. Judy knew all Beverly wanted to do was let Judy have it, tell her what a fuckup she was for walking away from her job. Scanning the call history, Judy felt stupider than ever.

As soon as Roger sat down, the waitress with the unstoppable smile pounced on him to offer him a drink. "A beer, please," he said, and he asked Judy if she wanted anything.

What she wanted to say was that she'd like to leave, but instead she ordered a martini.

"Have you seen our special drinks menu? Our choco-tinis are really yummy. You also can't go wrong with the key-lime-pie-tini."

Even an hour and a half ago, she would've found this girl tiresome, but now, after the shitstorm of self-doubt and self-hatred she'd endured, Judy tapped into a malignant growth of negative energy, the sort of dark force that would've made Darth Vader proud. She felt herself enlarging, strengthening, ready to tell this goddamn moron of a waitress what she needed to hear.

"Thank you, miss," Roger said. "But I think my lady here will have a regular martini, like she asked."

After the waitress left, Judy grabbed the knife and formed a hot, tight fist around the handle. She saw herself jumping out of her chair and stabbing Roger in the eye with it. She could see it happening, bloody ooze dribbling down his face, the image so violent that she immediately dropped the knife back on the table for the fear that she might actually do it.

"I'm not your lady," Judy said.

"I'm sorry," Roger said, "I didn't mean to call you that; it just came out. But I felt as if you were going to say something you were going to regret."

Judy let out a burst of bitter laughter. Was this some kind of a joke? "You made me wait for almost two hours, and now you're telling *me* how I should behave? Wow, Roger, this is like the best first date ever. You really know how to get to a girl. Now I understand why all you have in your cubicle is that shitty little photo of a cat, because that animal is probably the only thing that can stand you."

As Judy's heart pounded, Roger's very long, very Japanese face revealed nothing. His expression remained as still as a lake of Botox injections, and watching him, Judy realized how different they were. To most people, they looked alike, a pair of Asians sitting down for dinner, but Korea and Japan, the Land of the Morning Calm and the Land of the Rising Sun, were opposites in temperament. Koreans tended to be angrier, brasher people while the Japanese were famous for their infinite composure; it was the difference between red-hot kimchi and serene sushi, hard-hitting *soju* versus the elegant *sake*. Even the *kamikaze*, the Japanese suicide pilots who crashed their planes into enemies, possessed at their very core a steadiness that enabled them to keep their eyes open as they flew into their targets. This was the face Judy was staring into now, a bedrock of solidity, not smiling, not frowning, just being.

The waitress returned with their drinks and asked if they'd made up their minds. Roger surprised her by ordering linguini and clams; after her outburst, she thought for sure their dinner was over. She fumbled through the menu and asked for spinach lasagna. The silence that had descended upon their table continued to spread, and Judy wondered why she didn't just get up and leave. It was what she should do, what mature, grown-up people did in situations like this. Except she couldn't just leave because she'd drank all that water waiting for Roger.

"Excuse me," she said, and she left for the bathroom. She walked past the waiting station and pushed open the door with a silhouette of a Victorian-era woman sitting in front of a vanity, the word *ladies* prominently displayed in cursive underneath the art.

There was no one else in the dimly lit bathroom with its black tiles and stainless steel sinks that sat on top of the counter like woks. Judy hurried to the toilet and hiked up her skirt and rolled down her stockings and pulled down her lacy panties, silently cursing the fate of women who had to go through so much more shit than men to look decent. Even after she was done, she remained sitting in the blackness of everything: the toilet itself, the toilet paper holder, the metal walls of the stall. She wanted to stay longer, but she made herself get up and head over to the sink to wash her hands and touch up her face.

She'd never considered herself pretty even when she was young, but compared to now? Compared to these pouches under her eyes, the crow's feet threatening to become eagle's talons, she'd been beauty-pageant worthy. She reapplied her lipstick; she brushed her hair. As she walked out the door of the bathroom and back to their table, she chose the words she'd say to him: *Thanks for trying, but it'll be best if we go our separate ways.* That sounded good, that sounded calm and adult, except she wouldn't be saying anything because he wasn't in his seat. In fact, it was as if their entire table had been replaced, because where they'd been sitting, the napkins and the utensils were reset to their default setting. She was sure it was their table, but now it wasn't their table because he was gone and she'd be getting her coat. It was a relief, actually. She could now go home, released from the constriction of her clothes, climb into bed, pull the covers over her head, and slip into darkness.

"Over here, Judy," Roger said. He'd sneaked up behind her. He took her hand and led her to the other end of the room, the table next to the fireplace. He sat her down, pushed in her chair, then took a seat himself.

"I asked the waitress if we could start over," he said.

The light from the fire flickered orange, bronzing the right side of his face. For a moment he looked like a statue, never to move again, and Judy froze, too, wanting to be a part of this stable, dependable universe of his.

You could never start over. You could never take back the things that happened or the words you said. But she appreciated his gesture, even if she feared it was foolish.

S he had her martini, then she had another, and two more after that. She wanted to get drunk. Was it because she was happy? Or was it because she was sad? Or was it because she wanted to go home with him, for after four drinks, she had trouble standing up, never mind getting behind the wheel? *Way to go, Judy, way to play hard to get.* Why couldn't she just be like everybody else and have a normal date, one that didn't require a table change because she'd said such awful, mean things to this nice man?

She didn't know. And after finishing her dish of crème brûlée, the creamy sweetness lingering on her tongue, Roger, ever the gentleman, told her he'd drop her off at her house.

"That's very kind of you," she said slowly, trying to keep her words from sliding into one another. "But maybe you should take me to your place."

"Are you sure?" he asked. "I mean, you're . . . I just want to make sure this is what you want."

"I'm what?" she asked playfully. "Drunk? Is that what you wanted to say?"

Roger cleared his throat. "Well, yes, you do seem a little tipsy."

"You think so," she said, then added, "Roger?" On paper, it was a stupid-looking name, making her think of Mr. Rogers and his cardigan, but saying it was a different experience. The first syllable opened up her mouth in full, then it tapered down to a sensuous pout of her lips. *Rah-jur, Rah-jur, Rah-jur!* It was a muscular name, a sexy name.

Maybe she was drunker than she thought.

The check came, and Roger took out two one-hundred-dollar bills. Judy picked one up and stared at Benjamin Franklin, who stared back at her with a hint of a smirk. She remembered reading somewhere that he'd been a bad boy in his time, a player.

She darted a devilish look to Roger. Or at least one she thought— she hoped—was devilish. He laughed, which was good. It was nice that she was still able to make a man laugh.

"You know," Judy said, "just because I'm going home with you doesn't mean we're going to have sex."

"Fair enough."

"For all I know, I'll just fall asleep."

"Entirely possible."

"Or maybe it'll turn out that you have a tiny pecker."

It was supposed to be a joke, but instead of chuckling or retorting in an equally silly manner, he seemed embarrassed. Lord, *did* he have a tiny pecker? Asian men supposedly had smaller penises, though from personal experience, Judy couldn't say. To her, whether Asian or white or black, they all looked the same, all those eager phalluses akin to annoying, know-it-all schoolchildren who thrust their hands in the air when the teacher asked a question. *Me, me! Pick me, pick me!*

"It's of appropriate dimensions," he said, and she realized his embarrassment hadn't been for him but rather for her crude attempt at humor.

Outside, the chilly air shrank her pleasant round buzz. Roger opened the passenger door for her, and she sank into the leather seat. As she watched him make his way around the front of his car, she considered telling him to drive her home instead. In the restaurant, behind the soothing gauze of alcohol, the night had seemed full of passion. She'd envisioned stripping for him, unbuttoning her blouse one white disc at a time as he watched, until he got so hot that he couldn't wait any longer and ripped away her clothes so he could ravage her beautiful body.

Except she wasn't beautiful. She had love handles, which jiggled like Jell-O and felt like Play-Doh. The other day she caught a flint of silver in her pubic hair. She plucked it out with tweezers, but if there was one, there had to be others. And as she grew older, she'd become highly lactose intolerant, so if she didn't take her Lactaid pill, the cheese in the spinach lasagna she had for dinner would produce farts so foul she could hardly stand it herself. Jesus, had she taken that pill? Her stomach rumbled, but then she remembered slipping the foil cover of the pill tablet in the pocket of her skirt, and when she patted it, she felt the tiny, reassuring bulge.

"Halfway there," Roger said.

Already? She should've told him that she'd changed her mind, that she wanted to return to her home the second he got in the car, but now it was too late. Maybe it was what she wanted after all, because wasn't this better than being alone, even if she hardly knew this man? He had a cat, that's all she knew, but Judy had to remind herself this was how relationships worked, that every friend or lover at some point had been a stranger.

Still, this was too fast. She wasn't going to sleep with him.

"I'm not going to sleep with you tonight," she blurted out, and she couldn't believe how loud her voice was.

"Okay," Roger said.

"I hope you're not disappointed," Judy said.

"I'm not," he said, and her heart sank a little, but only momentarily. "And I am."

Judy had been so preoccupied with her thoughts that she hadn't noticed what a nice car this was. It was an old BMW, but it didn't look old. In fact, it looked as if it had come directly from a showroom, the black dashboard a polished obsidian, the chrome spokes on the steering wheel gleaming like mirrors. He must've had the car detailed for their date, and Judy realized that Roger must've had his own dreams for this evening, dreams that were no doubt shattered with his car breaking down and her bitchy attitude.

"Cool car," she said.

He told her about his BMW New Class 2002 Turbo. Only about seventeen hundred of them were made; this was one of the first ones off the assembly line, circa 1968. He bought it from a guy who specialized in restoring old Bimmers, so even though it looked authentic, almost nothing inside the car was original.

"Must've been expensive," she said, and she wondered how someone who worked in customer service, one of those headset-wearing lobotomites who answered the phones, could afford a car like this.

He shrugged. "I'm still paying off the loan, but you only live once, right?"

"Why this one?" she asked.

"It was what my dad drove. I have good memories of it."

"You like your dad," she said.

Roger nodded, chuckling. "Most people do, don't they?"

They crested a hilly part of Route 287, white and yellow lines of the highway disappearing over the black horizon.

"Maybe not everyone," he said.

"Maybe not," she said.

Growing up, she hardly saw her father's face, which was mostly hidden behind the newspaper. When he spoke, it was to tell her she'd done something wrong, and she'd given him plenty of opportunities: getting arrested for shoplifting, repeating tenth grade, breaking her ankle on prom night when she fell down a flight of stairs. Was it all to get his attention? Her various shrinks throughout the years thought so. He was a prototypical Asian father, content to keep his distance from his children. Why this didn't disturb her brother, she never knew. Maybe Kevin was a more accepting person than she was, a stronger, better person. Or maybe he was just different—different sex, different genes, different everything.

Roger lived in a gigantic development of townhouses called the Hills, in a section called Long Meadow. It was like driving through a maze, every corner looking like the one before.

"Are you sure we're going to your house and not someone else's?" Judy joked.

"I did get lost a few times in the beginning," Roger said. "But now it's home." He unlocked the door, and she stepped in.

As he helped her take off her coat, she noticed nothing particularly remarkable about the living room—a leather sofa, a widescreen TV, and a minimalist glass table—except for the reading lamp that lit up the corner when Roger had flipped on the lights. The lampshade, made of stained glass arranged in the shape of yellow and red flowers, glowed beautifully but looked out of place with the rest of the modern décor.

"It's a Tiffany," Roger said.

"Really?"

"A Dale Tiffany. A reproduction."

"Kind of like your car."

He tilted his head for a moment, then laughed, as if the thought had never occurred to him before. "I suppose you're right."

They walked over to the strip of a kitchen, where he poured a glass of water from the tap. Judy, beginning to feel the weight of the night, squinted as the fluorescent lights flickered on. She leaned against the counter and stared at the black handle of the microwave that had worn to a point where the silver underneath was coming through.

Roger handed her a full glass, and she chugged it, the kitchen filling with the sound of her gulping water.

"I never knew I had such a loud throat," she said.

"It's very impressive," he said.

She was glad he was still flirting with her, though she wondered how much longer she could stay on her feet. She wanted to keep moving, let momentum drive away the fatigue, so she was grateful when Roger suggested a quick tour of the house. In the dining room, which was really just an extension of the kitchen, there were two brown place mats on the wooden table, but only one was painted with ring marks and stains. Upstairs, the bathroom shower had no conditioner, just shampoo.

Roger's cell phone rang.

"One sec," he said, and he spoke rapidly in Japanese. He nudged his bedroom door open and gestured her to enter while he stayed out in the hall, talking on the phone. She'd always found that language frustrating to her ear, almost as if the syllables were in combat with one other. *Yes* was *hai*, but the long *i* was so shortened that it came out like a cough.

Judy knew what his room would look like even before she entered: dark-hued sheets (navy blue), two pillows maximum (bingo), blinds instead of drapes (vertical). How many bachelor bedrooms had she seen? Twenty, fifty, maybe a hundred? No, not a hundred, she hadn't been that big of a slut, but fifty was probably a fair guess. All those spartan bedrooms had been sadly similar in their own way, and she supposed the same could be said about her breed, the aging bachelorette.

Roger snapped his cell phone off as he returned to her.

"Everything okay?"

"Yes. Just some business I had to take care of."

"Must've been important, to call this late."

"It's morning in Japan," he said.

"Waaaaaah!" The sound came from under the bed.

"That's Momo," Roger said.

"That doesn't sound like a cat."

"The Siamese don't meow, they sort of wail."

"Does it do it all night?"

"Once we get quiet, he'll stop. He may even come out to say hello."

"Then let's get quiet."

"Okay."

She sat at the edge of the bed, and he sat down next to her. She took off her blouse, and he took off his shirt. She slipped out of her skirt, and he stepped out of his pants. She wasn't looking at him as she rolled off her pantyhose, and he wasn't looking at her as he pulled off his socks. When her left foot accidentally brushed against his right, both of their eyes were drawn to the point of contact.

"You have nice toes," Judy said.

"Thank you," Roger said, putting his feet together. "Yours are lovely as well."

Was this how people got to know one another, by talking about their toes?

"On three, let's look at each other, okay?" Judy asked.

"All right," Roger said.

They counted down together, and on three, Judy stared into the face of an angry dragon, its white fangs outlined in black, the flames inside the pupils of its bulging eyes matching the larger fiery breath exploding from its screaming mouth. Talons out, claws fully extended, a tattoo of this creature that existed in fairy tales was perched on Roger's left shoulder, and when he turned around, Judy saw the entirety of the dragon's snakelike body uncoiling itself down to the small of his back.

8

"Honey," Kevin said, "I'm home."

From the kitchen, he heard the familiar two-step greeting of Snaps, his German shepherd, who welcomed him with a quick bark that segued into a more robust, full-bodied howl that would've made any wolf proud.

He opened the kitchen door and out came his dog, jumping around him a couple of times to tell him just how much she'd missed him, and as she did, small tuffs of her fur flew off like confetti. If he didn't brush her today, he'd be seeing tumbleweeds of her hair in every part of the house.

He'd been gone for only a couple of hours, running errands and stopping at the grocery store, but for Snaps, time never held any meaning. When Kevin was here, she was happy. When he wasn't, she was sad. And when he came back, it was the best part of her day. Clichés existed because they were true: There was no purer love than the love from your dog.

Kevin grabbed the wire brush from the sideboard drawer in the living room, and Snaps was already sitting down, waiting to be groomed.

"Little genius," Kevin said, and she wagged her tail.

As he brushed her, he bestowed a silent thanks on Alice, because if not for her, he would never have gotten a dog. There were many things she'd introduced him to—like sushi. Even though he was the Asian, it was the blue-eyed and blond-haired Alice who got him to eat raw fish, on their third date. When he told her he would be ordering the teriyaki chicken, Alice frowned beautifully and asked him why he didn't want the tekka maki hand roll, which was supposed to be the best in the state.

"I'm not a fan of raw fish," he'd said.

"What don't you like about it?" she asked. When she saw his hesitation, she quickly assessed, "You've never had it."

She had a keen, almost eerie ability to see the truth in him: It was as if she took the shortcut while everybody else drove on the main roads.

"If you have a piece of my sushi, just one," she told him, "I'll let you sleep with me tonight."

"What if I eat thirty pieces?" he asked.

"Then we'll do it thirty times."

"That's a lot of sex in one night."

Her smile turned sly, fox-like. "That's a lot of sushi."

That was the most surprising thing about sushi, that even though they looked bite-size, he was full after one hand roll and twelve smaller pieces. He had tuna, spicy tuna, and eel. He liked tuna the best, because it tasted like nothing at all. It was more about the texture, the soft heft of the fish as it melded with the sticky rice and seaweed.

"You like it?" she asked.

"What's your guess?"

"I think you sort of love it."

He dunked the final wheel of sushi in the murky puddle of soy sauce and wasabi, let the liquid soak into the rice.

"Hey, that's . . . a little goes a long way, you know?" Alice said.

Kevin picked up the drippy sushi and popped it into his mouth before he could change his mind. It was like the most intense ice cream headache he'd ever had, except the burning/clearing sensation was in his upper sinuses. Tears welled up; he thought his nose was going to fall off.

"I have to admit," she said with a straight face, "nothing turns me on more than a man who can handle his wasabi."

That night they made love, and they didn't do it thirty times, just once, but it was more than enough. She smelled like baby powder. Her hair gleamed gold in the waning moonlight. When she breathed out, her face glowing with the sweat of her effort, her lips pursed out to form a perfect O.

His first memory of sushi, and now this, the sad supermarket version in front of him, black trays with clear plastic tops that displayed the upturned faces of the rolls. Kevin pried one tuna roll out of the tray and showed it to Snaps.

"Got your favorite," he said to her, and he tossed it into her dish.

On the kitchen island was the envelope Soo had given him last evening, and next to it, a business card, which had fallen out when he took a second look at the photograph. Kevin picked it up and ran a finger around its edges.

PICTURE THIS
Photos by Vincent DeGuardi
2318 Mission Street
San Francisco
• *Specializing in weddings, bar mitzvahs, and family portraits* •

The phone number on the front had been blacked out with a pen, but another one was written on the back. Kevin had dialed it last night, and he got the response he'd expected: Sorry buddy, wrong number.

Snaps, having devoured her treat, was at his feet and looked up with hopeful eyes as Kevin ate one sushi roll after another. When she tired of waiting, she scratched her side with her hind leg, thumping the floor as if it were a drum. With the final beat, Kevin heard a crack, and Snaps jumped away.

He checked the bottom of her paw and saw no damage, but the floor hadn't gotten off so lucky. One of the pumpkin pine boards was cracked and dented in, yet another part of this ancient house that was falling apart. Snaps tentatively approached the spot and sniffed it.

Kevin glanced at the clock above the sink. He had an hour before he had to be back at the tennis club, and this was a problem that couldn't be ignored, so he opened up the trap door and climbed down the stairs to the basement to get the spare board, the jig saw, a drill, and a couple of nails. Before coming back up, he checked on the two snapping mousetraps in the corner, which were thankfully still armed, but then he remembered the groundhog was back under the porch and he'd have to take care of that, too. Squirrels, snakes, bats, turkey vultures—sometimes he felt as if he were living in a zoo. Last week he heard a bear warning on the radio.

When Kevin and Alice had bought this aging colonial in rural Warren County ten years ago, it had seemed like a reasonable purchase. They were in love, and what better way to harness the strength of their spirit but to transform this house into their own? They would remodel the first-floor half bath, lift off the peeling linoleum, and lay down ceramic tiles. After that, the three bedrooms upstairs would get fresh coats of paint, and then they'd tackle the kitchen, replace the mismatching appliances with stainless steel, build a little pantry off to the side.

Unfortunately, they found out they didn't work well together. Alice started quickly and made adjustments as she went along, while Kevin believed in devising charts and sketches before he lifted a single tool. It was no different than how he'd approached his challenger circuit tennis matches, writing out a plan of attack the night before and sticking with it. Whether it was the location of a nail or the placement of a first serve, it helped to be prepared, because things always went wrong. But his wife disagreed, and when they butted heads, neither of them had anticipated each other's stubbornness, and it didn't take long for them to find excuses to delay the remodeling.

He should've sold the house after the divorce was finalized, but he didn't. He wondered why he didn't tire of being reminded of his marital failure, but the surprising fact was, he'd gotten used to this house. And with Alice gone, he was actually able to complete the tile job in the bathroom in a little more than a month. When he'd finished his grouting and admired the clean geometry of the straight white lines that patterned the floor, he picked up the phone but stopped himself from dialing her when he realized the stupidity of his notion.

As Kevin slid a large bit into the drill, Snaps watched him, sitting tall with her front paws together, the most regal pose of hers. He and Alice had gotten her as a puppy eleven years ago. The average lifespan of a shepherd was somewhere between ten and twelve. Did Snaps know that she was nearing the end of her life? If so, she never let on. Looking at her, he could almost pretend that she would be by his side for the rest of his days.

He held up the drill and triggered a burst of spin, like a doctor pushing out bubbles from a syringe. Kevin had done this repair job many times before, so it was routine. He drilled a half-inch hole at the broken edge for the jig saw blade to fit, then cut away the broken wood. He measured the length of the hole twice and cut off the necessary piece to snap into the void, and two nails later, he was almost done. He ducked under the trap door again and found two blocks of two-by-fours to support the new wood from the bottom.

The whole process took less than half an hour, and when he resurfaced in the kitchen, Snaps sniffed the new board. He'd have to poly it, but that could wait.

"Good as new, right?" Kevin asked her, and she plopped on top of it with approval.

There was a certain satisfaction to fixing up this house. He could point out all the other boards he'd replaced in the years he'd lived here. Not only did it give him a sense of pride, but it also made him consider the house as a living being that needed his healing hands to keep going. Kevin wondered if the houses of strangers would offer him similar satisfaction, if carpentry was a viable career choice for him. He'd always been good with his hands, but would the deft drop shot he employed with his tennis racquet translate so readily to a lathe or a chisel? He was forty years old, another thirty to go at least before retirement. Reaching that midlife milestone birthday had made him consider his future with more urgency, and the thought of teaching tennis for the rest of his working life filled him with dread. He was fooling himself, anyway—nobody wanted to be taught how to play a young man's game by a sixty-year-old geezer. Sooner than later he'd have to move into management, learn to keep his workers happy, do up the budget the way his boss Ernie did it at the club with his giant receipt-printing calculator and ledger software.

This Sunday afternoon, his first lesson was with Alexa. Usually he looked forward to working with her, but with what happened last time, he wanted to call in sick. The best part of his job, now ruined. And it all happened in a blink. *It's okay,* she'd told him after the kiss. *It's not the end of the world.* Maybe not for her, but for him, it was close enough.

Somewhere in this house, his cell phone rang. It was a muffled sound, meaning it was either under something or inside a pocket, and on the fifth ring, he found it, of all places, in the refrigerator. This was sad. This was the sort of thing that senile people did, leaving their keys in the freezer. The phone felt pleasantly cool on his ear.

"Kevin? Hey, it's me, Chuck. You called me last night about Vincent DeGuardi, the photographer? So I talked to my mom this morning, and you're not going to believe this. This number used to be Vincent's, many years ago. Because my mom got so many calls after he moved his business, she tracked down Vincent herself and they became friends. Maybe more than friends from what it sounds like, but anyway, not to bore you with the details, my mom still keeps in touch with the guy, is what I'm saying. You want his number?"

• • •

"So," Alexa said, "are you still all freaked out?"

She'd been waiting for Kevin because he was late. He picked up the metal ball hopper by the opening of the canvas curtains on the court and saw her on the other end practicing her serves. He was relieved she looked as she always did, in a no-nonsense gray T-shirt and blue cotton shorts. She tossed the ball, and he yelled, "T!" And sure enough, she served it down the middle. It was a drill he'd repeated in college, where his coach called out the location of the serve as the ball was being tossed. The point was to keep your opponent from reading your serve, which made it that much tougher to return the ball.

Alexa, her ponytail pulled through the back of her cap, tossed another ball.

"Wide!" Kevin yelled, and the serve missed the corner by a foot.

"Shit," she muttered, and she tossed and swung and clipped the line on her second try.

Kevin picked up the stray balls in his path, each sphere offering a satisfying resistance as he pushed down on them through the rungs of the hopper; it was the tennis equivalent of popping bubble wrap. Alexa tossed another ball, this time her second serve, slower but with a kick to the right.

He dropped the hopper by her feet. She twirled her racquet.

"Yes," Kevin said. "I am still all freaked out."

"Good. Me too."

They didn't speak. Kevin stood a few feet behind the net and fed her balls from the rolling cart, the mechanical Zen of the swing, the strike, the bounce emptying his mind. Never underestimate the simple power of repetition.

When the balls were gone, they both walked around the court to pick them up. They had started on opposite sides of the court with their respective hoppers, but now they were converging, meeting at the middle of the court, the white band of the net cord stretched tight between them. She took off her cap and dabbed the moisture off her forehead with her pink sweatband. She looked up at him with a face he didn't recognize, a face she must've reserved for discussing the unpleasant portions of her life. He wished he'd never seen it, but it was a fitting punishment.

"I'm sorry I kissed you," she said.

"It's my fault," Kevin said. "As the adult, I'm supposed to know better."

"I'm not usually impetuous."

"I know."

"You do know me, don't you? And I know you, too."

Kevin dumped the balls in his hopper into the cart, a makeshift mountain of neon green. "But you don't know me," he said. "All you know is the guy on the court. And all I know is the girl on the court."

Alexa handed her hopper to him over the net. "But we do talk. Like about your father; that's not something you tell just anyone."

"Yeah. I shouldn't have done that, either."

She picked up a ball lodged underneath the fold of the net. "But you did." She held it up as if it were some sort of evidence for him to see. "Now what does that mean?"

He snatched the ball out of her hand. "I don't know."

"Me neither," she said. "Nate, the guy I'm dating right now, he told me I'm frigid. Like an icebox, his words. Why do you think he'd say something like that? Because I'm totally not, as you now know."

Kevin cleared his throat. "Okay, drop shots. It's the least used shot in the game today. Let's work on yours."

"Very funny."

"Alexa, if I may be frank with you."

"Please."

"I don't want to talk about your love life."

"*Love life?*"

"See, this is really messed up now. I'm saying stuff that doesn't sound very good. You and I are a team, you know? You're my star student, and I'm your faithful teacher."

"What if my 'love life' is affecting my game? Isn't it your job, then, to coach me in that as well?"

His cell phone chirped, and Kevin couldn't remember hearing a sweeter sound.

"I'm sorry, but I have to get that," he said, and he ran over to the bench to pick it up.

"Mr. Lee?"

An old man's voice, it had to be him, the man who'd taken that photograph of his mother.

"Yes. And you are Mr. DeGuardi?"

"Correct. I can't talk for very long because of my arthritis, can't hold up the phone so long, you see. Karen, that's Chuck's mother, she told me that you were trying to track me down."

"You took a photo of my mother, many years ago," Kevin said. Alexa, who'd been pretending not to eavesdrop on the conversation, hurried over.

DeGuardi cleared his throat. "I haven't taken photographs in twenty years. And if God continues to hate me, I'll be turning ninety-three this year. So you'll forgive me if I don't remember her."

"I think you might, unless you took a lot of nude centerfold pictures."

Alexa stared at him with slack-jawed surprise.

"That takes me back," DeGuardi said, "I mean really, really takes me back. Those beautiful girls. No, I didn't take too many. You're Chinese, right? That's what Karen said."

"Korean, but close enough."

"Jade Asia."

"Excuse me?"

"That was her name. I did a few negroes, a couple of genuine Swedish blondes, but only one oriental."

"Jade Asia? That's what she called herself?" Kevin said.

"Probably not her real name," DeGuardi said.

In the distance, Kevin heard a bell. DeGuardi explained it was lunchtime in his nursing home. "I still have my files in storage. You're free to look through them, if you wish."

The second he got off the phone, Alexa was all over him. "Are you telling me your mother is also not your mother, and that she was a *Playboy* model? Or something? Oh my God, that's just like totally insane, wow, I mean *wow*."

Here he was again, revealing his personal life to her. "We still have another hour of practice." He walked back on the court and picked up his racquet, but Alexa remained standing by the bench, her arms crossed.

"You're shutting me out?" she said. "Why? Because I'm a kid? Because I'm your student? Because I'm stupid? Because I'm frigid?"

"Yes, yes, no, no. And your boyfriend, Nate—"

"He's not my boyfriend."

"He's probably just saying that so you will, you know, do things with him."

"Sleep with him."

"Yes, I suppose."

He watched her walk over to him, her racquet dangling, scuffling against the blue concrete. She looked older, a woman dealing with men problems.

She sat on the court, drew her legs into herself, and sighed. "I know all this, of course, but when he says it to me, it feels real. Knowing it doesn't stop the pain."

Kevin squatted next to her. "I could tell you that it gets better as you get older, but I'd be lying."

"What happened between you and your wife? You were married for a long time, right?"

"How did you know about my divorce?"

"I don't know," Alexa said, waving him off. "You might have told me at some point. You're old, remember? You forget stuff."

"I did leave my cell phone in the fridge this afternoon."

"See? You're just one step away from getting your own motorized scooter. Besides, it's not like I don't know anything about divorce. My parents are both residents of Splitsville. I live with my dad. My mom's out in San Francisco."

"That's where this guy is."

Even though he promised himself he wouldn't, he ended up recounting his whole sordid story to Alexa while they volleyed lightly at the net. Each bounce of the ball freed him a little more, tennis doing the work of therapy.

"Hey, you can totally stay with my mom," Alexa said, slicing his errant volley to keep the exchange going.

"Huh?"

"When you go out there. You will, right? You should, because this DeGuardi guy sounds like he might keel over tomorrow, and there might be more pictures of her there and other stuff. I mean it's possible that she's still there, don't you think? In San Francisco? She probably knows who your father is, too. Maybe they're together and they've been waiting to see you all this time so you can be a family again."

"I better get there before the carriage turns back into a pumpkin," Kevin said, though since he saw the photo of her, his mother did seem more real to him. To meet with a second family—what would that be like?

Kevin poked back a wide backhand from Alexa, but it floated over her head and their volleying came to an end. They must've kept it in play for at least a hundred strokes.

"And I can stay with your mother."

Alexa reached over for her water bottle.

"Absolutely."

"The parent you're not living with."

"She's the most selfish person in the entire universe. She thinks I should be as independent as her, so you can see why she makes a shitty parent. And yet she goes out of her way to help strangers, maybe just to piss me off, so yeah, you should stay with her. She loves to have company she doesn't know."

"Your mother sounds weird."

"She is."

It was almost four o'clock, the end of their session. They walked to Alexa's enormous tennis bag on the bench, big enough to hold six racquets. She sat down and unlaced her sneakers then took off her socks, her ritual after practice.

"You're still painting all of your toenails black, I see," he said.

"Might as well," she said. "The two middle ones are still all messed up after I jammed them."

Outside of her imperfect toes, everything about Alexa was new and hopeful, and maybe that's why he enjoyed talking with her: the infinite possibilities of youth, the unblemished, unknown future ahead of her.

"Thanks for the offer, but I'll opt for the hotel, if I go. I mean I can't just up and leave."

She stepped into her sandals and applied the straps across the gentle hills of her feet.

"Why not?"

"Because . . . I have a job?"

"That you don't like anymore," she said, and her words whacked him. All this time, he thought he'd kept his dissatisfaction to himself, and he felt sorry that his misery was affecting others like her.

"Is it that obvious?"

She stood up.

"No." She slung the bag over both shoulders like a backpack. "I'm just perceptive."

They walked toward the exit, together. She was almost as tall as he was already, their gaits in sync. She'd probably grow another two to three inches, about six feet, a good height for today's power game. If she kept at it, she could really be something, but did she have the love, the desire, the drive? At one point in his life, Kevin thought he had what it took, but he hadn't counted on how lonely tennis could make you. Even in boxing you could at least bear-hug your opponent or receive some words of inspiration from your corner between rounds, but tennis left you out there to suffer with no place to hide and no one but yourself to blame.

Kevin parted the canvas curtain for her to walk through.

"So this might be good-bye," Alexa said. "I don't like good-byes."

"Maybe I'll see you Tuesday evening."

She looked down at her feet, and Kevin looked down, too, at her shiny black nails, the gold chain with a red heart she wore on her left ankle. Even though she looked and acted like an adult, she was also a child, living in that awkward purgatory of adolescence.

He offered her his hand.

"Just in case this is good-bye," he said.

"No kiss this time?" She shook his hand. "You'll miss me."

"For sure," Kevin said.

She walked away through the opening, then turned around.

"But not for too long," she added.

"Why is that?"

He thought she was going to make a joke, but she remained serious. "Because that's just the way it is. People come, people leave, and we all go on."

She slipped past the slit in the canvas curtain, climbed the staircase that led to the lobby entrance, and pushed open the door. She didn't look back.

9

Judy had promised him they wouldn't have sex last night, but she'd made no such promise this morning.

Lying next to her in bed, Roger asked, "Are you sure?"

As the morning light beamed through the windows, she had watched Roger sleep, his lips slightly parted, his hands curled by his cheeks. He looked like a little boy, except for that screaming dragon on his shoulder. The juxtaposition intrigued her; it made him a real person. It made him sexy.

She answered him by slipping out of her panties and helping him out of his boxers.

"You're right," Judy said to him at one point, looking up at the flushed face that hovered over hers, "it is of appropriate dimensions."

It made him laugh, and it made her laugh, too. A perfect joke in the middle of their breathless, inspired lovemaking—she'd almost forgotten that this primal act was a talent of hers. In bed, she was as fluid as Jackson Pollock's paintings: bold, colorful, daring.

He continued to move with her, slow and quick and slow and quick, tiding in and ebbing away like an ocean wave. At certain moments, she stared at the face of the dragon tattoo, pretending that it wasn't a man who was making love to her but this serpentine creature. It was a weird fantasy to have, probably rooted in those Korean folk tales her mother used to tell many years ago. The most memorable one was about the *kumiho*, the nine-tailed fox. Once it lived to a thousand, the *kumiho* turned into a beautiful girl so it could marry a man. At the time, Judy had been fascinated with the story, even counting the number of tails when she saw a fox in a book or on television, but as she grew older, the story depressed her. A fox somehow manages to live ten centuries, and all it wants is to marry some guy? Pathetic.

But wait a minute. She really should've been paying attention to what was going on here instead of letting her mind wander, because her man was getting ready to blast off. She felt his entire body coil up, his muscles turning taut.

Right here was her favorite part of sex. Judy had borne witness to her share of masculine denouements to know of their obvious commonalities—the quickening of breath, the increased force of motion, the eventual spasm, and the long, satisfied sigh. But at the same time, they were as singular as snowflakes, and Judy believed she could tell a lot about a man from his brief ride through penile ecstasy. Because here, there were no walls, just a clear window into the vulnerable truth of a person.

He grunted, once. He exhaled as if he'd just finished some complicated task, an expression of relief rather than gratification, almost a "Whew!" Underneath his now-still body, Judy thought: *Who are you, Roger Nakamura?*

Roger was in the shower, and Judy was in bed, mulling over what just happened. She glanced out the window, at the neighbors across the way. Everywhere she looked, she saw the same beige house with brown trim, row after row. It was like two mirrors facing one another.

"Waaaaaah."

Having announced his presence, Momo jumped up onto the bed. His eyes were a deep, sapphire blue.

"Not so afraid of me now, are you?"

The tan cat with brown paws apparently decided she wasn't a monster after all. Judy kept perfectly still as he walked up to her face and sniffed her lips. He pushed the top of his head against her hand, forcing Judy to pet him. His throaty purring was a quiet, soothing combination of sound and vibration. She scratched his chin; the harder she scratched, the more he liked it.

If a man's orgasm was a fingerprint, then Roger's was a blank. Everything happened the way it was supposed to—obviously he had an erection, and she'd felt his penis pulse inside her as he came, but then there was this odd stillness in the end instead of the familiar release. It was almost as if he'd experienced no pleasure, that while Judy had gotten off twice, the second time stronger than the first, he was pretending to feel something. Was it even possible for a man to fake an orgasm?

The more likely explanation was some sort of sexual disorder. She'd never heard of such a condition, but what did she know?

"Hey?"

His hair was still wet from the shower, a towel wrapped around his hips.

"Hi!" she said.

"You were so deep in thought," he said.

She reached out and kissed him.

"You gave me a lot to think about," she said. Which wasn't exactly a lie, but at the same time, it was. So there it was, her first fib with her new boyfriend, if he was even her boyfriend. In the shower, as she lathered herself in the steamy dimness, she wished for better words, less frivolous words, than *boyfriend* and *girlfriend* for a couple in their late thirties.

They made breakfast together. It took a little doing to gather the equipment—they found the frying pan hiding underneath a giant bag of Doritos in the pantry, and they had to be creative with the ingredients, too. The loaf of bread on top of the fridge was pocked with mold, so while Roger scrambled the eggs, Judy warmed rice cakes in the toaster oven. The kitchen was as small as the one in her own apartment, not big enough for two people to walk by without touching each other, but that was okay. In fact it was more than okay when Roger, with a whisk in one hand and broken eggshells in the other, hugged her from behind and kissed her neck. She fell wholly into it, pressed her body against his. All she was wearing was an old T-shirt of his, and she felt him getting hard again, but instead of it exciting her, it tinged her with sadness.

It was possible that she'd been mistaken, wasn't it? That she'd made the whole thing up? Maybe it was another facet of her fear of intimacy, a way for her psyche to bring her to emotional ruin. The answer was simple: She'd have to fuck him again, perhaps as many as a hundred times to absolutely make sure, and the raunchiness of her thoughts made her smile.

They set the table together, her placing the forks on the left of the plate, Roger following her and sliding the knives on the right, the tiny clang of the metal salt and pepper shakers ringing like a bell. Usually the morning after was more awkward than this. This was a good omen.

The eggs were overcooked and the rice cakes stale, and outside, the landscaping crew for the townhouse association was out in full force, polluting the air with the numbing noise of their trimmers and blowers. It should've been a bad breakfast, but when Judy looked across the table, not a whit of the external unpleasantness mattered. Because there was Roger—long-faced, calm-faced Roger, forking up piles of egg bits and heaping them on top of the rice cake, trying to make an open-faced sandwich out of it.

"I don't think that's gonna make it taste any better," Judy yelled across the table to make herself heard over the landscaping noise.

She was trying to be funny again and was possibly failing. Roger smiled small and shrugged, then took a crunchy bite. While he looked out the window and chewed away, she watched him, and whatever spell she'd been under—possibly the afterglow of sex—was starting to shrivel.

Was he an overly sensitive guy? Would she have to watch her words, to make sure she wasn't hurting his feelings? Who exactly was he, anyway? She knew so little about him, and it would take work to find out who he is. And conversely, while she was finding out about him, he would find out about her, all her issues, her peccadilloes, her psychoses. All her previous relationships had ended badly, so why would this one turn out any different?

She was being pessimistic, but after Brian abandoned her, she didn't know if she had it in her to do this again. Maybe it was too soon. Besides, it wasn't as if Roger was perfect. He had this weird fake-orgasm thing, plus that enormous tattoo. The mysterious pull the dragon had on her had abated, and all that remained now was the harsh reality of what he'd done to himself. Who in his right mind defaces his body like that? Obviously Roger had his share of problems, and she had enough of her own, thank you very much.

"Well hey," Judy said. "I should get going."

Roger blinked a couple of times.

"I'm sorry, what?" he asked. In his left hand, he held a full glass of orange juice, and in the other, the remaining half-moon of the disgusting rice cake. In her sudden panic to escape, she hadn't even noticed that he was still in the middle of his breakfast.

"Oh, nothing," she said, and she forced a smile to her lips. She picked up her knife and fingered the smooth curve of its handle. It looked practically brand-new compared to the one by Roger, which made sense, since she hardly ever went deeper than a single layer of her own utensils tray. On one side of the blade were tiny engraved letters, GIORGIO and WALLACE.

Last night she'd been too drunk to notice, but he was a slow eater. *Slow* was a good adjective to describe him, actually. Even the way he sat down, it was like an old man aware of his delicate bones. He was careful while she was careless. He was patient while she was hurried. They were different people, but who knew, maybe they would have a good time for however long it lasted. With low expectations, everything was a gift.

Roger took his last bite and chased it with his glass of orange juice.

"Thank you," Judy said. "I had a nice time."

"Me too," he said.

Outside, the gardening crew shut down their machines, and the room overwhelmed them with silence. They sat there staring at each other, neither speaking, the moment elongating until they were both smiling.

"When's the last time you played this game?" Judy asked.

"I'm not sure if I've ever played it," Roger said.

"No siblings?"

"Just me."

"So what's the deal with the tat on your back?"

"Young and stupid."

"Anything else I should know about?"

"I like bread."

"Bread?"

"Plain bread, with nothing on it."

He had nice eyes, shaped like canoes, wider and bigger than her own.

"I can go on all day," Judy said.

"I hope you do," Roger said.

She lost, but only because she'd been double-teamed. At some point, Momo had sneaked down from the bedroom and scared the hell out of her when he jumped onto the dining table.

They drove back to Red Bank to get her car. She'd parked on Front Street by a busted meter, but that hadn't stopped the city from slipping a pink ticket underneath her windshield wiper for leaving a vehicle overnight.

"Fucking A," Judy said. According to the time scribbled on the parking ticket, they'd just missed the meter maid.

"If only Momo had come down a little earlier," Roger said.

Judy closed her eyes and felt the glossy paper between her fingertips. A warm breeze blew in from the Navesink River, birds chirped, and a little while ago, she was in bed with this very nice man, having a very nice time. Life was good, and this ticket was a small, inconsequential thing.

She opened her eyes when she felt a tug on the ticket.

"It's my fault," Roger said. "Why don't you let me pay for it?"

"No, I'll handle it."

"I really would like to."

"I said I'll handle it. Okay?"

Roger reluctantly let go, then thrust his hands into his pants pockets. "Okay," he said, and he leaned in to kiss her. It was a good kiss, longer than a peck and shorter than a faked-up romantic face-sucking, a solid B+, maybe even an A-.

Grading kisses. It was like she was back in junior high.

10

At the traffic light on Pittstown Road, Kevin cut a quick left at the last second and was almost rear-ended. As the long, angry car horn blared, he glanced at the rearview mirror and saw the driver, a woman in a red top, pound her hand against the steering wheel in frustration.

"Sorry," he said to no one but himself.

But he wasn't really sorry. As Kevin ramped onto the interstate and away from the tennis club, he was actually proud of himself. He'd always been a man of routine, taking the same road to work, slurping on the same medium cup of coffee bought at the same coffee shop, but this morning, he broke out of his pattern. He'd felt an impulse, and instead of quashing it as he had his whole life, he followed it.

Kevin flipped open his cell phone and speed-dialed Bill's extension and hoped it would go to voice mail; it did. He informed Bill about the Monday-morning game with Robert Weathers III, the CEO who had to win every game, telling him to take it easy, none of Bill's inside-out forehands because Robert's left knee was bothering him.

Now driving down Route 287, he got off at the Somerville exit and passed the large round insignia of a dancing stopwatch on the peak of Time to Eat Diner. On Fridays, he and Alice had met for lunch there. He would order the burger topped with a fried egg and crumbled blue cheese, and she would get the chicken francese with asparagus and roasted peppers. For how many years did they eat there? A decade or more, not that it mattered now.

After the divorce papers were signed and Alice had vanished from their house, the sudden void had shocked Kevin into a numbed stupor. It's like that, friends told him, friends who'd gone through the pain of separation. Strange to have all that emptiness, but they assured him he'd get used to it. But they were wrong. As the months rolled on, he thought of her more often, more than he ever did when they'd been together.

Kevin turned into the entrance of the Somerset Medical Center and followed the curves until he found the sign for Outpatient Services. He located her car after spinning around the parking lot twice. She'd removed the Obama bumper sticker he'd stuck on for her, but the remnants of the glue still remained. He hoped the gray rectangle remained forever.

He'd tried to get over her. That first month, he went out with a different woman each Saturday night, two of them certifiable knockouts, dinner and dancing and even sex with one of them. But by the second month, Kevin could start to feel an odd blooming inside him, the opening of some dark, sad flower. And now, eleven months after he lost his wife of fourteen years, there was a black bouquet embedded in his chest, wishing for the person who was no longer there.

As he stared at her car, he could imagine her so clearly, shutting her car door with an easy pitch of her hips, slinging her purse over her right shoulder, tucking a loose curl of her strawberry-blond hair behind her ear as she made her way toward the hospital. Wearing a beige blouse and a knee-length black skirt, she would be dressed as anonymously as every other woman heading toward the entrance, but she wasn't everyone.

Kevin parked his car in the visitor's lot and killed the ignition. He was here because he wanted to see her. Because he wanted to tell her everything that happened so far and what he was planning to do. Ultimately, she wouldn't care, he knew that, but that didn't matter. He opened the door. He rose and took in the crisp autumn air, wishing he'd worn something else than the white Izod shirt and the matching white shorts.

As he walked toward the entrance, he pictured where Alice would be, sitting in one of the myriad white and gray cubicles of the human resources department. Often someone like Kevin, someone who'd never worked in an office or for a corporation, would proclaim how terrible it was that so many people made a living in such bland, stifling conditions, but Kevin felt otherwise. Sitting in a cubicle all day would never be his thing, but how nice it would be to be a nameless cog in the machine of an enormous company. Maybe it was just a condition of wanting what he didn't have, but in his job, he always had to be on.

The security guard eyed Kevin as he approached the desk.

"Good morning, John McEnroe," he said.

"You can't be serious!" Kevin said.

The guard pushed the sign-in clipboard toward him. "That might be the worst McEnroe impression I've ever heard."

"Hence, my day job," Kevin said, signing the ledger.

He was glad he told the guard where he was headed, because the entire HR department had moved up from the second to the fourth floor. As he entered the elevator and watched doctors and nurses file in, Kevin recalled being here for Alice's fortieth birthday, a small surprise party her friend and coworker Eileen had set up. There weren't many fond memories from last year, but this was one of them, the conference room decorated with red roses, pink streamers, and yellow balloons, and Alice was genuinely surprised and happy to see Kevin there beside the chocolate cake ablaze with candles. He whispered "Happy birthday" into her ear as he took her in his arms, and she'd hugged back with such vigor, as if to try to force their bodies to merge. "Thank you," she responded in kind with a whisper of her own, her lips close enough for him to feel the warmth of her breath.

If only he could stop the video of his mind right there, but that wasn't possible, because on the very next day, Alice said she was moving out. Kevin hated the way these two memories were conjoined, how their embrace of love spoiled into an embrace of good-bye.

On the fourth floor of the main wing, Kevin followed the signs for HR and tried not to think of what Alice told him that night before she left, but of course he did. She said he wanted so much, more than she was capable of giving. So much of what? What was it that he wanted? What was it that she wasn't able to give?

Her answer: Everything.

He asked: Was it possible for her to be just a tad more specific?

Instead of engaging him in another useless argument, Alice turned silent. So that was the last word she'd spoken to him as his wife, *Everything*, which was ironic, because to him, it meant absolutely nothing. Nothing and everything; without one, there couldn't be the other, so maybe it did make sense in some twisted way.

He found himself in front of her office, bold black letters on a clean white oval sign announcing human resources. There was no door, just an opening, so he hugged the wall as surreptitiously as he could, peeking around the corner. He looked and waited and, oddly enough, didn't see a single person.

Even though HR was now on a new floor, the layout didn't seem any different to Kevin, a fact he cherished. It was good to see Alice's cube still behind Eileen's. A glance at a computer monitor opened to a calendar showed him why the place was deserted: There was a department-wide meeting going on in the fifth-floor conference room for another half hour.

He fingered the name plate stuck on the outer wall of Alice's cube, glad to see she hadn't reverted to her maiden name. Did that mean anything, or was it because she just hated the last name she was born with? It was a joke she liked to tell people, that she married Kevin because she couldn't stand another day as Alice Cooper, but even in jokes, wasn't there a sliver of truth?

This was the sort of thing that drove her nuts, his inability to leave molehills as molehills. Everything was a mountain with him, and no one enjoyed climbing it more than he did.

Kevin sat down in her chair and was immediately struck by her perfume, a flowery, baby-powdery scent she'd worn for as long as he could remember. Alice was a couple of inches shorter than he was, but the height of her seat fit him nicely.

This was her desk, but in truth it could've been anyone's. There wasn't a single photograph to be found anywhere. A stack of color-coded hanging folders were filed meticulously in alphabetical order on the shelf above while to the left of her keyboard sat an unruly pile of office paraphernalia: Post-It notes, paper clips, binder clips, all of them mingling together on a plastic dish that plainly offered separate compartments for each.

Her desk was half neat and half messy, which was the way she had been at home, her threshold of chaos much higher than his. He never thought he'd miss picking up a castaway sock off the floor or straightening up her wooden bin of magazines, but it was these kinds of menial tasks that reminded him of her absence as well as her physical body. It was what she did and how she lived that defined who she was. Kevin supposed that was the way it was with everyone, but he never quite realized it until Alice disappeared.

He couldn't resist any longer. He grabbed the plastic dish on her desk to sort it properly, and in reaching for it, he nudged the mouse of her computer to bring her monitor out of standby.

Actually, he'd been wrong. There was no mistaking whose cube this was, because there was a photograph centered on the computer's desktop.

From the way it looked, it was most likely taken with a cell phone, the length and angle of a selfie. There was Alice, giving the camera her best smile against the sky and the ocean, probably somewhere along the Jersey shore. And standing next to her was a man with an equally effusive smile, his cheek almost touching hers, a man he'd never seen before.

Who the fuck was this?

"Kevin?"

He'd been peering at the screen so intently that he hadn't noticed Eileen.

"Hey," he said.

She pushed up her eyeglasses and crossed her arms, waiting for him to continue.

"I know I shouldn't be here."

"For a number of reasons," she said.

He rose out of the chair and tucked it underneath the desk.

"I thought everyone was at the departmental meeting."

She walked over to her cube and searched through her filing cabinet. "I needed to get something for my presentation."

The man in the picture was blond with blue eyes that managed to sparkle even in this washed-out snapshot. Kevin had wondered who the next guy in Alice's life would be, and now that he was confronted with this image, he didn't know what to think. Would he have felt better if she'd gotten together with another Korean man like himself? Or would that have made her into some sort of an Asian fetishist? What did it mean now that she was with someone so different? Had he been such a rotten husband that she'd given up on Korean men in general? Or could this be interpreted as something perversely positive, that because Alice ran so far in the other direction, it meant she still held feelings for him?

It was all stupid. People were just people, and he felt like a dope for even thinking along such petty lines, but it couldn't be helped. These were unavoidable issues that bubbled up in an interracial relationship.

At least in the way he looked, this man was Kevin's opposite, and he was no doubt different in the way he talked, the way he thought, the way he touched. He figured Alice would find someone else, but to see actual evidence of it plummeted him to the basement of misery.

Eileen, a blue folder now in her hand, cleared her throat.

"I should be leaving," he said.

They walked to the bank of elevators together, sidestepping a caravan of bald little kids in wheelchairs. Hearing their animated voices as they rolled by, Kevin felt ashamed for even thinking his life sucked.

"Alice is doing fine?" he asked.

Eileen took in a breath and expelled a heavy sigh.

"I feel like I'm betraying her, Kevin, just talking to you. Not that she forbade me to talk to you or anything like that, but you came here uninvited, and if I didn't know you, I would've called security. Just step back for a second and look at yourself, right here. See you from someone else's point of view."

Eileen pointed to the shiny elevator doors, and Kevin stared at his reflection. Wearing his tennis outfit, he looked especially ridiculous in this corporate office, maybe borderline crazy.

She pressed the button to go up. He pressed the button to go down.

"Why *are* you here?" she asked.

"I had things to say. At least I thought I did."

The left elevator was coming down from the seventh floor while the right was coming up from the lobby.

"She's doing fine," Eileen said, then added, "without you."

Seven, six . . . two, three. It was a race, and Kevin wished the numbers would hurry the hell up. He wanted to tell Eileen that she'd known only the miserable Alice and not the bright light at the beginning of their courtship, but what was the point? There was no use in convincing Eileen of anything. What he needed more than anything else was to convince himself that his time with his wife, his ex-wife, had run out. The credits had rolled, and he had to get up and leave the theater of his old life once and for all.

This is it, he told himself. *I'm done.*

"Do me a favor?" he asked as both elevators opened up simultaneously. "Don't tell her I was here?"

Eileen was about to nod in assent, but then she caught the person walking out of the left elevator.

"Your PowerPoint's up," Alice said to her. "Everyone's waiting."

He saw her; she saw him. Human traffic streamed by them as if flowing around a pair of islands, and for the next few seconds, Kevin saw nothing, heard nothing, felt nothing as his world filled with the presence of his ex-wife. He swam in the blue of her eyes, lost himself in the forest of her hair, curled up against the curve of her neck.

He wanted to tell her about everything—his parents who weren't his parents, flying to San Francisco, the new tiles in the bathroom. And something else he now knew with absolute certainty: that today would be his last day at the tennis club. In her presence, as he always did, he found clarity.

Except he couldn't say any of this to her, because when he assembled the various parts of her face together, they formed an expression that wasn't so endearing. In fact, it was like seeing a piece of paper crumple.

"Oh my God, what *is* that?" he said, jabbing a finger at a point left of her. When Alice turned, he leaped toward the closing doors of the right elevator like Indiana Jones, his athleticism somehow adding grace to his desperate gesture of immaturity.

After the door closed, a pair of kids giggled as the elevator headed down.

"Man, I haven't seen the 'look over there' gag in, what, like since elementary school?"

"I think I've only seen it on TV!"

They held up their hands and he high-fived them, and for a moment he felt as though he got away with it, whatever it was. But then the other two people in the elevator, two old ladies huddled in the corner away from them, looked at Kevin with motherly disapproval, and he felt like the heel that he was. As he leaned against the brass railing and felt the cold metal touch his body, he wished this ride would last forever, pitch him down to the very center of the earth, sink him into the molten lava and melt him down to an organic puddle.

He looked at his watch and saw it wasn't even ten o'clock yet. This day, his last day of the life he knew, was just beginning.

Micah Braun. As soon as he gave up trying to remember, the name popped up as if it'd been there all along.

"Kevin? Did you see it?"

He had, and he hadn't. Kevin caught the spin of the ball and its subsequent bounce, but he'd missed which side of the line it had landed.

"No, I'm sorry," he said to Dinesh, a spindly boy of ten, who slapped the face of his racquet in frustration.

"Man, it was so *in!*" yelled the boy on the other side of the net.

"It looked out to me," Dinesh said. He looked at Kevin again, his face full of accusation. "You were right there."

Kevin held up his excuse, the final draw of the junior tournament to be held next weekend, which he was half-assedly filling out.

"If you think it's out, it's out. You're your own linesman. Them's the rules."

"I know," Dinesh said. "I'm just not sure. But he is."

Dinesh, being the gentleman, gave the point to his opponent, and soon the two boys were attempting to out-topspin each other with their lasso-whip forehands. Kevin moved away to the empty court, where he sat on the bench and scribbled the names of his kids above the empty lines in the draw. He wouldn't be here to see any of these matches. On one of the lines, he mistakenly wrote *Micah Braun.* Now that the name was out, he couldn't get away from it.

They'd both been twelve at the time, almost three decades ago. The winner of their match was two victories away from advancing to the National Spring Championship in Florida, where the top 256 kids of their age group would be competing. The ones who made it far in the tournament got noticed.

Micah was an older twelve, his birthday in January, while Kevin's was in December, so Micah had half a foot on him and probably a good ten pounds. But Kevin wasn't worried, because he had what Micah didn't: control.

Ultimately, that's how this game was won, to control the ball enough to create that space necessary to put the shot out of the opponent's reach. Spin, pace, and angle: Those were the tools, and Kevin's coach at the time taught him how to gain control by loving it. To love was to want, and to want was to have.

Kevin had always craved control, even as a boy. His favorite childhood toy had been a Pinocchio marionette; he spent uncounted hours making it do what he wanted. He always felt the safest when he had plans, when he had an itinerary, when there were lists to follow.

For this match against Micah, Kevin's parents were in attendance, and so was Judy, his family sitting with Coach Jimmy in the bleachers. Kevin wanted to make them proud, he wanted to win this match, but more than anything, he wanted control.

He had it in spurts. In the first set, for three consecutive games, it was almost as if he did have strings over Micah, pulling him in whatever direction he wished. His tennis racquet was like a giant, swinging remote control, every strike of the ball a click to place Micah in an untenable position. But then the remote swapped owners, and it was Kevin who became the puppet, his breath ragged from sprinting between the lines, scrambling backward and missing a lob by an inch.

Almost two hours later, Kevin won the match, but the final score or the celebration was not what he remembered now. They were tied a set a piece and deep into the third. Kevin dictated the point with precision, the ball cracking off the strings like an angry bullet. He thought he had won when he fired a shot down the right line, except Micah ran it down, untwisted his torso, flicked his wrist, and launched a crosscourt forehand aiming for the opposite corner, and now it was Kevin on the defensive, hurrying to catch up to this ungodly yellow blur from Micah; there was no way his opponent should've been able to hit the ball with that kind of depth from his awkward position—

Even now, Kevin could see it, the ball bouncing close to but grazing the line, and even now, he could hear it, his voice exploding, "Out!"

It happened so fast. He looked up to his dad, who had the angle to see the play, and Kevin braced for the frown of disappointment his father often saved for his sister. If he'd seen his son's lie, he didn't show it. In fact, he rose up and clapped, and now they were all up, not only his family and coach but everyone on the bleachers, the applause thunderous. Kevin raised his racquet in appreciation, then walked back to his ready position at the baseline, surprised at his poise and at the curious lack of guilt he felt.

He'd never forgotten that lie, and until today, until this very moment, he didn't know why he'd done it, or why he'd felt justified afterward. Of course: control. This act was the ultimate embracing of control, to forcibly change the rules, to own it. He would never steal an unwarranted point from another opponent again as a junior, but he wouldn't need to. Because after this match, he'd mastered this dark art to win games, to win people, to win a wife. Alice had always admired his sense of organization, his meticulous care over every facet of everything he did. Early in their relationship, he must've seemed like a capable person to her, able to shrink the macro world down to his micro, except she hadn't yet realized his insatiable hunger for control could also be an impediment to forward progress. A tennis match was a flow, one player finding his groove while the other withstood the onslaught, until there was some turning point—like a sure winner clipping the net cord or missing an easy overhead that a blind man would've hit in. The key was to wait for that moment instead of trying to force every point, and yet Kevin couldn't stop himself. Three coaches tried to teach him to let go. He wished he could, but even now, he'd failed. Look where he was this morning, standing in front of Alice like a knucklehead, making an ass of himself.

Micah Braun. What if Kevin hadn't called that ball out? He was certain he would've lost the match. The two following turned out to be cupcakes, straight set wins for him. He flew to Florida and reached the semifinals, the beginning of his professional tennis career.

Kevin left the court and walked up to the club's lounge, where the big-screen TV was showing a classic tennis match, Björn Borg against Jimmy Connors in their tiny white '70s shorts on the green grass of Wimbledon. There was no one on the guest Internet-connected computer in the corner, so he sat down to search the fate of his old opponent. A few clicks later, he found a photo of a man in a business suit accepting a golden plaque for some innovation in project management. Kevin imagined his own face up there, the red necktie tight around his neck, a fake smile for the photographer. If Kevin had called the ball in, would they have changed places, changed lives?

For all he knew, this wasn't even Micah, just some guy who shared his name. Feeling as if he'd wasted not only the last fifteen minutes but also the entirety of his life, Kevin closed the browser, pushed off the desk, and headed for the pro shop to gather his things.

11

Judy was crouched down, deciding between spending the extra twenty cents on a can of Goya black beans versus its Wegmans counterpart, when she saw her. But was it actually Alice?

A can in each hand, Judy jumped up to her feet too quickly and rammed her head against the red coupon holder jutting out from the shelf above. She was about to whack the stupid thing but then saw that the coupon it had just spit out was for any Goya canned product. Maybe this was her lucky day. She snatched the coupon, and with a whirl and blink of its red LED light, a brand-new one eerily slid into place.

Judy still had another dozen things to get from her shopping list, for a Tex-Mex fish taco and steak dinner she planned to make for her and Roger tomorrow night, but that could wait. She rolled her cart slowly out of the ethnic foods aisle, passing by the yellow jars of Old El Paso salsa and blue cans of La Choy lo mein, navigating past the throng of postwork shoppers.

Alice wasn't by the juices and milks, and though there was a lithe blond woman considering a wedge of Swiss cheese in the dairy section, she had two kids with her and didn't stand like Alice. Her ex-sister-in-law had the posture of a dancer, straight-backed and graceful, that made her easy to pick out. Judy had always liked her, quite a bit, in fact, and initially, when Kevin had told her that they were splitting up, Judy felt as distressed about her brother's loss of a wife as her own loss of a friend.

But were they friends? They had gone out clothes shopping on occasion, but most of the time, Judy had seen her with Kevin at family functions. Alice hadn't reached out to her since the divorce, and vice-versa for Judy, so maybe they had been more like family and less like friends, and for that reason, there was no reason to see each other.

Judy was about to turn her cart around when she caught a glimmer of gliding Alice, floating into and out of her vision at the end of the aisle. It was her. She remembered Kevin mentioning Alice had moved to Holmdel, which was about ten miles away from here. Judy abandoned her cart and sped after her, not wanting to lose her again, and she almost ran into her. Alice was inches away, reaching for the back of the milk shelf. Judy passed her and found what she was looking for, the spinning tree of bread loaves for cover.

The first thing Judy noticed was Alice's glossy black belt, how it wouldn't circumnavigate half of the female thighs in this supermarket, let alone their midsections. Alice had found her milk, and now she was onto orange juice, and as she leaned over and reached down, a perfect circle of her butt pressed against her black skirt, and her calves were toned and shaped like those out of a pantyhose catalog. Four men walked by her, and it was almost funny how their heads all swiveled like robots.

She should hate Alice, and maybe if she hadn't known her, she would. But last Christmas, the first one without her mother or her husband, when Judy saw her father and Soo saunter into Kevin's house, it was Alice who had saved the evening. She maneuvered Judy past Bill and the surprised faces of a bunch of Kevin's other friends and brought her to the deck, to the December evening air, so Judy could vent.

"I saw it, too," Alice said.

Soo, beaming with an irrepressible supply of yuletide joy, had been wearing a brooch on her sweater, a brooch that Judy had given her mother the year she died. It was a Christmas wreath made with tiny emeralds, accented with a ruby-encrusted red bow, which Judy had bought with money she didn't have. It would take her half a year to pay off the credit card debt from that present, but she knew it was the last gift she would be able to give her mother, and she'd wanted to make it count. Except it was now pinned on her stepmother's chest, glittering green like some gaudy lucky charm.

"That fucker," Judy seethed, "you know what he did? I bet you a thousand dollars he gave it to Soo as a present, a fucking regifter!"

Alice was freezing out here, hugging herself tight. Judy knew this was not what she'd wanted to do, stand listening to an angry tirade from her sister-in-law, but Alice pulled up two lawn chairs and gestured for her to sit.

"It's Christmas Day," Alice said. She cupped her hands and blew into them, the white steam of air escaping between her fingers. "The last thing your mother would've wanted would be for there to be a fight, right?"

Alice was correct, but this was not what Judy wanted to hear right now. She needed someone who'd agree with her and not make her feel small by lecturing on the obvious, which was what she wished to tell Alice, but she knew she couldn't. For almost twenty years she'd known her brother's wife, knew her almost as long as he'd known her himself, and yet she had no idea who she really was. There was personal information, of course, that Judy had come to know through overheard conversations and related anecdotes. That she was born in Boston, raised in Buffalo, went to college in upstate New York, and met Kevin at a doctor's office. That she liked ballroom dancing and ate kimchi more than her Korean husband. And yet none of these little factoids of her life and personality added up to anything, because this woman sitting out here with her, braving bitter pockets of winter wind, was still just a familiar stranger.

"Alice," Judy said, choosing to stand instead of sit. She grabbed the hollow metal of the patio chair, so cold that it numbed her hands, "who are you?"

Alice coughed up a nervous chortle of laughter. "That's an interesting question."

Somewhere in the distance, an animal howled. Kevin's house was in the middle of nowhere in Warren County, so a coyote wasn't out of the question.

"Never mind," Judy said. "I don't know what I'm saying."

Judy turned away and headed for the door, but Alice's voice stopped her.

"Happier," she said. "That's who I used to be."

For the next hour, they huddled together and talked. At some point Kevin came out, wanting to know why they were turning into icicles out here, and they both shooed him back into the house. In those sixty-odd minutes, Judy learned more about Alice than she had in all the years she'd known her. The reason why Alice looked like a dancer was because she used to be one; she'd been a theater major in college, and for a while, she had the dream of becoming a professional, but it didn't take her long to see that there were people who were just naturals, who'd always be so much better than she could ever hope to be. Still, an instructor had taken an interest in her and had told Alice she would work with her privately, but Alice refused.

"If I need someone's help, it's not worth doing."

Alice had spoken with such finality and determination that it verged on fury.

Judy had recalled that Christmas many times whenever she thought of Alice, because it was the first and only time they'd connected as real people, but now Judy saw it for what it had been. Alice hadn't shared a part of herself to get closer to Judy; rather, it was because she'd felt sorry for her and wanted to cheer her up. And maybe it went even further than that. Because a couple of months afterward, she and Kevin split up, which meant Alice had probably known it would be the last time she'd have to see Judy. The conversation had been a going-away present.

Judy sat down on an empty pallet next to the cartons of eggs. Leaning against the tower of squeaky Styrofoam containers, puffs of refrigerated air soothing her back, she knew her thoughts were silly fabrications in her head. What was real was that she missed seeing Alice on New Year's and Easter and Mother's Day, on their birthdays and the barbeque on the Fourth of July and Thanksgiving and Christmas. They'd pass the time talking about some vapid TV show or the latest popcorn flick, never talking about anything of consequence, but when you stacked up these incidental layers of small talk, they added up to a level of comfort impossible to duplicate in any other relationship. For all those previous years, she'd taken Alice's presence for granted, never knowing how easily she could disappear from her life. If Judy had known their ties were so tenuous, she would've tried harder—or maybe not. It was always easy to believe in hindsight.

Judy got up and dusted herself off, and when she scanned the dairy section, where Alice had been picking between tiny tubs of foil-topped yogurt, she was gone. Had Kevin also felt this way when Brian ceased to exist at the Lee family gatherings? Did he miss her ex-husband as much as Judy missed Alice? Her brother often played the role of a dumb jock, claiming he led an unexamined life and was quite happy to do so, but in reality, she knew he actually spent time thinking about these things, and probably more now than ever with his recent discoveries about his origins. She felt guilty that she hadn't called him since Friday. This was an extraordinary time for him; she needed to be a supportive sister.

Judy grabbed her cart and started to back away when a hand on her shoulder halted her.

"What the hell, Judy? What is this, some sort of a tag team?"

Judy didn't know what to say. Standing in front of her was Alice, who was not only beautiful from her butt down but also from the neck up. She had a face incapable of expressing displeasure, all watery blue eyes and chubby pink cheeks. That was always the funny thing about her, those squeezable, rosy cheeks of hers, in stark contrast to her slim body.

"Did you say *tag team?*" Judy asked.

Alice said nothing, just looked at her with what Judy supposed was her serious, penetrating glare: angled eyebrows, locked jaw, arms at her side. She waited until her eyes returned to their familiar fluidity, and when they did, Judy stepped forward and hugged her hard.

"I don't know what you're talking about," Judy said, "but I've missed you."

She hardly hugged back, but that's what Judy expected. Alice had never been a touchy-feely woman, and there was no reason to think she would've changed. But at least she was smiling when they broke their embrace.

"It's good to see you, too, Judy," she said. "Don't mind me. I had a strange day."

It felt comfortable to walk around the store with her, as if they shopped together every week. At the bakery, after sampling a toothpicked cube of cheesecake, Alice told her about her encounter with Kevin in the morning.

"Okay, so that's what you meant by *tag team,*" Judy said.

Alice nodded. "I actually saw you when you were standing by the shoe polish, but when you kept following me . . ."

"I was following you, wasn't I? Like a spy."

They laughed, and as they continued to push their carts through the brightly lit aisles of the supermarket, Judy resisted from asking Alice about their divorce. She'd heard the breakup only from Kevin's point of view, that they argued all the time, that they grew apart, that they'd reached a point in their relationship where separation seemed more natural than being together. But there had to be some other reason, didn't there? Two people who loved each other didn't just drift away from one another. Gusts of severance blew from many different directions, but there was always a source of the wind. For Brian, it had been Judy's sadness and anger, but who the hell did he think he married in the first place? What had given him the right to love her in the beginning and tire of her at the end, when she'd always been the same person?

"Judy?"

"Sorry," she said. This was becoming a bad habit of hers, zoning out. "I was just thinking about Brian."

"Oh." They'd somehow veered back to the bread section. Alice picked up a twin pack of English muffins and Judy got a loaf of cinnamon raisin bread.

She wished Alice would ask her about what happened between her and Brian so they could share in their mutual failures and maybe even learn something, but her ex-sister-in-law said nothing.

"Well, I guess I'm done shopping," Alice said.

Judy considered following Alice to the checkout lanes, but what was the point? Whatever this had been, whatever they had between them, it was over.

"I've got a few more things on my list," Judy said.

"Then I guess this is good-bye."

There were no hugs this time, just two friendly waves an arm's length away.

"Take care of yourself," Alice said.

"You too."

Alice rolled away with her cart, but she stopped and rolled back. "I'll be moving away again. In a month."

"Where to?"

"Boston."

So Alice was about to embark on a new life in a new town, perhaps with a new man, though Judy didn't get that vibe from her. As someone who knew loneliness more intimately than she'd like, Judy could see the same invisible cloak draped over Alice. Judy wanted to ask her why she was moving to Boston, but then she caught the flitter of discomfort in Alice's eyes.

Judy wanted to say something else, a few generic words of good luck, but the moment passed in silence and Alice leaned against the cart and pushed away. Judy watched her as she merged into the crowd of shoppers, disappearing from view.

12

The two suitcases on the bed had been a gift from Alice's parents. They were strong and light with smooth zippers and reinforced corners, but the black suitcases were also open cavities waiting to be filled up with a week's worth of clothes and toiletries and whatever else he'd need. After stacking four shirts and two pairs of pants, Kevin took a break.

He'd never been fond of packing, because the truth was, he never wanted to leave home. Out there, life was mysterious and uncertain. Hotels were basically the same no matter where he went, so they were all unfamiliar in their familiar ways, but that didn't allay his anxiety. He wouldn't consider himself agoraphobic, but perhaps that was in his future. If so, fine by him. He liked his house, his dog, and life would proceed even if he never again stepped a foot outside his front door.

There had been a few times, though, when he hadn't minded leaving, when in fact he'd been thrilled to toss in socks and T-shirts and little bottles of toiletries into a duffel bag. He'd been with Alice for barely two weeks when he suggested they go away for the weekend.

They were sitting at the breakfast nook of his old apartment in Montclair. She was wearing a Penn State shirt of his, nursing her morning coffee.

"Where to?"

He'd known he was pushing, that she had every right to say that they were rushing. In fact, that's what he'd been expecting, so when she saw how she'd stumped him, she laughed.

"You thought I'd say no."

"Yes."

"Then let's figure out where we can go."

After leafing through Kevin's collection of brochures and local magazines, they had it: Stokes Forest. It was an hour north, Route 15 up to Sussex County, where there were fifteen cabins in the state park. Only one was available on short notice, so Kevin made the reservation, and they were off.

It was Mother's Day weekend, almost twenty years ago. Alice tapped her feet to the Beatles on the car radio, "Here Comes the Sun." They got lost twice, but even that was pleasant, Alice thumbing through his ratty collection of maps, pointing out he had one for every New Jersey county except Sussex. This was the magic of a burgeoning relationship: Nothing could derail it. If they'd gotten into an accident, Kevin was certain they would've walked away from the wreck and laughed it off.

Their cabin was number 15, the most secluded of the lot, located underneath a giant silver maple whose thousands of leaves swayed like small hands conducting the wind. Consisting of a single large room, there were two sets of bunk beds inside the log cabin, the mattresses utilitarian slabs of vinyl-covered foam. They piled two of them together, which made it slightly less uncomfortable to sleep on, though they weren't doing much of that anyway. After making love that night, they walked out naked into their backyard hand in hand, letting the night's easy breeze dry their sweaty bodies. Alice stood like a living work of art, her breasts luminous moons, her hair strands of gold. Kevin supposed he didn't look half bad himself. After all, they were both in their twenties, their muscles and bones working in youthful concert, and it seemed logical to kiss and fall gently onto the ground and do what came naturally to them.

His knees sank into the soft, cool earth. The light from the cabin's window illuminated Alice's hair tangling in the blades of grass, and as they moved in rhythm, they fell deeper into their natural surroundings. They held each other and rolled over until she was on top, and now it was his turn to disappear into the greenery, to feel the night's dampness spread on his back, to smell the freshness of the forest intermingle with the human scent of this woman.

Next morning, they hiked down a nearby canyon. The stream was fast and clean with tiny waterfalls foaming up the water as they followed the path.

"We had sex," Alice said, "outside."

"I can't believe it, either," Kevin said. "I've never done it outside of a bed, to tell you the truth."

"Not even a car?"

"No."

"We'll have to fix that."

Alice jumped over a wet patch of earth and landed on the ball of her left foot, a set of movements that was as efficient as it was elegant. Her balance was impeccable, innate, and the same could be said of her temperament. There was an inner calm about her, a place he couldn't touch, at least not yet. It made him hungry for her, to know her, to be with her.

"Is this something we should expect, that we'll keep doing crazy things when we're together?" she asked.

Hearing her say that word, *together*, made him want to jump, so he did. He leaped where she'd leaped, over the wetness and onto the exact same spot, except he weighed another fifty pounds and the ground reacted differently. Something woody cracked underneath, and Kevin lost his footing and his right ankle turned a funny way. Luckily, he was able to avoid wiping out altogether by shifting his weight to his other foot and grabbing onto Alice's outstretched arms.

"You're hurt."

"I might be."

"Lean on me," Alice said. "We'll just backtrack and get back to the car."

They'd been walking for a good half an hour, probably a mile away from the parking lot. Alice was not a small woman, but Kevin was afraid she was overestimating her endurance. He tried to put weight on his ankle, but the pain made his head woozy.

"Don't be one of those men," she said, wrapping his arm around her shoulder. "We'll get through this, but only if you let me."

They passed the time by taking in the beauty around them. There were large clusters of hydrangeas along the path, a sudden burst of white, a subdued flare of lavender, a benevolent bouquet of yellow. It took twice as long, and they stopped several times for Kevin to rest his good leg and Alice to catch her breath. On the way, they met a father and his teenage son, and the man asked if they could help in any way. Before Kevin had a chance, Alice spoke up.

"Thank you, but no, we're okay. Have a great day."

She hadn't sounded confrontational, but almost. After they'd gone, she told him, "I can take care of you. Of us."

"I know."

"If I needed the man's help," she added, "I would've asked for it."

It was a lie, but back then, Kevin hadn't known that. He hadn't known how Alice would always be ready to extend herself but never receive in return. He argued with her that couples operated best on a balance, that give-and-take was an implicit contract to marriage, but she never budged. Eventually he relented and learned to live in her debt, which was what she wanted, what must've made her feel safe.

That Sunday morning at Stokes Forest, as he sat in bed and watched while she packed them back up for their return, he couldn't stop himself from making yet another ask.

"It's Mother's Day today," he said. "I think the best gift I can give my mom is for you to meet her."

Alice, done with her suitcase, moved onto Kevin's duffel. "And why do you think that?"

"You'd get along," he said. "She would like you."

"If she didn't?"

"Tough."

Her back was to him, but he could tell she'd liked that answer. He didn't exactly know how, but he felt it, like a puzzle piece snapping into place. He'd dated plenty of girls before, many he'd been fairly crazy about, but this was not the same. Being with a woman he liked had been like the quenching of a thirst, but with Alice, there was no release. His desire for her was a constant, pervasive hum, chugging along in the background of his mind.

Holy shit, he thought to himself. *This is love.*

He rode in the passenger seat of his sedan, a seldom-experienced perspective that let him feel like an outside observer to his own life. Riding down Route 206, past the canary-yellow clusters of forsythia in bloom along the road, they drove through the towns of his youth. He told her about Old Man Rafferty's in Hillsborough, where Kevin and his friends always ordered dessert first as the menu instructed ("Life is short!"). On the night of their senior prom, they walked around Harlingen Cemetery and toasted their beers to the dearly departed. And at Montgomery Cinemas, he'd seen his first foreign-language film, *Il Postino*, a movie he'd found so moving that his date asked him if he was all right when she saw him sobbing like a little girl.

"That was our first and only date," Kevin said.

"That last part, where the guy is playing the sounds he'd recorded for Neruda . . ."

"Stop, you're gonna get me all *verklempt*!"

As they neared Princeton, Alice pulled over at an Exxon station and grabbed her purse.

"Not Mother's Day without flowers," she said. Kevin reached for his wallet, but Alice put a hand on his arm. "My treat."

With a bundle of red carnations in his lap, he gave Alice turn-by-turn directions to his parents' house.

"Is there anything I should know?" Alice asked.

"Not really. My father doesn't speak much. He doesn't exactly have command of the English language, though even if he did, he wouldn't say much. My mother does translation work for the university, both oral and written, so she talks like a native."

"You have a sister."

"Still in college. Supposed to have graduated a couple years ago, but it didn't happen."

They made the final turn, but instead of parking in front of the white mailbox of his parents, they stopped behind a police cruiser.

Kevin sighed.

"You're not concerned," Alice said.

"Not yet, no," he said.

The commotion was where it always was, between his mother and her nemesis, Mrs. Fugate, by the Tolkien-esque sycamore tree that sat between the two backyards.

"So I take it this is not an anomaly," Alice said as they made their way over. Kevin's ankle was better, but he still leaned on her for support.

"No. The cop and I are on a first-name basis. If it wasn't my mother arguing with her neighbor, it was my sister, Judy, getting into some sort of fight, disorderliness, whatever."

"I like your family already."

"You can have them," Kevin said. "This has been an ongoing feud, by the way—the old neighbors moved, and the tree sits on the property line."

The cop on duty was indeed the one he almost considered a friend, Mitch. Kevin's mother was holding a tall tree trimmer, the kind with the blade at the tip and a rope on a pulley to snap the cut. She was in her gardening outfit of green gloves and Mets baseball cap, and she held the pole with both hands, looking as if she had no intention of letting it go.

"Kevin," Mitch said, grateful for his arrival. "Can you please talk some sense into your mother here? Your dad has given up—he went back in the house to make me deal with this mess."

"Mom," Kevin said with an open hand, motioning for the trimmer. "Please."

"It's my tree."

Mrs. Fugate, arms crossed, snorted her displeasure. "The hell it is."

"If she doesn't stop," Mitch told Kevin, "I'm gonna have to bring her in. I'm serious. I know it's Mother's Day, but Dr. Fugate plays golf with the chief, you know? I have to do something"—and now he was talking to Kevin's mother—"unless Mrs. Lee promises once and for all to modify this tree only if she and the Fugates come to a written agreement beforehand."

"They don't take care of it," Mrs. Lee said. "I've been doing this for a long time. It's my right."

"Kevin," Mitch said. "Please don't make me do this."

"Hi," Alice said to Mrs. Lee. "I'm Alice, a friend of Kevin's. I see the pile of branches you have here already. Do you have much more to cut?"

"Just one more."

Everyone looked up when she pointed her trimmer to the branch that clearly needed cutting, a dry brown bone of a thing, looking like a desiccated claw grabbing at the sky.

"Which is clearly on my side," Mrs. Fugate said. "I've had enough of this. I'm going to have my husband call Chief Maddox right now."

While Mitch attempted to placate Mrs. Fugate, Kevin watched his mother and Alice talk without talking. Alice smiled, then his mother smiled, and then she passed the trimmer to Alice and stood as a human shield against Mitch the cop while Alice excised the dead wood. It bounced from branch to branch, end over end, heading for Mrs. Fugate, who ran away screaming.

As it turned out, everyone got what they wanted that day. Mitch got to handcuff Alice, Mrs. Fugate got her arrest, his mother got the branch, and Alice got to give. And Kevin got what he wanted, too, bringing his mother and his future wife together. Now his mother was dead and his wife was no longer his wife, but back then, he'd been happy with the knowledge that these two women were very much alike and that he was their interconnection.

Kevin sat on his living room floor and gave Snaps a good brushing, thinking of that day. His dog whipped her head around and growled. Kevin, in his reverie, ran the metal brush through her tail, a no-no.

"Sorry, girl. I should be paying attention, I know."

Kevin's doorbell ding-donged, and Snaps bolted from relaxation to alert mode. It was too early for it to be Judy.

At the door, Bill thrust a six-pack of beer to his chest.

"Can't have you leave without a proper good-bye," he said.

Snaps, even with her bum hips, found the energy to jump up around Bill.

"Missy Snaps!" he said, and he gave her a good scratch on her nose.

Kevin sat on the end of the sofa while Bill took the armchair. Tomorrow Ernie would assign half of Kevin's clients to Bill, including Robert the Third and Alexa. It depressed Kevin to think that the club would go on without him. And not seeing Bill every workday—it was a different kind of divorce, another odd space in his life left open.

"You sure about all this?" Bill asked.

"I haven't liked the job for a while now. And this thing I told you about my parents . . ."

"That's no reason to just quit your job. I mean what the hell are you going to do, you know, to live?"

Ernie, being the sweetheart that he was, had told Kevin that if he changed his mind in a week, he'd be welcomed back, but Kevin told him not to bother. Ernie asked him the same question that Bill was asking now, and Kevin's response remained the same.

"I'm not sure what I want, but I know what I don't want."

Bill nodded. "You're okay financially? The airline ticket to San Francisco must've cost some Benjamins."

"Trent, you know, the pilot with the Connors two-handed back-hand? He got me on a reasonable flight at the last minute. Seemed like the right thing to do to go out there and see what I can find out."

"And your dad hasn't told you anything more."

"He says my mother took care of it all, whatever the hell that means."

Bill cracked open his can of beer, and Kevin did likewise.

"Love?" Bill asked, raising his can.

"Love," Kevin said, raising his own. "How long have we been doing that?"

"So long I don't remember."

They toasted. Aluminum never emitted the satisfying ring of glass, but it was better than nothing. As the carbonation effervesced in his throat, Kevin felt as if they should say something meaningful to each other, but all they did was slurp and burp. This is where it was better to be women, who'd hug and cry and promise they'd do lunch every week. Even though the sensitive man was in, it was for girlfriends and wives. Guys were still guys with each other, keeping their emotions in check, preferring to talk about last night's ball game than to dwell on their feelings. He and Bill had been together for more than half of their lives, and this was it. The morning after Alice had left, Kevin walked into the club and saw Bill at his court, waiting for him. His friend tossed him a new can of tennis balls, and together they pried open the lids, the whooshing sound of the vacuum seal breaking and the smell of untouched rubber familiar and cleansing. They hit the crap out of those balls, and as his anger and melancholy bounced away with each stroke, Kevin wished there were words to express what he felt toward Bill. It was gratitude, but it was also love. They could attach the word to a can of beer, but not to each other. It was understood, and maybe that made it more special, or possibly just tragic.

They exchanged a handshake that led to a half hug.

"You'll be missed," Bill said.

"Same here," Kevin said.

And then he was gone. Snaps laid down to snooze on the rug by the door. Above her hung a small oval painting, one that Judy had done of her as a puppy, standing on a pair of open hands that pointed out toward the viewer, offering the tiny dog to the world. Judy had used thick brushstrokes, the dog's fur like a relief map, the lines on the palms etched in. His dog used to be so small, so young. His sister was supposed to become a successful artist, and he a professional tennis player. He thought his parents would stay healthy and grow old together. He and Alice, too.

Kevin walked over to the window that faced the backyard and pushed it open. The air was damp and cool, evening turning into night, another autumn day coming to a close. Crickets chirped faintly, far away in the approaching darkness. He wished for something to occupy him until his sister came to pick him up, but there was nothing left.

13

On the kitchen counter, Judy found a small stack of pages.
"Oh, that," Kevin said, and from his guarded tone, she knew
she'd stumbled on something he hadn't meant for her to see. Kevin
had made seven copies, one for each day that he would be in San
Francisco. It read:

- ▶ QUICK WALK—MORNING
  - get plastic bag (in case she poops)
- ▶ FEEDING—MORNING
  - 1 1/2 cups of dry food
  - 1/2 cup of wet food (cover with plastic wrap and
    place can in fridge)
  - Fresh water in bowl, filled 3/4
- ▶ LONG WALK—AFTERNOON
  - get plastic bag (in case she poops)
- ▶ FEEDING—EVENING
  - 1 1/2 cups of dry food
  - 1/2 cup of wet food (cover with plastic wrap and
    place can in fridge)
- ▶ QUICK WALK—NIGHT
  - take her out so she can pee

Her control-freak brother, doing what he did best. At the beginning of each line item was an empty checkbox. Did he actually expect
her to take a pen and make a mark as she completed each task? If so,
he could just shove it.

Granted, the last time Judy house-sat for him, there was an incident.
Snaps ended up peeing in the downstairs bathroom because Judy had
forgotten to walk her that afternoon, which was totally bullshit because

she hadn't forgotten, she'd simply chose to delay it a little because it was the season finale of *Lost* and she had to watch the clips episode before it because there were a gazillion characters and more side plots than all the daytime soaps put together, and as for the finale itself, she couldn't miss even a minute because if she did, the show's title would become even more apt.

"What, you think I'm gonna screw up again?" Judy asked.

"No," Kevin answered, "of course not," and now his voice shifted again, this time to that of a placating big brother. These sheets of paper weren't just a collection of stupid checklists but also a time machine. Throughout her adolescence, those empty squares were always ready to report some future failure of hers. Kevin and her dad were the ones crafting these checklists and sticking them on the fridge, a happy fruit-shaped magnet clip (winking apple, grinning banana, laughing pineapple) holding up a clean white page with bold black letters, announcing chores that had to be done, family trips that necessitated preparation, groceries needed for the coming week.

She tossed the stack back on the counter, the sheets fanning out.

"You don't have to use them if you don't want to," Kevin said. He picked them up and piled them straight again.

"It's like you expect me to fail."

"You're reading way too much into this. I just want to make sure you take care of Snaps."

"If people expected more of me, I would give more of myself. It's a two-way street."

"Well, there was that accident last time . . ."

"See? That's all you remember. How about the fact that for the other six days, I was a spectacular success? Isn't that worth remembering?"

Snaps sauntered in, a stuffed duck in her mouth, because Judy had raised her voice. She remembered Kevin telling her how Snaps always appeared whenever he and Alice argued, almost as if she wanted to referee the verbal bout, though to Judy, the dog hardly looked like an official, circling twice and plopping on the rug underneath the breakfast table, peeking up at Judy and Kevin with doleful eyes. She let out a long, heavy sigh. If anything, Snaps looked sad and tired, like an old lady sitting at a bus stop. Kevin probably hadn't noticed since he lived with the animal, but Judy could see how much his dog had aged since the last time she'd seen her, her muzzle almost entirely white now, a shaky stutter in her hind legs.

"How long do German shepherds usually live?" Judy asked.

"What the hell kind of a question is that?"

"Jesus. Never mind." With her luck, Snaps would probably keel over dead while her brother was roaming the streets of San Francisco.

He squatted down and gave the back of Snaps's head a good scratch, and the dog lifted her chin in bliss. She might not have that much longer to go, but she sure knew how to enjoy life. Maybe in the week Judy was going to stay here, she could pick up some tips from the old dog.

"So you're all packed up?"

"Just about," Kevin said. "It's been a while since I went anywhere."

"You used to go away all the time," Judy said. "When you were playing those satellite tournaments."

Kevin rose and walked over to the garbage can. His fingers were laced with dog hair. "Can you brush her? Just a couple of times will do."

"I don't know," Judy said. "It's not on the list."

Kevin gave her a look that took her back, an impatient, exasperated raising of one eyebrow he used to level on her when they were kids. It made her happy to see it.

"You remember those trips I took?" he asked. "I only signed up for three of them. To give you an idea how long ago that was, satellite tournaments don't exist anymore. They're called Futures now."

"Futures," Judy said. "I like it. Sounds more hopeful."

"If you win."

She watched him add last-minute toiletries into his suitcase: an electric shaver with its cord wrapped around itself, a bottle of Pert Plus shampoo, a half-squeezed tube of Aquafresh toothpaste. She had to laugh.

"What's so funny?" Kevin asked.

"That's what you used when we were kids, the same exact brands."

He shrugged. "If I like something, I stick with it."

Her brother did have a knack for sticking with things. It was how he became such a good tennis player, staying out on the courts for six, seven hours a day to practice, hitting the balls until their fuzz wore off, downing gallons of water to stay hydrated during those scorching summer days. After high school, she'd seen him play twice, the first time at Penn State, where he handily beat his opponent on a muggy morning for the state title, a guy tall enough to play professional basketball. But the second time, at an indoor satellite tournament in Pittsburgh, it was a completely different story. Kevin lost in less than an hour to a bald man, a wily veteran who'd stuck around just to screw with the kids' chances, at least that's what it seemed like to Judy. The guy didn't hit half as hard as Kevin but he knew the angles, and the number of times he lobbed a ball just out of Kevin's reach—it was as if she were seeing two completely different games being played. She wished there was something she could do beyond clapping and hoping.

Kevin was now upstairs, his footsteps creaking the boards above. This was what she got for coming early to pick him up and drop him off at the airport, all this useless waiting. But she'd wanted to give him the right impression, that she would take care of his house and his precious dog in his absence.

"Snaps," she said, who was lying on her side with her legs stretched out, the epitome of relaxation. The dog looked clumsy getting up from her repose, and one of her limbs made a knuckle-cracking sound, but still she putt-putted her way over and sat up straight.

Judy stroked the back of Snaps's head and stared into her milky brown eyes. She'd seen on a PBS program that petting a dog lowered your blood pressure and made you live longer. It seemed like bunk, but as she sat and felt the softness of Snaps's fur on her palm, she noticed the repetition of the motion itself was like a mantra, and then there was the immediate feedback, too, that something Judy was doing was very obviously having a positive effect on a living creature. Still, a dog was a lot of work, but a cat like Roger's? Momo never needed to be walked and he went to the bathroom by himself. She would ask Roger about his cat when he'd come over later for dinner. Tomorrow made it a week since their first date, but it felt as if she'd been with him for much longer. Was that good or bad?

Snaps broke away from her and bounded to the bottom of the staircase, her tail wagging. Kevin appeared moments later holding what resembled a palm-size tennis racquet, except without strings.

"I knew I'd forget this," he said, finding the bag of toiletries in his suitcase.

"Your good-luck mini-racquet charm?"

"It's my tongue scraper," he said, examining the green plastic object under the kitchen lights. "That's weird. I never thought it looked like a racquet."

"When did you start scraping your tongue?"

Kevin said nothing and slipped the device into his bag.

Alice, of course, and Judy wished she hadn't asked. These are the gifts we're left with when our loved ones leave us—a tongue scraper for Kevin, a press pot for her. Before Brian, she'd brewed her coffee with a coffee maker, but after he showed her his French coffee maker, she never went back. Now she couldn't imagine making coffee without pressing down on that plunger, and she was sure Kevin would never consider his mouth clean without having his tongue scraped.

"I forgot to tell you," she said. "I saw Alice."

He froze. "When?"

"Monday. At Wegmans."

"Oh," he said, and he brought both of the zipper handles to the top.

"You saw her in the morning, and I saw her in the evening."

He looked away, embarrassed. "So you spoke with her."

She wanted to tell Kevin that Alice was moving to Boston, but she couldn't do it. It was the way he was standing there, holding on to the handle of the suitcase, almost for support.

"She's not seeing anyone," Judy said.

"Is that what she told you?"

Her face got hot. "What do you mean?"

"In her office, there was a picture on her computer, with some guy. Some Eurotrash asshole."

"That doesn't mean . . ."

"Oh, please," Kevin said, and he yanked on his suitcase. "You didn't see the picture. They weren't pen pals. Come on, we're gonna be late. I can't believe she'd bullshit you like that."

Judy followed him out and didn't know what to say. Maybe it was better that he was now angry at Alice. At least this is what she told herself to stave off the guilt.

He shoved his suitcase into the trunk and got in. The car was cold, her breath fogging up the side window. She cranked the engine.

"It doesn't surprise me she lied to you," Kevin said. "She probably just wanted to get away and do her shopping."

"Oh," Judy said. "I see." Though she didn't see.

"She never really liked you. Or anyone in our family. Or me, for that matter, obviously."

Judy knew Kevin was just angry, but his words still hurt. Alice never liked her, probably complained about her behind her back after all those holiday get-togethers. Judy could see it, Alice prettily sitting on the edge of the bed, brushing her hair and telling Kevin what a screw-up his little sister was, how annoying it was that she had to sit next to her and listen to some sorry story in her stupid life.

"Fucking bitch," Judy said.

"Right on, sister."

She slammed on the accelerator hard enough to sink them both into their seats.

J udy parked the car at the curb of Terminal C, the passenger drop-off section of Newark Airport. Kevin yanked out his suitcase and gave her a quick hug.

"A week and a day from today," he said.

"Okay," she told him. She couldn't help but think of the last time she was here at the airport, with Brian. She'd kissed him, he'd waved good-bye, and then she never saw him again. The more she tried to fight the tears, the more she cried, so she stood in front of her departing brother and just let herself weep as cold rain fell.

"It's all right." Kevin embraced her once more. "I'll be back before you know it."

She was always the one left behind: her mother, then Brian, now her brother. Leaving someone was a lesser form of death, wasn't it? Because the fact was, when Kevin walked away from her, he would be gone from her life for the next eight days. For all she knew, he could very well be dead the second he stepped off the plane, fall flat on his face from a brain aneurysm. When the automatic doors of the terminal parted and Kevin gave her a thumbs-up, she felt another wave welling up from her chest.

Even though Kevin had satellite radio in his car, Judy kept it off on the drive back and listened to the tires cutting through rain, the occasional swoosh of the passing vehicle. The reflectors embedded in the yellow median of Interstate 78 glowed in the wetness, and slip-streaming through the black highway stretched out in front of her, she was fine, in a buoyant mood, even. She'd always liked Kevin's old house, which was way roomier than her one-bedroom apartment, and this was gonna be like a vacation, especially with Roger visiting. Actually, that was what she was supposed to ask on the drive up, if that was okay with Kevin, but why wouldn't it be okay? As long as she changed the sheets at the end, who gave a shit?

What she liked most about his 160-year-old house was the first floor, which was preserved in its original configuration and materials: tongue-and-groove walls, pumpkin pine floorboards that stretched twenty feet long, a pair of wooden columns supporting the structure that looked hand-chiseled. Sitting in his living room was like being transported to *Little House on the Prairie* times, the very definition of quaint. It was drafty as hell, but right now, the nights didn't get colder than fifty degrees, so she'd be fine wrapped up in a down blanket. She'd borrowed a couple of DVD sets of TV shows from the library and couldn't wait to start vegging out.

What she liked least about his house was its location. He lived minutes from the main drag of Harmony, but once she made the mountainous drive up Coleman Hill Road, it was Unabomber country. Even though she'd driven to his house at least a dozen times, she still had to keep an eye on the trip meter after passing the sign for the dairy farm, because otherwise, she'd miss the quick left turn. Which she just did.

"Goddamnit," Judy said, and she spun a U-turn.

The place was creepy dark at night, but when she pulled into the gravel driveway, the motion floods thankfully kicked in. Kevin had replaced all his regular bulbs with low-energy compact fluorescents everywhere in the house, so she'd just leave them all on. She felt like a little kid for thinking like this, but she'd never been a fan of rural areas. Even though she hardly knew her neighbor in her apartment complex, their proximity trumped their anonymity. When she killed the engine and stepped out of Kevin's car, the trilling of insects was as disturbing as a continuous scream.

Judy hurried from the car to the door and almost ran into the garbage can, which had been pulled out from the side of the house and left directly in her path. Kevin must've done that to make sure she pulled it out to the curb, not so much for this week but the next one, because he assumed she would forget otherwise. She thought about not doing it just to spite him, but it was overflowing. She could conceivably do it in the morning, but as she recalled her brother's instructions, the garbage truck came at six.

She pulled the handle and dragged the hulking vat of plastic down the driveway. In the distance, something howled. After pulling it halfway, she had to pause to catch her breath and felt a twinge in her left ankle. Fantastic—she probably tweaked something. She felt it again, and now she heard a noise cutting through the fallen leaves. It sounded sort of like those rumba shakers that the teacher shook in the modern dance class she took last year, except it was at a faster beat. And there it was again, coming from somewhere below, and then she saw it, a shiny long thing slowly slithering away from underneath the wheels of the garbage can.

She'd never seen a snake in the wild before, and strangely enough, her first reaction was one of admiration. It must've been at least five feet long, and under the faint light of the crescent moon peeking through the rain clouds, its sleek, smooth skin sparkled like metal. And then there was the sound again, the rattle, and the twinge Judy had felt in her ankle turned to a numb sort of burning, and now the full realization of what just happened shocked her cold. She backed away and circled wide of the snake and stumbled to the front door and dropped her brother's ring of keys as she tried to unlock it because her hands were shaking so badly and her entire right foot now tingled like it had gone to sleep and was it panic or venom that made her breathing so fast?

She fumbled open the door and felt for the light switch.

How long did it take for this poison to work through her body? Was she supposed to suck it out? Everything was blurry—was her vision affected? No, it was tears, tears of fear. She had to get herself under control. Even if she were to scream until her voice box blew, no one would hear her because her stupid brother lived in the middle of fucking nowhere.

She wiped at her eyes with the sleeve of her sweatshirt. It was still possible that all this was a psychosomatic reaction to looking at the snake, that what happened was nothing more than a muscle strain from dragging that garbage can. She sat on the floor and reached for her ankle—if only she'd worn her black leather boots—and saw what she already knew. There were three sets of bite marks, tiny red eyes looking back at her. She'd been bitten not once, not twice, but three times. How was that even possible? Did the snake have three heads?

Judy felt a strong vibration on the inside of her hips, and the sensation was like nothing she'd experienced before. What was happening to her? And as quickly as it came, now it was gone. And then again it was there, like a warning, stronger than ever. She tentatively put her hand on her hip and found a hard, round nodule—her cell phone.

Maybe it would be funny later, but right now, her emotions jumped from terror to relief. It was the alarm she'd set for herself, but what was it for? No matter—she dialed 911.

"Nine-one-one, what's your emergency?"

Now her lips were tingly, too, and her fingers felt fat and slow.

"A rattlesnake bit me," she said, "three times."

"Can you tell me your name?"

"Judy Lee."

"Do you need an ambulance?"

"Yes."

"Where are you?"

"In my brother's house," she said. As soon as she'd said it, she realized how idiotic her response was. But the dispatcher wasn't fazed.

"Can you give me an exact address?"

She knew it was on Buckhorn, but for the life of her—and it might very well be her life—she couldn't remember the number. She'd always hated math in school, all those numerals and operations and variables and angles a frustrating mystery to her.

"Miss Judy? Can you tell me the house number and the town?"

The woman's voice was getting softer, as if she were on the radio and the volume knob was turning down. It seemed to Judy as if she were no longer here, that she was watching what was going on from elsewhere.

"The town is Harmony. The street is Buckhorn Drive. It's one mile from the sign for Makepeace Farms. There are two cows sitting in lawn chairs. On the sign, not actually. Sixteen. That's the house number."

"Okay, Miss Judy. The ambulance is on its way."

"That's good," Judy said. And it was. Maybe that meant she wouldn't die alone. "Are you allowed to stay on with me, or do you have to go?"

"I'll stay with you until the paramedics arrive," she said. The woman had a deep, reassuring voice. As Judy closed her eyes and felt the faint rhythm of her own heartbeat, her ears filling with something between a bee's buzzing and white noise, she thought back to her mother. When she'd been a child, the best part of getting sick was having her mother at her bedside, her concerned face hovering over Judy's. That was so long ago, and yet it seemed so very real. If she reached out, Judy was certain she would touch her.

PART II

•

THE MONTH OF OCTOBER

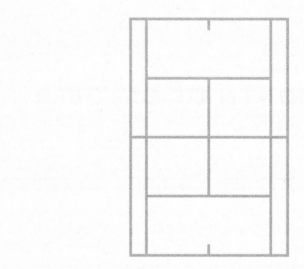

14

With his rolling suitcase in tow, Kevin stood at the foot of Powell Street and considered the hill ahead of him, and the hill above that one. Who in their right mind would build a city on terrain like this? But build it they did. None of the surrounding structures were as tall as the skyscrapers of Manhattan, but like any big city, every conceivable space was occupied by restaurants and stores and galleries and, of course, Starbucks.

Twenty-five years ago, his mother was attending a weekend conference for Korean translators in San Raphael, and his father had gifted an airline ticket to Kevin. He didn't think it was such a great trip, but his opinion changed the night his mother drove them across the Golden Gate Bridge and down Lombard Street. To go from the vertiginous expanse of that suspension bridge to the ski slope–inspired one-way road—this wasn't a city, it was an amusement park. Kevin had never been so far away from home with just his mother, and as they walked down Fisherman's Wharf, past the crying cluster of sea lions and the bright beacon of Alcatraz, she seemed more like a friend than his mother. He accompanied her to her sessions held in the hotel ballroom, and they ate lunch together with her colleagues. He'd never felt more grown up.

He wished his mother were here now, for a variety of reasons, but mostly so they could revisit these streets. After crossing three intersections, Kevin's heart pounded and his calves burned, a shameful surprise since he was technically still an athlete. He paused in front of what looked like a park: palm trees swayed in the October breeze, a tourist posed next to a heart-shaped metallic sculpture, and rectangular patches of grass sprouted in between concrete stairs that led up to a stage where people danced the tango. As Kevin neared them, he heard a trio of musicians in the corner, a violin, a keyboard, and a man squeezing a palm-size cousin of the accordion. Couples twirled about the dance floor, one of them having gone all out, the pencil-thin mustached man wearing a one-piece all-black suit like an ice skater while the woman was in a skin-tight red dress with ruffles. Her hair was pulled into a bun, and when they touched their cheeks together and marched in lock step with their hands clasped and arms extended, the audience clapped and whooped.

Watching them, Kevin recalled the time he and Alice enrolled in the beginner dance class at the studio located in a strip mall. The place was called It Takes Two, and before it was a studio, it had been a candle shop, and even though nothing of the old store remained, the smell of those candles lingered on. Depending on where they stood, a different scent would assault them: vanilla near the entrance, cinnamon by the water cooler, a bouquet of roses by the stage where the teacher demonstrated the dance of the evening. The class had been an anniversary gift to her, and what he remembered most was watching Alice dance with other men. That was something the teacher had insisted on, that they switch partners to get acquainted not with the people but with the moves. Even though Kevin had never taken a single dance lesson, he was good at it, nimble on his feet and loose with his hips. Tennis required muscle control, the execution of small steps at a much quicker pace than introductory dancing. The women complimented him as he waltzed and jitterbugged and swung, but Kevin found himself time and again looking across the room for Alice in another's arms, laughing and twirling like a stranger. What he felt wasn't jealousy but rather curiosity. Seeing her with another man was a pleasantly dislocating sensation, as if he were in a parallel universe where they had yet to meet. It was exciting to pretend they could start over, that they could somehow do it better this time around. When it was his turn to reunite with Alice, she took his hand, and he pulled her close to him.

They were doing the foxtrot, spinning around like the rest of the couples in the room, the instructor shouting "slow, slow, quick-quick" to the rhythm of a big band version of Frank Sinatra singing "The Way You Look Tonight." Since Alice had majored in dance, her movements were more defined than every other woman's. For a moment he was beset with pride: *This is my wife, and she's the most beautiful, most talented woman in the room.*

"Why are you smiling?" she asked, smiling herself. She leaned back and away from him, her neck as elegant as a flower stem.

"It's like you're somebody else out there."

"Who am I, then?"

Before he could answer, the instructor clapped twice, signaling another change in partners, and she ducked under his arm and pirouetted away from him, laughing as she snapped onto the next lucky guy. Except now, his memory was playing tricks on him because the new dancer's face was the same as the man on her computer screen in her office, he and Alice staring at the camera cheek to cheek. Kevin felt a hollowness in his belly, as if it had been scraped out.

Perhaps it was just hunger. He hadn't eaten since the stewardess served some sort of a chicken-and-carrot stew in a boiling-hot mini–casserole dish that had tasted like ramen noodles. He dragged his suitcase down the stairs of the park, every drop of the wheels onto the concrete like an angry complaint. To his right was a square-shaped beige building owned by Saks Fifth Avenue, the West Coast sister to the New York store. As he trudged past the Marriott, Kevin wished he'd reserved his room there. According to the online map printout quickly becoming soggy from his sweaty palm, he still had to cross two more streets, but these weren't streets, they were mountains. The last one was a doozy, the sidewalk grooved to provide traction when it rained. At the corner of Powell and California, Kevin leaned against the wooden pole that had two lights mounted at the top. Above him was a yellow sign:

CROSS STREET

CABLE CARS

DO NOT STOP

What did it mean? Was it telling him to cross the street, or not cross the street? Or was *cross* not a verb but an adjective, the three-stanza poem merely stating facts? It all became clear when one did come tumbling down on its track without bothering to slow down, clinging and clanging right by him. A commercial jingle from Kevin's childhood played in his head: "Rice-A-Roni, the San Francisco Treat." His stomach growled, but he wanted to check into his hotel and get settled in first. Luckily, the Stanford Court was right here, the sign in gold and burgundy, the main entrance underneath an arch big enough to allow two cars through.

This was not the sort of place Kevin normally stayed, but the airline pilot in the tennis club who'd gotten him the last-minute tickets had a relationship with the manager of this luxury hotel and was able to get him rock-bottom rates for the week. Walking through the arch, Kevin was bathed in a yellow light spread by an enormous stained glass dome above a water fountain. The main entrance doors were made of artsy translucent glass, and the woman behind the marble counter, in her navy-blue uniform, looked as unique as she sounded, her accent a hybrid of Caribbean and British.

"Welcome to San Francisco, Mr. Lee," she said as she handed him his key.

His room was on the seventh floor, and when he spread open his curtains, he had a view of the bay, tiny white boats bobbing on the blue water, and of the city, too, the Transamerica Pyramid jutting out from the skyline. Even though there were hundreds if not thousands of people in a hotel, it was a place of collective loneliness. No matter who you were—a couple vacationing, a businessman on a trip, a conventioneer—you were away from home, from all the things that made you who you were.

Kevin pushed the pillows on the bed aside and fell backward, his body sinking into multiple layers of comfort, swaddled like a baby. He touched the headboard, which was velvet smooth and cushioned. Everything in the room was a soothing shade of beige, and Kevin didn't even realize he'd fallen asleep until he woke up half an hour later.

By now Kevin was famished, so he took the elevator down and, with the help of the map he'd picked up from the lobby, walked just two streets to Grant Avenue, and here was perhaps the most endearing thing about a cosmopolitan city like this one: At the corner was a red brick church, Old Saint Mary's Cathedral, and if he were to continue down on California toward the bay, he'd pass by monolithic corporations and high-class hotels, but on Grant, the landscape transformed to the Orient, right down to the streetlight shaped like an ancient lantern with a sinewy dragon entwined at the base. Someone had erected an old-school pagoda on the top of an apartment building, and across the street, the ordinary square-bricked structure that housed the Chinatown Food Court was topped with sweeping gabled rooflines, the corners curved up like a ski jump. Taken singly, these buildings were vortices of intercultural disarray, but standing side by side, they made their own kind of weird sense.

Kevin stopped at a small café that had a banner hanging above the door that piqued his curiosity: ginger milk. They also had a sun-faded poster of various dishes on the window, and standing in the shade, Kevin wished he'd worn his windbreaker. He'd heard that San Francisco was like this, that you could go from spring to summer to fall, all on a single street.

The wind chime attached to the door rang as he pulled it open. The café was just a strip, barely enough room for two people to walk by the counter, but in the back it opened up to a cozy circular room with three tables. He ordered a ginger milk plus a plate of beef lo mein and was told it would take about five minutes, so Kevin took a seat next to a foursome of teenage boys, dressed in what must be the de rigueur skater gear: ski knit caps, black T-shirts, torn jeans. A skateboard leaned behind each kid, and they were busily dissecting their plates of egg rolls with chopsticks. Kevin couldn't understand what the kids were saying because they were speaking Chinese, but it was plain they were having a great time together. These kids were about Alexa's age, and maybe even her type; he remembered at some point hearing that her not-boyfriend Nate was an avid skateboarder. If he were back in New Jersey, he'd be warming her up, hitting to her backhand first, then to her forehand, and then she'd be up at the net, her eyes fixed on the ball as he'd taught her years ago when he'd used colored balls and had her yell out blue or red or green as soon as she saw it.

Except he was wrong, because it was actually seven o'clock on the East Coast now, three hours and three thousand miles separating him and home. Alexa was long gone, and so was he, on the opposite side of the country. Jesus, what the hell *was* he going to do when he got back home? With his life? With everything?

A bellhop ding: His food was ready.

The ginger milk came in a bowl, and what was inside wasn't a liquid but rather a light custard, its consistency like that of silken tofu. The warm milk was sugar sweet, but the ginger kicked his tongue around. It was absolutely delicious. He dug into the center, excavating a white chunk shaped like the Rock of Gibraltar and slurping it like Jell-O, which he hadn't had in years. It had been his favorite food growing up, and even though his mother always felt guilty for making it, thinking rightly that it was just a vat of jiggling candy, they had it once a week. He'd been so small then, and his mother had made all his decisions for him. What was that like, to have a little person to take care of, day in and day out? He didn't know, and chances were unlikely he ever would. Alice hadn't wanted children, and Kevin hadn't felt strongly one way or the other. He'd read somewhere that the final stage of maturity was raising your own kids, to give up your own life for the next generation. Some people never reached this point, and whether Kevin had actively decided or not, he was now one of them.

He was almost done with his ginger milk when his cell phone buzzed. It was a number from the 510 area code, which was Oakland, where Vincent DeGuardi's nursing home was. A woman who sounded harried was on the line.

"Mr. Lee, were you going to visit Mr. DeGuardi this evening?"

"That's right," Kevin said, confused. "Was I supposed to make an appointment or something? He told me I could just come by."

"Mr. DeGuardi passed away yesterday," the woman said.

"You've got to be joking."

A pregnant pause.

"Excuse me?" she asked.

He apologized for his insensitivity. He couldn't have gotten out here sooner than today, and now DeGuardi was dead.

"Marilyn is his daughter. She told us to forward all correspondence to her, so she would be the person to call. You're lucky we found his calendar—he had your name and your number written on it. You'll want to copy down this information."

Kevin walked up to the counter and borrowed a pen. He copied down the name Marilyn and a phone number onto a paper napkin.

He thanked the woman for saving him the trip out to Oakland and ended the call. Kevin forked up a tangle of lukewarm lo mein and felt anything but lucky.

15

A clear teardrop caught the morning sun. Slow-dripping into the syringe was a rectangular bag of liquid on a hook, and the mouth of the syringe was connected to a tube, and the translucent tube squiggled down and over and into Judy's right arm, where it disappeared under a band of white tape. She tried to lift her arm to get a better look, but what she wanted from her arm and what her arm was willing to give were two different things. Every part of her body felt heavy, as if she were covered by an iron blanket.

There was a bird to her left. At least that's what it had initially sounded like, but now the chirping was shortening to a steady beep. And now Judy could smell the familiar antiseptic scent around her. This was a hospital room. She'd been bitten by a snake. She wasn't dead.

"Well, hello there," a voice floated down from above.

It took forever for her head to turn. A young man with fashionably disheveled hair stood with a stethoscope wrapped around his neck.

"Hi," Judy said, but what came out was a quiet cough. She tried again and this time successfully whispered her greeting.

"I'll let the doctors know," he said. "It's good to have you back." He whipped the blue curtain around her as he left, the fabric swaying off the circular rail.

Little by little, her body returned to her. She stared at the source of the beeping and found the cardiac monitor, as small and thin as an iPad. There were four graphs running from right to left, the top green one peaking with the beat of her heart. Her pulse was 54, her blood pressure was 90 over 61. That seemed low, but she'd just woken up from being asleep for how long? She'd dropped Kevin off at the airport at six at night, so by the time she got back to his house, it'd been almost nine. Outside, the sun had risen beyond her window, so morning was ending. She'd slept about twelve hours, which wasn't actually out of the ordinary on the weekends. She sank into her pillow, closed her eyes, and let her thoughts drift to prom night, the last time she'd been a patient in a hospital.

She'd worn a green satin dress with black spaghetti straps that hugged her chest and hips and then flared out to the top of her knees. As she walked down the stairs of her house, the beige carpet plush underneath her three-inch heels, her mother snapped one photo after another, the continuous flashing of the camera her own private fireworks. Kevin stood at the landing, back from Penn State, whooping at his grown-up little sister while her father sat on the sofa with his legs crossed, his face behind the open newspaper. The last sound she heard before she began tumbling down the steps was him clearing his throat.

Judy reached out for the railing that was no longer there, and if not for the athletic quickness of her brother, she might have suffered a far greater injury; his hands somehow managed to cradle the back of her head, preventing it from smashing into the last step. Her left ankle, however, got lodged between two oak banisters, her black heels with red bottoms, the ones that had cost as much as the dress, still on her foot but turned in a way no foot should ever be, her toes pointed sideways while her knee pointed up.

At the ER, the doctor explained she was fortunate to have suffered a clean break that didn't require surgery. She'd be in a cast for two months and then start on physical therapy. Her mother thanked the doctor and asked Judy if there was anything she wanted from the cafeteria. She didn't, and she was surprised when her father declined to accompany his wife and Kevin.

"Go," he said, "I stay."

He took off his glasses and cleaned the lenses with the front of his shirt. He'd gotten them only a month ago, but she was already used to him with them on, his eyes naked and vulnerable without the frame. There were deep pink half-moon indentations left by the nosepiece, like small wounds.

"Old carpet," he said. "Tiny shoe get stuck."

"Yup," she said.

Under the glaring fluorescent lights of the hospital room, Judy's dress shimmered gaudily. She felt ridiculous, wishing she could change into a pair of shorts. She pulled the top piece away from her breasts momentarily, grateful to get some air circulating in there.

"Dress too tight," her father said.

"No," she said. "It's just hot in here."

"Too tight," he said again, but the way he'd said it again was different from before. There was a sadness there, perhaps a father's sorrow at seeing his girl looking like a woman. At least that's what it seemed like to Judy now, though who knows what twenty years would've done to the state of her memories.

The next day, as she lay on the couch with her foot in a cast, she watched him yank off the run of the carpet and put down a new one, the same color and width as before. He'd rented some kind of a hammering staple gun, and he was slamming and banging at the staircase steps as if they were sets of drums. He'd always been a physical man, enjoying the pleasures of simple, repetitive tasks. Back then, taking on a home improvement project like that was nothing to him, but now—now he was waiting to die.

Her curtain whipped open. Two doctors approached her; one checked the chart while the other fiddled with the drip.

"Good to talk to you, finally, Judy," the chart doctor said. She was an Indian woman who was all eyes and cheekbones, her long black hair flowing down to her shoulders. "I'm Dr. Desai. How are you feeling?"

"Tired," Judy said, "but all right, I suppose."

"One more," the other doctor demanded, a little Asian man who didn't even bother to introduce himself. He not only resembled her father physically, he walked like him, too, a penguin-like gait as he took a vial from Dr. Desai and prepared whatever it was he was now doing, hunched over the counter with his back to her.

The Asian doctor removed the IV bag and replaced it with a new one.

"Dr. Chang's giving you a final dose of the antivenin," Dr. Desai said.

"Hello, Dr. Chang," Judy said.

He nodded curtly, then hung the bag and left without another word.

"A regular chatterbox, isn't he?"

Dr. Desai smiled and scribbled on the chart. "He's one of only seventeen doctors in the entire country who's able to do what he just did for you."

"And what did he do for me?"

She slid Judy's chart back in its holder. "That's the eleventh antivenin you've received since your arrival, all but the first delivered by

Dr. Chang, who helicoptered over from Long Island. Usually we can deliver antivenin by injection, but you had an unusual allergic reaction to it, so it had to be administered through a drip. The doses had to be scaled precisely, and Dr. Chang knows how to do that better than anyone I know. If not for him, we might have lost you."

Almost dead. There was life and there was death, and even though the division seemed stark, there really wasn't much of a barrier.

"So I've gotten just about a dose an hour. That seems like a lot."

"It would be," Dr. Desai said. "Except it was every three hours. You've been in bed for a day and a half."

With that, she was gone, leaving Judy to consider that it was now Sunday, not Saturday. This bothered her, but exactly why she couldn't remember, not yet. But before she could get her head straight, Dr. Chang barged back into her room.

"Excuse me," he said. He stared at the cardiac monitor screen and compared the numbers against a printout he held in his hand.

"You're excused," Judy said.

It was as if she weren't in the room. His attention to the monitor was fanatical, his eyes magnified by his thick glasses, watery dark pupils staring unblinkingly at the ever-changing digits on the screen. Closer up, he looked like her father's twin. Her father, whose kidneys were shot.

Her own kidneys weren't exactly virgins, but at least they worked. So yes, it was within the realm of possibility to give one of hers to him. But to save the life of the man who, when it mattered most, chose money over her mother's life—it was wrong. This equation would only balance with his demise. She could forget about all his past transgressions against her, but to do what he did to his own wife—he did murder her. He may not have fired a gun or stabbed a knife, but there were other ways to kill someone.

It had been the day after her mother's birthday, and if Judy had been a stronger, more confident, more successful person, maybe then her mother would still be here. But she'd been none of those things when her mother grabbed at her belly halfway through her dish of spaghetti and meatballs, one of the few American meals she enjoyed, which Judy had cooked for her. The night before, Kevin had taken their parents out for a proper celebration at a restaurant, but Judy made up an excuse to not go because she couldn't afford the meal and didn't want Kevin to pay for her, too.

"I'm fine," her mother had said, but sweat beaded on her fore-head. She popped a Rolaids into her mouth and chewed it with her front teeth like a rabbit, the crunchy-crumbling sound of the tablet making them both laugh.

"At least your teeth are strong," Judy said.

She took a long drink of water. Like most Asian women, her mother was blessed with good skin, her eyes just starting to show crow's feet, the lines around her mouth faint underneath her makeup. She'd always been a tough little woman. She'd get a cold once a year, but that was about it.

"Don't worry. I went to the doctor last week," her mother said.

"And what did he say?" Judy asked.

"Some test they want to run, but I don't need it."

"Big money," her father said. "Nine hundred dollars."

That was the cost of the CT scan that her doctor wanted to do, their health insurance with its sky-high deductibles making it unaf-fordable. Maybe the test wouldn't have mattered at that point, the cancer already firmly rooted into her colon, but the fact was, he'd just slapped a price tag on his wife's life. Nine hundred dollars. What Judy should have stated was obvious, that they should do the scan regardless of the cost, but she stayed silent because she was afraid of what he'd say.

Oh, you want test? Good. You pay test.

His unspoken words rang in her ear. She could hear their bitter cadence, every ugly syllable spitting out of his mouth. He'd made her complicit in her mother's death by saying nothing. This was why Judy was now stuck in this hospital bed: simple karma. Whatever other acts of misfortune awaited her, she deserved them.

"Okay," Dr. Chang said, and he nodded to himself in approval. "That's the last antivenin delivery."

"Thank you," Judy said. "I heard you had to fly here in a helicopter."

"Yes," he said. "I don't like them; they're very loud. But they're fast." Now that he was done with his job, he seemed relaxed, almost jovial. But then Judy heard a faint buzz, and Dr. Chang reached for the cell phone hanging off his belt. He scanned the readout, and his business demeanor returned.

"Another helicopter ride?"

"No, this one's drivable, over in Connecticut."

"You're like a superhero, hurrying from crisis to crisis."

"Antivenin Man," he said, posing his arms like Superman before takeoff. "Be well. Let's hope we never meet again."

She watched him leave and realized she was wrong. He was actually nothing like her father. This man was a successful doctor, he possessed a sense of humor, and most of all, he wasn't nearing the end of his life.

According to Kevin, the average wait for a kidney to become available off the national waiting list was between three and five years, and her father's nephrologist predicted that within six months, his liver would fail without a kidney transplant.

"Ms. Lee?"

Standing at the door was a woman in a black business suit, about her age. As she approached, Judy saw her high heels underneath the cuffs of her pants, stabbing the floor with every step. Her hand thrust forward, her lips stretched into a forced smile, and she introduced herself as Connie from AR.

"That's accounts receivable. I don't know if you remember this, but you gave this to us when we admitted you."

In her hand was Judy's insurance card, the one provided by her temp agency.

"I don't even remember riding in the ambulance," Judy said. "But since you have it, I guess I must've given it to you."

"Are you still employed by the company?"

It wasn't so much a question but an accusation. With each passing second, Connie was transforming into her true self, a bill collector.

"Why wouldn't I be?" Judy said, defiant.

"Because according to the insurance carrier, your policy was terminated last Friday."

Which was when she'd walked out of her last assignment. Judy had dodged a flurry of phone calls that day from Beverly at the temp agency, but three days ago, there had been more calls from her. Judy had been certain Beverly was still trying to berate her, but maybe she'd wanted to tell her about something else. Like continuing the coverage of her health insurance. Even with insurance, hospital stays were expensive, but without it? How much did it cost to be in this bed? Probably thousands. Judy felt panic prickling her skin.

"Could you get my purse for me?" Judy asked, pointing at the chair.

Connie brought it over for her. When she saw Judy taking out her cell phone, she said, "You're not supposed to use your cell phone here."

"Oh," Judy said, snapping the clamshell shut.

"But since this is important, just keep it short. I'll be back in an hour for a status update."

There were eleven messages on her voice mail; the first one was from two Fridays ago, from Beverly, as Judy had suspected, her high-strung voice coming through as clearly as if she were standing right here, barking into her ear.

"Judy, goddamnit, call me back. Right now!"

Judy deleted it and moved to the next one, recorded fifteen minutes after the first.

"I can't believe this. I can't believe you fucking walked out. It's incomprehensibly irresponsible. I mean, you are an adult. It's one thing if you're being mistreated or something, but you just walked out, without telling anybody there. Do you have any idea what you did? You—"

Judy pressed 3-3-7, and poof, the abuse disappeared forever. It gave Judy a modicum of pleasure to cut her off. Beverly wasn't saying anything Judy hadn't heard before.

The next four messages were also from her ex-boss, the last one telling her that because she'd left the last assignment, Judy had failed to make thirty-two hours for the sixth consecutive week, which meant her medical policy would be canceled unless she took the proper course of action. Judy could opt to get on COBRA and pay for her own insurance, but she had to get back to HR before the end of the week. It had been her final warning.

That was Friday. Judy remembered the notice that came in the mail, a certified letter she'd tossed onto the pile of to-dos that became don't-cares. Before she could sort out the terrifying implications of what she'd just learned, the next message played on, from her brother.

"Hey, it's me. I've run into some complications here—the guy I was supposed to meet, Vincent, he passed away. Great timing, right? I know that sounds crass, but there it is. So it sounds like I'll be here probably until the end of next week—Vincent's daughter is flying in from Minnesota, but I can't get her on the horn. The funeral will be held on Tuesday, the day I'm supposed to fly back, so I hope I can count on you to keep taking care of Snaps. Thanks, sis. I'll be in touch."

Holy shit, the dog. By now it must've peed and crapped all over the house, upturned the garbage can in search of food, howling night and day to broadcast its injustice to the world. Snaps wasn't in great physical shape to begin with, and this was just the sort of thing to push the beast over the edge.

"Hi, Judy, it's Roger. I'm right here at your brother's house. I guess you stepped out or something? I'll be here waiting for you."

She should've never checked her messages, because this was turning out to be a running log of her recent failures. Poor Roger—she hadn't even thought of him until now. She'd had such high hopes for their night together.

The last three messages were all from Roger. The first was from yesterday morning, where he expressed his concern for her continued absence. The second one was from that night, where he told her he called the police and discovered her whereabouts. Emotional highs and lows, and yet Roger spoke with his usual brand of quotidian calmness no matter the situation. It was nice listening to him talk, especially the final recording from this morning, made from this very room.

"They say you'll wake up soon," he said. "I have to go to work now, but I'll be back for lunch. It's strange talking to you like this, because you're right here and you can't hear me. It's feels like we're in a play or something. Anyway, Snaps is all taken care of, so don't worry about anything. Just be well."

"No cell phones, miss."

Judy thought the nurse was coming to take the phone away from her, but instead he snatched up the empty vial of antivenin from the stainless steel tray to the right of Judy.

"Connie said it was okay," she said.

The nurse, a skinny black man with wild hair like Buckwheat, peered at the vial in his hand. "If Connie said it was okay, that's not good news. You got bitten?"

Judy poked her right foot out from under the covers for him to see. "That's the eleventh one they gave me."

"Six thousand dollars."

"Jesus," Judy said. "That's almost six hundred dollars per bottle."

The nurse shook his head. "Each."

Judy stared at the empty bottle in the nurse's hand. Six grand. She'd never earned more than thirty-five thousand dollars a year any time in her life, and now two years' worth of her best earnings was coursing through her bloodstream to keep her living. The concept

made sense—you take the drug to fix you—but six thousand dollars for the liquid in this tiny bottle . . . was it made from crushed
diamonds?

"Don't mean to scare you or nothing," he said.

"I think I have three hundred dollars in my savings account," Judy
said.

A little later, when Connie returned, she brought the estimated bill
in an envelope. The total was $109,125.47.

"That's if you're discharged this evening," Connie said.

What made Judy laugh out loud was seeing the last two digits of
the unfathomable total, forty-seven cents. *Well, that*, she thought, *that
I can pay*. It might as well have been a million dollars. Connie, whose
job no doubt entailed breaking ruinous financial news to the under-
funded and the overwhelmed, said nothing as she stood by with her
arms crossed, shifting from foot to foot ever so slightly, like an elm
swaying in the wind.

16

Kevin tried talking to the manager, then that manager's manager, but he got nowhere. The rate he'd gotten for his stay at the Stanford Court Hotel was a special deal that was no longer being offered, and if that wasn't bad enough, his credit card was denied when he tried to settle up the current bill.

"There must be a mistake," he told the hotel associate at the desk, who handed the now-tainted Visa back to Kevin. As soon as he'd said it, he wondered how many others had relied on the same exact phrase, the same sad song of the financially blighted.

"Of course, Mr. Lee," she said. "Would you like to use our phone to contact your bank?"

From behind, Kevin heard a wail. A couple with a young boy were waiting to check in. The mother was trying to shush her kid, but he ignored her, throwing up his arms in protest.

Kevin held up his cell phone. "Why don't you take care of these folks while I straighten this out?"

He dragged his suitcase over to the cluster of latte-colored leather chairs and dialed the number on the back of the card, where he learned that his credit limit had been reduced from ten thousand dollars to two thousand.

"Aren't you guys required by law to tell me that before you do it?"

"Yes, but not if you have a variable-rate credit card, Mr. Lee. Which is what yours is. As a courtesy, we do send out a letter to you, but it usually takes about a month after the adjustment."

"That's useful," Kevin said.

The rep told him it was nothing he did, that it was part of risk management that the company had enacted across the board, to all their customers. Kevin asked for an emergency extension of credit, and after being put on hold for a good five minutes, the guy returned with more bad news.

"I think if you hadn't missed that one payment back in January, we might allow it, but the officers are vigilant nowadays. I'm sorry, Mr. Lee."

That was the month his divorce became final, when the last thing on Kevin's mind was making sure the check got sent to the bank. He thought about mentioning this but decided against it. It didn't feel right to use one failure to fix another.

Kevin hung up and opened his wallet. He could attempt to use his debit card to pay for the hotel, but he was fairly certain he didn't have enough there, either. His final check from the tennis club wouldn't be deposited until Friday. He had some savings bonds he could cash in, but that took days.

In restaurants, when you ate without paying for the meal, it was called dine and dash. What would it be for what he was about to do— snooze and split? They had his credit card on file, so it wasn't like he was completely bagging them, but still, he felt terrible. The couple with the angry son was taking the hotel associate's full attention, making her recheck their reservation. Kevin rose from his seat, pulled on his suitcase, and crossed the length of the lobby. Hotel employees were everywhere, from the concierge behind the podium to the bellhops rolling their archway-shaped brass luggage carts, and Kevin made himself look at each and every one of them in the eye, a smile plastered on his face while the grip on his suitcase turned clammy.

"Hope you enjoyed your stay at the Stanford," the doorman said. He was big enough to tackle Kevin to the ground if the woman behind the counter yelled out to him.

"I certainly did," he said. "Thank you so much."

The doorman pulled the door open, the gust of wind knocking Kevin back.

"It's nippy out there, sir," he said. "Take care of yourself."

Kevin turned left and walked away at a reasonable, normal pace, even though every part of his body wanted to run. Like the road leading up to the hotel, the one he was on now was also cresting up a hill, though gentler. Kevin hazarded a glance back at the hotel and saw the doorman out on the street, looking as if he was trying to find someone. Most likely he was hailing a cab for a patron, but Kevin picked up his pace anyway.

Whether it was from guilt or fright, Kevin managed to miss the gray elegance of the enormous church until he was standing at the foot of its multitiered steps. From the front, Grace Cathedral resembled Notre Dame, with its rising towers and the round rose window in between, and he recognized the tall front doors, too, ten bronzed panels called the Gates of Paradise. He'd seen both of these original structures on his honeymoon. Alice had always wanted to go to Europe, and that was reason enough for them to empty their savings accounts to spend two weeks in France and Italy. As he stood in front of this church now, seeing a bit of Paris and Florence here in San Francisco made the world smaller, more intimate, and all he had done was be physically present in both locations. Like the saying went, half of life was just showing up.

They'd both shown up, as a newly minted couple, watching the throng of people gathered in front of Notre Dame, snapping photos, buying trinkets, offering prayers. He remembered Alice's hand in his hand, their fingers interlocked, her cheeks apple red from the spring chill, and her face, childlike in its display of joy, how back then her happiness had been his happiness. And so, when he felt a buzz from his cell phone amid the swirls of good memories, Kevin was certain it was Alice calling him, their hearts fused together through time and space, but it wasn't a phone call but a graphic of a yellow envelope in flight, shooting into a gray mailbox.

READ TXT NOW?

backhand sux 2day. help! wish u were here.

He clicked on the Reply button and leaned against the railing as he struggled to type on his microscopic keypad. He persevered to compose a response, except instead of sending the message, he somehow turned it into a draft and couldn't figure out how to edit it.

He dialed Alexa's number, and she picked up on the second ring.

"I bet you gave up trying to text me back," she said.

Listening to her familiar voice, he felt homesick. He thought of his house, Snaps nestled in her corner of the kitchen, her nose tucked under her bushy tail. Which reminded him, he hadn't heard from Judy, but then again, he hadn't expected to.

"You're turning your shoulder early," he said. "Your backhand. Just slow down your stroke and you'll see what you're doing wrong."

"Bill's schedule doesn't coincide with mine, so Artie's my hitting partner now."

Artie wasn't the best, but he wasn't the worst, either. "He's a good guy. He played Boris Becker once, did he tell you?"

She laughed. "Twice today, which makes it something like a hundred times altogether."

A gust of wind came out of nowhere, and his suitcase teetered. From above, church bells rang to signal the start of a new hour, their resonance felt as much as heard.

"Those bells," Alexa said.

"It's a beautiful city."

"So my mother says."

"Listen," Kevin said, and he told her of his hotel escape. If aliens came down from their spaceships and wanted to know what human happiness was, Alexa's laugh would be an apt example.

"Snooze and split, I love it," she said. "So maybe you'll take up that offer to stay with Mommy dearest?"

Was he really going to do this? Go to the house of a complete stranger and crash on her couch like some kid on break from college? His bank account would appreciate the sacrifice, but it felt like yet another failure in what was quickly becoming a string of failures on this trip out West. But desperate times . . . desperate measures.

"Are you sure it's okay?"

"I already told her you might be coming, so this will make her day. There's no such thing as a free lunch, though. You *will* pay with your sanity."

"The funeral's later this afternoon, so it'll just be for a couple of days."

"Don't say I didn't warn you."

From Grace Cathedral, it was almost two miles to Alexa's mother's place, nineteen streets away, information easily retrieved by Alexa's phone, which was able to provide Kevin with step-by-step instructions via Google.

"Walk over to Sacramento. That way, you'll pass by Lafayette Park, which looks pretty cool. And after that, go up another street to Clay, and four intersections later you'll see Alta Plaza to your right. I can see the Street View, but only the steps leading to the park. Looks like you'll have some pretty good views. I wish I was there."

He was never great with directions, but he thanked her and promised to send her phone photos. By the time he reached Lafayette Park, he received another text message, this time with a snippet of a map, complete with a translucent blue line that led him to Alexa's mother's house, marked with a green lollipop. For the first time this trip, he relaxed. Now that he could see where he would have to go, he could enjoy the scenery.

By the time he climbed the multitiered steps of Alta Plaza, the afternoon sun hid behind a flock of fluffy clouds, like a flashlight shining through a bedsheet. The view here was as spectacular as Alexa had promised, the busy expanse of the city's buildings scattered in front of the low hills beyond. It felt very Californian, and Kevin took out his phone and took a picture for Alexa. When he passed by a group of pug owners with their squishy-faced companions off their leashes and frolicking in the grass, he took two more and sent them, too. The dogs of his youth—Samson and Delilah were the ones his family had way back when, and Kevin could almost see his father chucking tennis balls for them, two at a time to keep them both happy. His old man wasn't so old then. Kevin hoped he was having one of his good days today, that he wasn't in too much discomfort.

He received a reply when he was two streets away from the house.

qt pics! luv the dogs. 3022 washington st. 4got2tellu her
name is claudia. dont let her scare you.

Kevin hung a right on Divisadero and gawked at a row of houses, all of them typical San Francisco Victorians, somehow managing to be both capricious and grand as they stood stacked next to one another. One house was decorated with golden fleur-de-lis buckled atop each window frame, while another displayed its family shield above the porch, the copper face shiny like a mirror, while carved wooden sunflowers adorned the molding of its enormous bay window. Every house was flawless, neither a beam crooked nor a window askew, the paint so perfect that it looked plastic.

The house at 3022 Washington Street was something else entirely. There was an oddness to this tall two-story Victorian that could very easily have been three stories. There were four doors in front, the two giant ones in the middle large enough to fit a delivery truck through, and jutting out to the sky in one corner of the roof was a steeple-shaped bell tower. When Kevin reached the front steps, he saw the four letters embossed above the doors, SFFD, and two brass plates to the left of the knob, each with its own door bell, announcing firehouse and cookhouse. San Francisco Fire Department—that's what those letters stood for. Alexa's mother was living in what once must've been a fire station.

He didn't know which doorbell to ring. Most likely, they both triggered the same alert, but to be on the safe side, he pressed the cookhouse button; food seemed like a safer bet. From inside, he heard the most beautiful throwback ding-dong, a sound right out of *Leave It to Beaver*, and waited. Considering the depth of the house, if Claudia were on the second floor in the back, it might take her a couple of minutes to open the door.

Across the street stood a more normal home, cedar shingles and white trim, nothing gold. In the window above the garage door, a black cat parted the curtain and made itself comfortable on the sill to soak up the temperamental flits of sunlight.

"Kevin Lee, I presume."

A deep yet feminine voice, a voice of confidence, had come from the open door. Wearing a purple bandanna cinched around her head Aunt Jemima–style, the woman stood on the porch with her arms akimbo. She was as tall as he was, and even though she was wearing a loose white T-shirt and baggy jeans, he could see how much she resembled Alexa. They both had short torsos and long legs, their shoulders pitched straight and broad like oversized clothes hangers.

"Hi," Kevin said, and he offered his hand. "You must be Claudia?"

It was like shaking a wooden branch, knotted and rough. "And you must be the man who made out with my daughter."

The words themselves alluded to jocularity, but her delivery suggested otherwise, except she wasn't angry or disapproving, either. Kevin tried to think up a reply, but he stood frozen, Alexa's last text message filling the void: *Don't let her scare you.*

"Yes," Kevin finally said, thinking that honesty was the way to go. "That's me."

"You seem ashamed, unhappy about it."

"Not my finest moment."

A faint smile crossed her face. She was older than he was, probably on the cusp of her fifties, though she could easily roll back ten years if she wanted to. Claudia wasn't wearing any makeup, and curls of brunette hair sprouting underneath her bandanna were salted with grays.

"But when you were kissing her, that very moment your lips touched, was that pleasurable for you?"

Kevin cleared his throat.

"Would you rather I make small talk, like a normal person?"

Kevin nodded.

"Nah," Claudia said, her smile deepening. "This is what we should talk about because this is fun. It's fun for me, and I'm enjoying it, so that's why we're having this discussion."

"But what if I'm not enjoying it?"

"You can stop. But if you were to tell me what I want to know, it'll give me pleasure. But if in your telling, this causes you pain, then you must decide—is the pain you'll be experiencing in equal measure to the pleasure I will experience? If that's the case, then we have a net zero in our positive and negative energies, a canceling out, so to speak. You'd be sacrificing, which, I must tell you, is something I never do, so don't do this in hopes that in the future, you'll receive some sort of emotional payback."

"Okay," Kevin said. "What was the question again?"

"When you were kissing Alexa—just think back to that specific point in time, disregarding the obvious dose of guilt you felt afterwards—were you happy?"

It didn't seem like Claudia wasn't going to let this go, so Kevin closed his eyes and did as he was told. Initially his brain filled up with multitudes of thoughts, most of them having to do with this eccentric woman standing in front of him—what kind of antipsychotic medication she might be on, if she was married to some rich guy or if she'd bought the house on her own, and if so, what she did for a living—but then his mind did focus on Alexa, though not the moment of their kiss but rather her in action on the court, her ponytail flailing as she lined up a forehand, the liquid follow-through of her whip-fast backhand. She was a beautiful, talented girl, and when he recalled the event in question, when he saw her face floating over his, he opened his eyes and shook his head to get away from the image.

"That was awful," he said. "I feel terrible all over again."

Claudia clapped her hands together with great satisfaction, then walked right up to him, took his face in her hands, and kissed him right on the mouth. And then she bear-hugged him.

"Well, there you have it," she said into his ear. "Now you'll never do it again, because you know it didn't give you pleasure."

"If you say so," Kevin said.

She released him from the embrace but held him at arm's length.

"I do. See, at the core, that's really all we are as human beings. We are pleasure seekers, which is what we were as children, but then due to societal and religious and cultural limitations, we learn to suppress our very nature. And that's wrong. It's not healthy for anyone, but I can talk about this until the day I die, so let's move on. Let's get you settled, shall we? I'm so very happy you came, Kevin."

She grabbed his suitcase and ushered him through the door. The ceiling rose twenty feet high, and to the right, a golden fireman's pole shot down from an octagonal hole. There were enormous paintings of Claudia hanging on the walls, all of them featuring her plaintive face, her half smiles expressing regret more than joy. By the entrance was the famous Dali painting with the melting clocks, except all the clock faces were actually Claudia's face—languidly stretching, forever melting. Others were just as strange, the one next to the Dali homage depicting a spaceship that had crash-landed into a red barn, shards of real metal protruding from the canvas, tethered by thin wires. The iridescently green-skinned alien, whose limbs petered out to points instead of hands or feet, was undeniably Claudia, too, even with moony black eyes and a shovel-shaped head. This masculine, other-worldly version of her stared back at Kevin, and the funny thing was that the creature looked, more than anything, bored, as if this sort of thing happened all the time. The juxtaposition of the explosive sur-roundings and the placid alien face was jarring in a way that drew him right in. In all the paintings, the level of detail was startling, a photo-realistic quality that brought these impossible scenes to lush life.

"I hope the paint fumes don't bother you," she said.

He hadn't noticed until she pointed it out. Some of his best child-hood memories involved painting with his father, Kevin working the roller while his dad took care of the details, cutting around the trim and the windows. And once, just once, everyone had participated in a project, to repaint Judy's room. It was the summer before she started high school, and even though it'd been scorching with all the windows open, that was the day Kevin would always remember when he wanted to think fondly of his family, the four of them sweating together, working together to turn Judy's room into that deep forest green she so desired. Of course Judy and his father argued—they wouldn't be who they were if they hadn't—but there had been a kidding quality even to that, the two of them butting heads almost for show.

In the far corner of the great room were a pair of vast panels where two Claudias faced one another, on the left a child walking among heaps of old bones, on the right an old woman in the middle of a verdant meadow, and yet their bemused faces were identically middle-aged. Standing underneath these enormous paintings was a canvas on an easel, about as big as a double-hung window, tiny compared to the rest of the works on the walls. Kevin walked over and saw that the edges were missing swatches of colors.

"I'll be done with it today, I think," she said.

They were two eyes zoomed in close, but instead of where eyes usually were, side by side, these were placed top and bottom. The individual eyelashes were crafted with such meticulousness that they looked alive, like tentacles. Reflected on each iris was Claudia's face, the top one missing her left eye, the bottom one missing her right.

"What does it mean?" Kevin asked.

"I don't know."

"But you painted it."

She picked up her gear, a wooden palette with the middle hole long broken. Claudia slipped her thumb through a loop made of frayed duct tape. She dabbed gray paint onto her brush and outlined the top of the eyelid, giving it more definition, making it appear almost three-dimensional.

"That's why we have critics, so they can interpret what I do."

"I want to make it right," Kevin said. "That's what I feel when I look at it. I wish there were moving parts I could shift around."

"Like a Mr. Potato Head."

"Exactly."

"That's a really good idea. Not for this, but for something else I've been thinking about. I could attach a steel plate to the back of a canvas and place magnets behind the movable pieces. The ephemerality of art—is that even a word? If not, it should be."

"You're always in your paintings?"

"Artists always put something of themselves into their work, and instead of pussyfooting with style or mood or whatever bullshit, I just made it physical. I am my work, and there's no better way to convey that than to have myself in it. Besides"—she yanked on the red silken fabric to reveal a standing full-length mirror to her right—"the model's always available."

Kevin stepped into the reflection, which was wide enough for two people. Here he was, in this palace of a house with this very odd woman. Life had gotten very strange, almost dreamlike since he left New Jersey, but seeing himself with her in the surface of the mirror grounded him. A little added distance between her eyes and the shift in angle of her eyebrows made Claudia look like a stronger, bolder version of Alexa. When she smiled at him, Kevin hadn't realized he'd been staring at her.

"You don't get tired of painting yourself?"

Claudia added a few more eyelashes to the bottom eye, stepped back to assess the entire canvas, then nodded to herself satisfactorily.

"Not yet. I've painted other things, other people. But then I had a vision. Have you ever had a vision?"

"Probably not."

"You'd know if you had one."

"Then I'd have to say no."

"I'll tell you about it one of these days. In any case, that's when I started to do what made me happy, and everything you see here is because of that."

Kevin took in his surroundings again, his eyes lingering on the chandelier, its golden branches draped with sapphire orbs and crystal teardrops. The room tapered down to an opening in the back where a staircase spiraled up to the second floor, whose open landing overlooked this room. He saw a ceiling-to-floor bookcase up there.

"You must be famous."

"Kim Kardashian is famous," Claudia said. "I'm just a painter."

"Are the bigger ones more expensive than the smaller ones?"

"Not always, but usually. The one here's a bargain, three hundred big ones."

"Three hundred . . ."

"Thousand."

"That's a lot of money."

"Depends on how much you have."

Even if he had a billion dollars, Kevin couldn't imagine spending that kind of money for a single painting, and yet it must happen at some gallery somewhere, for sums far greater than three hundred thousand dollars.

"So Alexa tells me you'll be attending a funeral," Claudia said.

He looked at his watch. "About two hours from now. It's at the San Francisco National Cemetery."

"Really? Only high-ranking ex-military are interred there. It's been a while since I've been to a funeral. I'd like to come with you. Is that all right?"

Kevin didn't know what to say. He had a feeling this was something that was going to happen often with Claudia.

"I think it's open to anyone, so yes, I don't see why not."

"Good, then it's settled. Besides, I've been talking your ear off. This way, you can fill me in about who you are while we drive out to the Presidio."

But before the Presidio, they drove downtown because Claudia was hungry for the best croque monsieur in the city.

"We're going the opposite direction, but we have time," she said.

"Okay," Kevin said. "Sure."

Kevin had no idea what a croque monsieur was—it sounded like something a French person would yell out in exasperation—but right now, he was afraid to say anything. Claudia drove with the distract-edness of someone texting while drunk, the car slowly veering to the shoulder until she jerked it back into the lane. Thankfully, buckled all around the cabin of her whisper-quiet Mercedes convertible were oval airbag logos.

"Hey," he said, pointing at a street sign, "we're on Mission Street?"

"Mission Street in the Mission District. Lots of Latinos live here, though not as many since the housing boom."

He dug through his wallet and found Vincent DeGuardi's business card, the one in the envelope containing his mother's centerfold.

He asked her to stop at 2318, which was just a block past where they needed to go. The Mission was more blue-collar than where he'd been staying, but there was a certain charm to the place, like the Chinese grocery on the corner with a mural painted on its side wall, the scene depicting a gaggle of children running around and playing soccer on a bed of white and aqua-blue swirls. At 2310 was a furni-ture store, and 2318 stood beyond it. MISSION JEWELRY & LOAN CO., the white letters announced on the forest-green background of the sign. And just in case that wasn't clear enough, a canary-yellow box jutted into the sidewalk: PAWNBROWKERS, and underneath it, MONEY LOANED. No doubt it lit up at night so desperate people could find its services. A line of electric guitars hung down from the ceiling, abandoned by their cash-craving owners, serving as a warning for those dreaming of a career in music.

"Do you want to go in?" Claudia asked.

Somehow, it seemed fitting that the place where his mother posed naked so many years ago was now a pawn shop.

"No," Kevin said. "That's all right."

They parked in front of a nondescript storefront without a sign. If it wasn't for the line of people snaking from the door, Kevin would've thought it was closed. When he opened the car door, he was welcomed by the yeasty scent of baking bread.

"I'm starving," he told Claudia, and she nodded knowingly, as if this was how everyone who came to Tartine Bakery reacted.

The queue moved quickly, and once inside, Claudia surveyed the seating situation. All the communal tables were occupied, so she found them seats at the bar facing the window and asked Kevin to sit while she got them their lunch. When he tried to give her some cash, she ignored him.

The mysterious croque monsieur turned out to be a fancy grilled ham-and-cheese sandwich on a thick piece of crusty bread, and it was as exquisite as Claudia had promised. Chunks of roasted tomatoes were like tiny bright bursts, and the pickled carrot was an unexpected surprise, a sweet and vinegary chaser to the rich meal.

Alice would've been proud of him. Breaking down a dish to its component parts was something they both enjoyed doing. They'd either find restaurants in the Zagat guide or the local newspaper's food section and devote their gastronomical senses wholly to the experience. Even when things were bad between them, they still found solace in a plate of vodka penne or a seared filet mignon, talking only about what was on the table, what was on their tongues.

He told Claudia about the significance of the Mission Street address on their way to the funeral. And once he started telling her about his centerfold mother, it led to everything else he'd gone through these last few weeks.

"I like it," Claudia said.

"Excuse me?"

"Your story."

"I didn't make it up. It's real."

"I know. Real or fake, our lives are just stories we tell ourselves. You'll be better off for it, believe me."

Kevin didn't agree, but he didn't see the point in arguing.

Claudia turned onto Presidio Boulevard. The city fell away to a dense forest of straight, sky-pointing trees, and with less traffic, Claudia's driving became calmer.

"It's beautiful here," he said.

"My favorite part of the city," she said. "Mostly eucalyptus trees, here at the national park, and they're taking over. Every year the rangers plant pine and cypress to even out the numbers, though I think they're wasting their time, fighting nature."

"But what if it makes them happy to fight nature?"

She smiled. "You already know all there is to know about me."

A few curves of the road later, gray tombstones rose from the green grass behind a black wrought iron fence, carefully aligned into stately rows on the hill. Four stone pillars stood sentry at the entrance, the gate wide open for them to drive through. They parked in a lot next to the main building, which looked large enough to hold services indoors. A soldier directed them to a path, and they walked up a slope, the tip of the Golden Gate Bridge becoming visible. The cemetery seemed endless, one end fading into the horizon.

"I don't like funerals," Kevin said.

"I find them invigorating," Claudia said. "Makes me want to do more with my life while I'm still alive."

"You sound like someone who hasn't lost anyone close."

Claudia considered his words. "It's true, everybody in my family is alive, even my grandparents. It must've been tough to lose your mother."

Even now, he could recall only slivers of that horrible day. They were like fractured bits of a movie: the heavy coat of lipstick around his dead mother's lips in the open casket, his sister's tears streaking down her cheeks, and worst of all, Judy and him at the crematorium after the service, huddled around the window that displayed the view into the basement facility where they incinerated the bodies. The director twice asked if they were sure they wanted to witness this, that while it was the last time they would see their mother, it was ultimately their choice. His father and their spouses had declined, but they were the children, and they didn't want to abandon their mother as she left the world for good. Yet in retrospect, he wished he'd stayed with his father because what he saw was a mechanical procession of human death. Because his father opted for the cheaper plan, where the show casket was a rental used only for the service, the actual coffin was just a beige pine box, lying on a conveyor belt. A short distance away was a silver door. A large man wearing an orange hazard vest stood by a control panel.

"If you're ready," the director said.

Kevin and Judy nodded.

He pressed on the intercom and gave the man below the go-ahead, and the bright green light above the silver door turned red. The door slid open, and flames danced against the coffin, which slowly, inexorably headed for its fiery destination, like a medieval sacrifice to appease an angry god.

Judy held his hand and clasped it tight, a tiny, involuntary sound like a chirp escaping from her clenched mouth, and just like that, they were motherless.

Except not for him, because apparently he now had a spare mother, like a tire in the trunk of a car. He had accepted the fact that the people who raised him had lied to him for all these years, but then he would imagine the moment of the transaction, his birth mother handing over a tiny, swaddled version of him, putting her baby into the arms of a stranger and then walking away. He hoped it had been a difficult moment for her.

Up ahead, people sat in white folding chairs, while seven armed soldiers stood by the oversized American flag draped over the casket. Kevin and Claudia were in black like everyone else, he in a suit, she in a dress, the uniform of the mourning.

At the ceremony, an army general in military regalia praised Vincent DeGuardi for his valor in the Korean Conflict. He held up a silver star with a sky-blue strap, the medal received for saving the lives of his platoon. After his speech, a woman introduced herself as Marilyn, a short, gray-haired lady in horn-rimmed glasses who looked nothing like what Kevin had envisioned on the telephone. From the way she'd given him directions to the cemetery, he'd expected a female drill sergeant who stood six feet tall. In fact, her immediate authority had prevented him from asking her about her father's photos, but now that he put the voice to the face, she seemed more approachable.

The soldiers shot their rifles three times, the burnt smell of gun-smoke spicing the air, and after the casket was lowered into the plot, the ceremony was over.

"I'll hang back while you do your thing," Claudia said. "Unless you want me to go with you."

"You've fed and chauffeured me," Kevin said. "You've done more than enough."

"Good. Then I'll go say hi to General Atchison."

"You know him?"

"He bought a painting of mine, years ago, when nobody wanted my paintings."

As she walked away, the pleats of her dress swayed with each step. With her loose, silver-streaked dark curls cascading down her back, everything about her flowed. Like Alexa, she moved like silk, as if she were gliding on skates instead of walking.

People surrounded Marilyn to offer her their condolences, and he waited until the crowd dispersed.

"I'm Kevin Lee," he said, offering his hand. "I'm sorry about your father."

"Thank you," she said. "Were you friendly with him?"

"I spoke to him a week before his death. He took a photograph of my mother."

She brightened. "He loved taking pictures, especially of families. When was it?"

"A long while ago. 1973."

It was as if her smile were a flame that had just extinguished.

Kevin continued, "He told me he had his old photos in storage and that I could look through them."

"Yes, well," she said, hitching up the strap of her purse high on her shoulder, "I don't think so."

It seemed so desperate, confessing to yet another stranger about his recent discovery of his origins, but maybe this was something he would have to get used to if he wanted to arrive at the truth. He had to at least try after hauling his ass all the way over here to California. "I'm forty years old and I just found out I was adopted. Your father took a photo of my mother, the only picture I have of her."

"So you want to get more naked shots of her? What would that accomplish?"

"Maybe there's information there in his files, I don't know, an address or something."

Marilyn cleared her throat. "Do you really think the purveyors of smut would've kept copies of driver's licenses and birth certificates? Do you have any idea the kind of people my father consorted with?"

"Look," Kevin said, trying to keep his composure. "What is the harm in having me check through boxes of his old photos? Why are you giving me such a hard time?"

"Is everything all right here?"

It was one of the soldiers who'd shot the volleys.

"I'm fine," Marilyn said. "Wait for me at the car."

The soldier left, but not before giving Kevin a lingering stare.

"He's my son," Marilyn said.

"I am a son, too. Trying to find my mother."

A heavy pocket of clouds muted the lush landscape of the cemetery. A field of headstones away, a red-tailed hawk floated down, its wings spread wide, the end feathers splayed out like fingers, landing on a white obelisk that resembled a miniature Washington Monument. Once again in the San Francisco shade, Kevin shivered. More than ever, it felt like weather fit for a funeral. Marilyn hugged herself as she spoke.

"Mr. Lee, you have no idea what that part of my father's life did to his family. So please don't lecture me about hard times. In any case, I don't mean to argue with you. My father does have an archive in storage, but none of those photographs are there because I got rid of them a long time ago. Everything from that time period, I burned. He trusted me to take care of his prized possessions, so I guess that makes me a bad daughter. I don't know. But I do know that I have nothing for you to see. I'm sorry."

As he watched her go, Kevin wondered if she was lying. But why would she? Besides, even if the photos had survived, she was probably right. They wouldn't have yielded much more than another embarrassing glimpse of his mother.

He felt a hand on his shoulder.

"Didn't go well, I take it," Claudia said.

"Nope."

In another part of the cemetery, far away from them, a tour was being conducted, a woman walking slowly backward while a crowd followed her at a short distance, their heads swiveling in unison as she pointed out the famous graves. Claudia hooked her arm into his as they followed the path back to her car.

"I can introduce you to a PI," she said.

"Magnum?"

"I wish. No, this guy looks like an accountant, but he's as good as they come."

Kevin got into Claudia's Mercedes. He was about to strap on the seat belt when he caught a glimpse of something through his passenger-side window. A man had just gotten into the car parked next to Claudia's, a man whose hair was gray, whose wrinkles were carved deeper than his—

"Hold on," Kevin said.

This can't be happening. This is not who I think it is.

He stepped out. The man's car reversed, was about to pull away. Kevin ran in front of it and held up both hands.

The man met Kevin's eyes. It was like looking into a magic mirror that added twenty years to his face.

17

A day after Judy was discharged from the hospital, she got a phone call from Kevin, who prattled on about his San Francisco trip. She pushed the speakerphone button on the cordless and stood it up on the coffee table, then carefully lowered herself onto the couch, an involuntary yelp escaping from her lips when her bitten ankle nudged the arm of the sofa.

"Hey, you all right?" he'd asked.

"Fine," she said. "Everything's good."

He'd seen his birth father at a funeral of all places. Just amazing luck, as his father was paying tribute to the man who'd brought him and his future wife together, Kevin's mother. Judy told him how happy she was for him, and it wasn't a lie. Kevin had found his dad, and this was without a doubt just the beginning, the rest of his blood family waiting to love him.

"I'm gonna be out here longer than I thought, so I hope you can house-sit for another week or so?"

"Of course," she said.

"Are you sure you're okay?" he asked again. "You sound exhausted."

She almost told him, but she held back. He had enough going on, and she didn't want to burden him with her problems, too.

Now, she was sitting at the breakfast table in the kitchen of Kevin's house with a calculator, a legal pad, and a pen. She stared at the numbers again.

$109,125.47.

Her left ankle was propped up on the chair next to her, the throbbing now mostly gone, though maybe the low-level ache had relocated itself to her brain. On her calculator, she divided the number by 4 and got back 27,281.3675. Twenty-seven thousand dollars. That was better, a number she could deal with. It was the cost of a nice, new, semifancy car, though she'd never spent any more than ten thousand on any of her used clunkers. That time she got promoted at the ad agency before getting fired a year later, she'd made thirty-five thousand a year, and that was before taxes and rent and food and everything else in the world that conspired to make her poor. This debt would take a decade, if not more, to pay back, and from the way the finance woman at the hospital had sounded, they weren't willing to wait that long. That meant collection calls, repossession of her assets, all leading up to the empty shame of bankruptcy. Judy wiped away her tears and blew her nose. Snaps puttered up to her and laid her head on Judy's thigh.

"Your aunt is headed for the poorhouse," she said, raking fingernails over Snaps's furry dome. The dog's eyes glazed over, but as soon as Snaps heard the slam of a car door, she ran to the back entrance and emitted her customary low growl.

That was Roger, who'd called her twice a day since she was discharged and was bringing dinner. Should she feel happier than she actually did? She was grateful he'd taken care of Snaps while she'd been hospitalized, for bringing flowers and visiting her. He'd done all the right things, and maybe that was the problem. Not that Judy was a fan of mind games or unkindness, but a little play was welcome, a little resistance to let her know that he was a person with his own specific set of wants and desires. Sparks flew when metal struck metal; if she was iron, Roger was a bowl of cotton balls, a memory foam mattress.

Snaps gave one bark, then two. Her tail wagged, which meant Roger was about to enter.

She imagined what he'd look like: his mop of black hair in a state of low dishevelment, the red knit scarf wrapped around his neck, brown leather bomber jacket zipped up halfway. He would be holding sagging yellow plastic bags from ShopRite or the twine handles of the Chinese takeout place. Dependably predictable, predictably dependable. And yet on his back was that crazy tattoo, which she'd found out on the Internet could be a sign of the yakuza, the Japanese mafia. It just didn't seem possible that he could be a gangster. What did he do to his enemies, bore them into submission?

"Hey," Roger said. The only thing she hadn't guessed correctly was the color of the plastic bags. Instead of ShopRite yellow, it was Wegmans white.

He had no reason to do anything for her, and yet he fed her, kept her company, smiled sweetly. Was it because he loved her? But love wasn't forever. In fact, it should come with an expiration date, because then she'd know when it would spoil.

Roger placed the bags on the kitchen island and leaned over for a kiss. His lips were chapped, so she rubbed her lips over his side to side in an effort to transfer her lip gloss. It made him laugh, which delighted Snaps, who pranced around him in a tight circle.

It was the only way she could get Brian to take care of his lips, and now she was doing it to Roger, and somehow it felt wrong to hand down this particular move to another. Like an aging comedy bit, it needed to be retired. Or maybe it was she who needed to be retired from men. If only she could, but the fact was, she'd been lonely. Before Brian, there had been a steady diet of live-in boyfriends; this was the longest she'd ever been by herself, and as much as she found a relationship taxing, it trumped being alone.

"What are you up to?" he asked, looking at the calculator. She clicked on the red C button before he could get a look.

"Just squaring away some financial stuff."

"Oh," he said. His eyes lingered over the statement. The total was folded underneath, but the hospital logo remained visible. "You're set with everything? Insurance and stuff?"

He'd reduced her predicament into the simplest of all answers, a yes or a no. Tell the truth or continue to lie.

"Fine," she said, "everything's good." The same exact words she'd told her brother. Maybe later she'd have the courage, but right now, she just wanted to have a nice meal.

When she tried to help set up, Roger made her stay put, so she watched him assemble their dinner.

"I got spinach lasagna," he said, taking the rectangular plastic containers out of the shopping bags and opening them up one by one. There was broccoli sautéed with garlic, steamed artichoke hearts, a loaf of cheese bread. Roger offered each dish over to her like a sommelier showing a bottle of wine. Everything smelled divine, and despite the cloud of financial doom hanging over her, she was glad to feel hunger, something she could satisfy.

She told him it was delicious, and it was true. The lasagna was a delightful combination of chopped tomatoes and spinach and ricotta, a touch of nutmeg, a medley of earthy flavors. Did she tell

Roger at some point that Italian was her favorite cuisine? She didn't think so. He was a thoughtful guy. Maybe she just wasn't trying hard enough to like him, though that made her feel even worse, that even her inability to fall in love with this man was somehow her fault.

Halfway through the meal, the phone rang. Roger rose to get it, but Judy told him not to bother and let the answering machine pick up.

"Ms. Lee, this is Warren Hospital, accounts receivables department, Connie speaking. This is the third time we've tried to reach you regarding the forms for payment . . ."

Judy ignored Roger's protestations and limped her way to the living room to grab the phone. So it was starting already. It was almost seven o'clock—these people never went home.

"It's in the mail," Judy barked into the receiver. "I signed and sent the forms this afternoon, okay?"

"Thank you, Ms. Lee," Connie answered. "I apologize for calling at this hour, but because this is a priority account, we need to keep all the steps moving along."

There was a pause, and Judy could almost feel the question that Connie wanted to ask: When can we expect you to pay? But she didn't, because she knew as well as Judy that they were headed for something ugly down the road.

"Well, you have a good night," Connie said.

When she doddered back to the kitchen table, Roger was reading the bill.

"That's my stuff," she said.

He placed it back on the table.

"That's a lot of money," he said.

She sat down and took another bite of the lasagna, but it'd gone cold, the texture turned glue-like, sticking to the roof of her mouth. She chased it down quickly with a slug of red wine, and then another. If she'd been so concerned with Roger finding out, she could've taken the bill with her. The truth was, she was in a terrible place, and there was no one else she could get mad at. She was the living definition of a bad person, somebody who took out her ills on a bystander.

"Was that them on the phone? This Connie Peterson?"

"I don't need your help," she said, and even as she was saying it, she knew it was ridiculous. That's all Roger had done since her snake bite, help her. Had she even bothered to thank him?

Roger moved to her side, and she sank her face into his belly as he stood by and rubbed her back. It felt good to give herself wholly to her predicament, and when her tears tapered down to sniffles, Roger said something she thought she'd misheard.

"What did you say?" She blinked hard to clear away her blurry vision.

"I'll take care of this."

"You have a hundred grand just sitting around. That's why you work at your shitty job answering customer-service calls."

"I can get the money," he said, and then he dialed down his voice to almost a whisper. "I can take care of you, Judy. If you'll let me."

He was being serious. He could get the money. Meaning it was money he didn't have but somehow had access to. He could take care of her, whatever the hell that meant. She looked at him intently, so much so that she felt as if she had x-ray vision, and then she did sort of have it, or at least through her memories. Roger pulled at the collar of his powder-blue dress shirt, and she could almost see the tattoo underneath, the head of the fire-breathing dragon perched on his shoulder.

"I'm going to ask you something," she said. "I think it's time I asked."

Roger took his seat again.

"All right," he said.

"Are you a member of the yakuza?"

Roger rubbed his palms together, flexed his fingers, drummed the tabletop.

"It's complicated," he said.

"It's actually a pretty simple question."

"I was," he said, "but it was a mistake, and it was a long time ago, when I turned eighteen."

"So you're not one now."

"No. Though I suppose I always will be mistaken for one, thanks to the tattoo." He picked up his glass of water and drank it down. "I was in the Yamaguchi-gumi family. For a month."

"A month?"

"Like I said, it was a mistake."

Judy didn't mean to laugh, but she couldn't help herself. "Was it a trial offer? Your satisfaction guaranteed or your money back?"

Roger said nothing, just shrugged.

"So how is it that you're offering to pay for my enormous medical debt if you aren't the Japanese Tony Soprano-san that I thought you were?"

He mashed the remaining piece of spinach lasagna on his plate with his fork, thin pillars of goo rising between the tines.

"I'm afraid to tell you," he said. "Because if I do, I think it might ruin what we have."

"And what is it, exactly, that we have?"

"Good," he said. "Something good. I hope."

"I hope so, too," Judy said.

In the morning, after Roger left for work and Judy leaned into the bathroom mirror to put her face on, she thought about their conversation last night. It was, without a doubt, one of the stranger discussions she'd had with anyone. But not boring, which was good. Not that she wanted to have her life filled with drama again. In her early twenties, she'd dated a drug dealer, a strip club owner, and an ex-con, and even though those relationships had their wacky moments, she eventually found their instability tiresome. If there was a truism in life, that was it: No matter how titillating somebody or something seemed in the beginning, the newness invariably faded to an oldness, so there was little reason to go through police raids and drug overdoses when, in the end, it all devolved to the status quo.

Her favorite lipstick was almost gone, so she used a brush to dig out what she could from the wall of the plastic tube. It was twenty bucks the last time she bought it, an outrageous price for a tiny stick of makeup, but she couldn't find a cheaper knockoff that had the same deep, professional shade of red perfect for the office, which was where she was headed today, to another temp agency. As much as she'd appreciated Roger's offer, she told him no, not only because the money's origins were shrouded in mystery but also because Roger was right, it would without question ruin what they had. An action as large as that would shift the balance of any relationship, especially a new one like theirs. And besides, Judy wasn't in the panhandling business. This was her debt, and as a responsible, grown-up person, it was her problem to deal with, and she had no intention of pushing it off on anyone else.

The October morning was windy, her little Toyota jostling on Shrews-
bury Avenue. The empty lot next to the STS Tire Center hosted makeshift swirls of maple leaves, tiny whorls of brown and yellow rising and
falling. She pulled into the parking lot of the temp agency, a square,
redbrick building that held six different businesses according to the
directory bolted onto the wall in the lobby. Judy was thankful there was
an elevator, because she was wearing a stability boot and the last thing
she wanted to do was climb stairs with only one good foot.

Trilling Personnel Services wasn't her first choice, but after walking
out on her last assignment, Judy knew she couldn't go back to her old
agency, and she didn't want to trek over to Neptune or anywhere further. There was no permanent sign on the gray metal door, just a laminated card with the name of the company printed in bold black ink,
and inside, a frizzy-haired secretary with a mole on her cheek greeted
her. Stuck on the outer edge of her desk was a name-tag sticker, and
it read:

HI! MY NAME IS
DOTTIE

"Hello, I'm Judy Lee. I called earlier?"

"Yup. What happened to your foot?"

"Bad luck," Judy said, and when she said nothing further, Dottie
looked disappointed.

"Frank will be right back from killing himself," she said. She held
her pen like a cigarette and mimed a few puffs.

Judy thanked her and sat in the only chair in the waiting area that
didn't have a stain or a rent in the fabric. She picked up a dog-eared
issue of *Newsweek* with Barack Obama on the cover, and as she flipped
through it, she recalled her final smoke with Roger, thinking it would
be the last time she'd see him. It seemed so long ago, and yet it hadn't
even been a month. She tried to think of a future with Roger, tried to
envision him at family gatherings, making small talk with Kevin and
humoring her father and her stupid stepmother at the dinner table,
sitting in the same seat that Brian sat in. It irked her to think of Roger
as a replacement for her ex, though she supposed any man she'd
bring home would be regarded as such.

"Ms. Lee?"

Frank, beads of sweat threatening to roll down his forehead, extended his hand. He was a big man, a fat man, even his bushy mustache bearing a significant amount of weight.

It was like shaking hands with a slab of raw beef. He motioned for her to follow him to the back wall, walking past dark, empty cubicles, some of them turned into makeshift storage spaces for boxes and extra chairs.

In his office, Frank wheezed so much that the sound of his breathing took over the entire room; the more Judy tried to ignore it, the louder it became. When he looked up from reading her resume, she smiled so hard that she probably looked insane.

"So looks like there's a gap in your employment history," he said.

Judy hadn't put down her latest stint with the temp agency, for obvious reasons, and had already prepared her reply to this inevitable query.

"Yes," she said, and she lowered her voice a notch. "I've been taking care of my brother. He's been having some personal problems."

She said this without any guilt, because she and Kevin had a long-standing pact that they could use each other as excuses. It was one of the brighter spots of having a sibling.

"Oh," Frank said. "I'm sorry."

"There are days when he's as normal as anyone," Judy said. She got into it, like an actress locking into character. "But then he has these episodes, and he trusts no one but me. No one else can go near him. That's why I'm still temping after all these years."

Frank angled the framed photo and pointed at one of the boys in the family picture, the one obviously with Down Syndrome.

"The sacrifices we make," he said. "You're doing God's work. Let's find you something good, huh?"

There were possibilities: a two-month gig at a doctor's office, filling in for a receptionist on maternity leave, or a three-month assignment at a law firm, working as a personal assistant.

"Sleep on it and let me know which one will work for you."

"Thank you, Frank," she said, and she double-stepped out of his office and out the door.

As she drove away, she scrolled through the call list on her cell phone and dialed the hospital. The best way to alleviate her guilt was to put her future earnings to their intended destination.

"Good morning, Ms. Lee," Connie said. The friendliness in her tone was so unfamiliar that for a second, Judy thought she'd misdialed.

"I wanted to talk to you about my bill," she said.

There was a pause, and it was as if Judy already knew what she'd say.

"There is no bill," Connie said.

"Because it's been paid in full."

"That's correct."

"Thank you," Judy said, and she snapped her cell phone shut.

She pulled her car off the road and onto the shoulder. The highway uncoiled in front of her, harsh sunlight flashing off the roof of each passing car. She listened to the tick-tock of her right turn signal, attempting to let its metronomic rhythm bring her a sense of calm, but it didn't work. So she drove. The wealth of conflicting emotions— relief and injustice, gratitude and violation—jolted through her like a continuous electric charge. She should dump Roger right now, tell him what an asshole he was for—

For being there when she was in the hospital bed, unconscious?

For taking care of her while she recuperated from her injuries?

For rescuing her from certain fiscal devastation?

For the rest of the drive, she blasted the heavy metal station on Kevin's satellite radio. This was one genre of music she didn't listen to, but having a bunch of angry-sounding men screech and yell over the crash of guitars and drums cleansed her, their collective noise too big for her to think about anything.

Judy had hoped she would have time to sort things out, but when she pulled into Kevin's driveway, Roger was there, leaning against the hood of his BMW.

She killed the engine but stayed in the car. She watched him through the windshield as he tapped a cigarette out of his pack. He had trouble lighting it, going through three matches before he was able to cup his hands around the temperamental flame and catch the fire. He took in a long drag and exhaled through his nostrils, watching her watching him.

She opened her car door, lifted herself out of the seat, and stood up. It'd been warm in the car, but outside, autumn wind raked through her hair.

"I know you probably hate me," Roger said.

No, she thought, *but I don't love you, either. I wish I did.*

"To tell you the truth," she said, "I don't know what I feel."

Judy pushed her door shut and walked up to Roger.

"Why?" she asked.

Roger flicked the ash off his cigarette and took a second long drag.

"I knew doing it would make you angry. Because you told me not to. And yet I wanted to do this for you, because I have money. A lot of money. And it isn't blood money from a gang. I lost both of my parents within a year of each other, and they left me millions."

"Millions?"

"Over a hundred, the last time I checked, which was three years ago, so probably more than that now."

"Can I have one?" Judy said, pointing to his cigarette. She used the end of Roger's to light hers. "And yet you work the phones in that brain-dead job."

"I do."

"Why?"

He shrugged. "It keeps me busy. I like the people. I've been there for seven years."

"This is the most fucked-up thing I've heard yet, and I've heard a lot of fucked-up things," Judy said.

"I thought doing this for you would make you happy, even if you said it wouldn't."

"And do you always do things to make other people happy?"

Roger took a final drag, dropped the butt, and crushed it with a quarter turn of his shoe.

"I try."

"There's something wrong with you, isn't there," Judy said.

Roger nodded. "I've never been happy. It's not depression—it's different. I've gone through every drug, every treatment. It's always been this way."

Judy took him in her arms and cradled his head against her chest. She wished she could say something, anything, to make things better, but what good were words now?

"I don't know, Roger." And she didn't. At this point in her life, she'd gone through enough self-analysis to know that being with somebody like him, somebody in this odd condition, wasn't going to be easy for her.

"That makes two of us," Roger said.

Holding hands, she led him to the front door and opened it for him. Even though it was the middle of the day, it was dark inside because she'd left the blinds down. She followed him, into the gloom that awaited them.

18

Kevin hadn't known anyone named Norman personally, but now he did, his birth father. At one point during their first dinner together at a little French bistro near the Civic Center, they traded driver's licenses to laugh at their similarly awful pictures. Reading the last name printed on the card, Kwon, Kevin sounded it out in his mind: *Kevin Kwon*. It wasn't bad, the alliterative *K*'s downright sing-song. Of course, had he been raised by his birth parents, he probably wouldn't have been named Kevin. What had they called him? Kevin thought he wanted to know but then changed his mind. It was sad to consider the boy he didn't grow up to be.

There was more sadness as the evening went on. When Kevin asked about his birth mother, Norman closed his eyes for a moment before continuing.

"I knew you were going to ask about her, but it's still hard for me to say that she's passed on," he said. "I'll tell you more about her later, but not tonight. Right now, let's enjoy this meal, shall we?"

"Just one thing," Kevin said. "Her name?"

"Grace."

Norman and Grace Kwon. Who had they been? Why did they give their son away? There were so many questions, too many.

On their second evening out, Norman suggested they meet in the town of San Leandro, and when they walked by a three-story gray building off Davis Street on their way to dinner, Norman acted as if it was some sort of cosmic coincidence that they happened to be in front of his office.

"Would you like to see it?" he asked Kevin. "Since we're here and everything?"

Kevin wanted to tell him that there was no reason to go through any pretense—Norman was his father, so why wouldn't Kevin want to see where he worked?—but that felt like a lot to say. So he assured him, "Of course. I'd love to."

Norman had told him he was a licensed therapist, and the nameplate on the building corroborated this fact: PRESENCE PERSONAL COUNSELING—NORMAN KWON, LPC. Norman led him down the beige-carpeted corridor until they arrived at the third door on the right.

The walls were the same color as the carpet outside. There was a high-backed wooden armchair, a brown sofa, and a coffee table, all sitting on top of a circular oriental rug. In the corner by the window, a narrow secretary desk was left open, its oval door flipped out like a tongue. It looked like a cramped living room of someone's city apartment.

"So," Norman asked, "is it what you expected?"

It was a question loaded with entirely too much baggage. Truth be told, none of it was what Kevin had expected, and the least expected of all was this man who looked like a fast-forwarded version of him. Kevin hadn't exactly counted on his existence, maybe because having seen and held the photograph of his mother, his focus had been entirely on her. Or perhaps because he assumed she'd been a single mother, a woman who'd gotten in trouble with an unwanted pregnancy. Kevin didn't quite know what to do with Norman. They resembled one another, which made the emotional disconnection even more alarming.

On the coffee table, Kevin glanced at the stapled stack of papers.

"That's what we counselors call the intake," Norman said. He pointed to the sofa, which was a three-seater crowded with throw pillows. "Take a look."

Kevin moved a few pillows out of the way and sat. The form was five pages long, asking for basic biographical information plus sections for psychological services history, family history, substance use, spiritual activities, just about everything that could be queried about someone's mental health.

"It's baseline stuff, what I ask when people come to see me, though mostly it's for insurance and liability purposes. Once we have the basics down, it's all about presence."

Kevin nodded, though he didn't understand what Norman meant. "Do your clients lie down when they talk to you?"

"They can do whatever they want, as long as they don't talk about their mothers," Norman said.

Presence therapy, Norman explained, was about accepting the present moment as the only reality. Traditional psychotherapy involved the client discussing his past while the counselor listened and analyzed to bring subconscious issues out into the conscious. Once these wounds are dragged out, then the healing supposedly began, until the client, free from his emotional distresses, became a complete person.

"But it doesn't work that way," Norman said. "Believe me, I know, because I used to be one of those therapists. The root of the problem isn't what happened in the past, but rather what you do with the present—the ego and the mind. As humans, we're gifted with our wonderful brains, which spend a lot of time with the past and the future, none of which apply to the present. The goal is to learn to look inward, into the nature of our own minds through systematic self-observation. That might sound like a lot of mumbo-jumbo, but it's the only truth I know."

Norman had a tendency to hold a gaze a second or two longer than what Kevin felt was comfortable, and he was doing it now.

"You're not saying anything, Kevin, but I can tell you're not buying it."

Kevin didn't want to disagree, but what Norman had said struck him in a personal way.

"Ignoring your past—it seems like denial."

"Fair enough. Let's take your situation. You wish your adoptive parents hadn't kept this secret from you. And now it's causing you pain. So to choose to not look at the past feels like a form of denial to you."

Kevin nodded.

"But the revelation of this secret—this happened weeks ago. So why are you still thinking about what happened in the past? What good is it doing for you? Think it, and then let it move through you. By looking at the past and latching on to it, you're actually in denial of the present. So be here instead, in the now. The Buddhists call this *sati*—mindfulness. For you to not be lost in anticipation or worry of everything that's not here."

Over the next four days, they shared three more meals, and as much as Kevin tried to see things from Norman's philosophical point of view, he couldn't. The idea of presence seemed like an excuse, a justification, for Norman to not reveal his past, and ergo, Kevin's past. When he told Norman how he felt, his father agreed.

"I understand," Norman said. "Which is why I'm almost ready to tell you everything, Kevin. Almost done, just give me one more day."

Done? What did he mean? But Norman wouldn't say anything further.

The following afternoon, they were sitting at an outside table of a tiny Mexican restaurant. Straw sombreros dangled from the ceiling and swayed with the breeze.

Kevin hurriedly wiped his taco-greased fingers on a napkin. His father held a jewel case containing a homemade DVD. The words *For my son* were scribbled in thick black marker on the rainbowed surface of the disc.

"I don't understand."

"You will," Norman said. "I'm usually good talking face-to-face. After all, it's my job. But you mean a lot to me, and that complicates things. So in this case, I'm better on camera than in real life, if that makes sense."

Claudia was standing in whiteness when Kevin returned from lunch. He was about to greet her but stopped when he saw the position of her body in front of a blank canvas. She held a wide paint brush in one hand and a bucket of red paint in the other, except instead of looking like a contemplative artist, she resembled a tiger about to jump on its prey.

Today was Sunday, which meant he'd been staying with her for almost two weeks, and even though he'd gotten more familiar with his surroundings, he still woke up each day in a slight daze. The only other time he'd been as unmoored from life was the summer after college, when he did the backpacking thing with Bill to Europe like many recent grads, but the circumstances then weren't comparable. He'd been a kid finally shorn of his educational contract, and as he toured the cobblestoned streets of Paris and listened to people who spoke words he didn't understand, the world had never seemed more open.

Kevin tiptoed around Claudia and ascended the stairs like a thief. Since Alice moved out, he'd been alone, and he was once again reminded of the challenges of living with another person, the self-awareness it required. Claudia wasn't a difficult housemate, spending many twelve-hour days at her gallery, and whenever she was in the mode of creation, he let her be.

The single television in the house was in the office, which didn't make much sense to Kevin until Claudia explained it. For her, the TV was work, where she watched the videos artists sent to her or a documentary on some arcane subject, like the history of the pushpin or how soy milk was made. Even when she did catch the rare show, it was still a job to her, a way for her to glean whatever she could to improve her art. Everything she did was for the service of her paintings, and there was something undeniably honorable about that. In spite of the nutty hedonistic side to her personality, he liked her.

He was placing the DVD in the tray when he heard Claudia behind him.

"What the fuck am I doing?" she said.

She threw herself facedown on the couch and screamed into the cushion, which didn't work too well because it was made of leather and not exactly sound-absorbent. Without her bandanna, her hair spilled out over the couch slowly, like melted chocolate.

Kevin grabbed the remote and sat down next to her. Most leather couches tended to be cold in winter and sticky during the summer, but this one was different. According to Claudia, it'd been treated with some sort of space-age chemical to make it feel and act like fabric.

"Why didn't you just get a cloth-covered couch in the first place?" he'd asked.

Her laugh was like a cough that expanded to a minor explosion. "That's a very good point. See, this is why I need someone like you, because you think simply."

Which was different than a simpleton, she assured him, and she then chuckled some more.

He ran his fingers through her hair. It was odd how quickly they'd become comfortable with one another. Some of it had to do with Claudia, who was not shy about touching or being touched. He hadn't felt this cavalier with a woman since college, when it seemed as if there was an infinite supply of female bodies to discover. He couldn't decide whether this was a progression or a regression on his part, to re-experience this form of carefree human contact two decades later.

This was different, though. Back then, it was the haze of alcohol that created the false sense of closeness, while with Claudia, it was her uncompromising demand for emotional honesty. She wanted nothing less than for him to act on and follow his desires, and the moment she noticed his hesitation on anything, she would call him on it. Like last night, when she'd pulled open the freezer and taken out the chocolate ice cream and asked him if he wanted some, she pounced on his microscopic pause.

"What is it you really want?" she'd asked.

"What are you talking about?"

"You"—she pointed the silver scooper at him—"don't really want"—now pointing to the tub of chocolate ice cream—"this. You want something else, but despite what I've asked of you, you continue to lie."

"We're still talking about ice cream?"

She slammed the door of the freezer, the hanging pots above the kitchen island clattering. Scooper in fist, she walked right up to him, the tips of their noses almost touching. She stared at him as if she wanted to take a battering ram to his face.

"This is about what you want, and you asking for what you want. Now tell me, Kevin, what is it that you want?"

"Vanilla," he said. "I have always preferred to put chocolate sauce on top of vanilla ice cream. In fact, if I can be perfectly honest . . ."

"Yes, please."

". . . I have never believed in the need for the existence of chocolate ice cream. Because by itself, it's too chocolaty. But vanilla is vanilla enough that you can add whatever you want and make it to your satisfaction."

Claudia put the scooper down on the table, gripped his arms with her incredibly strong hands, and kissed him on the lips, hard enough to hurt.

"Thank you," she said. "I ate the last of the vanilla ice cream this afternoon, so we don't have any."

They drove to the store and bought six tubs. This was life with Claudia. Kevin had hoped for her company and clarity today, and he was glad to have her by his side. Maybe he was just overreacting, but he was scared of the DVD. On the subway ride back to Claudia's from Norman's, it had gained the heft of a horror movie, and it was always preferable to watch scary films with someone else. Kevin held up the DVD case and filled her in.

"So instead of actually talking to you in person, your bio-dad chose to make this film. That might mean he used to be an actor or has worked in some other capacity in the film business before he became a therapist. Maybe he's a transplanted Angeleno; lots of them here."

Kevin nodded, though he couldn't see Norman as an actor. He didn't have the demeanor associated with people in the dramatic arts, with their loud voices and confident strides. But maybe when he stepped in front of the camera, he kicked into a whole different personality.

"Are you waiting for an invitation?" Claudia asked, tapping on the remote in his hand.

"Right," Kevin said, and he clicked Play.

On the wide flatscreen, a red bedroom glowed, definitely not his father's. Kevin had visited his bungalow a couple of times and was given the requisite tour, so he knew this footage wasn't taken from his house. In front of the wine-colored walls, there was a garish four-poster bed from Victorian times, a gauzy curtain draped between the posts.

"Interesting," Claudia said.

And now a man, holding a wooden chair with canvas backing and seat, the type that movie directors sit in, walked into the frame. It was Norman, and he was naked.

"Really, *really* interesting," she said.

The quality of the video was startlingly real, high definition enough to see the hairs on his arms. This man, his father, placed the chair down on the floor and stood upright next to it, without a hint of embarrassment or titillation, as if what he was doing was nothing at all. For a man in his early sixties, Norman was in fine shape, possessing the lean, muscular body of a runner, and he just let it all hang out there, his penis jutting out of the forest of his pubic hair like a totem. Norman was uncircumcised. Kevin had seen his share of penises in the locker room, quick sideways glances to see how he measured up against the competition, and in the process he noticed how everyone had their foreskin removed. And now here was Norman in full, binding them together through this private physical trait.

"He did write *for my son* on the disc," Kevin said.

"Do you want me to leave?" Claudia asked.

"No. I mean how much worse can this get?"

"Have you seen the website goatse.cx? Or Lemon Party?"

Kevin shook his head.

"Then you probably don't know how much worse this could get."

Norman, as if somehow sensing the conversation between them, turned and reached for the arm jutting from the right that was holding a robe.

"There's somebody else there!" Kevin said.

Norman put the robe on and sat in the chair, his legs thankfully crossed.

"There's lots of somebodies there," Claudia said. "This is a set for a movie."

Norman cleared his throat. He looked directly at them, the camera slowly pushing in until his face filled the screen.

"Son," he said, "I'm sorry if that shocked you, but I wanted to get this out in the open. For the last hour, I tried speaking to the camera like a regular person, but I couldn't do it, not without feeling like a liar. I thought I'd shed the shame that's associated with my business after all these years, but it looks like it came right back when I had to tell you what I did for a living. Even though I have my own counseling practice, I work exclusively with the pornographic industry. I understand these people because I was one of them. I was a porn actor, and so was your mother. That's how we met, and that's how you came to be."

Kevin turned to Claudia, and if his jaw could fall any further, it would be somewhere in the fourth dimension.

"This is, without question," Claudia said, "the best movie I've ever seen."

"I've always been most truthful in front of the camera," Norman said. "I'd like to tell you about my life. Even though none of it matters now, in the present, I know you feel differently, and I owe this to you."

They sank deeper into the couch and listened.

Just how is it that I became a porn actor? It's the question I'm most frequently asked. And like most things in life, it's an unplanned event. Things are different now—there are men out there who actually decide and pursue this line of work as if they were going for their MBA, but that's because there's a viable infrastructure. It's all about money, of course: Last year, pornography brought in more than six billion dollars. But back in the day, we were just having fun. We got drunk or stoned, or a combination of the two—don't forget, this was the late '60s/early '70s, when everybody was smoking dope and dropping acid—and we were living in a gorgeous house owned by a very rich friend, a guy named Montaigne, and the guy was having a lot of sex with a lot of women, and me and this guy Rick were a part of his entourage. So when he tired of certain girls . . . we got his sloppy seconds, I guess you could say. When he wasn't fucking, Monty liked to take photos, and it wasn't long until he got himself a video camera and started recording us.

So this is how it starts. There are all these cute naked girls, there's plenty of alcohol and drugs to go around, you're young, you're beautiful, you're horny. The camera rolls, and you don't even see it. You're just goofing off. Then Monty says let's play, why don't you, Norman, pretend like you're a plumber, and Jane, you're a bored housewife. Then he actually starts getting props and costumes, and that makes it even more fun.

The first movie wasn't scripted at all, one scene after another, just loops made with the Super 8mm with some corny music and amateur dubs added later, but it indeed is a feature-length film because it ran for eighty-one minutes and we were actually trying to tell a story. Granted, it wasn't much of a story, about a wife cheating on her traveling salesman husband while he was away, but there was an attempt to write a script and to act like a proper actor.

There was a strip joint in the Tenderloin that showcased nudie films after midnight, so that's where we had our premiere, supposedly. I wasn't there because it was all done without any of our knowledge. There were some girls who were pissed, and initially Rick and I weren't thrilled, either, but then we started getting recognized—by a tiny subset of the population, of course, and not always the most desirable. Still, it was something, because at the time, we were both down on our luck and couldn't really see a way out from the blackness of our future. I mean, you're so different than me, son. You are a professional, someone who has already conquered this mysterious world. For me, I saw a life of lifting boxes or digging ditches. I had no skills and, to tell you the truth, didn't want any. After barely passing high school, I never kept a job for more than two months. I couldn't imagine working in an office for the next forty years, and besides, I saw it as a sort of a spiritual suicide. It was the '70s, in San Francisco. I wasn't the only hippie in town.

As you've seen, I'm not particularly hung. Many of the men in this business are well-endowed, but I'm normal Norman. Rick, on the other hand, he was big, "eight and a quarter inches of pleasure," as he often liked to say. But size doesn't do you any good if you can't get hard, and for Rick, that's what happened to him. He was good for about four pictures, but then he started having trouble, which isn't surprising at all. By that time, Monty had a studio built in his basement and had two cameramen and a lighting guy on the payroll, folks who worked in the mainstream doing commercials and wanted to make some extra money at night. The techs get those lights really close up to your genitals, and they're hot. And sometimes the cameraman has to brace himself right against you to get the money shot, and maybe the guy ate garlic bread or kimchi for lunch. Then there are the girls—usually they're pretty young things, but many of them take drugs to get through it, and I've had times when a deep throat goes down a little too deep, and she ends up vomiting all over you. Not to mention that just like any other movie shoot, there are workers milling about, extras to fill a scene and caterers setting up the spread, and all these people have to get paid whether or not you can maintain an erection.

Fifteen years ago, you saw all sorts of guys doing my work: old, ugly, fat, what have you. That's because staying hard was a gift from above, and usually God gave you a magic dick and not much else. But that changed with the introduction of Viagra and other ED drugs. That's why all the recent porn actors are handsome and sport six-pack abs, because they can just pop the blue pill before they face the camera. Some of the girls don't like it, because it makes them feel less attractive and sexy, that a guy has to use drugs to perform, but this is the present reality.

Call me lucky. I've had my blood tested, and my testosterone level is still higher than most men in their twenties. The toughest part for me was keeping from coming inside a woman. Because if there's one rule you cannot break in porn, it's that you have to ejaculate outside, for the camera.

In some ways, women have it easier than men in this business because they can fake it. And of course they do. In all the movies I've made, and I've made my share, 193 to be exact, there have only been a handful of women I worked with who actually orgasmed with me, one of whom was your mother. I'm sorry if that shocks you—I can't imagine many children wanting to hear about their parents and their orgasms—but sex, to me, is a commodity, a way to make a living, no different than the way an electrician may consider his voltmeter. But I'm getting ahead of myself, Kevin. There's so much I want to tell you that it's difficult not to stray.

After the first four movies, I had to find a better porn name. Ironically, Rick was born with one, last name Strong. The thing Monty liked most about me was how easygoing and relaxed I was, so he dubbed me Mellow Yellow. Maybe today I would've been offended by the racial connotations, but it all seemed fine back then. There weren't many Asian porn actors working in the States, so more than anything, I was grateful that I was getting paid to fuck a lot of women. In fact, I think there was only one other, a big Chinese guy they called Long Dong, so you can imagine what his specialty was.

Many people who get into this business do so as an act of defiance, because they were brought up in strict religious households, where they prayed every day, never heard a single curse word, weren't even allowed to think about sex until marriage, and maybe not even then. It's a terrible situation to be in, especially when you're a teenager, puberty exerting itself in every which way, like a bomb waiting to go off. Believe me, I know, because I was one of these unfortunate people. My parents were Catholic missionaries, their entire lives devoted to the church and all things Jesus Christ, and what they wanted was for me to be a priest.

A priest!

It's funny now, but there was nothing funny about my adolescence. Do you believe in God, son? That's perfectly fine if you do; in fact, I applaud you if you do, because I've never been able to believe. In my heart of hearts, I know there's nothing else for me, for any of us, outside of what we have here and now. And I'm not pulling some sort of a Nietzschean nothingness here. I just know that we are, in essence, alone in this universe. Why wouldn't we be? Why would we want to look to some ethereal, higher being for guidance of any kind? We are our own gods.

Okay. Let's get to me and your mom before I turn down another philosophical alley.

We met at Monty's birthday party. It was 1971, and Grace Kim, that's your mother, was invited by Vince DeGuardi, the photographer. It was just a couple of weeks after we had our movie premiere at the O'Farrell Theatre, so both Rick and I were semicelebrities. That's where the movie Behind the Green Door was shown a year later. It was when everyone saw Deep Throat and the concept of pornographic films became more palatable to the general public, a time dubbed the golden age of porn. I can't agree. As usual, the past is often seen through the forgiving filter of nostalgia, and what I remember about that time period is nothing of the sort. Drugs were everywhere, the mafia was involved with both the backing and the distribution of the products, and as it was a time before AIDS, there was no regard for the sexual well-being of the actors. At the same time, the movies back then had larger budgets and longer shoots, so the claim isn't entirely unfounded. The Internet has both been a blessing and a curse, making for easy delivery of materials but also bringing in an enormous wave of free amateur porn, but it's not as if the adult film industry is the only one that has suffered at the hands of new technology. Look at what's happened with record companies.

Sorry I went off on another tangent, son. It's not often that I talk about my past, especially to my own blood. Which reminds me—I haven't told you that you have a sister. Half sister, I suppose, but blood is blood. When we see each other again, I'll be sure to get you in touch with her. She wants to meet you. Denise lives in Oakland, just a few BART stops away.

Your mother was eighteen years old when we met, and she was a beautiful girl. The photo that you have is from 1973, and by that time, she'd spent almost three years working in the industry, and it destroyed her. She didn't admit it to anyone, especially herself, and her cause of death was determined to be an accidental overdose, though I think it was as accidental as someone dying of lung cancer after smoking three packs a day for his or her entire life.

When I met Grace at the birthday party, her feet never touched the ground. There is no better way to describe her youth, her air. Here was a girl who knew how to have fun, whose hair was so long and so dark that it touched the small of her back.

I know an orgy sounds like some weird, kinky thing, but it's nothing more than a lot of people fucking at the same time. You might think there's all sorts of swapping going on, like some kind of a naughty square dance, but in the numerous orgies I've partaken in, that's actually pretty rare. This will sound strange, but it's more like the thrill of watching a great movie in a crowded theater versus watching it at home by yourself. What's special is the shared experience of the moment, that you're not alone. Nobody thinks about this because, well, it's not something that normal people ever have an opportunity to think about in a different way, but sex is a lonely thing. Yes, it certainly is less lonely than masturbating, but have you ever considered the fact that when you are orgasming, you're almost always experiencing it by yourself? As everyone knows, simultaneous orgasms between two people only exist in romance novels. In the real world, if the girl is lucky, she gets off before the guy does. When you're in a room with a hundred people groaning with pleasure, bodies dripping with the sweat of lovemaking, it's guaranteed that there's somebody else reaching their climax at the same time as you. There's nothing that makes you feel more human.

So that's how we met, at Monty's birthday orgy. Human bodies fell around us like trees, female legs spread wide and reaching for the sky, grunts of pleasure echoing all over the house. At eighteen, Grace's body was as fresh as a summer's morning. Touching her skin was like getting high; never would I meet another woman who'd have that kind of an effect on me. I can still remember her inner warmth, like an all-encompassing embrace. That was the magic, Kevin, that our bodily union was like a hug. We felt so safe with each other.

Sharing in this very intimate act with other people is why I've stayed in this business. Most people have a very low opinion of the kind of work I do, and maybe you do, too. But I believe I'm doing some good in this world, for this world. There are men out there who would never be able to get a girl to bed, ugly men, disabled men, obese men, shy men. But they're still men, and they need an outlet. That's why there's pornography. Maybe a husband isn't getting the frequency of sex he desires from his wife, so instead of having affairs or getting a divorce, he beats off while watching one of my movies. We've all been conditioned by religion and society to be shameful of sex for too long, so it's not going to change overnight, if ever. Even though pornography has become more mainstream, America's Puritanical roots will never allow us to enjoy our lives without guilt. But that doesn't mean I won't stop trying.

Because what I do, son, what I do is an expression of freedom. I'm not talking about some Larry Flynt–First Amendment soapbox but rather the act itself. It's something that didn't occur to me until many years later, but when you're naked and there's this girl who's naked and there are cameras whirling and people all around you, watching and filming this very primal moment—I wish I could convey to you how free you feel. There are no rules, it's animal, it's the very essence of life.

I'm sorry to say your mother and I were in only one film together, and the only reason why it even got made was because Monty owed a Chinese opium dealer some money and wanted to appease him. Unlike most folks, who wanted to see interracial couplings, this guy wanted to see two Asians going at it.

That reminds me—I forgot to tell you that in about two-thirds of my films, I played a Mexican, which I could get away with, with my dark skin and my convincing accent. With a bushy mustache and darker eyebrows drawn in, I became Juan Grande. So if you ever come across some vintage porn starring a Mexican who could pass for an Asian, it's probably me. Not that you would find any of my old movies. Most of those films were stolen or trashed. It wasn't like we were making The Godfather or Gone with the Wind, safeguarding our masters in vacuum-sealed vaults.

Our film was titled One Night in Bang Cock, the name of the city intentionally misspelled. That was the name of Grace's character, Bang Cock, and it was filmed mostly in Monty's backyard, at night, hence the title. Monty's backyard was as manicured as a golf course, so it made for a suitable backdrop. The story was that she was waiting for her husband to return from a war, but she was this nympho, so she ends up having sex with everybody—the mailman, the gardener, the girl babysitter. It's actually a pretty funny movie, because the whole time, she's in false agony, like, "I miss you so much, husband," and then the next minute, she's blowing the exterminator. But the last twenty minutes of the film is just us. The costumers had me in a samurai suit, with the sword and the armor and the iron helmet that was like having a house on my head. It took a good five minutes for me to just get out of all of that gear, but was it ever worth it. Being on camera with my future wife—it was the spring of 1971, a full moon rising high in the night. When you look back on your life, son, can you find a single moment that makes life worth living? Maybe it's sad, that of all the years that I've lived on this planet, I can shrink down the best of my life to a single shard of time. But I've lived that scene many times over in my mind, us sixty-nining on the grass, then I'm on top and not even seeing the cameras anymore, your mother's breasts cupped in my hands, her nipples as hard as erasers, our bodies moving as one, and now the director is screaming because he can see it on my face, it's something he'd never yell at a professional like me, but there I am, breaking the only unbreakable rule in this business.

That was you, son. I know it was you because nine months later, you were born.

The movie paused, his father's mouth frozen in midword, looking as if he'd encountered some mild, pleasant surprise. Kevin lifted his elbows to see if he'd accidentally pressed a button on the remote, but the remote was in Claudia's hand.

She pointed it at the TV and clicked the power button, the light extinguished, the room darkening.

"Claudia?" Kevin said.

She looked as if she wanted to kiss him, and that's what she did, her lips pressed against his, moist and full. She tasted like salty caramel, and it was as if some switch had been thrown, more in his pants than his head. He wasn't exactly turned on, but he wasn't exactly not turned on, either, and that was more than enough. Kevin returned her passion in equal measure, holding her close, pulling her closer. She unbuckled his belt; he unbuttoned her blouse. Her hands were as scratchy as a cat's tongue, raising goose bumps when she ran her palms over his chest. She laughed, and he laughed, and they were on the couch and then the floor and then back again, her hair in his mouth, her fingernails digging into the flesh of his ass as she yanked him onto her, into her, through her, their bodies melding into a single creature. Wasn't that lovemaking, a flesh connection? At the core of it, that's what fucking was, a man and a woman joined at the front of their respective hips to achieve a symbiosis of sorts. He'd always enjoyed the physicality of it, the well of pleasure filling up before the grand release of orgasm, and now, as Claudia rode him like a mechanical bull, her breasts bouncing with every pump, it occurred to him that his appetite for sex was something else that ran in the family.

He never used to be so ruminative during sex, but it'd been like this since Alice, and now he thought of her, the last time they made love. She was on top but facing away from him, leaving him with the view of her backside as she rocked rhythmically down and away from him. It wasn't his favorite position because he enjoyed seeing her face while they were doing it, and this was exactly the opposite, as anonymous as sex can be between two people, especially for her, since she was turned away completely.

For a second, Kevin thought Claudia was going to strike him, but she slammed both hands by his ears instead.

"Holy Jesus Christ!" Claudia screamed. "I'm coming, oh my fucking God, I'm coming!"

An orgasmic tsunami, hot waves of vibrations through a gush of sticky wetness. And just like that, he was on the edge himself. He wrapped his arms around her thighs, squeezed her and pumped into her, his movements no longer his own.

Was it this good with Alice? Maybe in the beginning, but if so, he honestly couldn't remember. With Claudia slumped over him, her breath as ragged as his, he hugged her sweat-slick body and realized he was doomed to forever compare every new woman to the love of his life. At the same time, he knew he was being melodramatic—there was life after Alice, whether or not he wanted to recognize it. Because this was what that afterlife was: making love in San Francisco, meeting his porn-actor biological father. He needed to open his eyes and consciously experience what was in front of him.

"I've always been a messy fucker," Claudia said. "When it's good, that is."

Kevin looked up at her. "I like messy."

When she ran her hand through her hair to tame the wildness, Kevin found her self-consciousness endearing. She lay down next to him on the Oriental rug, shoulder to shoulder, arm touching arm. They stared at the chandelier, crystal teardrops twisting lazily.

"Thank you," she said. "You could've said no."

"I suppose. But why?"

She giggled. She propped her head on his chest and walked down the expanse of his stomach with her index and middle fingers, her paint-spattered nails barely grazing the surface of his skin. Her fingerfeet waded through the jungle of his pubic hair, digging and lifting through the thicket. She held his limp penis between her thumb and index finger and flopped it back and forth.

"It's one thing I'll never know, what it's like to have one of these."

"If you keep doing that, he'll wake back up."

"Really?"

"It might take a little while, though. I'm not as young as I used to be."

"Are you one of these guys who names his penis?"

"No, but I do say *him* and not *it*. Come on, it's a penis. Of course it's a *him*."

They watched him grow back in size; it was like seeing a time-lapsed photograph of a flower blooming.

"I'll miss this," he said, "when I'm old."

She wrapped her hand around his shaft, and the enclosed warmth made him harder.

"It's just sex, but it's so much more, isn't it," Claudia said. "It's power, it's life, it's everything for a man. No wonder all those boner drugs have been a godsend for big pharma."

"I don't know if it's everything, but it is more than just sex."

She climbed on top of him again and kissed his lips, her hair falling over his face like a million little hands, and she sighed ever so slightly when he slipped inside. She was warm and wet, and he cradled her ass in his hands as if he owned her. She laughed and rocked and threw her head back, her hair still a tangled, untamed mass.

"I have to say," she said, "it—I mean he—is quite a trooper."

After they showered together and noshed on cold leftover pizza, they returned to the couch and turned on the television. His father came back exactly as they'd left him, except now it was they who were different.

"We look like him," Kevin said, and it was true, in their matching his-and-her bathrobes, the white terry cloth plush like a fresh towel.

She picked up her glass of water and took a sip. "This was a little weird, huh? Because when you really think about it, we fucked because your father and his sex stories turned us on."

Kevin leaned back and slung his arm over his eyes.

"Can I just blame this on you?"

"Of course you can," Claudia said. "But it does take two to tango, and as I recall, it was you and I who tangoed. Naked. Like right there, where that wet spot still is?" She pointed with her bare foot. "I'll have to get that rug cleaned."

"I bet this would make him proud. If I told him that watching his movie led us to this."

Claudia nodded. She filled his empty glass with the decanter of water sitting on the side table and handed it to him. "Are you okay? I can't even pretend to imagine what's going through your mind."

Kevin took a long drink. He wanted to know what he was feeling, but all he could sense was the cold water going down his throat and settling into his stomach. A deep chill spread through his body.

"Let's finish this thing," he said, and he clicked on the remote.

To this day, I still remember the first moment I held you, marveling at your impossible, tiny hands. Everything about you was so small and yet so fully formed, a human being in miniature. Of course that's what babies are, but when you see your own, it really is true, your life changes. For seventeen days of my twenty-second year, I was a father. On your birth certificate, we put down Norman, but we called you Little Man. That was, as I'll always remember, your name.

We couldn't keep you, Kevin, because we weren't ready, it was as simple as that. For two weeks we pretended we were, but your mom was still taking a cocktail of drugs, and I knew I couldn't do this alone. One day we had to rush you to the ER because you wouldn't stop crying, and when the doctor looked at you, he asked one of the nurses to get a bottle of formula. It turned out that we'd forgotten to feed you and you were just really, really hungry. Your mother had thought it was my turn and I'd thought the opposite, and you were crying so loudly that we panicked like frightened children ourselves.

So we gave you up. I'm not going to lie and tell you this was a diffi-cult decision. We knew there was no other way, and we were still young enough to fool ourselves into thinking that there was a future ahead of us. Grace died two years later, a day shy of her twenty-first birthday. To wake up in the morning and find the woman you love dead in your own bed—it's a day I wish I could erase from my memory banks, but I can't.

Here I go, getting ahead of myself again. To this day, I'm not exactly sure how the transaction transpired because Grace did it alone. We had a horrendous fight the night before, because she wanted to keep you, even though she was in no condition to. So if you want to blame someone for your abandonment, blame me. When I threatened to leave if she kept you, it was she who disappeared for two days. When she returned, you were gone, so I didn't even get a chance to say a proper good-bye. All she told me was that you were in good hands, that you would be raised without prejudice and as if you were the couples' own baby. She would never bring you up again, even though she thought of you every day for the rest of her days.

She just got worse from that point forward.

Don't get me wrong; it wasn't as if every day was misery. There were many moments of happiness, especially after a long day of shooting. Many people find it surprising that a couple who make porn movies can stay together in a normal relationship, but what those people forget is that sex is not intimacy. It can be, and it often is, but they are not mutu-ally inclusive. Passing a box of popcorn while watching Three Days of the Condor, listening to her breathing as she drifted to sleep, sweating in the kitchen as we cooked up our favorite dish, duck à l'orange—these became our secret couplings. That's not to say that we didn't have sex—I don't think we ever went a day without fucking. To some eyes, we might have been sex maniacs, but would they reserve the same judgment for Michael Jordan if he shot hoops every day? If you're good at something, you do it because it gives you pleasure.

But your mother was unhappy. For most of her life, she'd been unhappy. A fair number of people who come into pornography do so because they were sexually abused or suffered some other form of child-hood trauma, and so it was with your mother. She hated to talk about her past, but eventually I pieced together that she had an uncle who started touching her when she was eight years old and it just got worse until she ran away at sixteen. In this business, there's a decent chance that you're working with somebody who's emotionally damaged, and here's the thing: If you're fucked up coming into it, you're not going to find any answers here. If anything, it'll just fuck you up more. The business drew your mother in, sucked the life out of her, and shit out what remained. Left her in the toilet is what it did.

I'm sorry if I sound bitter. I try not to be because I owe my livelihood to porn, but I can't forget the broken people I've worked with, especially women. That's why I'm still with the industry, trying to do what I can to make it better, working from the inside. I listen well and I've been through a lot myself, so I know I can help. I'm a survivor. And I don't give up—look at us, you and me. Even though I knew there was virtually no chance of me finding you, here we are. I've been searching for you for almost twenty years. I'd contacted various adoption agencies, even hired private investigators to track you down, but because Grace gave you up secretly and through nonstandard means, I knew it would be almost impossible to find you.

But we are together now, son. Through perseverance and luck and the generosity of whatever power that may or may not be out there, you are hearing about how the three of us came to be. I wish I had the courage to tell you all of this in person, but this is the best I could do. Which is also true of forty years ago. Your mother and I did the best we could, which we know wasn't good enough. Whatever hurt you have been harboring since you found out about your adoption will remain with you for the rest of your life, but if it's any consolation, you can count on me to be there for you going forward. I'm well aware you already have a father, but there can't be any harm in having another person who loves you, who cares for you—is there?

Thank you for listening, Kevin. I hope you'll find it in your heart to call me so we can talk about this and whatever else. And I want you to meet your sister before you go back to New Jersey. We are a family. I'm happy. I'm so very, very happy.

19

For fourteen days Judy woke up to the distant cry of gulls. As she made her way to the bathroom half asleep, her bare feet warm from the geothermal heat rising off the marble floor, she squinted against the sun-reflected surface of the bay. Iridescence and tranquility assaulted her from every window, and there were a lot of windows. None of this felt real, and yet it was absolutely real, especially when she sat down on the toilet to pee.

Snaps uncurled herself from the plush shag of the black bearskin rug that sat in the middle of the room. She placed her two front paws together and arched her back for a full stretch, her bones cracking like popcorn, then trudged over to greet Judy.

"Hey, girl," Judy said. She scratched the top of Snaps's head, the shape of which had always reminded Judy of a horseshoe crab. Even though it was more than a decade ago, she could see the puppy in this old dog, that day Kevin and Alice had gotten her. Snaps had stood up in her palms, two tiny paws balanced on each hand, the entire dog cradled in the span of her outstretched fingers. Most of Snap's muzzle was gray now, as were her whiskers.

This ridiculous expanse of a bathroom, its dimensions roughly the size of her apartment's living room, seemed just as foreign as it had two weeks ago, when Roger had brought her to his home in Cape Cod. The Jacuzzi bathtub was big enough for the Brady Bunch, its inside walls lined with jets to soothe every muscle, and it was adorned with a circle of track lighting above that not only dimmed or brightened but shone different hues to enhance the mood. There were two enormous sinks, each basin large enough that Judy and Roger could stand side by side and still have plenty of room. The stand-up shower, which was shaped like a bottle, had just one showerhead, but it was as wide as a tire and rained a warm drizzle that was as nurturing as a mother's hug.

She was living an illusion, but she didn't care. This was the power of money, the greatest illusion of all.

"You don't care, do you?" she asked Snaps, who stared with her mouth ajar, pink tongue ensconced within the fence of her bottom row of teeth. Her lower canines jutted out like stalagmites, yellow pillars streaked with brown. They were all bone white in her puppy days.

Judy had always been afraid of death. Even as a child, she'd never experienced the fascination like so many of her friends or her brother. The games often involved someone getting shot or pushed over the precipice to the imagined abyss below, the kids clutching their chests, twirling and swaying in an elaborate dance of demise. Not wanting to be seen as a party-pooper, she reluctantly went along, but her deaths were always quick, never dramatic.

She couldn't watch nature shows where some poor animal got his neck broken by the jaws of a tiger; she averted her eyes at the deer lying on the side of the road with its legs at odd angles. Even dead insects bothered her, Brian the designated sweeper of the upturned shells of the stink bugs and ladybugs from the windowsill.

Judy got up from the toilet and flushed. Snaps rose with her and followed her to the sink, then sat and performed her scratch-and-thump routine, her back leg drumming against the floor. Judy blasted the hot water then turned it down immediately, forgetting that in this modern marvel of a bathroom, the water was instantly hot. She washed her hands and dipped her face to the basin, and as she gave herself to the fluid darkness, she felt a sense of déjà vu. She'd been in this exact position in a bathroom not unlike this, the one in the hospital, on her mother's final night. Of course that bathroom had an antiseptic, industrial quality, but it was as quiet as this one.

As she'd splashed cold water on her face, she'd known with absolute certainty that her mother's death was imminent. It wasn't something she had seen, but felt, a coldness that had descended on her mother's hospital room, the moonlight from the window turned fainter, frayed. To see her own mother die—that was what was waiting for her. To hear her take her last breath, her soul evaporate into nothingness, the dreaded finality of death. Judy walked into a nearby stall and sat on the toilet and stared at the metal olive-green door, as if it held answers.

After what felt like an eternity but was not even fifteen minutes, she dialed Kevin.

He sounded like he'd been asleep, but he forced his voice to clarity. "What's the matter? Is everything all right? Is it Mom?"

"I don't feel good," she said. Her brother had spent all day here, and the night was supposed to have been her shift.

She told him it was her stomach, that she felt like throwing up. It was an excuse as old as time itself, one she'd used to get out of situations as a child. Certainly Kevin should've sniffed out the bull-shit, having heard it himself a thousand times, but perhaps because he'd been half asleep, he fell for it wholeheartedly. When Kevin told her he was on his way, Judy resented him for not offering more resistance.

What she should've done was to tell him the truth when he arrived, but when she saw the concern on his face, all she wanted was to get the hell out of there.

They met outside their mother's room. Kevin was wearing a Penn State T-shirt and a pair of baggy sweatpants. Maybe it was the harsh fluorescent lights of the hospital, but her brother looked old to her, sinewy and weathered like a piece of leather left out in the sun too long. He looked like an athlete beyond his prime.

"I'm all right," she told him when he harped on her about her stomach issue. "There's just a lot going on, that's all."

"Okay," he said, sounding anything but. "Should I call if her condition changes?"

"Of course," she said, annoyed. "I'm not going into a cave in Afghanistan, just back home, for Christ's sake."

But when the phone rang that night, she didn't pick up. She'd been in bed, trying to will herself to sleep that wouldn't come, when the simulated electronic ringing shocked her through the surrounding blackness. Brian was working the graveyard shift at the Quick Chek, the vacancy of his side of the bed an unfamiliar void. The apartment was quiet enough that she could hear her brother's broken voice playing on the answering machine in the kitchen.

"I just sat there and watched her," he said. "She's gone, Judy, our mother's gone."

And now, in the most luxurious bathroom she'd ever been in, she lifted her face and watched the wetness roll down the concavity of her neck. Rivulets formed like rivers down the front of her body, cresting over the rounded hills of her breasts, rolling down the knoll of her stomach, the final stream pooling in the crater of her belly button.

With her arms propped against the sink, Judy leaned forward toward her mirrored reflection. What was she doing in this ocean-front mansion of Roger's? She was trying. She was trying to make something of herself, yet again. Because she'd almost died, because she and Roger had talked about where to go from where they were, and it wasn't just a physical place, it was purpose, it was meaning. It all sounded so self-absorbed, but she had to stop the *think* and start the *do*.

There was a time in her life when Judy considered herself an artist. Even just remembering this brought on a sense of egoism that she found discomfiting, not to mention horrifying, considering just how little she'd managed to accomplish toward this goal. It was true she wasn't that old yet, but certainly time was running out, as it did for everyone. There were always heartening stories of a schmuck who finally published her first novel at the ripe old age of eighty or an actor finding stardom at the same time he received his Medicare card, but not only were those serious exceptions to the rule, they also were still tales of regret. Because even if they found success late in life, the majority of their lives were spent in struggle and disappointment, those precious years long gone.

Judy never had grand ambitions, just a reasonable-sized one, to make a living using her God-given ability to see what she saw with her eyes and transfer it to paper with accuracy and ownership. As long as she could remember, she knew how to do this. She never even real-ized it was a gift, which was exactly how a talent like this was supposed to be; the whole point of an inborn ability was to take it for granted, which she did until high school, when her art teacher told her how fortunate she was that she could do something that took people years to learn, if at all.

But in college, there were many precocious talents to rival hers, and when Judy failed to garner one of the five fellowships that the school offered, she began to doubt her future. It certainly didn't help that when she reported the rejection to her parents, her father's response was as curt as it was brutal: "Maybe you good, but not very good." Growing up, she'd heard two conflicting voices, her father publically criticizing her every move, her mother privately reassuring her that none of it was true. As much as she'd appreciated her moth-er's support, the words that squeezed her heart were her father's.

But wasn't there a statute of limitations on parental misguidance?

She was two years shy of forty, and she was still blaming her dad. At this point, she'd spent enough time in therapy to be a psychiatrist herself, and if there was a time to break out of her old ways, this was it.

Judy picked up the silk robe hanging from the hook and wrapped it around her, cinching the belt tight against her belly. She grabbed her box of Marlboro Lights on the counter and tiptoed past the bed, where Roger still slept, his cat Momo curled up against the back of his neck like a stole. For two weeks they'd slept together, and so far, it had been a nonexperience. Brian had been a tosser and a turner, broadcasting his presence to her with every shift of the mattress, but Roger's breathing was as shallow as a yogi in deep meditation. Not that she wanted to be woken up by a flailing arm or a kick to her shin, but she wouldn't mind being aware of the person sleeping next to her once in a while.

Maybe this was her true talent, the ability to whine about anything, no matter how ideal or perfect the situation. She was living in a house only a millionaire could afford, and she was still somehow managing to bitch about it.

Two doors down from the master bedroom was the study, where a giant ceiling-to-floor window encased in a thick mahogany frame looked out over Hen Cove and its bevy of sailboats bobbing on the early-morning blue water. She approached the glass drafting table sitting in the middle of the room and sat on the stool, its cold metal surface like a slap on the butt. She tapped a cigarette out of the box and lit it, then watched the smoke curl away.

This was where she was supposed to draw, to do her work, first thing in the morning when her brain was at its clearest. But her mind wasn't empty, it was full of junk as always, what she'd have for breakfast, the silly sitcom they watched last night, and her brother, who called just shy of midnight, forgetting that he was on West Coast time.

"I really can't thank you enough, Judy," he had said. "Taking care of Snaps and the house and everything for all this time, I'm really glad I can count on you."

"You bet," she said, watching Roger teach Snaps how to pray. He'd hold his arm out for Snaps to hang her paw on, then he'd hold a treat underneath so she'd dip her head, and just like that, it looked like the dog was leaning against a pew, talking to God. He caught her staring at them and gave her an exaggerated bow.

"I'm not just saying that," Kevin said. "I'm really glad you're my sister."

Hearing the unbridled sincerity in his voice while watching Roger rub Snaps's belly, Judy felt a gush of guilt. Laziness was not the sole reason why she didn't want to tell Kevin all that had happened with her, it was shame, shame for receiving this unplanned gift of food and shelter from a man she barely knew, for the poisonous luck of a rattlesnake's bites. There was only one way to stop this cycle of negativity.

"I'm not at your house," she said into the phone. "I'm in Cape Cod."

There was a sizable silence on the line until Kevin spoke again.

"Excuse me?"

She told him everything, about the snake bite, the huge hospital bill, Roger and his money and his house in Pocasset, Massachusetts. During her recounting, Roger came over and planted a kiss on the top of her head. Her admission wasn't just about her, it involved him, too, and even if he didn't feel joy like everyone else, she could see this meant something to him.

Laughter was not a reaction Judy had imagined from her brother.

"Life, sis, is truly weird. You're not gonna believe this," Kevin said, "but you and I have been leading very similar lives on opposite coasts."

And now it was his turn to tell her about where he was staying in San Francisco, the woman he'd met (and had obviously slept with, from the way he was playing it down), and his father the porno actor. What was the universe trying to say by having both of them live in the good graces of one percenters?

Now, sitting in front of her sketch pad, taking in the oceanic vista, Judy picked up her charcoal and poised her fingers over the empty whiteness. Earlier in the week she'd tried the obvious, the seascape in front of her, a sailboat, a man and his son walking along the shore, but none of it came out the way she'd wanted it to. There used to be a synchronicity to what was in her brain and what came out on paper, but not anymore. Maybe she'd been away from it too long; it had been years since she last tried to draw anything. She was probably being too tough on herself, something her brother often told her. The first time she tried to hit a tennis serve, she cleared the fence, and when she continued to fail—bouncing the ball before it hit the net, hitting the net, missing long, missing wide—Kevin took her racquet away and made her listen.

"The toss is where it all starts," he'd said. "If it isn't perfect, then you try to compensate for that imperfection, throwing all that follows off-balance."

"Are you talking about my life or my serve?"

Ignoring her, Kevin demonstrated again, slowing down his motion, his left arm reaching for the sky, his right arm holding the racquet as if it were a hammer. He could've passed for a Greek warrior, but what was really impressive was how every part of his body was tuned to this pose, all the muscles and ligaments and bones aligned in precise formation.

"Did you hear a word I said?"

"Yes, yes," Judy said. "Go on, big brother, show me how it's done."

He instructed her to swing the tossing arm up with the wrist and elbow locked, like a stiff stick, and at the pinnacle of the lift, to open the hand as if it were a flower and let the ball bloom straight and true.

On the pad in front of her, she started with a hand shaped like a sunflower with the long, delicate petals for its fingers. She'd never imagined such a thing, and yet it now felt so real that she was no longer drawing a fabrication but rather tracing an existing model. Instead of using charcoal, she opted for a permanent marker, adjusting its angle against the paper to achieve lines of varying thickness. She widened the stem of the flower and transformed it into a human arm, the transition from plant to mammal seamless. The final touch was the tennis ball, in the middle of its flight, which she'd completed halfway when she felt a hand on her shoulder.

"I don't know a thing about art," Roger said, "but I know that's beautiful."

He brought her an egg salad sandwich with a half spear of a sour pickle. How did he know what she wanted? He was always paying attention to her, something she wasn't used to receiving from a man in a long time.

When she'd started, the morning sun was still near the horizon, but when she looked out onto Hen Cove, it was nowhere to be found. The boats weren't casting any sizable shadows, which meant it was probably about noon. Three hours, just gone, for all the right reasons.

Roger leaned over to kiss her, and she turned away.

"I haven't brushed my teeth!"

He gave her a peck on the cheek. "Life is good?"

"Yes, it is."

But that was a lie, too, because as nice as it was to be taken care of, she felt like a housewife, her existence dependent wholly on that of Roger, her husband-equivalent. It almost felt like dying, a giving-up sensation, and yet for the history of humanity, women have been doing this as if it were nothing. Even now, in the age of the Internet, there were still many women who were homemakers. Judy might have had trouble keeping a job for long, but she'd always worked. And now that she wasn't, now that she was living off of someone else, there was an unshakable sense of weakness that grew inside her. She'd tried to convince herself that she lucked into this, that it was like hitting the lottery, or like receiving an anonymous grant from some academy to pursue her art, but the fact was, this was neither.

"Do you feel like going to a tennis court?" she asked.

"Sure," Roger said. "It's not like we have anything else to do."

They found a pair of courts at the corner of Tenth and Union in Wareham, by a set of swings in the elementary school playground. Only one was in use, two young mothers dressed the part but barely able to dink the ball back to each other. Off to the side were two baby carriages, their hoods down to protect the kids from errant balls. It was like watching the Special Olympics, but the women were none-theless delighted to be out here in the wide-open October air, the breeze as light as a fleeting touch.

Judy took a seat on the bleachers and listened to the women chatter as she considered her surroundings. After sketching Kevin and his flower-serve, she had the idea to see if she might draw inspiration from the sights and sounds of the game. Many years ago, when she'd been the most productive, she'd immerse herself in whatever subject she had chosen, and she desperately hoped it would work again, though sitting here, what she felt was a whole lot of stupid.

"I wish I had a talent for something," Roger said.

"This is my talent, right here," Judy said, pointing to the spotless pad.

"You're too hard on yourself."

"My mother used to say that."

He sat down next to her and offered her a hunk of bread.

"Challah? You brought a loaf of challah with you?"

He held up the clear bag. "I like the taste."

She couldn't help but laugh. "You and your bread."

He shrugged and took a bite, then washed it down with a sip of bot-tled water. "See? This is what having money does to a person. They end up bringing challah everywhere they go."

Judy stared at her marker, its black cap so shiny that it looked liquid. She knew the last thing Roger wanted was for her to feel guilty, but it was hard not to. "Are you sure this is what you want, to be here?"

"I want to be where you are," he said.

It sounded sincere, and Judy knew Roger's intentions were good, but what of his heart? If a person had never experienced pleasure, then why did he do anything at all? The other day, she read up on his condition on the Internet, anhedonia, personal anecdotes from people who suffered from the disease. Some couldn't feel happiness, but there were others who felt nothing at all, their lives just one continuous numbness. There was no cure.

The women took a break to sip their lime-green bottles of Gatorade and tend to their babies. From this distance, Judy couldn't tell if the babies were boys or girls, but as she watched the mothers pick up their respective children and heft them into the air and bring them down for coos and kisses, what was certain was the outpouring of joy in these four faces, an almost embarrassing amount of it.

"You okay?" Roger asked.

For a while it'd hurt too much to even look at mothers with their babies, but now it wasn't so bad. There was so much Roger didn't know about her. Once he did, once she did reveal all there was to know about her, what then?

"We don't have to be here," Judy said.

"I know."

She placed the sketch pad next to her and capped her pen.

"I'm not an easy person to be with. I'm moody. I complain. Sometimes I hate myself so much that I want to hate other people. That other person might be you, probably already has been you."

"Okay," he said.

"Okay?"

Roger spun the bag of challah and watched it wind and rewind. "What do you want me to say?"

"I don't understand why I'm here, with you. Why you put up with me."

"I could ask you the same question."

"It's not the same. I'm at your place, in your mansion of a house. I don't understand why I'm here."

"You said that already."

Judy placed her face in her hands and crouched. She knew she was making no sense, but the confusion she felt was so omnipresent that it was as if she were dipped in it.

"I love you . . . ?"

She sat up and opened her eyes and laughed. Those three words were just that, words, and as Judy well knew, their proclamation could be broken at any future moment. But they were still nice to hear.

"Perhaps I should have said that with more conviction," Roger said.

"No," Judy said. "Doubt is good."

One of the women was walking over with her baby in her arms.

"Excuse me," she said. "But are you an artist?"

Judy didn't know what to say, the question so filled with implications. The answer was more like a pronouncement than a job. An engineer built bridges, an architect built houses, a doctor cared for patients, but an artist?

"She is," Roger said.

"Oh, that's great! Could I . . . ?"

Judy flipped her pad to her work from the morning and showed it to the lady. Her fingernails were painted pink and black, split in a diagonal zigzag from one corner to another, and her long, thick eyelashes were like a set of shelves hanging over her eyes.

"Oh my God, you're amazing! I was wondering—would you consider doing us? We'll pay you whatever you want."

"Whatever I want?" Judy asked.

The woman giggled. "Well, you know, within reason. Like two hundred dollars? I know I have that much with me in cash. It's my girlfriend's birthday, and it would be *so* cool."

"It might take an hour or more," Judy said. She looked at Roger. "You're okay?"

"Absolutely," he said, and he smiled, except there was nothing behind that smile; it was an act. But then again, who didn't put on an act? Only toddlers reacted truthfully with their emotions, like the baby that the other woman was trying to calm with a bottle of formula. His anguished cries diminished now that he was receiving what he wanted.

"I'll do it for a hundred," Judy said, "so you can take her out for a nice dinner."

"You're so awesome!" she said, and Judy and Roger watched her skip back to the bench.

"Can you give us like ten minutes?" she yelled from across the court. "I'm gonna feed my baby, too."

Judy told them to take their time. Two women cradling their babies and feeding them, their legs crossed neatly, their pleated white skirts fanned out like a pair of moons: instead of a pen, Judy wished she had a camera. She did the next best thing, which was to close her eyes and take a picture in her mind, except her mind saw it with a twist: Instead of babies, the women were each holding a large tennis ball, about the size of a basketball, swaddled in a blanket. And then the picture in her mind further transformed, with the women breastfeeding the balls, but their breasts were vaguely tennis-ball shaped and there was a connective goo that ran between the baby and the mother, elongated like a stretched piece of rubber.

She'd never been a fan of Salvador Dali, finding most of his stuff more frightening than strange, but she had to admit, these ideas seemed very much in his mode. In her mind, the two women were biting tennis balls, biting them hard enough that they looked ready to burst. She'd never been a fabulist illustrator, always sticking with what was in front of her. This was new.

"I'm sorry, what did you say?" she asked, not hearing what Roger had said.

"It's nice of you to do this, I said."

"If I was really nice, I'd do it for free."

"A girl's gotta eat."

She snatched the bag of challah from him and pinched a piece herself. It was sweeter than she'd expected, not sugary but a gentle sweetness, like that of a semiripe banana.

"This *is* really good," she said.

"What did you see, just now? I know you saw something because it was like you weren't here."

"I'm not sure, to tell you the truth," she said. "But I know what I'll be doing when we get back home."

He stared at her face as if he was searching for something.

"You're happy," he said.

It might have been the saddest thing she'd ever heard.

"I am," she said, "thanks to you."

• • •

The sketching took less than an hour because it was nothing more than transferring what her eyes saw to the paper underneath her hands. Roger played the role of her assistant. He made sure the women kept their poses, and when one of the babies started crying, he rocked it in its cradle until it quieted down.

"You looked like you knew what you were doing there," Judy told him later, when they'd returned home from their outing and were sitting out on the front porch. Snaps lay on her side, her back paws bicycling lazily, as if dreaming of a slow-motion chase. This was Judy's favorite part of the day, the late afternoon sun casting golden beams of light over the water and the coast of Bassetts Island beyond. Roger was flipping through the day's paper, gazing at the photos and headlines, while she was in the middle of her odd sketch of the two women and their tennis ball babies. It was turning out just the way she'd imagined.

"I was a nanny for a while," he said.

A cardinal flew onto the giant bird feeder hanging off the railing, its feathers the color of red chalk. Inside the house, Momo jumped up to the window ledge and pawed at the glass, but the bird knew it was safe, leisurely pecking at the seeds, almost taunting the cat.

"A nanny?"

"I was trying . . . stuff, I guess. I don't know. I was a little lost."

It seemed to Judy that every day, she found out something new about Roger. What she knew so far was that he had no one left. Both of his parents passed away before he turned eighteen, his mother from a brain tumor and his father in a car accident just a few months later. He was an only child. Neither of his parents had siblings, either, and his grandparents were long gone. There had always been someone there for Judy, no matter how much she craved to be alone. If Roger got hit by a truck, who would mourn? He had no close friends she could see, his lawyer being the only person she'd heard him talk to on the phone since they'd been at the Cape.

His father's death messed him up more than anything. At least with his mother, the path of her disease was telegraphed, but when his father failed to come home one night, when Roger saw the police cruiser glide up to the curb, he knew he was alone. Orphaned and with a mound of cash from his father's inheritance, he left New Jersey for Japan and joined the yakuza.

That sounded crazy but actually wasn't all that different than applying for a new job. Because unlike the mafia, the yakuza had offices out in the open. The Yamaguchi-gumi family was the largest yakuza in Japan, and because their newest boss was promoting an expansionist policy, when Roger walked through the doors and wanted in, they didn't ask many questions.

"But why would you do something like this?" Judy asked him. "I've heard of people joining the army or the navy to jump start or change their lives, but the mob?"

"It's not anything I planned. It was a dark period of my life, literally —I slept during the day and lived for the night, content to stay in my Eastern Time Zone, you could say. I rode the train from city to city, ate dinner when I should've been eating breakfast. I couldn't stay in the States after losing both of my parents. I grew up in Japan until I was ten, so it was still a sort of home for me, and as a kid, I looked up to these sunglass-wearing, tattooed men. They were so unlike everyone else, walking around Tokyo like they owned it, and it wasn't as if they were all hardened criminals. Remember those terrible earthquakes in Kobe back in '95? The city was too slow to react, and it was the Yamaguchi-gumi clan who lent a hand for disaster relief, distributing food and supplies to the afflicted. So one late night in Sapporo, I was walking by an old canning warehouse, and there was a wooden sign hanging off a rusty loop of chain with the family's insignia, a samurai sword inside a diamond. I went in and joined."

They asked only one question, the biggest of all, why—why he was here, why he wanted to join—and Roger told his *shatei gashira*, the local boss of his gang, the truth.

"Satoru was his name," Roger said. "Smart guy. I think he could've done a lot of other things than run a gang, but it was just how it turned out. I told him that my parents were dead and I didn't know what to do. My situation wasn't that far off from the rest of the members there, actually—many of them were either orphans or exiled from their families in some way. Satoru patted my hand and said, 'You're here because you want to hurt the world.' Pretty simple, right? I did want to hurt the thing that hurt me."

In the basement office of their headquarters building, he and Satoru drank from the same sake cup, and he was now a yakuza, though he didn't feel any different.

"Tattoo," Judy said.

"Unfortunately, yes."

Because money wasn't an issue, Roger found the best tattoo artist in the city, and the man was fast. Still, it took a week to complete his dragon design, and another week for Roger to be able to move normally.

Of his month as a member of the yakuza, Roger spent a quarter of it filing paperwork in the office. And after he'd recovered from his tattoo, his only responsibility was to go to the horse track each morning and make various bets for Satoru.

"It was no different than any other brainless job," Roger said. "Almost like a corporation, the way they held meetings where they talked about the current budget and upcoming financial forecasts and whatnot. I had as much chance as a worker at Apple running into Steve Jobs as meeting Yoshinori Watanabe, who was then the *oyabun*, the head boss of the Yamaguchi-gumi. I never even saw a picture of him."

"I thought you joined the yakuza for life. Like the only exit is inside a coffin."

He laughed, then dropped his voice down a notch, emulating the baritone of the movie previews voiceover, "In the sinister world of the yakuza, there is only one way out. But Roger Nakamura has a different plan."

"Roger, that's pretty good! If you ever run out of money, I think you've found your calling."

"Thank you. Maybe if I'd been some higher-up guy, they would've flinched, but I was nobody. Satoru felt sorry for me, and I think he was actually glad to see me leave. I still talk to him about once a month."

"Was that the phone call you received on our first date?"

Roger nodded. "He invests some of my money. Not in anything illegal—like I said, he's a real smart guy, and he's done well for himself in the Nikkei exchange, which is really saying something considering how terrible the Japanese economy has been for the last twenty years."

After his underwhelming stint in the Japanese underworld, Roger returned to the States, no better off than when he'd left, but not any worse, either, and if he had an ally, it was the passing of time. He knew he would never get over the loss of his parents at such a young age, but every day was a new day, and money was something he'd never have to worry about. At the urging of his lawyer, Roger got himself a trio of help: a cook, a maid, and a psychiatrist, all of whom he'd employed throughout his twenties. But the year he turned thirty, he let them go.

"Why?" Judy asked.

"I got better. I wanted to live the life of a normal person, and I'm still here, so I guess it worked out."

And this was the Roger of now, this man sitting across from her with his feet up on the wicker table, his ankles loosely crossed, leafing through the sales circulars in the Sunday paper. What a strange life he'd led, and now she was a part of it, a part of that strangeness. Where was he going? Where was she headed? She had no idea where or why or how. Maybe some of Roger's indifference was rubbing off, because she was okay with the not knowing, at least so far.

20

Saturday night, September 1988. Kevin couldn't remember the exact date, but it was the first day of the Summer Olympics in Seoul, which for some odd reason was held in the fall of that year. Kevin was excited because for the first time in more than six decades, tennis was officially included as part of the games, but that wasn't the only reason why he'd been looking forward to this day.

"He's your older brother?" he'd asked his mother.

"By two years," she'd told him. "Just like you and Judy."

His name was Myung Hoon, and he was flying in from Korea for business. Kevin had never met him before, and he could hardly wait for him to arrive. After vacuuming the carpet and mopping the floors, he and Judy showered, then dressed to impress, Kevin putting on his argyle vest over his ironed shirt. His sister wore a black dress to go with her black nail polish, her color of choice now that she was fifteen and grumpy.

"You forgot your bow tie, Poindexter," she said when they reconvened in the living room.

"And how many funerals will you be attending today?"

"Just stop smiling for a minute. I mean he's just her brother, not fucking Santa Claus."

"You're not even a little curious?"

Judy shrugged, plopped onto the couch, then turned on the television. When he saw she was about to change the channel, Kevin snatched the remote out of her hand.

"The VCR is recording that," he said.

"Whatever."

She crossed her arms and watched the massive procession of Olympians walking slowly around the stadium track and waving at the cheering crowd. It was Sweden's turn to be on camera, its blue and yellow flag flying high, and Kevin caught a glimpse of his favorite tennis player, Stefan Edberg, his spiky blond hair turning silver every time a flash popped.

Underneath Judy's disaffected demeanor, Kevin was sure she was just as intrigued as he was to meet Uncle Myung. Theirs being a nuclear immigrant family, visits from the extended Lees were as rare as a comet sighting. The last time was so long ago that Kevin could hardly recall his grandmother, not that he even wanted to. All he could remember from her brief stay was her demand that he massage her legs, so he did, feeling as if he were performing some strange custom as he kneaded her tissue-thin skin.

Thankfully, when Uncle Myung arrived with his parents from the airport, he did not want a massage. He was as short as his own little sister, but what he lacked in size, he made up in energy. For a tiny guy, he was unexpectedly strong. He gave Kevin a bear hug and lifted him off the ground a couple of inches, and he even elicited a genuine giggle from Judy when he gave her the same airy treatment.

"Gift!" he said, pronouncing it *ghee-poo-too*. He pinned a small fuzzy figure on each of their chests. It was a friendly, smiley tiger, making a peace sign with its right hand and wearing a black derby on its orange head.

"*Hodori*," he said. "Name, *Hodori*."

"*Ho* is *tiger* in Korean," his mom said. "*Dori* means boys. The mascot for the games."

For the rest of the evening, the three adults chatted while the Olympic Games Opening Ceremony dragged on in the background with dances and fireworks. His dad opened up a bottle of Chivas Regal he'd been saving, and soon the men's voices got a little louder. Judy went to bed, but Kevin stayed up, pretending to watch the television. He'd planned to surreptitiously observe Uncle Myung, but something odd happened: He ended up watching his mother. For as long as Kevin could remember, she had been the caretaker of their household, probably because she was the one who spoke fluent English while his dad struggled. His father still made his share of decisions, especially when it came to money, but Kevin always considered his mother their benevolent leader. But in front of Uncle Myung, whom she referred to as *ohpa*, the Korean term for an older brother, his mother did something he'd never seen her do: fan her hands delicately in front of her mouth when she laughed. And she laughed a lot. Even though Kevin couldn't understand what they were saying since they were speaking Korean, he knew her girlish giggles were a gesture of respect more than humor. Just the way she sat in her seat, ready to spring into action for any little thing her brother wished— who was this woman?

A few days later, Uncle Myung was gone, and so was this other version of his mother, but Kevin never forgot that night. There had been this whole other person inside his mother, someone he did not even know existed.

As Kevin waited underneath the curved wooden sign that read CHEZ: PANISSE in Berkeley, he thought of his mother and Uncle Myung. Would he, too, change into a different Kevin when he came face-to-face with his new sister? Half sister, he supposed, since they shared a father, but not a mother. He was going to ask Norman for a photograph of her, but Kevin stopped himself. Knowing what she looked like meant he'd have the upper hand, and he didn't want that. Or, more accurately, he did want it—control, as always—but this time he fought it, and it felt good to let things be, for them to be equals.

Would she be like Judy, arriving half an hour late? He hoped not, because according to Claudia, this was one of the best restaurants in the Bay Area, if not the entire country. In the morning, Kevin had tried to be vague about his plans, but Claudia wouldn't have any of it.

"What, were you afraid I was gonna force you to take me along?"

"Well," he'd said, "yes."

"You had every right to worry, but looks like it's your lucky day, because I'm not allowed in there anymore."

Claudia insisted it wasn't her fault. She'd ordered the lamb special, but they'd just run out, so Claudia stood up and asked the dining room if anybody would like to give up their dish for a thousand dollars.

"I can see you doing that," Kevin said. "Easily."

"It made the woman who volunteered very, very happy."

"And you were happy, eating what you wanted to eat."

Unfortunately, it was the last meal she'd have there, as word got back to Alice Waters, the proprietor of the restaurant, who personally called Claudia to say that what she did at Chez Panisse would never happen again.

"So there might be a poster of me at the hostess's podium, for all I know," she said. "Do not serve this woman, she's armed and dangerous with a checkbook."

As Kevin waited for Denise's arrival, he watched a mother and a daughter at an ATM across the street. The mother lifted up her girl so she could swipe the card and punch in the PIN. Claudia, too, had been as young as that girl once, and the more Kevin thought about it, the more he believed her current philosophy of doing what she wanted, no matter the consequence, was a deeply childish behavior. Like the way the adult Michael Jackson had tried to re-create his lost childhood, maybe purchasing that last rack of lamb was Claudia's Neverland.

Kevin checked his watch, and now it was noon on the nose. So officially, Denise was late, or was she right on time? Because here was an Asian woman walking toward him right now, heels clicking on the sidewalk, long hair billowing like a dark curtain. Except, like all the Asian women who had passed him so far, she was too young to be his sister. He knew there were a lot of Asians in California, but it seemed as if every other person he saw today was one. Maybe it was the university, which probably had a fair number of Asians in its population, and thinking of all those book-smart black-haired folks strutting to class with their backpacks in tow, talking of math proofs and chemical formulas and the hidden meaning behind some unreadable Shakespearean play, sent a wave of unease over him. As an Asian, he'd been an anomaly, terrible at math and not much better at any other academic endeavor.

He was saved by his body and his mastery of it. The thing that most people didn't know was how much intelligence it took to perfect an athletic maneuver. Adjustments both inside and outside the body had to be made on the fly, and that ran beyond the realm of the physical. Sometimes the TV commentators compared tennis to chess, except Kevin thought that was a disservice to the players, because chess geeks weren't outside, battling for four hours under 120-degree heat, drenched in sweat and out of breath.

In a way, he was not unlike his father, who'd always been good with his hands, building a deck all by himself, repairing the engine of his riding mower . . . except Kevin was forgetting, yet again. He didn't have any of his railroad engineer father's genes, just the sad DNA of his porno dad and mom. If he had picked up anything, it was purely nurture, not nature, and the lie that was his childhood gnawed at him. Would he always feel as if he was robbed?

"Kevin?"

She was an Asian Barbie doll. There was no other way to describe this woman, this perfect creature of made-up beauty. Her face didn't have a single blemish on it, a Photoshopped sheen to her skin, and her bright red lips were like two pieces of molded rubber. If she stayed in the sun for a little while longer, he was afraid her face would start melting like the villain's at the end of *Raiders of the Lost Ark.*

"You must be Denise," he said, and they did the awkward dance of a handshake segueing into a hug. She smelled like a fresh bouquet of flowers. Norman had told him she was three years younger than him, and it was obvious she took care of herself. She was wearing a yellow sundress, and her bare arms were tan and toned, the sort of body that belonged to a health-conscious California girl.

They went in and sat upstairs, just beyond the bustle of the kitchen, a pair of vest-clad waiters jockeying to grab their dishes from the counter. On the shelf next to Kevin sat an overflowing pot of white and yellow chrysanthemums. He tucked a tendril of leaves around another to stop it from grazing his forehead.

"It's all about nature and sustainability here," Denise said. "They've always gotten their meats and vegetables from local farmers. Nobody really did that before Chez Panisse."

"You've been here before."

Denise nodded. "For a place this good, it's actually decently priced. I've eaten at this very table at least a dozen times."

There was a directness to her that he liked, a no-nonsense tone in the way she spoke. When the waiter arrived, she ordered not only the appetizer and the dinner, but the dessert as well. Kevin hadn't even looked at that part of the menu, so he followed suit and ordered her choice, the pear tart.

"I hear Daddy made you a home movie," she said.

"That he did."

"He told me about it, and he was afraid of your reaction. That's probably why he set us up here, so I can report back to him."

Their drinks arrived, his beer and her cosmo. When she lifted the pink liquid and yellow twists of lemon for a toast, it was like an ad

out of a magazine, her red lipstick and canary-yellow dress comple-
menting the colors of her mixed drink. He downed half his beer and
placed the glass back on the little square napkin.

"I'm all right," he said. "I mean yeah, I was shocked when I saw it,
but I think his heart was in the right place."

"It's just his brain that goes on the fritz once in a while."

Kevin smiled and nodded and didn't know what to do with his
hands, so he went back to the glass and drained the rest of the beer.

"Thirsty, are we?" she asked, raising one curious brow like Mr.
Spock.

He'd always found first dates to be nerve-wracking, and that's
what this encounter reminded him of. The only time he didn't feel
this way was in a tennis match, playing a brand-new opponent, and
that was because it didn't involve talking, just doing, his body taking
over what his mind didn't want to face. But that wasn't true. His
first date with Alice was in a restaurant not unlike this one, a fancy
joint where the servers scampered to the table to refold your napkin
when you left for the bathroom, and yet he hadn't felt any of his
usual jitters.

It was pathetic how much she still occupied his thoughts. It was
even more pathetic how he recognized this and yet still couldn't
make himself stop.

The waiter returned with their appetizers, sardine toasts for him, a
cucumber-avocado-melon salad for her. Kevin almost acceded when
the waiter asked him if he'd wanted a refill on his beer, but he didn't
want to give Denise the impression that he needed alcohol as a social
lubricant.

"Your salad's good?" he asked.

"Always. Yours?"

It was simple and delicious, baguettes buttery and crunchy, the sar-
dines ground up and spread on top like a dip. The flavor of the little
salty fish was so present within the paste that with each bite he felt as
if he were eating their very essence.

"Dad tells me you played tennis professionally."

"If by playing you mean losing, then yes, that's correct."

She sipped her drink and smiled like he did, the left corner of her
mouth rising and abutting the crease of her cheek. For all these years,
he'd assumed his and Judy's naturally curly hair were bestowed by
their mother, but now he knew it was mere coincidence. Here, it was

different, because this woman sitting across the table was of his blood, and this shared smirk of theirs was an instant bond.

Their main course arrived, a pork shoulder basting in a bed of corn for Kevin, a chicken leg with little yellow beans and fried artichokes for Denise. His pork looked as good as it tasted, roasted in a garlic sauce that drew out the fatty richness of the pig.

"I played Andre Agassi once," Kevin said. "If you know who he is."

"Even people who don't care about tennis know Agassi," Denise said, chopping her artichoke hearts into bite-size pieces. "Anybody who marries Brooke Shields is gonna be famous no matter what he does for a living."

"And now he's married to Steffi Graf, former number one female player in the world."

"I've seen a commercial with a pretty blond woman, so I guess that's who you're talking about. So how was it, playing a legend? And more importantly, did you beat him?"

"Somewhat," Kevin said, and he began to tell his story.

It was in August, the summer of 1997, in Binghamton, New York, the Gouldin & Thompson Tennis Challenger. It was the sort of tournament that somebody like Agassi wouldn't have played since he turned pro, since the champion was awarded only seventy-two hundred dollars. But earlier in the year, Agassi had fallen out of the top one hundred, far from the elite player he'd once been.

"It sounds very exciting to me," Denise said, "playing as a professional athlete."

"I think *sounds* is the operative word. Piling into buses that cart you from the Best Western to the city park, being pretty much forced to attend golf outings and donor parties in the evenings—I mean yes, I'm not scrubbing toilets for a living, but there's not much glamour in playing Challenger tournaments."

"And having to win," she added.

"That's why you're there in the first place. In '99, Agassi would reclaim his number one ranking, so when we played, he was already finding his form," Kevin said. "But for a couple of games, it looked like maybe I'd have a chance."

Agassi was known as the best serve returner in the game, but on that Thursday morning in the second round of the tournament, Kevin had him for a little while. He was up a break, leading five games to four, and was about to serve out the set, leading 40–15, when the

Buddha of tennis struck back Kevin's kick serve with what felt like twice the speed.

"The only way he could've taken such a monstrous swing was if he knew where I was going to go, which serve I was going to hit."

"Did he know?"

"Not in the beginning, but he must've figured it out. It's not surprising—the best players can read a 'tell' that a player has. For example, Boris Becker, who was a phenomenal player and played Agassi many times, had a habit of poking out his tongue right before he served, and the opposite direction of where his tip pointed was where the ball would land."

"Agassi saw that from that far away?"

"Seventy-eight feet, to be exact. I guess in addition to being blessed with ridiculous reflexes, he also had perfect vision."

"So what's your 'tell'?"

Kevin sheared the browned meat of the pork from the bone. "You'll have to ask Andre."

Never again would Kevin play anyone as accomplished. That year was the highest he'd ever rank on the ATP, 293. He was in his latter twenties then, well aware that his dream of playing in the US Open would remain just that, a dream. He'd seen enough world-class talent to know that he could never compete for anything beyond the first round of a Grand Slam tournament, but he would never make it to the big stage, advancing only to the second round of qualifiers that year. Of course he would've been trounced by whomever he played next, and with his luck it probably would've been Pete Sampras or Agassi himself, but to play a match in the gladiatorial expanse of Arthur Ashe Stadium—he'd wanted that. He'd practiced as hard as he could, even working with a sports psychiatrist to be more free and less controlling, and yet it still wasn't good enough. Maybe he shouldn't have been so accepting of his mediocrity, or maybe he should've tapped into anger like John McEnroe. When things weren't going their way, many of his opponents slammed their racquets hard enough onto the concrete to warp the frame, garnering warnings from the chair umpire, but as a pro, Kevin never threw a fit. He never saw a reason for getting mad at the ball or the equipment or the linespeople, because even when he was losing, he wasn't exactly unhappy to be on court.

Because at the core of it, he loved to play the game more than he wanted to win it. Which meant he lacked the killer instinct that all champions have, that drive that gave them the impetus to win at all costs. Even against Agassi in Binghamton on that sun-beating August afternoon, there wasn't a moment he wished he were somewhere else. After losing the first set 7–5, there was no mercy from the other side. Kevin did everything he could, mixing it up with serve-and-volley points, risking drop shots from the baseline, slicing his backhand low until the fine fuzz of the tennis ball kissed the tape as it floated over the net, but he was no longer playing a human being. That was what separated the best from the not-so-best, the unfathomable, robotic consistency. No matter how well a rally was going, Kevin knew it was just a matter of time until his ball either dumped into the net or sailed long. The first set had taken more than an hour. The second, the one he'd lose 6–0, winning 4 points total, took twenty minutes.

At 5–0, with Agassi about to serve out the set and the match, Kevin forced himself to take in his surroundings, to remember this day because in a few minutes, it would be over. The seats to his right were gray folding chairs five rows deep, and you couldn't slide a bookmark between the packed spectators, a number of them standing in the aisles. Beyond the chain-link fence of the park, people were leaning out of the second-floor windows of their houses with binoculars, trying to catch a glimpse of the match. Everyone wanted to witness the resurgent legend beat him, though maybe not this badly. At least Kevin had given the crowd a good first set; this second one was just a display of the innate unfairness of life. A decade later, Agassi would tell the world in his autobiography how much he'd hated the game that gave him everything, how much emotional and physical toll it had taken, and yet for almost two years, there was no one on the planet who was better than he was. To be the very best at what you despise—was it possible for life to be any crueler? It was like something out of Greek mythology.

Kevin bounced from foot to foot as he waited for the last serve, Agassi up 40–15, match point. Agassi would probably aim for Kevin's body, a shot which had already handcuffed him so many times that his racquet felt like a shield. When Kevin was grooving, his racquet was an appendage, fitting into his hand with the rightness of a key sliding into its lock. Those feelings were a distant memory now, and as Agassi tossed the ball into the air, Kevin made his decision: He would slide to his left, sidestep the ball's intended destination and swing his forehand as hard as he could for the crosscourt corner. Agassi's serve was a blur of yellow, but luck was on Kevin's side, as his plan worked to perfection, a clean winner.

The crowd cheered, hoping he could somehow work another miracle and push the game to deuce, but no, the next serve was too good, down the T, and unless Kevin could turn into Plastic Man and extend his reach by another two inches, there was no way he was even nicking that ball with the frame of his racquet.

"I shook his hand at the net," Kevin told Denise now, the memory of that day faded but not forgotten. Agassi smiled over a frown, patting him on the shoulder before they walked over to the umpire to shake his hand.

"You must've been a little cowed."

"Oh yeah. It isn't every day that I got to play someone as famous as he was. Andre didn't say anything memorable, just the usual exchange of pleasantries passed from the winner to the loser, but he has such an expressive face, and I'll always remember how genuine he was."

A year later, Pete Sampras would easily beat Agassi in a forgettable Wimbledon final, except for the winner's ceremony, where he quietly motioned to Sampras that his five-o'clock shadow had trapped bits of terry cloth like Velcro. Andre wanted to make sure Pete looked good to hoist his trophy. Perhaps it was an insignificant gesture in the grand scheme of things, but for Kevin, that moment defined the man's kindness.

Their waiter returned to clear off the table, removing every last crumb with a pen-size dustpan tool that Kevin had seen before in high-class restaurants. Their desserts were on their way.

Denise excused herself for the bathroom, and he watched her walk down the aisle. He saw a number of eyes, both men's and women's, follow her confident strut, her head held high like a runway model on a catwalk; a busboy darted out of her way because if he hadn't, she might have plowed into him and kept going. There was an air of athletic grace about her that made him feel closer to her, though it was possible it was in his head, trying to find whatever way to forge the tenuous familial bonds in the limited time he had remaining here. As much as he liked San Francisco, he wasn't staying here forever.

By the time she returned, their tarts were in front of them, with a dollop of pear ice cream on the side, molded in the shape of a pear, a shard of chocolate for the stem.

"Now you know all about me, but I still know nothing about you," Kevin said. "What do you do for a living?"

She forked a wedge of the tart and popped it into her mouth. She considered him, he could see, deciding.

"I'm a porn actress."

"Oh," Kevin said. He didn't know how to respond to this. *Good for you? Congratulations?* He hoped his nonreaction wasn't making her uncomfortable.

"Dad told me I was supposed to lie to you, say that I was the head of a nonprofit organization. Which actually isn't a lie, because I am, and I can't do what I do forever."

"You still look . . . fine," Kevin said.

"Thank you, but I'm gonna be . . . older next year, let's just say, and this is a young person's game more than ever. Even as little as five years ago, things were different, but with high-definition video, you can see every single wrinkle, and there's no bigger turnoff than seeing frown lines on a vagina on a sixty-inch flatscreen TV."

It made sense, Kevin supposed, that Norman's daughter went into the family business. Or did it? It wasn't like his father was in a line of work that was socially acceptable. If anything, he probably would have steered Denise away, but who was Kevin to judge? Perhaps she was happy being a porn star. She certainly came off as a grounded person, at least so far. Outside of the meticulous attention she paid to her looks, she seemed pretty ordinary.

"Do you want to hear about what I do?"

He hadn't meant to hesitate, but his mind ran in six different directions, leaving his mouth in a coma. He was imagining her face in false ecstasy, pretending as all porno actresses must, screaming their fake climaxes to the rolling camera.

"Of course," Kevin finally managed to blurt out.

She clicked her red fingernails on the table, once, then again. She stared at him, but not as she had just before; this was a penetrating glare. Not exactly angry, just full of command. "Do you have an issue with what I do?"

Kevin clasped his hands on the table, as if in prayer. He could use a little miracle right now, get him out of this potentially ugly situation.

"It's what you do," he said, feeling like no matter what he said, it would come out wrong. "I respect that."

"Really? You'd respect me when I'm on all fours with a cock in my mouth? Or one in my butt? Maybe at the same time? After seeing that, you'd still respect me?"

She said this with such dispassion that a fellow diner, unless he was eavesdropping, would think she was describing a day at the office. Which, Kevin realized, was what she was probably doing. He no longer met her eyes, fixating himself on his melting ice cream. The white liquid spread out ever so slowly.

And then there was her hand over his hand, and he looked up to see a bemused Denise smiling at him.

"Relax," she said, "I'm just busting your chops."

She patted his hand and dug into her dessert, and Kevin breathed again. "To tell you the truth, I haven't done a DP in years, let alone an airtight," she said, speaking what must have been porn lingo. He didn't have anything against pornography, but there was something sadly reductive that happened with it, everything devolved into the most crude elements. At its core, it was sex without love, and for him, there were few things more depressing than to wake up in the morning next to a strange woman after a one-night stand.

"You do rougher stuff when you start out," she continued, "though a lot longer if you're not attractive. I don't mean to sound cruel, it's just how the business works. The ugly girls are the workhorses, the ones who do gangbangs day and night. As you can imagine, they're the ones who need the most support. That's why Dad and I formed the AWS—Adult Workers Sanctuary—to give our people a break they need."

There was a softness to Denise's voice as she talked about the Sanctuary, curves to her hand movements as she described the Zen-inspired décor of the house, the strong sense of community within, all the work to keep it going, work that was primarily hers. It was a pleasure and a relief to see such genuine enthusiasm from her, but he had to admit, it also made him a little envious, reminding Kevin of how little passion there was in his life right now. They weren't so different, after all; like athletes, porn stars also had a short shelf life. They both needed a second act to their lives, and it looked as if Denise had found hers.

Denise picked up the check, reassuring Kevin that it was a gift from their father. "He really does feel bad about chickening out with the movie like he did," she said.

"I'll give him a call later today."

She signed the credit card slip. "A good son. That's what you are."

They left the restaurant and walked along Shattuck Avenue, past the Berkeley post office and a tobacco shop. People on the street glanced at her then at him, in that order, which only made sense since she was the kind of woman who turned heads. Did they look like brother and sister? Kevin wanted to stop and ask them. Denise clicked on her key fob, and a white Toyota Prius blinked its headlights at them. Their lunch had gone by so fast. Kevin hadn't expected to fit a lifetime in two hours, but there was so much he didn't know.

She opened her arms wide for a hug. As they embraced, he said, "Hey, how about if you take me to the Sanctuary sometime?"

Denise held his hands. He could almost feel the pathways her neurons were taking, the words she was considering as she considered him. Her glare was scientific.

"Are you just saying that or do you mean it?"

He squeezed her hands. "I'm saying it and meaning it."

"Okay," she said, and she let him go.

He saw her eyes reflected in the rearview mirror as the car pulled away. *There she goes,* he thought. *My sister.*

21

Roger was switching DVDs of *The Wire* when Judy's cell phone rang. Snaps, who'd been snoozing near the door, barked, and Momo, who'd been sleeping on Roger's lap, yowled his displeasure.

"I love this. And because I love this, I love you."

"Excuse me?" Judy said.

She heard a man's voice in the background, but the woman on the phone ignored him.

"The drawing you sent to your brother. The sunflower, the tennis ball. You are the one responsible for this work?"

Judy was glad she didn't have to lie to her, because even if she hadn't drawn the illustration, she might have agreed. The woman sounded as if she'd expected Judy to already know what this was about, why she called.

After a scuffling sound, a familiar voice came on the line.

"Sorry, sis, that was Claudia."

"That drawing was for you," Judy said, miffed that he'd shared it with someone else without asking her first. "Please don't show it to anyone else, okay?"

"Ummm . . . I think . . ."

More scuffling, and Claudia came back on the line.

"I'm not usually like this, but then again, I haven't been this excited in a long time. Let's start over. I'm Claudia St. James. Since you're an artist, you might know me better as—"

"Claudia X?"

"Oh good, you've heard of me."

Heard of her? Kevin was shacking up with Claudia X. Holy mother of Christ.

Roger muted the television and asked, "Who's Claudia X?"

She wasn't as famous as Pablo Picasso or Andy Warhol, but that was only because she wasn't dead. Everyone in art knew Claudia; her intensely personal paintings where she thrust herself into the oddest places. Judy's favorite painting was *Army of Eros*, where Claudia painted one hundred soldiers shaped like upright, erect penises, each proudly displaying plump bare breasts and a vagina where the shaft met the testicles, and if the comingling of the male and female sexual genitalia wasn't enough, each duck-footed creature held a handlebar mustache for a shield and a spear shaped like a stretched lipstick. And of course, Claudia's face was on the head of each penis soldier, a horde of one-eyed faces staring at something off to the right, some unseen force available only to the viewer's imagination. The wall-sized painting had fetched more than three million dollars last year at a Sotheby's auction, which was in the news and reason enough that more people should know who she was, but then again, the art world was a tiny subset of the general population. Besides, with the likes of Bernie Madoff and the mortgage crisis, maybe three million was not as newsworthy these days.

Another scuffle, this time with more background shouting, and Kevin came back on the line.

"Judy, you don't have to do anything you don't want to." Then his voice moved away. "Isn't that right, Claudia? Good. That's what I thought." Then back to her. "I'm really, really sorry. She's just like this. I can explain later."

Judy spoke quietly. "Do you have any idea who Claudia is?"

"She's an artist."

"That's like saying Rafael Nadal is a tennis player."

The metaphor seemed to do the trick, as her brother paused before speaking again.

"Really?"

"One of the top five artists working today."

"So you're okay if she keeps talking to you."

"Maybe you can put her back on the phone."

As the phone exchanged hands, she heard a simple "Ha!" in the background.

"Thank you for being so accommodating," Claudia said.

Claudia had just thanked her. Judy almost wanted to ask Claudia to say it again, to make sure it really happened.

"You have other works I can take a look at?"

"Two others," Judy said. After the one of the ladies and their tennis ball babies, she'd completed another drawing, of a tennis racquet weaved among the squares of a tennis net. It gave off a trapped feeling, like an insect caught in a spider web, or at least that's what Judy hoped. If she were to add a few more racquets and configured them just so, it would make the insect metaphor more overt.

"I want to see you," Claudia said. "In person. I'm having a gallery opening for some upcoming artists next weekend, and I want to include this and anything else you bring. There's something primitive and raw with what you're doing, and I think it'll fit right in with the others."

Judy had heard the words that had come through the tiny speaker of her tiny phone, but it was taking her brain longer than usual to process them. *In person, gallery, next weekend, primitive, fit right in.* Did any of this make sense? Was this really happening?

"Okay," she said.

Claudia told her that one of her assistants would call Judy tomorrow and set up the flight, the lodging, everything that would be required for her to come out to San Francisco, all expenses paid, for both her and Roger.

"If there's something you can do for me," Claudia said. "Can you fly out of Newark?"

What she wanted was to have her daughter fly out to see her at the same time. Even though Alexa was old enough to fly by herself, Claudia felt safer if she was accompanied by an adult. Roger, as expected, had no issues with any of this, and Judy realized more than ever that the greatest gift money provided wasn't this fancy house or luxury cars or a private yacht; it was the freedom to do whatever, whenever.

"Fantastic," Claudia said. "Thank you, Judy. I can't wait to meet you."

She handed the phone back to Kevin.

"Good news, huh?" he said.

Judy laughed. "You could say that." Snaps trudged over from her spot by the door, tail wagging. "I think your dog wants to say hello."

Kevin told her what a good dog Snaps was, and Snaps, despite Momo's wailing protestations from the top of the staircase, barked and barked. Their greeting ended with the now-familiar duet, where Kevin howled into the phone and Snaps howled with him, her long snout raised to the ceiling, holding her single baritone note out of her O-shaped lips, her best wolf impression.

"Are you coming back?" Judy asked him. "Or have you found California that lovable?"

"Going with the flow, sis," Kevin said. "Not easy for me, so I think it's good practice."

"Well, take as long as you need. Though Snaps misses you a lot."

"I talked to Dad yesterday," Kevin said. When Judy said nothing, he continued. "I know you don't particularly care, but Dr. Elias needs to see him again in order to keep him on the donor recipient list. Something to do with a policy change in the way the hospital deals with transplants."

"You're right," Judy said. "I don't particularly care."

Even though Kevin was thousands of miles away, she could feel his sigh. She could see his face, too, cheeks deflating like a sagging balloon. "I'm telling you this for a reason. I need to ask a favor."

"You gotta be kidding me. Like I haven't done enough for you?"

Kevin wanted her to go see the doctor with her father because he was going to need someone who could translate. Even though her Korean was no better than Kevin's, according to her brother, it was better than nothing.

"But I'm not in Jersey, Kevin."

"But you will be."

The appointment with the doctor just happened to be the day before the flight to San Francisco. It was almost as if Kevin had formulated an itinerary that Judy couldn't refuse, and she told Kevin so.

"You're absolutely right. I called Dr. Elias and changed the appointment so you could do this. So please, Judy, just do this, okay?"

"Fine," she said. "But you're a sneaky ass, you know that?"

"You can call me whatever you want," he said. "Thank you, sis. It'll be great to see you, and wait until you check out this gallery for yourself."

Judy ended the call and sat back in the sofa. Her drawings were going to be in Claudia X's gallery. She couldn't even claim this was a dream come true, because she'd never even dared to imagine something so ludicrous. The whole thing sounded insane—it took months to put a gallery show together—but this was how Claudia worked from what she'd read in profiles and interviews, following her instincts wherever they led her.

Roger came over and broke her out of her reverie. He put his hands on her shoulders.

"Congratulations," he said.

She wanted to jump up, dance and laugh, hug and kiss him and fall onto the floor together in a moment of unadulterated glee, but it all seemed so gratuitous.

"It is good news," she said, and kissed she him as gently as she would a child's wound.

The next morning, after a fitful night of uncomfortable dreams and frequent awakenings, Judy was back at the study. In her sleep-deprived state, the phone call from the night before had felt more like a dream, but on the table was evidence of its certain reality, an overnight express envelope containing plane tickets for her, Roger, and Claudia's daughter, Alexa, for a week from Saturday. Judy hadn't seen old-school tickets like these in years, with their mechanical sans serif font printed on card paper stock, stapled together on the white perforated tab. This was how all plane tickets used to look, but now people printed bar codes at home or sent them to their smartphones for check-in. Judy held the stiff stack of paper in her hands. How sad it was that so many things that used to exist didn't exist anymore. Everything, no matter how permanent it seemed, had a future date with oblivion.

The first time she flew, her mother had held tickets like these. The occasion had been a solemn one, a funeral of her grandmother on her father's side, so Judy fought to tamp down her excitement, but once they arrived at the airport, the smile of a seven-year-old knew no restraint. How marvelous that the sole purpose of this enormous building was to receive and send off airplanes! It was so much more than just pilots and stewardesses that she'd seen on television. Judy watched two men move a truckload of suitcases into the open belly of an airplane. She sounded out the named placards held by chauffeurs in black suits: MATTHEWS, WARD, ROTHMAN. A motorized cart beeped by, elderly passengers riding backward. An old man twirled his cane for her like a baton, and Judy turned to her father to ask him if she could ride it, except this man who stood next to her, who glared at her, looked nothing like the father she'd known.

Even now, gazing at the tranquility of Hen Cove, she could feel the weight of his unhappiness. His disappointment frightened her so much that she burst into tears. When her mother asked what was wrong, she couldn't even say. True, her father had been upset about the death of his mother, but it was more than that. It was the beginning of their separation, of her father choosing to step away from her life, for reasons Judy still found mysterious. All she knew was what she felt, which was that when he saw her, he wished he saw someone else: turning away, closing his eyes, the rising of a newspaper wall. Wasn't it a genetic requirement for a father to like his daughter? It didn't make sense.

For a while, she tried to make him like her. In preparation for one Father's Day, she spent two months weaving a sweater, a difficult project for an adult, let alone a ten-year-old, and even though he'd held it up against his chest and thanked her, she never saw him wear it once. Which was fitting, because it wasn't what he did or said that telegraphed his feelings, but their very lack.

More than thirty years had passed since that day at the airport, and yet the emotional laceration was ready to bleed. Had she been born with such thin skin, or was this a by-product of her father's withholding? It was like the chicken or the egg, which came first. Judy picked up a piece of charcoal from her tray, aligned the sketch paper on the desk, and started with his eyes. Thick circles and curvatures, black and bottomless as a well, these were the disapproving pupils that stared at her when she wore her ratty Salvation Army jacket, her silver nose ring, black stockings with Swiss cheese holes, the rebellious accoutrements she embraced in her adolescence because he never embraced her.

She flicked the charcoal to create a pair of prickly eyebrows, then drew a shadow of a nose, and finally, filled in a straight bar for a mouth, completing his default facial mode, which was somewhere between exasperation and annoyance. After she left for college, things got better between them, mostly because they didn't see each other as often, though there was a massive blowout when she suggested he talk to a psychologist about his past trauma. As a senior psych major, Judy had thought that she now possessed the right to speak to her father about his horror of running over that mother and child in his train back in Korea. She'd even taken Korean that semester to better communicate with him, but when she returned that Thanksgiving and attempted to reach out to him, what she received was a literal slap in the face, his open palm smacking her so fast that she thought some foreign object had flown out of nowhere and struck her. Her mother, after making sure Judy was all right, followed her husband to the den.

"I don't think he knew that you knew that story," Kevin had told her.

"So that gives him the right to hit me?" Judy asked.

"Of course not," he said, helping her into a chair. "It's just a bad situation."

For the rest of the long weekend, Judy waited for the apology that never came. Her brother and her mother did what they could to salvage the holiday, making sure that one of them was always around when Judy and her father were in the same room, but that felt like a tacit acceptance of the violence that had occurred. What Judy wanted was to leave and never come back home, but she knew she wasn't that strong. She needed her mother. She needed her brother. Without them, she was alone.

"Knock knock."

Egg salad and pickle on a plate, served by Roger.

"Thank you," she said, and she took a bite of the sandwich. There was a hint of curry this time, a slight change of pace that was welcome to her palate.

He glanced at her sketch. "Angry."

"My father," she said. "What he looked like when he slapped me."

Roger furrowed his eyebrows. "How often did he hit you?"

"That one time."

"Oh."

"What does that mean? That it's okay if it's just once?"

"My parents didn't spare the rod, so you're probably talking to the wrong person."

Roger ate the other half of the sandwich while Judy summarized the incident for him. She didn't want to sound like a whiner, which probably meant she did.

"My dad was like yours. Even with my issue, he wouldn't have been pleased that I saw a shrink. He was from a different generation, where only crazy people went for help."

"We just never jibed, he and I. Never saw eye to eye on anything."

"Are you sure you want to take him to the doctor yourself? You don't think I can help?"

Judy shook her head. "That's not it. I'd rather just do this alone. Maybe I don't want you to see the ugliest side of me. My father is dying, and I'm sort of glad. I'm a shitty daughter."

"You are who you are, and that's fine with me," he said.

Roger left after finishing the sandwich, and she was once again alone. Next to her father's face, she quickly sketched her mother's, then her brother's and hers as kids. In her opinion, her family had never been a cohesive unit, but this was as close as it got, her parents in their early forties, the kids in elementary school. Until Kevin started to play tennis seriously and attended junior camp, they summered at the Jersey shore, renting a two-bedroom cottage in Long Branch. It couldn't have been any more than a few years that they went to that white house by the beach, but they were memorable ones. One evening they drove up to the carnival that had ridden into town. She watched her parents share a cotton candy, ride the Ferris wheel, toss rings at a hundred cola bottles. Judy understood how they fit together, how only she and Kevin could belong to this exclusive permutation of people. It might have been a momentary illusion, but at the time, it felt as real as Kevin's hand she was holding.

A week from now, she would be standing next to Claudia X. People would watch her, scrutinize her works. Judy wasn't ready for any of it. She wanted to have a few more drawings for Claudia, but her mind was a blank. Staring at the eyes of her father, she wanted to blame him for her shortcomings, but that wasn't going to do her any good. She'd have to work, to produce, to make something of herself. She flipped the sketch board over to a fresh sheet of white, picked up her Sharpie, and drew a line.

22

Unlike Claudia, Denise was a model driver, signaling when she changed lanes, her eyes on the road at all times. Once again, Kevin was being chauffeured around by a woman he hardly knew. Back home, the passenger seat of his car remained vacant, a spot that had been occupied by Alice because whenever they went anywhere, she preferred that he drove. He'd loved it when she wore a skirt, the short, clingy black one with silky black stockings. On the street, her beauty was available to everyone, but inside his car, the view of her legs, together and leaning slightly to her right like a piece of human sculpture, had been exclusive to him.

Except now it was exclusive to someone else, probably that douche bag in the background photo of her work computer. Kevin sat up straighter, trying to get himself back to the here and now. He forced himself to watch the buildings to his right blur by as they left the city and drove down to Oakland on I-980, racing toward the wide open sky.

"Should we be talking about ourselves or something?" he asked.

"Since we're sister and brother," she said, "and we have a lot of catching up to do."

"Don't you think?"

Denise drummed the steering wheel with her fingers to some beat in her head, seemingly mulling over his request as she ramped off the highway and got on another.

"You know, there's just so much," she said. "Even if we were to live together in the same house for the next ten years, it wouldn't be possible for you to know who I've been, and vice versa."

"Time only moves forward."

"I'm glad it only goes in one direction. Whatever I've done, good or bad, that's it, no do-overs."

"No regrets."

"A waste of time, or maybe not exactly a waste but a rerun, a repeat. Who wants to watch a rerun of a TV show?"

"Unless it was a really good episode," Kevin countered.

"But is it as good the second time around?"

They drove up Thirteenth Avenue in Oakland, in what Kevin assumed to be a less affluent part of town, houses with paint so chipped they looked as if they were shedding, rusted chain-link fences surrounding browned-out yards. Denise parked in front of a large beige house with black shutters, perhaps the best maintained structure on the block. A small wooden sign ran down the mailbox post: A. W. SANCTUARY. It almost looked like a name of a person.

As soon as Denise opened her car door, two young kids ran out from the backyard, a boy and a girl.

"Auntie D!" they screamed in their high-pitched voices, their identical blond curls so gold they looked manufactured. When she bent down to embrace them in each arm, Denise gave herself wholly to the children, folding into herself, disappearing.

"Who are you?" the boy asked.

"A friend," Denise said. "His name is Kevin."

"That's my name!" he said, and he looked at Kevin with great curiosity. "You must be cool."

"As cool as you," Kevin said.

"This is Betty, Kevin's sister," Denise said. The girl waved without meeting his eyes. She slinked behind one of Denise's legs and hugged it like a tree.

"Nice to meet you, Betty."

The kids led the way to the back. Denise slipped out of her heels and walked barefoot, and Kevin followed them. She looked professional today, a white blouse and a navy-blue skirt, and her face was still perfectly porcelain. The fenced-in yard was big enough for a set of swings, a verdant vegetable garden that wrapped around the perimeter, and what looked like a crude maze created with football-size stones laid in concentric circles. The kids ran to the swing and jumped into their seats, launching themselves into the air instantly.

"I didn't want to tell them you're my brother because they get very attached."

"I understand." It felt like an excuse, but he let it go. "Who are they?"

"Technically, they belong to Amy, but she's gone, so right now, they sort of belong to the house."

"Gone?"

"She'll be back. She's done this before, just takes off for a couple of weeks without telling anybody."

"And you guys take care of the kids until she returns."

"It must sound crazy to you, but the kids have been coming here for years."

"It seems like Amy could use some professional help. I don't think a mother is supposed to abandon her children, do you?"

Denise took his arm and walked toward the starting point of the maze, a cedar garden arbor with ivy climbing over and around the lattice and the arch. "This must not sit well with you, considering what you've recently discovered about your own past history."

He watched the kids in their swing, their limbs dangling in the air, and listened to the chime of their laughter. They were so little.

"Have you ever walked a labyrinth?" Denise asked.

She stood in front of the arch and shook her arms loose, raised and lowered her shoulders like a runner. In the distance, a church bell rang, and a neighbor was probably doing the laundry, as Kevin caught a whiff of artificial freshness in the air.

"There's no right or wrong way to do this, but the point is to follow the path, get to the center, then follow the path back out. First thing is to focus at the entrance, to become quiet and centered. I like to bow, to give acknowledgment to what the structure offers us."

"I'm not much of a spiritual person," he said.

"Neither am I." She curled and uncurled her toes in the grass. "Every time I come here, I do this. It clears my head, sets me straight. You don't have to do it, but either way, you'll have to wait."

He shrugged and removed his sneakers and socks. The grass here was more like the St. Augustine variety, harsh and stiff, but it still felt nice to be free of his shoes, closer to the earth.

Denise bowed, and Kevin stood behind her and did likewise.

"Remember, just walk. That's all you have to do. Some people ask a question before they start."

"Do they hear a response?"

"If they're lucky," she said, and she walked under the arch and over to the other side.

With the sun out in full, her silk blouse turned iridescent, glowing as if powered by electricity. He'd been so involved with his own situation that he hadn't even asked her how she felt about him coming into her life. Had she even known that he'd existed, or did Norman keep the knowledge of Kevin away from her until he was found? As he followed her slow, methodical steps around the curves of the stone-lined pathway, he chided himself for not being more empathetic, for being selfish. Oh, that word—his favorite word for Alice. Whenever there was something he wanted to do and she didn't, he'd accuse her of selfishness, while she'd counter with a call for mutual independence. Wasn't it better if they both got what they wanted instead of one person bending toward the will of the other, for the sake of forced togetherness? Shopping had been a frequent battleground, him wanting them to walk the aisles together like a normal couple, while she wanted to break away and do her own thing. Museums, too, where Alice preferred to take in the gallery at her own pace, encountering the works of art by herself instead of waiting for Kevin to finish.

Looking back, it seemed so incredibly stupid that they'd even argued about such inanity. But these evidences of their incompatibilities had a way of accruing. Even after it had been fully established that his threshold for mess was much lower than hers, ultimately, she never got neater for his penchant for order and he never became more accepting of her entropic inclinations. Neither was able to compromise, and it was just a matter of time until friction burned them.

But he loved her, still. How was that possible? It was more than just wanting her body, though he did want it, every inch of it, the firm curves of her breasts, the tensile sinews of her thighs, the soft sweetness of what lay in between. He loved to make love to her on a weekend morning, right after waking up, spooning leading to a lazy, slow sex that felt so right for both of them, riding the crests of their pleasures until they fit inside each other like an infinite set of Russian nesting dolls.

Then they would talk, just ordinary stuff like what was going on with the world, some annoying part of their jobs, the goofy TV show they watched the night before. Lying naked with his wife, chatting about the mundane: It was the epitome of comfort to discuss the leaky faucet in the kitchen or recaulking the tub in the upstairs bathroom. They were supposed to take care of each other, grow old together.

Maybe it would've helped if they had children like everybody else, but who really knew. He remembered the horror Judy went through with her miscarriage, how it had cast a shadow over her relationship with Brian from the get-go. No matter what, life was a minefield of failures and regrets.

Denise put out her hand to stop him from running into a bronze statue. He hadn't realized that he was in the eye of the labyrinth. It wasn't much to look at, a couple of shrubs in various states of struggle, a gray ceramic pot with a lid.

"Deep in thought, were we?" Denise asked.

"The labyrinth is doing its job."

"Good. His name is Fred, by the way," she said.

It was a happy, fat ceramic Buddha, sitting down with one knee up, a bunch of tots climbing all over him. He was fairly large, his shiny bald head coming up to Kevin's waist. "I didn't know Buddha had a first name. What's in the pot?"

Denise knelt down, lifted the lid, and removed a small notepad and a pen sitting on a bedding of folded pieces of paper.

"Some people jot down a secret. It could be something you want, something you're hoping for, almost like a wish list. Or maybe something you want to kick out of your life." She offered the pad and pen to Kevin. "If you feel like it. I'm going to just stand here for a bit and pray with Fred."

There were two large, flat stones flanking Fred, and Denise sat on one and Kevin on the other. The notepad was spiral-bound and opened from the top, like something reporters used in old movies. About half the sheets were gone, saw-toothed remnants of the ripped-out papers stuck in the tunnel of wire, evidence of the hopes and dreams and mysteries and pains of the people who came before him, who walked the same path he had just walked. It seemed like a useless thing to do, something that felt more like magic than logic, but at the same time, what was the harm in it? At the very worst, he'd be throwing his particular ideas into an anonymous pot, and that would be the end of it. He uncapped the pen and wrote:

I wish for happiness.

He read it over and instantly felt like a loser, and seeing the words in his own handwriting made it worse. How many others in that pot asked for the same sad wish? Kevin was tempted to shove his hand in there and read a bunch, but instead he crossed it out and tried again.

> *I want to lead a meaningful life.*
> *I want Alice.*
> *But I can't have Alice.*
> *I want to stop thinking about Alice.*
> *I don't want to be who I am.*
> *I don't want to live where I live.*
> *I wish my mother were still alive.*
> *I wish both of my moms were still alive.*
> *I hope my father finds a kidney before it's too late.*
> *I hope Judy is happy with her new relationship.*
> *There seems to be so much wrong with my life right now, I don't know where to begin.*
> *What am I doing here in this strange city, with these strange people? I'm nowhere closer to understanding anything, but I don't want to go home because*

He flipped over the sheet.

> *there's nothing there for me, except my dog. I miss Snaps. I envy her. I envy my dog, probably too much and too often.*
> *Everybody dies, everything ends. I'm forty years old. I'm at the halfway point, a place when most people have direction and stability. They have kids, families, jobs they can tolerate. I don't have any of those things, and I'm scared.*
> *I'm fucking terrified.*
> *And I don't know what to do about any of it.*
> *How did I get here? And how do I get out?*

Kevin was about to go over to the next sheet, but he stopped himself. He ripped it out of the notepad and savored the zip of tearing. He folded the paper twice to make a thin long piece, then folded the two ends in opposite directions and brought them together to lock them in a knot. He tossed it onto the pile in the pot, then closed the lid with the pen and pad inside.

"You're done writing your novel?" Denise said, peeking around Fred.

"My hand hurts."

"You look good. You look alive."

She led the way out of the labyrinth, and he thought of absolutely nothing but the steps he was taking, the brush of grass underneath his feet, the sparks in the stones, the fading perfume of the laundry. By the time they were out, it was almost four and noticeably chillier.

"Now that we've detoxified our souls, it's time for the tour." She grabbed his hand and took him through what looked like a small loading dock that led to the kitchen.

It was a large kitchen, big enough to run a small restaurant. But instead of having industrial-size equipment, they had two of everything: two white fridges side by side in the pantry, two gas ranges and ovens, two islands pushed together in the middle of the space. Nothing matched, the appliances most likely donations, but everything was clean and neat.

"We take turns cooking." She picked up a crusted pan on the island and added to the mountain of pots in the sink. "We take turns cleaning up. Some are better at it than others."

"Ugh, you're like one of the shoemaker's elves," a voice said behind them. Even though she was wearing a baggy, faded Pink Floyd *Dark Side of the Moon* T-shirt, there was no hiding her enormous chest. "Always cleaning up whenever you walk in here."

"Angeles, meet Kevin, my brother," Denise said.

Although she could pass for a college student, the way she held herself suggested otherwise. Her cool blue eyes shined behind a film of hardness.

"Are you good or bad?" Angeles asked.

It was a strange question, but being with Claudia had given him plenty of practice. "Depends on the day."

"I like that answer, brother of Denise."

Three other women came in soon after, and as soon as Kevin was introduced to each of them, he forgot who was who. Amber and Susan and Stacy were facsimiles of one another, a trio of stacked blondes with big smiles and long legs, each wearing tight shirts and short shorts, as if they'd leaped out of a beer commercial. They were girls, probably barely old enough to legally drink, but even these nubile beauties carried a shadow of fatigued knowledge, like young war veterans who'd come home after their tour of duty. They were here to clean up because it was their turn to do so, according to the chart on the corkboard hanging off the wall. There was a column for *kitchen,* which included subcolumns for cooking, waiting, dishes, pots and pans, and floor. Then a column labeled *bathroom,* dividing the duties for the three and a half baths in the house, a footnote attached to each one, referencing a laminated sheet pinned underneath the chart that detailed the required steps to deem the task complete.

"You did this?" Kevin asked Denise.

"I'm a woman of many talents."

"You should work at my tennis club." He flipped past the current month's assignments and compared it to December's. "Half of my time is taken up formulating lineups for the leagues. People always complain I don't vary their opponents enough."

Denise held the swinging door open for him, which led into the dining room. It looked like a time portal to the '70s, warped wood veneers on the walls, the trim painted in a psychedelic shade of Yellow Submarine. Like the kitchen, the dining room was a collection of mismatched castaways. Six tables were pushed together into a U shape, and sitting around them were wooden and wrought iron and metal folding chairs of all sizes and shapes and colors. There was even a pair of white plastic patio chairs at the end.

"It's a work in progress." Denise walked down one side and pushed the chairs in to their rightful places. "I'm doing everything I can to raise money, but it's tough in this economy."

Kevin followed her lead and neatened the opposite side. "I imagine it's not easy, trying to get philanthropists to throw money your way."

"Not exactly the sort of business that Bill Gates wants to get involved with. Though I bet you my last dollar that Bill has seen his share of girl-on-girl action."

The dining room led to a four-way intersection: a meeting room to the left, a TV room ahead, and stairs to the right. The meeting room must've been a library at some point, with built-in bookshelves on all four walls, but now it looked like a place of congregation, with couches along the sides and chairs lined up like a wedding, leading up to the wide, cafeteria-style table beneath the trio of windows that looked out onto the weedy yard. Two men sat at the table, playing cards.

"Fresh meat?" one of the guys asked Denise.

His name was Tony, a name he shared with his younger counterpart. They were the only two male residents right now, and neither of them looked like what Kevin imagined porn actors to be. Old Tony was a dead ringer for Jackie Gleason, and Young Tony was so thin that Kevin wondered if he was suffering from an illness.

"My brother, Kevin," Denise said.

Kevin shook their hands. In the next room, laughter erupted like a bomb, so sudden and intense that it sounded like a recording someone had blared out of a set of loudspeakers.

"*Anchorman,*" Old Tony said. "The movie. If we hadn't seen it yesterday, we'd be over there with the ladies."

Denise and Kevin let the guys resume their card game and headed over to the TV room. She told him the two Tonys were cameramen taking a week off. "They're just burned out, making the same movie day after day," she said. "Nobody gets out of film school thinking they'll be shooting porn."

The TV room was crammed full of people, so many that Denise didn't bother to introduce him. The TV was one of the older rear-projection units that was as large as an armoire, and as Kevin watched a snippet of the film, Will Ferrell and Christina Applegate fighting like pro wrestlers in the newsroom, Kevin thought about what Denise had said, if she, too, had expected something more from her life. Who wouldn't? This was the sad truth about anyone working the sex trade: Nobody ever expected to be there. It was an industry built on a foundation of failures, a place of last resort. Some of the folks watching the television were older women, and yet they continued to dress like girls, skin-tight tops fighting to contain surgically ample breasts, their hair platinum blond to wash out the grays. From sexy babes to MILFs and, eventually, hunchbacked octogenarians in nursing homes; it would happen to all of them.

Denise asked him what he was thinking.

"Death and decrepitude," Kevin said.

"Decrepitude," she said, and she nodded approvingly. "That's one of those words that sounds the way it means. Almost like it's falling apart as you say it."

They climbed the stairs to the second floor, wide, imposing red-rugged steps with oak banisters and railings, except half the rungs were missing like fallen-out teeth and most of the rug was frayed, stained, or ripped out entirely.

"This must've been a beautiful house once," Kevin said, then wished he could take it back. He hadn't meant it as criticism, but he was afraid it had sounded that way.

"I wish I could see pictures of the way it used to be," she said. "I mean I can imagine it, but it would be nice to have a real, visible goal to strive for, the sort of thing I can tape on the wall and show people: This is it, this is what we want to accomplish. Some of the residents aren't afraid to do a little repair work, and I think it's just a matter of time."

Either Denise was deluding herself or she was the most positive thinker he'd ever met, because from what Kevin could see, this house needed more than a hammer and elbow grease. The plaster on the ceiling was fissured as if by an earthquake; a gap in a window was patched with folded newspaper. He'd toiled enough on his own house to know how much time and skill was required to make even the simplest repairs. If the externals were in this poor shape, it was highly likely that the unseen—the electrical system, the plumbing, the heating—were equally in trouble. His sister was a realist except when it came to this house. But that was love, wasn't it? Blinding everyone in its wake, making a fool of everyone caught in its jet stream.

There were six bedrooms and three bathrooms on the second floor, all of them spartan, the rooms each furnished with a bed, desk, chair, and lamp. There were no prints on the walls, no photographs encased in frames, one room as anonymous as another. Denise had described the décor of the house as Zen, and now it made sense to Kevin, the barren simplicity of these rooms lending themselves to a quiet, meditative spirit. The larger rooms were divided with bamboo screens to accommodate multiple residents, though they were nothing more than skeletal reeds, easy to see through.

"They're more symbolic than actually providing privacy. The girls who come here, they don't exactly have boundary issues with their bodies."

Kevin nodded, but the more he heard about the porn world, the more it seemed like a foreign culture that he would never truly understand. On a bedroom door was a sign that read:

LIGHTS OUT BY 10 PM

"You have a curfew?"

They climbed up another set of curving stairs, one of the steps creaking as if it was about to give way.

"We voted on it. We run a democracy. We also voted on no sex, which really doesn't need to be enforced. You can imagine it's the last thing the residents want to do."

"Sort of like having plumbers at a plumbers' conference put in a sink."

"And here we come to the end of our brief but informative tour."

The third floor was a wide-open space set up as a dormer, double bunks with white sheets and pillows. It resembled an army barracks. A puffing air freshener was installed near the entrance, filling the room with the scent of lavender.

"We can accommodate up to eighty people in total, and although it's rare to have a full house, it happens from time to time." She sat on one of the beds and tapped the space next to her. When Kevin sat down, he could see the labyrinth through the small round window by the staircase. The Buddha was surrounded by dots of stones, two birds perched on his bald head.

"So," she said, "what do you think?"

"It's fantastic, all of it," he said, and he was glad he didn't have to lie, and even gladder that just a couple of days ago, all he had was a name, and now he had this very real person sitting next to him. She may not have been a lawyer or a doctor, but she was his sibling, and he was glad to know her. "Denise, I think you're awesome."

She clapped her hands and laughed. "Well, I think you're awesome, too, Kevin."

Two sisters. He had two sisters now, and yet they didn't know each other, but that could change this Saturday at the gallery opening. Kevin knew having Denise there would mean more to him than anyone, but he was the link between his sisters, and it seemed important to bring them together, a sense of opening up and also of closing in, a connecting of the two familial worlds he now inhabited.

"What are you doing this Saturday evening?" he asked.

"I'll check my planner, but I think I'm free. Why?"

"There's someone I want you to meet," he said.

23

Right up until they were due to drive back to New Jersey, Judy pushed herself. She sat in front of her drafting table in the study for two six-hour shifts each day. She modified the racquet-and-web drawing to make it more insect-like, then she started and finished one more, a close-up rendering of a tennis ball's surface in a planetary mode, replacing the fuzz with a dense forest and a rushing river through its curvy, rubbery groove. Then she had the idea of blacking out the sky, as if the drawing were shot from outer space, like those majestic photographs of the Earth from the moon. It was a simple drawing but not exactly easy to complete because she used a fine-point pen to create each tree. Filling up a poster-size sketchpad with tiny trees was work for the mad, but Judy found herself entering a trancelike, meditative state, and as she raised each trunk and grew every branch, she remembered why she loved doing this in the first place.

She forgot to eat again until Roger tapped her shoulder, her egg salad sandwich on a plate of gold. It was her favorite china of his, a set of dishware coated with gold paint. It made her feel like Cleopatra. This time, she tasted parsley and cucumber, a summer salad in each bite.

"Thank you," she said, and she devoured the remains. Thankfully Roger wasn't watching her eat like an animal; he leaned against the window frame and perused the tranquil bay.

"I'd like to go with you to your father's," he said.

She pushed her plate away and sighed.

"Can we discuss this later?"

"We're leaving tonight, right?"

"We already talked about this."

"We did," he said. He turned to face her. "But I'd like to talk about it again, if you don't mind."

She did mind, because what she wanted was to refuse his request, but then again, Roger had never asked anything of her until now. Not that she owed him—he'd made that absolutely clear that she wasn't beholden to him—but saying it and feeling it were two different things.

"Why do you want to be there?"

"Just to meet him," Roger said. "I'll be seeing your brother in San Francisco, so this way, I get to meet your whole family."

"They're not that interesting."

Roger walked over and wrapped his arms around her from her back, placing his head next to hers. "In case you haven't noticed, Judy, I like you, and when you like someone, you want to get to know them better."

Judy leaned into him, their cheeks touching, appreciating this moment for what it was, this man wanting to get closer to her. It was a romantic gesture, and there was a warmth spreading from within her, as if her sleeping heart was slowly waking up. She'd hoped that this time alone with him would stir something, and now that it was here, she was quietly terrified because here was Brian, butting into her brain. For a little while she'd loved Brian so completely, and what good had it done? She knew Roger was not Brian, far from it, but Roger was still a man and had the capacity to hurt her.

"I don't have much in common with my father or my brother," she said. "It's not like you're gonna discover some deep, revelatory connection."

Roger disengaged himself from her and kissed the top of her head.

"But they've known you your entire life. That's enough for me."

Judy gazed into her sketch of the tennis planet in front of her, points of stars peeking through the inky darkness of space. At some point, she'd have to give herself to Roger, pry her fingers off the railing of her heart. Maybe it'd already happened. That's how it always was; by the time you realized you were in love, it was already too late.

She didn't want to be angry, but two streets from her father's house in Princeton, the house of her childhood, she felt the pointy roots of her past dig in.

Roger drove, and she told him to make a right onto River Road, past the white Victorian on the corner where she used to play with a girl, the one with the birthmark on her cheek whose name now escaped her. They were just a street away, and Judy's heart thumped.

"Take the next right," she said, and the same green street sign was there, Caldwell, shaded by the overhanging branches of red maples that lined the street. Three houses later, they were at the curb, and by this point, all Judy could do was stare at the crooked mailbox. She didn't dare look at the house itself, because she didn't want to be reminded of all the things that were no longer there, especially her mother's garden. How Judy had despised that patch of green, its perimeter cordoned off with wooden posts and chicken wire. In her youth, she used to get so jealous of it, resentful that her mother spent so much time there. It had been the equivalent of a man's garage, an oasis of tinkering and solitude; even her mother's fingernails looked like a mechanic's, so full of dirt that she had to use a toothbrush to clean them out after working the beds. Her favorite plant to grow had been Korean radishes, white oblong root vegetables that she diced and cubed to make kimchi. Judy remembered them as winter harvests, her mother grasping the leafy protrusions like a head of hair, then yanking them out of the ground, her breath a white smoke in the December air as she mooed with each pull. "It's not a cow," Judy used to tell her, but her mother still said it, and it soon became a private joke between them. In Korean, that's what the radish was called, *moo.*

But now all that was left of the garden was the chicken wire, a rusty web fallen over the overlapping heap of weeds. Standing over the mess, Judy couldn't decide whether to be disgusted or impressed by the sheer virility of the unwanted greenery before her.

"We should get him?" Roger showed her his watch.

It was the sort of thing that Kevin would've said, except Kevin wasn't here. When had she last visited her father without her brother acting as the human buffer? Maybe the day after her mother's funeral, when she'd stood at these very front steps, brimming with hate, but that was more than a year ago. She'd been avoiding him, which wasn't hard. She was supposed to come to that kidney transplant info session last month but hadn't. And now that she was standing by the red front door, her index finger poised to press the well-worn oval of the doorbell, she thought back to what she'd told him on that awful day they buried her mother.

"It's your fault," she'd said. "That's why she's dead."

He stared at her with bloodshot eyes. He'd been drinking, she could see it and smell it. "Okay," he said. "But no change. You scream, I scream, no change."

At that moment, she hated him for so many reasons, but more than anything, for being right. His wife, her mother, was gone. She'd given everyone enough time to witness and accept the gradual metric of her permanent departure, but the fact that Judy would never be able to see her, talk to her, be with her again, felt impossible.

Roger wrapped his hand over hers and nudged her finger forward. The button rang the familiar ding-dong, a sound she'd always associated with coming home, and Judy heard movement on the other side.

Behind the open door stood Soo, drying her hands on her apron. Every time Judy saw this woman, Soo was in the middle of cooking. In every way, Soo was different from her mother, from the tight perm on her head to her ridiculously tiny feet, and yet for some reason, she was her father's second go-around at love. Had Judy expected the new woman to be a copy of her mother? Absolutely not. In fact, that would've been more disturbing. During her mother's sickness, Soo had been a welcome fixture, feeding her father and doting on her mother. But then her mother died, and Soo never left. While Kevin believed her father and Soo got closer because of their mutual love of their mother, to Judy, it always felt as if Soo had crept in, then attached herself to the hull of their lives. Not even six months later, Judy found out from Kevin that Soo and her father had gone to city hall to get married, and the invasion was complete. Now, standing face-to-face with this woman, Judy was glad the bulk of her distaste still remained.

"Good morning," Soo said. She looked at Judy askance, reminding her of the way Snaps acted when she was caught misbehaving. Judy could see she wanted to know who Roger was, probably salivating at the possibility that she might be able to feed him, but Judy didn't want to give her the satisfaction.

"Father ready?" she asked. "To go?" She pointed to the car.

"Yes, yes," Soo said, and she scurried away.

"That's your stepmom?" Roger asked.

"So they say," Judy said.

He asked her if they were going to go in. Even though she'd rather stay out here on the front porch instead of subjecting herself to her past, Roger was here for her to do exactly that. Judy pushed through the door.

"It's a nice house," Roger said, and it was true. As they ascended the stairs, her left hand tracked the curve of the banister. It felt as it always had, the wooden handrail cold and slightly sticky. She'd lived eighteen years of her life here, longer than any other place, and even though she was a grown woman with her own apartment, when she thought of home, what materialized in her mind's eye was this staircase and the family photos lining the walls. From the landing up, it was like traveling through a time machine, with portraits of Kevin and Judy as infants, Kevin posing with his bat in his Little League uniform, Judy awkwardly airborne in a pink tutu. After a pair of graduations, there was no evidence of the future failure of two marriages, and finally, a shot from some nondescript birthday. Somebody must've given the camera over to the waitress because everybody was there, Kevin and Alice and Judy and Brian and her father and her mother, sitting around a table, their hands clapping, a fireball of a birthday cake burning in the middle. She couldn't remember whose birthday it had been. How many countless other houses displayed a visual path of family history like theirs, the children growing up and living out their lives, only to die themselves and continue the great game of life with their own children?

There was a change to the wall at the top of the staircase, a small portrait of her father and Soo at the dinner table, looking truly happy. Both of their hands were on the table, each holding a shiny knife and fork, ready to dig into a feast, their faces beaming as if they'd just heard the funniest joke in the world. Judy would bet a hundred bucks that Kevin took this picture, he must've asked for them to pose this way, and she felt a pinprick of jealousy. To imagine herself in Kevin's place, camera in hand, composing the shot, then telling her father to grab the utensils and be silly—it was a possibility that was an impossibility. Her photo would've been an error; her father's natural grimace and Soo's simper would have been evident in their unwilling smiles, captured onto the digital grid, the ugliest possible arrangement of their pixels.

"Was this your bedroom?" Roger asked.

Every year of her childhood, she had counted the footsteps it took to walk from her bedroom door to the first step on the staircase. She stopped doing that when she could do it in nine steps, but now, she was able to get there in just five quick strides. How little that child must've been, how utterly unrecognizable from the sullen woman she'd turn out to be. Judy stood at the border of her adolescence, tentative to cross the threshold, as if breaching this invisible line would mean she'd transform back into the happily helpless, helplessly happy girl.

Her mother had warned her that she was planning to convert Judy's bedroom into her craft room, but it never happened. Some of her mother's stuff had migrated here, the largest of which was her floor loom, looking more like the skeleton of a piano than a machine that created tapestry. Judy's bed was still in the same position, and her desk, too, except instead of her books on the hutched shelves above, spindles of yarns of different colors and shades were crammed tightly between the boards of wood. Judy had been the first one to abandon this room, and now with her mother's departure, this space felt like a tomb.

"Boy George?" Roger pointed at the poster that still hung on her closet door, its edges curled inward like an ancient scroll.

It was a blow-up of Culture Club's first album cover, with a head-shot of Boy George in his signature black bowler hat looking pouty, contrasting the neon-bright extensions in his hair and liquid pink lipstick. Three round insets showcased his bandmates in sleeveless T-shirts, the silliness of '80s fashion in full display. Staring at the poster, Judy had trouble believing she'd once been enough of a fan to have gone through the numerous steps it took for this piece of paper to exist in front of her. She had to have asked her father or mother to drive her to the mall, where she handed over babysitting money to the cashier to buy the poster, and then to bring it back home, unroll it, tack it on with enough poster putty for it to still hang here a quarter of a century later? It was exhausting just to think about it.

"The less said," Judy said, "the better."

Roger sat on her bed and leaned back against the wall.

"Thank you for doing this for me," he said. "I know you didn't want to."

She sat down next to him. "There are some good memories in here. Bad ones, too." And now that Roger had been here, he, too, joined the cast of previous characters occupying this room, and Judy couldn't help but think which one Roger would be years from now, good or bad? Maudlin lyrics from the old Culture Club hit floated back to her. *Do you really want to hurt me? Do you really want to make me cry?*

She was living in the present but was preoccupied with the future's past, doing exactly what years of therapy had told her not to do. You

were supposed to live in the moment, because that's all there ever
was, and yet it was maybe the hardest thing to do.

From below, she heard her name being called in that inimitable
way of Soo's, two dragged syllables ending with an uncertain lilt:
"Joo-dee . . . ?"

"Okay," Judy yelled back.

Roger offered her his hand, and she took it. They rose together.

"It's a nice room," he said. "I can see you in it."

She could, too, and so much more: the twin tracks of scuff marks
on the floor where she pushed back her chair, the left leg of her bed
she'd banged into so many times that she'd wrapped a sock around
it, a shadow of the old forest-green paint peeking through the peach-
colored walls. Her father had helped her repaint this room. She hadn't
asked him, he just came to work with her, and the only words they'd
exchanged pertained to the task at hand. She'd been fifteen, and the
night before, she was caught shoplifting a skirt at the mall, the stu-
pidest stunt in a series of stupid stunts that summer, and he'd been so
angry that her mother had stood between them, turning herself into
a shield against his acid words and flailing arms. He screamed that
Judy was growing up to be a terrible person, human trash, a person
with no moral center. She called him a coward, a drunk, anything else
to hurt him.

And yet the next morning he was here, dipping a roller into the
paint tray, blotting out the deep dark green with his troublemaker
daughter. In retrospect, there was no better antidote after a fight
than painting, covering the walls that had absorbed the brunt of their
bitterness. With every roll or brushstroke, it was as if they were witnessing the gradual emergence of a brighter future, and they could
almost pretend that this would be a new start for them, a peaceful
coexistence between father and child. Of course this hardly turned
out to be the case, what with driving and sex and alcohol and drugs,
all those vices lining up ahead of Judy's high school years, ready to
blow up like a series of time bombs, but for that one afternoon, there
was enough hope for the both of them to trust the ephemeral conge-
niality of their shared fiction.

Ever since she tripped and broke her ankle on prom night, Judy
made a habit of holding on to the handrail, and she did so now as she
descended the staircase. Her brother wasn't here to save her this time
if she took a tumble. He was far away in California, and thinking of

Kevin and her drawings gave her a solid, palpable sense of joy, until she saw the man waiting at the landing. She hadn't seen her father in months, and bundled up in a puffy winter coat, he looked far frailer than she'd remembered, the few white curls of his hair as wispy as windswept clouds. She knew she was supposed to feel sympathy, which was what Roger was obviously feeling, the way he laid a kind hand on her shoulder, a gesture of pity and understanding if there ever was one. Judy wished she felt something, but there was nothing there. Was this empty void better than hatred or disgust? She didn't know. Maybe it was an improvement, to see her father as what he was, a task to be performed because her brother asked her to.

"You not have to come," her father said.

"Yes," Judy said. "I know."

"You late."

The house could be burning down, and she could be carrying him in her arms, jumping over the flames and out the door, and he'd still find something to criticize.

Roger opened the door for Soo.

"Thank you," she said.

"I'm Roger," he said, and he bowed to both of them.

Judy's father gave him a once-over. "You Japanese," he said, not a question.

Roger nodded.

"Okay."

Judy didn't know what that meant, whether because Roger was from Japan, or that Judy was with a Japanese man, or that her father had guessed correctly. In the end, it didn't matter, because whatever or whomever the word had been bestowed on, it was right.

24

H idden in the North Beach district of San Francisco was the Hive, Claudia's gallery, which from the outside looked more like a warehouse. There was no sign, just a single metallic sculpture of a beehive and a bee flying toward it, with a tangled squiggle of dotted lines to show its flight path. Inside, it was as if someone had taken a space as tall and wide as a high school gymnasium, filled the room with white paint, and drained it out. Everything, from the ceiling to the floor, was white. Kevin had been here only once before, and the first thing he pointed out was how clean the floor was.

"It's a trick," Claudia had told him. "There's a full inch of a clear coating on top of the white enamel. So as long as the coating doesn't yellow, which it isn't supposed to, ever, considering how much it cost, I'll always have the snowiest gallery in town."

The cavernous space had been mostly empty then, but now it was filled with art. According to the sign leaning on the easel by the entrance, there were six artists being showcased. The fourth one down on the alphabetical list was JUDY YOON LEE.

"That's your sister, Judy?" Denise asked.

"Your sister, too, in a roundabout way," he said.

How many times had Judy sat in the bleachers of his tennis matches, under the relentless sun or inside a sweaty tennis club, to cheer him on? Standing here and taking in her name embossed in gold capital letters, he was grateful to be able to pay her back in part for all those hours she'd spent on him. And the woman who was making it possible, Claudia, was at the opposite end of the room, wearing a cerulean bandanna, guiding a worker to relocate a gigantic sculpture shaped like a matchbook. The head of a match was as large as a human head, but the piece was made of some light material because the man had no problems pushing it into its new place. The matchbook was open with four matches remaining, three clustered together on one side while one stood alone on the other. There was tension in the grouping, the lone match versus the trio, and it probably wasn't a coincidence that the three had yellow bands below their orange heads while the single had a black one. At Penn State, Kevin had taken a course in modern art, and the artist he ended up liking the best was René Magritte, because not only were his paintings really cool to study, but also it seemed as if they took him some time to compose. Someone unfamiliar with art may not understand the cultural or artistic significance of the green apple obscuring the man's face, but Kevin could still appreciate the workmanship. When Claudia looked his way, Kevin waved, and she motioned him toward her.

They met halfway across the room, at another featured artist's work, a head shot of a woman's face that when seen close up was a mosaic of black and white pushpins. The woman's hair was a glittery clump of paper clips, her sweater a collection of curled up Post-It notes. The mixed-media canvas was encased in a clear material like Lucite, but instead of a flat surface, it had waves, as if the material had been put in liquid motion before being flash-frozen in place. It was remarkable, and large, too, a circle about six feet in diameter, and it hung suspended by a cable from the ceiling.

"This is amazing," he said.

"Wait for it," Claudia said.

The artwork slowly started spinning on its axis, stopping when it revealed its opposite side. Initially, it looked like a black-and-white landscape seen from an airplane's window, the white houses tiny and the streets laid out like black ribbon, but when Kevin considered the entire canvas and not the individual components, a face emerged, a man's face, a winding swath of the grassy park transformed into his beard, a swimming pool shaped like a nose. Before he could get a better look, the painting spun again.

"Pretty nifty, eh? It's titled *1:59*, and we're still trying to figure out how Jarkko worked those numbers into the piece. For example, that's how long it waits until it turns again, a minute and fifty-nine seconds. There are 159 houses on the other side, and there's one house that's bigger than all the others, at a scale that is 1 to 59 to an actual building. It's the one with the roof open, and inside, you see little figurines of the man and the woman, sitting down on a sofa and staring up at a two-sided painting."

Between this and the matchbook sculpture was Judy's section, her lone sketch looking like a brightly lit postage stamp next to these behemoths. There were three empty frames surrounding her drawing, spotlights pointed to each one, waiting to be filled with additional sketches she must be bringing. Kevin didn't know whether to be worried or impressed, because if Claudia considered Judy's work on the same level as these others, that was some high praise.

As if noticing his concern, she laid a hand on his shoulder and said, "I can't wait to put the rest of Judy's works on display. This is going to be a wonderful show."

"Thank you," Kevin said. "What you're doing for my little sister . . . you're gonna change her life. You've already changed it."

"I'm not doing it for anyone but myself," Claudia said. "You know that as well as I do. Now who's that woman you brought?"

Kevin had been so entranced by the artwork surrounding him that he'd forgotten about Denise. And she'd made herself easy to forget, sitting on a bench off to the side.

"My new sister. I'll bring her over."

Denise was admiring a painting, a nude woman sleeping on her side on a mattress of roses. Every rose contoured to her body, and she was half awake, her green eyes slightly open, peering furtively at the viewer. The rest of her face was obscured by a bouquet of white roses.

"What do you think it means?" Denise asked.

"I have no idea. Sometimes I think it's enough for a work of art to be beautiful."

They wended their way through the sudden thicket of gallery workers who moved with a heightened sense of immediacy. Heels and shoes clicked on the immaculate white floor; the level of collective noise elevated the din to a noisy clatter. Caterers wearing classic white tops and black slacks set up the drinks and hors d'oeuvres on the north end of the room while a sunglasses-wearing DJ set up shop on the opposite side. Claudia directed with a yardstick, showing the lighting guy where to nudge a pair of halogens above the rotating painting, while a cadre of assistants and underlings with clipboards and tablets consulted with her. When there was a lull in the commotion around her, Kevin snuck in front of her with Denise.

"Claudia, this is Denise."

"Norman's daughter. Nice to have you," Claudia said, extending her hand. She then turned to him and said, "A family gathering. I like it."

"That rose painting," Denise said, "just out of curiosity, how much is it?"

Claudia tapped the yardstick on her shoulder, thinking. "Rosalind sold her last painting for somewhere around thirty grand, but that was before her show in Milan, so you're probably talking about thirty-five now, maybe forty if she's got the balls to ask for it."

Denise let out a whistle. "Everything good I've ever wanted in life, I've never had enough money to buy it."

Soft jazz gradually, quietly flooded the room, the music coming from everywhere, and Kevin remembered Claudia mentioning something about this, how she'd flown in one of the lead engineers from the Bose Corporation to build a sound system that used the walls themselves as a giant speaker to provide the most organic listening experience. As the saxophone and piano meshed into a harmonious whole, Kevin saw the double doors of the entrance swing open to reveal his sister.

It hadn't been that long, hardly a month, but as he excused himself from Denise and Claudia and made his way over to see her, his heart tightened. He hadn't felt a swelling of nostalgia this strong since college, when he'd returned his freshman year after fall break. As he watched Judy hand her leather portfolio to the girl by the front counter and then pull off her coat, he couldn't shake the idea that he'd known her for her whole life. He'd been a month shy of turning three, but when he saw her bundled up in the hospital bed, sleeping in the crook of her mother's arm, he climbed in and proclaimed, "I like you." At least that's what his mother had told him for so long that it had become an implanted memory. Judy used to gift him her dolls, sling the arm of the plastic baby in a dramatic arc and into his hands, her smile so guileless. She loved to sing the Korean folk song "Arirang" with her mother, belt out the chorus with abandon.

"Little sis," he said, and she turned around. There was a glow to her skin, her hair shiny like a long, wet stone. She wore a simple black dress that made her look older and assured.

"Big bro," she said, and there was that same kid smile on her face, just a bit wider with the passing of a few decades. It felt so good to hold her. Their mother was gone, and when their father left, then it would be just the two of them.

"What is this?" she said when she caught his eyes welling up. "That's usually my job."

"Maybe we've switched places," Kevin said.

She scanned the room and slowly shook her head. "I have to stop saying that I can't believe this is happening. Holy shit, is that like a giant matchbook? I wonder if it works. I wonder if it's made by one of those artists who'll set it on fire at the end of the night."

A media crew arrived through the entrance, lugging their cameras and AV equipment, a stream of burly stagehands grunting through the door while a pair of well-coiffed media folks, a thin man in a Euro-cut suit and a woman in a skin-tight red dress, stepped gingerly over the threshold. Judy and Kevin stepped off to the other end of the counter to stay out of their way.

"I took him to see Dr. Elias," she said. Still she avoided using the words *father* or *dad*. Maybe he was expecting too much—the fact that she'd followed through was an accomplishment.

"You did?"

"Don't sound so surprised."

"Well, you didn't call when I rang you. How's he doing?"

"About the same. Maybe a little worse."

"You don't get better from renal failure."

A caterer paused with a silver tray in his hand, holding flutes of champagne and glasses of wine, and Kevin was glad to see Judy decline.

"So," she said, changing the subject. "I brought Roger with me."

"And I'm looking forward to meeting your man." It had been a while since he'd seen her so happy, which was good but also imbued him with trepidation. Judy had a way of falling hard for people, and though after Brian she'd become more guarded, Kevin didn't notice her holding anything back as Roger Nakamura walked through the door. He was about Kevin's height and build, and looking at his face was like staring at one of those traditional Japanese flat paintings where the eyes were thin and wide and the faces were horsey-long, almost like caricatures.

"You must be Kevin," Roger said. He spoke with equanimity, each word its own island.

"And you must be Roger. Thank you for taking care of my sister."

"It was just a few weeks. She healed up quickly."

"Still, I wasn't there. I'm grateful."

The three of them made small talk. Judy regaled Kevin about the first-class flight from Newark to San Francisco where they sat in a recliner-like seat and were given bibs for their lobster dinner. Kevin looked around as he listened, trying to find Denise, until one of Claudia's assistants interrupted them.

"We need you, Ms. Lee," she said, "you and your artwork. Our installation people are ready."

"I can use Roger's help, too, so we'll let you catch up with your former star student," Judy said.

"What are you talking about?"

"Look behind you," she said, before being whisked away with Roger.

He'd never seen Alexa like this, decked out and dolled up. Her normally straight blond hair, which was always tied back in a ponytail, was waved out to a luxurious fullness, and her black satin dress was a tube of elegance. As she approached him, he saw that the dress wasn't all black but varying shades of darkness, the gradations shifting with each step.

"Surprised to see me?" she asked.

"I guess I shouldn't have been."

"But surprised nonetheless."

He leaned over and gave her a quick, innocuous hug.

"So," she said. "Mom told me you guys had sex."

Kevin's mouth and his brain were not cooperating, and he was certain he looked like a guppy out of water.

"Yes," he finally said.

"I'm not judging you," she said, sounding exactly the opposite.

"Well, thank you. Claudia felt the need to tell you this, I see."

"She feels the need to say a lot of things she shouldn't," Alexa said. "So do you feel complete now? Are you satisfied with your life, your *longing*? Are you in *love*?"

She was trying to sound funny and sarcastic, but mostly what came across was her hurt, of exactly what, Kevin didn't know. He had a feeling Alexa didn't, either. There was a complicated dynamic of emotions at work here, and as the grownup, he thought the best way to diffuse the situation would be to play it straight.

He kept his voice as neutral as possible as he asked, "What do *you* think?"

It did the trick. Alexa's shoulders fell, then they rose up to a nonplussed shrug. "I think . . . I think maybe we should talk about something else."

"Small talk."

"Tiny talk."

"You're out here visiting your mom."

"It was her idea. I haven't seen her in a couple of months."

"How's your tennis going?"

She picked up a flyer on the counter, rolled it into a baton, and mimed a perfect drop shot.

"That's totally Bill."

She nodded. "I'm working with him now. It's different. He's a very different player than you. A very different person. It's fine, but it's . . . different."

"The way we play is who we are," Kevin said.

"Oh, and I just got accepted to the Bollettieri summer camp," she said. "Some advanced techniques thing."

"That's fantastic!" Kevin said. It was the premier tennis academy in the country, where top players like Maria Sharapova, Pete Sampras, and Andre Agassi developed their skills.

"I suppose. I don't think I'll learn that much more, considering how much you and Bill have already taught me."

"Spoken like a true teenaged know-it-all."

Behind and beyond Alexa, there was something going on, something that sounded like more than the chatter of pre-opening excitement. Claudia was vehemently shaking her head, and Judy was holding on to one of her mounted sketches.

"It's my mother." Alexa grabbed his hand and pulled him toward the now full-blown commotion, a crowd forming, the savvy media folks already rolling the camera. "Before things get out of hand, which I guarantee they will, let me just apologize ahead of time for her being who she is."

"You don't have to tell me about her eccentricities," he said. "I've been staying with her for almost a month now."

They'd reached the eye of this widening gyre. "I'm sorry," Claudia said to Judy, "but I just can't."

"What's going on?" Kevin asked.

"She says she won't display my drawings," Judy said, her voice disembodied, a ventriloquist's dummy. "She says they're no good."

"No, please, that's not what I said. What I did say is that they're not going to work here. I made a mistake. It's me who fucked up. And I am deeply, deeply sorry for that, but I just can't let these go on."

"But she's here," Kevin said. "You brought her here."

Claudia, looking exasperated, closed her eyes as if to blot out the mess she'd created. "You're not helping."

Judy looked to Roger, who had his hands in the pockets of his pants and met her eyes with the same, utterly composed face. Kevin remembered Judy telling him that Roger was medically unflappable, whatever that meant, but if there was ever a time to flap, this was it. Judy dropped her gaze, dropped her head, and dropped her framed piece from her hands, and as it made its inevitable, awful descent, Kevin saw that it was one he hadn't seen before, a tennis ball–shaped planet in outer space, her largest work yet. The glass shattered as the corner struck the floor, the noise amplified with the unnatural hush that had fallen over the gallery.

It seemed as if everyone was frozen under a spell until Judy ran out. Roger followed, their footsteps hammering echoes in the silence.

"What happened?" Kevin asked Claudia. "What the fuck?"

Claudia sighed, tightened the bandanna around her head. Kevin knew he was pissing her off, but he didn't care. "Right now, Judy's work is one of desperation. The first one she sent you, that was real. I can see it in her strokes, the confidence, the attitude. With each subsequent sketch, it ebbs away until this last one has none of it, not a whit." She held up another one Kevin hadn't seen, two women in tennis skirts sitting on a bench, topless as they breastfed the tennis ball they each cradled in their arms. "They've been neutered, as if they were started by her but completed by someone else. Displaying her works as is would be like showcasing the decline of an artist, and that's not what this show is about."

Kevin peered at the drawing to see the certain mistakes that Claudia saw, but what was the point? This was her domain, and he knew how immutable her mind was once she made it up. All he saw in his sister's work was wonder, how she took a blank canvas and drew something that had existed only in her brain. It was magic, this act of creation, and Claudia had sullied it.

"Bullshit," Alexa said. "All of it, all utter bullshit, Mom."

Claudia crossed her arms and addressed her daughter. "Now you know better than that."

"Contrary to popular belief, this is what she does better than any- thing else," Alexa continued, ignoring her. "It's positively Olympic, her ability to screw with your mind."

"I meant every word I've said. That's called integrity."

"She hasn't told you, has she," Alexa said to Kevin. "She hasn't told you what happened when she suffered her nervous breakdown, excuse me, *vision*, when she stopped being a reasonable person and became the monster that she is."

Claudia clapped twice, and the circle around her began dispersing. "We still have a gallery to open in less than half an hour, folks." She turned to Alexa. "You can keep talking, but no one's listening, my dear."

"You and your stupid fucking Tiny Claudia," Alexa said, and she headed for the exit herself.

Already Claudia's assistants were at work in the background, removing the panels that were supposed to showcase Judy's works. Hammers unhinged nails; pieces of the beige matte boards passed from one assistant to another like a fire brigade.

Kevin clutched Claudia by the arm with enough force for her to emit a small yelp of complaint. He wanted to keep his voice steady, but he could feel himself losing his cool.

"Everything was ready to go here," Kevin said. "All you had to do was just let it go. If you'd just let your people do their fucking jobs . . ."

"I can't go against myself." She yanked her arm free of his grip. "That's what it would've been, me doing something that no longer felt true." She picked up Judy's painting off the floor, the shattered glass an intricate spider web that obscured the sketch underneath. "This might feel like the end to your sister's career, but have faith that it's just the beginning."

"No," he said. "There has to be a limit."

"A limit?"

"You're a child, Claudia. You're worse than a child, because you're an adult but you don't act like one."

Claudia shook the broken shards into a garbage can, the pieces sounding like white noise as they hit the metal. "That's how you really feel?"

"I've never been more sure of anything in my life."

She placed the framed sketch on a rolling cart and stood in front of him, close enough that he smelled her familiar scent of paint and sweat. "Then we're done, you and I."

"Fine," Kevin said.

"It is. You're not the first one to no longer understand who I am, and you won't be the last." Her voice was about to break, but then she fought it off. "I know this is my lot in life."

With that she walked away, toward the gap where his sister's works were supposed to be tonight, a white space that was now being populated with long-backed white chairs and round white side tables, an area where people could gather and debate the finer points of art and all its elusive definitions.

He felt a hand on his shoulder.

"It seemed best if I stayed out of the way," Denise said. "With what was going on."

"I'm sorry," he said. "You didn't even get to meet Judy."

"That's all right. I've gotten my fill of art and artists for the evening. Possibly for my lifetime. What should we do now?"

"What I want," he said, "is to go home." Except home was across the country, and getting a ticket tonight would basically bankrupt him. Still, he tried, calling the airline as Denise held the door open for him. The please-hold Muzak annoyed his ear.

Outside, the air was cold, and sitting on the stoop was Alexa, her legs pulled in close.

"Hey." He crouched down next to her. He handed his phone to Denise, who nodded and took it.

"My mother's crazy," she said. Her eyes were red, her voice gravelly. "I'm sorry I ever mentioned her to you. She wasn't like this, always. She used to be a normal person."

"'Tiny Claudia,' you said. What did you mean by that?"

"A hallucination. She's always been a manic depressive, but one night she had a huge fight with my dad and she was gonna kill herself. Emptied her bottle of sleeping pills and had shoved them in her mouth when she saw a tiny version of herself at the bottom of the bottle."

"A tiny version . . . ?"

"She swears it was her."

"She hadn't actually taken the pills yet. So this hallucination was not drug-induced."

"That's why she insists it was real. She spit the pills out, rinsed out her mouth, told my father to go fuck himself, and became who she is.

Somebody who does what she feels, regardless of the consequences, because to her, going against herself is taking those pills."

"Claudia's theory on life is like communism," he said. "On paper, it's great, but its actual execution leaves much to be desired. Do you want to go somewhere or something?"

She shook her head. "Eventually I'll have to come back here. She's still my mother. I have no other place I can go, except home."

"I got somebody," Denise said, and she handed Kevin's cell phone back to him.

He introduced the two ladies to each other then took the call. The best the rep could do was to book a flight three days from now, one that had a pair of connections, from San Francisco to Dallas to Denver and finally Newark. He still had to pay another three hundred dollars, but he took it.

"Back in Jersey on Tuesday," he said.

"You're not coming back to Mom's tonight, are you," Alexa said.

"We're gonna stop there now so I can pick up my stuff," Kevin said, "but no, I won't be sticking around."

"And you're not coming back to the tennis club, either."

"Maybe as a member, like you."

"I have a match next Saturday in a local junior tournament. The girl I'm playing is six foot one with the wingspan of an airliner. Ridiculous serve. Would you consider being my coach?"

"I don't know how much help I'd be," he said, and he meant it, because in the end, tennis was a long-distance boxing match, you against your opponent. "But I'd be honored."

"Good," she said. She dusted herself off, looking once again like a prom queen in her strapless dress. "Then this is still not good-bye. Because I hate good-byes. In fact, I'm just going to walk back in there now so I don't have to say it."

They watched her do exactly that, disappear into the squinty brightness of the Hive.

"I like her," Denise said. "One of your students?"

"Was," Kevin said. "I quit my job at the club."

As they were about to leave, the thin man who came with the media crew hurried through the door and hailed Kevin.

"Someone told me you're the brother of the artist Judy Yoon Lee?"

"That's right."

"I'd like to talk to you, but I have to go back to the opening. Can I get your number?"

Kevin gave him his number, the man typed it into his smartphone, and then he was gone as fast as he'd come.

"The saga continues," Denise said.

They walked down the Embarcadero to get to Denise's car, past the giant gray Pier 35 building until the bay came into view. At night the city was a living jewel, lights from the distant Treasure Island twinkling gold. Sailboats glided through the darkness while inland, a pair of skyscrapers was outlined like neon lights. The beacon atop the Transamerica Pyramid was a cold white orb.

"You can stay at the Sanctuary, if you like," Denise said. "I know we have beds open and you're only gonna be around for a couple days."

"That's really kind of you," he said. "My wallet thanks you as well."

"I have a shoot tomorrow, but the next day I'm free, so I can come by to see you off."

Denise clicked on her key fob, and her car blinked its headlight eyes in response. They both got in, but before she pressed the starter button, she turned and looked at him. Under the street light, her Barbie doll made-up face looked wrong, because she was frowning.

"What's the matter?" Kevin asked.

"We leave our lies behind in the Sanctuary. We're not there yet, but we will be soon, and I'd rather get this out in the open now than later."

"All right," he said.

"I'm not your sister," Denise said. "Not your half sister, not even one percent."

Kevin breathed into his belly, breathed out, puffing his cheeks, then again. He was doing his stroke breath, right before he approached the tennis ball and struck at its center. It used to calm him down; he hoped it still worked.

"Why?" he asked.

"Because of Norman. He's helped me through a lot of hard stuff, and I didn't think he was asking much, but as it turns out, he was, because I like you, you're a good person, and I'm no good at lying anymore. I used to be better at it."

"He asked you to pretend to be my sister?"

She nodded. "I thought it was crazy, too, but he loves you, and he doesn't think he alone is enough to keep you."

"Keep me? What the fuck does that mean?"

"I don't know. It's what he told me, and I'm probably fucking that up, too. He should tell you himself. He comes every Monday, tomorrow, for counseling sessions at the Sanctuary."

"I can't believe people take advice from this man."

He knew this was a slam against Denise, but he didn't care. To be lied to like this—it was just an awful thing to do to anyone, but from his own father? But maybe it made sense. Making a home movie like the one Norman had, the man clearly had problems.

"I'd like to explain at least my portion of this mess," Denise said.

Kevin said nothing. Just when he thought this day couldn't get any shittier, it did. He sank into his seat and turned away from Denise. She started the car and they drove down the street, the environmentally friendly hum of the Prius's hybrid engine filling the cabin. The girders of the Bay Bridge rose like mountain peaks as they approached it from the south, the cars in front and the cars in back sharing the common goal of leaving this city behind.

PART III

•

THREE DAYS IN NOVEMBER

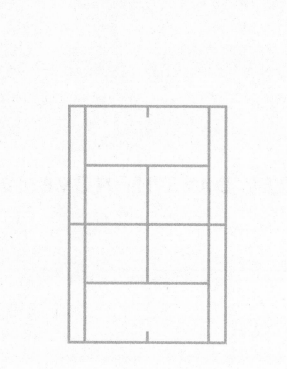

25

Judy watched Roger choose pastries from the buffet table as she sat on one of the many leather couches in the first-class lounge of the San Francisco Airport. She didn't know whether she was mad or disappointed at him or her brother or Claudia, or maybe it was just everything and everybody, all at once. She felt she possessed the right to be pissed at anything.

From the end table, she picked up a discarded copy of *SF Weekly* and was surprised to find a story about the Hive opening, and even more surprised that the piece was more about her than the show itself. It was an essay in the entertainment section, and the headline captured her thoughts perfectly: "Claudia X: Genius or Bitch—or Both?" Judy's name was mentioned several times, and a photograph of her first sketch was prominently displayed with the article. "What egregious offenses did Claudia X find in the works of Judy Yoon Lee? Take a look for yourself, dear reader, and see if you can discover anything beyond what I witnessed: the quirky, beautiful, bold work of a professional. Once again, a budding artist is caught in the crossfire of Ms. X's runaway ego." The writer was an art professor at San Francisco State, and it was obvious that he was no fan of Claudia and, maybe for that reason, was a fan of Judy.

"Pick what you like." Roger sat down next to her and held up the dish like an offering, a smorgasbord of baked goods: a croissant, powdered donut, blueberry muffin, and cheese Danish. Back on the East Coast, it was two in the afternoon, so she really should've been hungry, but she wasn't.

"You have to eat something," he said, nudging the plate.

Judy grabbed the croissant so he'd leave her alone. She had trouble looking him in the eye, a sign of her remaining anger. Like a record on repeat, her mind kept returning to the moment last night when she'd held her tennis planet sketch close to her heart and waited for him to say something, anything, to save her from the horrible creature who told her she wasn't good enough. *Desperation* was the word Claudia had used, and the worst of it was that Judy knew she'd been right. Only with her first sketch had she left it raw, unrefined, the strokes catering to no one, not even to herself, the work existing for the sake of existing. The women breastfeeding their tennis ball babies, the racquet caught in the web of the netting, the tennis planet—with each successive sketch, she'd become less certain of her intent, more generic in her overall effect.

But her shortcomings as an amateur artist did not justify Claudia's actions at the gallery. Late last night, Kevin had called Judy to apologize and to let her know why Claudia was the way she was, some cockamamie story about how close she'd come to killing herself. As far as Judy was concerned, the only unfortunate part of the tale was that she hadn't succeeded.

"I'm coming home, for real, on Tuesday," he said.

"What, you've gotten your fill of your new family?"

He had, and when Judy heard the insane story, with the porn and the girl and the house and the lies, she laughed.

"It's not funny," he said. "You know, you laughed when I told you I was adopted, too. What is it with you?"

"I think it's hilarious," she said, "that your blood family is just as fucked-up as your adoptive family."

"Possibly more," Kevin said.

At least her brother had tried to stick up for her in front of Claudia, but Roger, he'd just stood there. Judy bit into the crusty croissant and watched the buttery flakes rain onto her plate. What could Roger have done, call Claudia names, punch her out, threaten to set the place on fire? The woman's mind had been made up, and she was the queen of her gallery. But still.

"You just stood there," Judy said.

Roger took a sip from his orange juice, then held on to the glass with both hands like a talisman, as if it could explain the unexplainable. "Last night, you mean. At the gallery."

Judy nodded.

"I should've defended your honor," he said.

"When you put it like that, it sounds stupid."

"That's not what I meant," he said, and he placed the glass on the table.

"With you, with your anhedonia, I just don't know what I am to you."

"It's possible that I'm just a coward, and that I didn't want to feel the wrath of that unstable woman."

"But I know you're not. It looked like you were observing—not in the situation but outside it, unaffected."

"And maybe this is how you feel about me, that I see you objectively. Simply put, that I don't love you. That I can't love you."

They were just talking, but the words still stung her.

One of the reps at the front desk came over to inform Roger and Judy that their flight would start boarding in ten minutes. Everyone was so kind here, so ready to help. First class was a side of travel that Judy had never seen, all of it now available to her thanks to Roger. Considering how much he'd done for her, she felt terrible for bringing any of this up, but at this point in her life, she knew herself enough to know that the longer she kept something bottled up, the worse its eventual aftereffects would be.

"I'm never going to be like everybody else," he said.

"Don't say that."

"It's true, though. This is who I am, and I can't blame you for the doubt you have about my feelings for you."

"Love," Judy said. "I don't even know what it's supposed to feel like, if I ever did."

He kissed her then, his lips on her lips, his warmth becoming her warmth. She reached out for him, and he took her in. He was here, and so was she.

The rep came back and cleared her throat to warn them once again.

Judy opened her eyes and took in his unwavering gaze.

"I don't know what happiness is—I'll never know—but I know I want you to be happy," he said.

"Okay," Judy said.

They rose from the couch, held hands, and walked through the automatic frosted glass doors of the executive lounge and out into the fray. Judy looked forward to getting back on the plane, to fly high above the clouds and head back East.

• • •

Roger's mansion on the Cape didn't feel like home for either of them, since he used it for only a month in a given year and Judy had been there only for a couple of weeks, but there was one thing that made it seem more homelike: Snaps, whose ears perked up into a pair of pyramids when she heard their return. No matter how comfortable she seemed in her plush circular dog bed, she got up to greet them at the door. Her steps weren't as sure as they used to be, but still she came, her scruffy muzzle, her eyes cloudy with cataracts. The pet sitter who took care of Momo and Snaps told them that all the dog did was watch the door and wait for them.

Judy had lived with Snaps for more than a month now, and she'd almost forgotten how much Snaps used to annoy her. Like most German shepherds, she was overly territorial, scaring the hell out of Judy every time anyone came near Kevin's house. There was no greater threat than the UPS truck, a sound the dog could hear well before the brown vehicle rolled into the driveway. Every time she'd gone over to her brother's, Judy had to brace herself against Snaps's piercing onslaught of barking, which was so sudden and harsh that it felt like a stab.

But the years had mellowed Snaps out, and now she was the perfect dog. Judy crouched down and gave her a full-bodied hug, sank her face into the dog's neck and came up covered with fur.

"Always a mistake," she said, picking out hairs from her mouth.

On the return flight, she and Roger agreed to spend one more night at the Cape, then drive back to Jersey on Monday morning. It had been a good time, a productive time for her. Even if it all went to hell in San Francisco, she'd worked well here, and she didn't want to forget that. In the end, that's all that mattered, what she'd put down on paper.

She helped Roger close up the house for the coming winter. They drew the curtains and lowered the blinds and cinched the cover around the gas grill on the deck. Judy felt a vibration in her pocket, and for a moment she thought back to the snakebite, when she thought she might die, and now here she was, able to laugh about it.

On her phone was a man named Cody who sounded so effete that he seemed like a gay character from a *Saturday Night Live* skit. He called her sweetheart, he said he saw the *SF Weekly* piece and thought it was fierce, just fierce, what she was doing, and told her that it would be an honor if she would bring her works to his gallery in the Lower

East Side, because nothing would make him happier than to show-case sketches that didn't live up to Claudia X's "standards."

"You know she's *loco*, right? Well, of course you do. You just dealt with her ass-crazy bullshit. The number of artists who have felt the sting of her insanity as you have and gone on to do great things? Dozens, love, dozens. Claudia X has her share of admirers, but there's a tribe of people she's pissed off for no good reason."

Judy took the cell off her ear, swallowed a long lungful of air, then expelled it. Cody was still talking, his munchkin voice blaring off the phone's earpiece.

". . . which is why I think she's as double-edged as a sword can get. I mean I'm not gonna lie to you, the woman is supremely talented, a giant in the art world. But she should stick to what she's good at, is all I'm saying."

"Thank you, Cody," Judy said. "Is it okay if I think about it?"

"Think on it, sleep on it, fuck on it. I'm here for you, Judy. Ring me and we'll get it going, and it's worth it, you know? Art that isn't shared is cry-worthy. People should see what you're doing, because there's nothing else like it. Remember that."

Roger was emptying the dishwasher when she walked in to tell him about the phone call.

"That's great news," he said. "Isn't it?"

While he placed the cups back in the cupboard, she sorted the utensils into their appropriate nooks in the drawer.

"I suppose. It's funny—Kevin told me that before he left, Claudia told him that though this might feel like the end, it's just the beginning."

"Of your career as an artist."

"If you're being positive. If you're being negative, it's the begin-ning of the bullshit that goes along with being one. I still can't make myself say that, by the way. Artist."

"But that's what you are, like it or not."

"It just sounds pretentious, vacuous. Like I should be wearing a beret and speaking with dramatic hand gestures."

"I think it's good to be good at something," he said. "It's a gift, to have a designation for yourself. Not everyone gets to have one in their lives."

He was no doubt referring to himself, his rudderless existence. She pushed the drawer closed and went to him.

"All of this is because of you," she said. "You saved my life in more ways than one."

"Thank you," he said, and she could see he meant it, and yet the disappointment remained on him like a stain, and she couldn't exactly say that she felt any better after the phone call, either. In the end, she'd still wake up each day in the same tired body she'd occupied her whole life, and it all just seemed so meaningless. Maybe she'd contracted Roger's anhedonia, or maybe it was her own proclivity to favor the darker side of things.

"I'm not suicidal or anything," she said, "but sometimes I do wish it all to be over."

Roger put the last dish in the cupboard and slid the rolling racks back into the dishwasher.

"That's a curious thing to say after receiving such good news."

"What is the point, when we're all doomed? Every one of us, all heading toward our eventual, singular demise. And yet we all go on."

"Because this is all we know of, this brief life of ours."

As if to demonstrate her agreement, Snaps walked over and lay down by Roger's feet, on top of the rug by the sink, one of her favorite spots. Roger sat down on the floor and rubbed her belly, and Judy leaned back against the oak cabinets and stroked the back of the dog's neck.

"Maybe crazy Claudia is the only sane one," Judy said. "Do whatever you want, fuck the consequences."

"There are downsides to every philosophy," Roger said. "I can't imagine the woman has many friends. Mostly I feel sorry for her, for being a slave to her every whim. It almost feels like she's living out a curse."

"Either that or a bad movie. Like that one Jim Carrey was in, where he was always forced to tell the truth and got into a whole lot of trouble."

"*Liar Liar.* I actually found it sort of funny."

Judy stopped her petting and looked at him. "I thought because of your anhedonia, you don't . . . you can't . . . ?"

"You've seen and heard me laugh, haven't you?"

"I didn't know if, you know . . ."

"If I was pretending, going through the motions."

"Something like that."

At this, Roger laughed. "Sometimes, Judy, I think you see me as an android, like Data on *Star Trek*. If it's funny, I laugh. It's just that it doesn't elevate my mood. I guess you could say I don't enjoy it."

"It's something I can't even pretend to imagine, that disconnect. Laughter *is* enjoyment."

"Yeah," Roger said. "Well."

For their final meal at the house on the Cape, they ordered in, a pizza with pineapple and ham toppings and a loaf of cheesy garlic bread. Snaps watched them eat with great expectation, hoping for the crusts to be tossed into her dish. Momo, perched on the middle shelf of his cat tree, yowled his disapproval and batted at her butt as Snaps paced back and forth.

That night, as Judy and Roger made love, she felt every touch, every drop, everything that his body offered, as if through her hypersensitive efforts at seeking her own pleasure, she could enjoy it enough for the both of them. She couldn't, of course, and as he drifted to sleep under the cold darkness of the November Massachusetts sky, she stayed awake and stifled her tears. For all her problems with her job or self-worth or whatever, she had her health, and yet Roger did not. Was it selfish of her to want him to feel what she felt? She loved him, she knew this now, but he would never be able to fully return that love.

Somehow, night turned to morning. Judy was woken up by a shake on the shoulder and Momo at her face. For a second, she thought it was the cat calling her name.

"Judy," Roger said, "I think there's something wrong with Snaps."

26

The woman had climbed to the top of the flat roof of the Sanctuary, stood tall with her arms at her side, up against the ledge. Up there, three stories and an attic high, her hair whipped around in every direction at once so that under the morning sun, she looked faceless, an oval mass of flying golden strands. All she had on was a silky white bathrobe cinched loosely against her body, the belt billowing like an angry flag.

Kevin stood in the yard with Angeles and a handful of other Sanctuary residents, watching as Norman climbed up the fire escape. According to Angeles, the only person Amy would talk to was Norman. She was the mother of the two young kids he saw last time.

"She's jumped before," Angeles said, shading her eyes against the two figures. She was in her bathrobe, too, one of her ample breasts barely contained. "Luckily she only broke her leg. But that was before she met your dad."

"So it's an improvement that she's now threatening to jump instead of actually jumping."

"Baby steps," Angeles said, "baby steps."

Norman, having climbed all the way to the top, now skulked his way toward Amy. He moved with the grace of an old dancer, and once again Kevin was reminded of how much of this man's genes were passed down to him.

Everyone lived within the confines of their genetic makeup. It was a box big enough that you could take a little walk and back, but no matter how hard you tried, you could never escape its borders. There were parts of this strange man in him, a pathological liar who talked suicidal porn stars out of committing the irreversible, as he did now, his legs swinging and dangling from the roof's edge as he sat down next to Amy. He spoke to her as if this were the most normal thing to do on a Monday morning.

"You talk with him, too?" he asked.

"Wednesdays at three."

"So he's good at what he does."

"We talk, we look, we meditate," she said. "I don't always feel like spinning cartwheels after our sessions, but I learn something. So yeah, I'd say he's very, very good at what he does. I've seen shrinks with degrees from Harvard and Berkeley, but dealing with people is an instinctive art, you know? You're born with it."

Up above, Amy was no longer standing but sitting next to Norman. She talked with her hands, throwing them up and slicing the air, and Norman nodded and listened. Bits of Amy's voice, high-pitched like a young girl's, shot down like stray bullets: *trespass, motherfucker, hopeless.* Norman offered his hand, and she placed it over her heart.

"You're pissed at him," Angeles said. "About the whole Denise half-sister thing."

"You know about that?"

"We all live in this house. Nothing stays a secret for long around here."

"Don't you think it's a pretty strange thing to do?"

"I'd agree with you on that. But I'm sure he had his reasons."

"So this doesn't change anything for you. You'd still listen to him."

Amy was off the roof's edge and headed for the steps of the fire escape, with Norman close behind her. Angeles stretched out her arms, yawned, then tightened the belt around her robe.

"What the man does with his own life has little to do with his talents. Unless his own failings bleed into his counseling, I have no problems with him. Sorry. But you can discuss this with your fake half-sister." She pointed at the car pulling into the lot.

"Very funny."

"I try," Angeles said. She ran up to Denise, and they walked back together arm in arm to where Kevin was standing. In a pink hoodie and a pair of well-worn jeans and with her hair tied back in a ponytail, his nonsister looked collegiate. All Denise needed was a book bag slung over a shoulder to complete the illusion.

"He's still mad at you," Angeles said. "If you need me so we can gang up on him, you know where to find me." She blew Kevin a kiss, and then she was gone, too, and now it was just the two of them, Kevin and Denise. Fat clouds the color of steel wool floated across the sky, blotting the sun with their puffiness.

"I got here as soon as I heard. Everything's okay?"

Kevin zipped up his windbreaker against the rising wind. It felt as if a rainstorm was coming. "Norman worked his usual miracle, apparently."

"He often does," she said. "I don't know what I'd do without him."

"Wish I could say the same."

"Listen," she said. "Would you at least give me a chance to tell you my side of the story? You were too mad last night to hear me out, but I was hoping that you'd be more open after a good night's sleep."

"You're going to lecture me on reason?"

"I know you want to light into Norman, but please don't, at least not until lunchtime. I've scheduled him for three sessions this morning, and all of these people need him at his best."

"So I'm supposed to wait my turn to tell him how nuts he is."

She took him by the arm and led him to the back door and into the kitchen of the Sanctuary. According to the clock on the wall, it was almost eight, prime time for breakfast, but it was deserted.

"They're all fasting today," Denise said, rooting through the bottom cabinets until she found what she wanted, a cast-iron skillet that looked heavy enough to have its own gravitational pull. "Have a seat. I'll make us some breakfast."

The ruckus had woken him up, so he hadn't had a chance to wash up or even brush his teeth, but Denise waved off his complaints. From one fridge she got out a carton of eggs and a block of butter, and from the other fridge, a carton of milk and a jug of orange juice, both of which she opened and sniffed approvingly.

She pointed at the stool by the island with her spatula, and Kevin sat. Denise slid him a glass of orange juice and took a long, satisfying drink from her own.

"I don't like to talk about myself," she said, "so it helps if I do something." She turned on the oven. "First, I'll make the batter, and then I'll make us some eggs. How do you like yours?"

"Scrambled."

Denise lifted a tub of flour onto the counter; a puff of white dust announced its arrival. "Remember me telling you last night that you're a real sweet guy? See, this is why. I know you don't really care to eat breakfast now. I also know that you'd like nothing more than to tell Norman off. But you're here, sitting with me, humoring me, even."

"You might be mistaking sweetness with stupidity."

"I just complimented you," she said. "Don't turn it into the opposite."

It was words like those that made him like her, her straightforwardness. "What are you doing?"

"It's a surprise. What I can tell you is that it's easy to make, easy on the eyes, and tastes as good as it looks. It's the only thing left from my childhood that's worth remembering."

"You don't owe me anything," Kevin said, surprising himself as he said it.

"The hell I don't."

"To take a page out of Claudia's book, tell me whatever you plan to tell me only if it'll give you pleasure. Not because you feel guilty and you want to appease me in some way."

Denise dumped eggs into a large bowl and sliced a third from a stick of butter.

"I can't lie, of course."

"Not in the Sanctuary."

"It may not give me pleasure to say what I have to say, but I believe it will give me satisfaction. Is that enough?"

"Probably," he said. "It's not like I'm an expert in living selfishly."

Denise stayed silent during this final part of the preparation, adding milk, nutmeg, and vanilla to the bowl, but Kevin could see she was figuring out what she wanted to say and how. She set the timer on the oven for nineteen minutes.

"That's pretty exact, nineteen," Kevin said. "You've done this before."

She pulled up the empty stool next to Kevin. "I was gonna make some omelets for us while we waited."

"To further distract yourself."

"Even with Norman, when I have my sessions with him, I'm doing jigsaw puzzles, knitting, anything to keep me from feeling the feelings I should be feeling."

"And how does that make you feel?"

She smiled, and it was a thing of beauty. Kevin hadn't known that all the smiles preceding this one had been guarded, careful. He wished he could see her without her makeup, the way she looked right after she woke up.

"If you don't mind, just listen, okay? Until I'm done."

They were interrupted by Kevin's ringing cell phone. Area code 617—it was an unfamiliar number. He sent it to voicemail and swtiched it to silent mode.

"I'm ready," he said, and Denise spoke.

"The reason why I agreed to play along with this ruse of Norman's, Kevin, was because you and I share something that most people are fortunate enough not to experience. Like yourself, I, too, am an adoptee, but unlike you, I was aware of my situation as soon as I was old enough to question why my face looked nothing like the faces of my parents.

"I was adopted when I was four months old. I don't know who my birth mother is, and I don't care to know. From what Kay, my adoptive mother, told me, I was no different than most of the kids who get abandoned in Korea, cast out from a single mother who did not want to bear the stigma of having a bastard child. This was in the late '70s, and the country was nowhere as rich as it is now, but here's a statistic that might disturb you: One in two hundred children who are born in Korea, today, are still sent overseas. Considering that our mother country has twice the gross domestic product as Switzerland, why is it that children are still sent from there for adoption every year? Right now, South Korea has the lowest birth rate of any developed nation, and yet Koreans decline to adopt one of their own due to societal pressures. Because back there, it's all about the bloodline.

"I can rail on about this forever—the way single mothers are ostracized, the lack of government-sponsored programs to help them, et cetera. It wasn't that long ago that the country refused to consider orphans legal citizens, if you can believe that. Changing the viewpoints of a culture is always slow. There was a time when I thought I could make a difference, volunteering for transnational adoptee support groups to hold meetings, put up flyers, make cold calls, but you really can't help others if you can't help yourself first, and I had my own demons to beat out of me.

"So it was Kay and Robert, my adoptive parents, and my sister, Jenny, and me, in the flat little town of Skillen, Illinois, where I was one of only three nonwhite kids in my elementary school. I went through the usual troubles transnational adoptees go through, feelings of abandonment, the inability to fit in anywhere because I wasn't blue-eyed and blond-haired like my family, nor was I Korean, since I didn't speak the language and wouldn't have known kimchi if it hit me in the face. I felt inadequate most of the time, that there was something wrong with me. It all comes back to the inescapable fact that I shouldn't have been born. I know that sounds cruel, but it's the hard truth for anyone who's an adoptee. Yes, your mother chose to have you instead of aborting you, but that's because she didn't have the guts. You and I, Kevin, are the products of fear and regret.

"Kids made fun of me, of course, as kids do. Running up to me with fingers pulled at the corners of their eyes, telling me my hair looked like a dirty mop. Big sister Jenny did her job, protecting me as much as she could, but she couldn't always be there, and soon she had her own problems to deal with.

"I don't want to tell you what I'm about to tell you. I just don't. It's what I'll be working on for the rest of my life, to move beyond this, though really, it isn't possible. Because you can't unsee what you've seen, you can't unhear what you've heard. When Jenny turned twelve, her father, our father, started touching her inappropriately. It was subtle, the way it began—a hand that lingered on her shoulder, then down lower to her back, a hug that felt a little too close. It might be unkind to call our mother an idiot, but that's what she was. A homemaker who only saw goodness in people, she never saw her husband as anything but the most perfect human being. They'd met at some sort of Jesus camp, and they were devout Christians. My father was a salesman for a tool company, and he was extremely good at his job. The few times I've revealed this part of my life to people, they've all asked the same question: How is it that someone like him could qualify to be an adoptive parent? The screening process has become more rigorous since the '70s, but I still think no agency today has a chance against the charms of my father. I never did understand why he ended up with my mother, when he could've talked any woman into marrying him. Maybe it was that she adored him so completely. Or maybe it was because he knew with her, he could get away with anything.

"He started coming into our room at night. Jenny and I shared a large bedroom, but even if it had been the size of a football field, it wouldn't have been big enough for me not to know what was going on. Neither of them uttered a single word, which amplified all the terrifying sounds of sex: the top bed sheet sliding off, wet kisses my father would plant on my sister's body, the squeaking of the mattress springs as he violated her again and again. I squeezed my eyes shut and pretended to sleep, and I'm positive that my father knew that I was pretending. Not that I had anything to worry about, as he never laid a hand on me, not once, not ever. Not that he didn't want to—as I hit puberty, I could feel him, his hunger. And yet on the nights he sneaked into our room, it was for Jenny and never me. Why was that? Was it because I was adopted, that I wasn't actually his daughter? Shouldn't that have made me an easier target? At some point, I convinced myself that he'd made a deal with himself, that if he could keep away from me, he was saving himself in some small way.

"Is it wrong for me to wish that he did touch me? Because that's the truth. That's the hideous truth that I've kept locked away from myself until I was finally able to face it. Norman says it's a variant of Stockholm syndrome, where the kidnapped eventually comes to love the kidnapper. I wanted my father to fuck me. I wanted him to want me the way he wanted my sister. It's sick, and now it must be clear to you why I ended up in the sex industry. So many girls I've met in this business are damaged, and I'm no different. Why would any woman with a normal upbringing want to lead a life where she gets fucked by strange men, having her cunt filled with foreign cocks, foreign objects, while other men direct cameras and boom mikes to record the close-ups of her penetrations, to capture the sounds of smacking flesh and the ridiculous screams of fake orgasms? Sex is natural, but pornography is not. In order for us to make the sexual fantasy come alive on the screen, we have to be dead inside. There is something deeply wrong with me, and there always will be.

"Life is strong. You can go on, you can forget about the night when it's morning. After a while, things fall into a pattern, and getting raped by your father is just something else that happens. Jenny and I brushed our teeth and took our showers and ate breakfast before we went off to school, until one day, my sister didn't come home.

"There's a walking bridge in our town, one that doesn't rise above a rushing river but rather a cavernous crevasse. It hangs over what used to be a limestone quarry, and it's one of the quietest places I've been. There's one part, not the deepest point but near it, that's pitch black except for two minutes each summer, when the sun is at a certain height and angle to make it shine like a bed of stars. Jenny and I had been there many times on cloudless days, waiting and watching for that brief moment when there was light in that darkness.

"That's where the police found my sister's mangled body the next morning. She left no note, though it was obvious to me why she'd climbed the six-foot railing and thrown herself into the abyss. A day after the funeral, I packed up a suitcase and hopped on a Greyhound bus to Los Angeles and haven't been back home since. Once a year, I call my parents, though I don't speak to them. I don't know why I do this. Almost always it's my mother who answers, and occasionally it's my father, but in either case, I just listen to their repeated hellos until the eventual hang-up. Once, just once, he'd guessed right. This was a long time ago, just a couple of years after I'd left. He said he was sorry that Jenny died and that I was gone and that he wanted to make things right, but no matter how much he begged and cried into the phone, I said nothing.

"Maybe I'm waiting for the number to be disconnected, or for someone other than my parents to answer. Maybe I want them dead, because then I can move on for good, though it's not like I pay them any mind. Maybe I miss them, and this is the best way for me to deal with what's happened to my life. I don't blame my father entirely for the path I've chosen. There are women who are sexually abused at an early age, who don't turn into strippers or whores or porn actresses— all the jobs I've held to survive in this world. I don't know why I wasn't strong enough to build a regular life for myself. This is my life, and I have to find ways to accept it. To accept what is, because in the end, that's all that we ever have.

"The oven timer's about to ring, and the dish we're about to have is best served hot. I just want to tell you one more thing, not about me but you. Kevin, I know you're very hurt that you just found out about your adoptive past, but I hope you can also see how fortunate you were by not knowing. I see it as a gift from your parents, not a sin they've committed. With me, it wasn't a possibility for me not to know, but your adoptive parents saved you from what every adopted kid feels at one point or another: that they don't belong. No matter how much love they may be showered with by their adoptive family, that core sense of abandonment never leaves. What you sense now is betrayal, which isn't exactly a cakewalk, either, but oh, Kevin, what I would give to feel what you feel instead of the hollowness that has lived inside me since I was a little girl.

"Obviously my view of your situation is biased. It may even be wrong. But it's the way I feel and I wanted you to know. And now, let's eat."

Denise called it "the big pancake," though if it were up to Kevin, he would've named it a "walled pancake." The batter had climbed and risen above the rim of the iron skillet, forming a brown buttery crust that was flaky and light. The pancake itself was thin and moist, and after she had squeezed half a lemon and sprinkled powdered sugar over it, it was sweet and sour perfection.

"This is extraordinarily good," he said.

"Thank you."

"And I'm so sorry about—about everything. You haven't had an easy life."

"There are people worse off," she said, neatly cutting off a small triangle of the pancake. She picked it up like a miniature pizza and nibbled on its pointed end. "But thank you. I'm not one of those people who get angry at pity, so if you feel like pitying me, go right ahead. I can always use all the good wishes I can get."

"I find it heartening that you've survived and that you keep on surviving," Kevin said.

"Now if you call me a hero, that—that might piss me off."

"Then I'll be sure never to call you one."

It was entirely too delicious, especially when she brought out a jug of maple syrup.

"Now that's just not fair," Kevin said.

If it took Denise half an hour to make the pancake, it was gone in five minutes.

"I'm glad you enjoyed it," she said. "There's something deeply satisfying about seeing someone eat your food. I'm fairly certain it's a basic mothering instinct that kicks in."

"Have you ever thought about having one? A kid?"

Denise used the last bit of her pancake, a strip of crust, to wipe and soak up the remains of the brown syrup. "I'm past my expiration date, so to speak."

"Not really. Even women in their fifties have kids nowadays."

"Courageous women. Or rich women. Even if I were younger, no, I don't think so. It still surprises me how so many people do end up having children. I suppose I should be thankful, because if every woman were like me, we'd die out as a race. What about you?"

Kevin shook his head. "My ex-wife didn't want any, and I was fine with that. Considering what's happened to us, it was the right decision."

They cleared the table together, and in the kitchen, he washed while she dried.

"I like talking with you," she said.

"Me too."

At one point, their arms crossed paths, their skin touching, sliding along in a way that surprised them both, making them whip their limbs back to their sides. They looked at each other and laughed, and then she was in his arms, his back pressed against the warmth of the oven, and then a kiss, a tentative pressing of her lips on his own. This time they literally jumped away from one another, the water in the sink in between them, the drain glugging and burbling like someone quenching their desperate thirst.

They both reached for the faucet, Kevin turning off the hot as Denise shut off the cold. Usually he knew when he liked a girl, knew it right away. That's how it had been with his first, and it was how it had been with his last, Alice. But this was different. Denise had somehow snuck in, gotten under his subconscious, and it disarmed him.

"Well," she said.

"Well, indeed."

"That was weird."

"But not as weird as if you were my sister."

Then they were laughing again, and this time, they couldn't stop. When was the last time Kevin had felt this kind of unabated, primal rush of humor? Years. Maybe never. He couldn't catch his breath, his diaphragm was in spasms, and he wished it would never end.

"God, it hurts so much," he said, and they laughed even harder and kept on until they saw Norman standing in the doorway between the kitchen and the back hallway.

"Please, don't stop! I've dreamed of this, and now it's come true. My two children, my two happy children." Without warning, he crushed Kevin with a hug, squeezed the air out of his lungs. "This is my patented hug that I give to all my clients, and now to my son, too."

Looking over his shoulder, Kevin looked to Denise, who shrugged sheepishly. So she hadn't told Norman anything. Tomorrow Kevin would be leaving, and a part of him wanted to tell Norman off, but Kevin had to admit, what Denise had told him did make sense. He probably was lucky that he had discovered his adoption at an age where it didn't make much of a dent in his personality or his psyche, and maybe there were worse grievances than his birth father wanting to please him so much that he fabricated a sister. Kevin could just walk away, the way Norman had walked away from him when he'd been a baby. Logically, the equation balanced out, but emotionally, not so much. Here was a better calculation: Kevin was the one who'd been given away to be adopted, and now it was Norman's turn to be taken in by Kevin.

"I don't want you getting jealous now," Norman said, and he unclasped himself from Kevin and embraced Denise.

"Let's all go out to dinner tonight, huh?" Norman said. "My treat. We'll go to Betelnut. It's a great Chinese fusion place. They brew their own beer, and the calamari is outrageous." He offered a hand to each, and Kevin and Denise took them. "I'm so glad you guys are getting along so well."

"I feel very close to Denise," Kevin said, and she bit her lip to stop herself from laughing.

"That's just what I'd hoped. I'm not going to lie to you, Kevin. Nothing would make me happier than to see you as much as I can. You can always come out here, and I hope I can come out to see you, too."

"Of course," he said, then added, "Dad."

Norman's eyes filled up.

"I didn't mean to . . ."

"No," Norman said. "I hope that word will always make me cry."

Norman reminded Denise it would be her turn to be counseled in fifteen minutes, and then he took his leave.

"So," Kevin said. "Whatever happened to 'There are no lies in the Sanctuary'?"

Denise hung the skillet on the hook above the counter. "I suppose you could say it's more of a guideline than a rule."

He felt his cell phone buzz in his pocket. It was the same number from before, and this time he picked it up.

"Hello, Kevin?"

Kevin recognized the stately voice at once. "Mr. Cooper."

"Every time, I have to tell you to call me George."

"It's because every time, I forget." Which wasn't true at all. Kevin could never make himself call Alice's father by his first name unless he was prompted to do so, because he was a tall, silver-haired man best described as kingly. He always wore a suit, and even when he was relaxing at home, he wore pressed slacks and button-down shirts. He was a man of education, having been a high school principal, then serving as the superintendent of his school district, which was why Kevin always felt that George was disappointed at his daughter's selection of a jock for a husband.

"How are things in White Plains?" Kevin asked.

"We haven't been in White Plains for about three years. No, we're near Boston now."

"Boston?

There was silence on the line, punctuated by a throat clearing. "I shouldn't be surprised that Alice didn't tell you. By this point, I should know my own daughter well enough, but I suppose I still don't. Yes, she's here now, and she's not well. In fact, she's very sick."

Kevin heard the words, but he didn't process them.

"Hello? Are you still there?"

"Yes," Kevin said, "I'm here. But could you . . ."

"You heard me right. Alice isn't well, not at all, and that's why I'm calling. I'm taking the initiative to let the people she cared about know, because time is growing short. It's a brain disease. I don't know if . . ."

Kevin snapped his phone off, walked out of the Sanctuary and onto the driveway, and hurled the device with every bit of his strength against the asphalt. It burst into a hundred glittery pieces. His chest felt so tight that he thought it a heart attack, but no, it was just anger. He hated George for calling him, for dispatching the news to him without warning. It was a classic case of shooting the messenger, but what choice did he have? As he stood there with the electronic guts of the phone splayed on the blacktop, he was hard-pressed to think how else information of this magnitude could've been conveyed. Would it have made any difference if George had offered some stock bit of comfort—brace yourself, you better sit down, that sort of bullshit? No, not at all. This was a tragedy, and there was no real way to shine any light into such blackness.

Alice. His Alice. What the fuck could've happened to her? She'd always been slight, always the envy of her girlfriends for her ability to eat whatever she wanted without ever gaining a pound, but she'd been a dancer, and dancers were not weaklings. They were healthy, they were every bit as fit as tennis players, and she was going to die? She was barely forty years old. It didn't make any sense. It had to be a mistake.

But it wasn't a mistake. It was, he knew as well as anyone, how Alice would handle it. Was this why they'd broken up, because she didn't want him to witness her demise? No, it was more than that, but it had to have played a part. The only people she'd let in at this point were her parents, because she owed them. But what about him, didn't she owe him anything? They were married, husband and wife. This was beyond selfish, it was cruel.

He squatted down to pick up the pieces of his shattered phone. Denise came out the back door and walked over to his side.

"What happened? Are you okay?"

He would tell her, but not now. Right now, what he needed was to sink into this pain and sadness, drown in it, let it wash over him like some twisted baptismal waters.

27

Judy had never heard Kevin sound the way he did. It was like talking to a corpse, his voice not even monotone but no tone, nothing at all. He was not flying into Newark tonight but rather Boston Wednesday morning.

"Kevin, do you want me there? Because I can do that. We're still here at the Cape, and it's like an hour and change from Pocasset to Logan."

"Oh," he said. "Why? I thought you drove home yesterday."

When her brother had called, she had planned to tell him what was going on with Snaps, but after hearing about Alice, she figured the last thing Kevin needed was to hear that his dog was dying, too.

"Roger had some business to take care of," she lied. Roger was on the other side of the living room, on the phone with the vet. "We'll probably be here for another couple of days. But never mind us. I'm worried about you. I've never even heard of this . . . ?"

"Creutzfeldt-Jakob disease," Kevin said. "It's like Alzheimer's, but it happens really fast. There's no cure, and . . ."

And here was another frightening sign, Kevin crying to the point where he couldn't speak. He was not one to break down like this. Even when he'd delivered the news of their mother's passing, he'd managed to compose himself.

"It's going to be hard to see her, I'm not gonna lie," he said. "But no, Judy. It's between me and her. I'll manage."

After they exchanged good-byes, Judy sat back in the sofa and felt as if she'd been punched. Alice, dying. The last image of her was at the supermarket, where she'd looked as healthy and normal as anyone, but even then, she must've been sick. Had Alice known? She must have, because she'd been on her way to Boston. Judy looked at her hands, turned them slowly back and forth, like a queen's wave. Times like these, it seemed very true that human bodies were nothing more than temporary vessels formed of unreliable flesh and bone.

She made herself get up and walk over to Roger, who was sitting where he'd sat all day yesterday, by Snaps's side on the circular dog bed in the kitchen. He stroked her fur. The dog didn't look any worse this evening, but she also didn't look any better. Eyes glazed, she stared off into the distance as she lay on her side like a fallen horse. Her breathing remained shallow.

"The vet will be here in half an hour," he said. "What was that all about?"

She told him, and Roger listened. "Your brother must be devastated. From what it sounds like, he's still in love with her."

"They were married for fourteen years. And they dated a bit before that, too, so we're talking close to twenty years, half his life."

"What went wrong?"

Judy thought back to that conversation she had with Alice last Christmas on the balcony, and her determined words echoed in her ear: *If I need someone's help, it's not worth doing.* It seemed preposterous; the whole point of getting married was so you wouldn't die alone, and yet the more Judy considered her ex-sister-in-law, the more it made sense. Alice had always been a tough girl, and now she was making her toughest stand.

She shared her thoughts with Roger, and he agreed. "Everyone has their own way of dealing with death."

That's what the vet informed them when he came and listened to the faint beats of Snaps's heart. "There's not much we can do for her at this point," Dr. Gordon said, wiping his glasses. "The numbers from yesterday's blood work aren't good. Her organs are shutting down; she doesn't have long to go. If you want to euthanize her, I wouldn't argue with you."

"But it's not what you'd do," Judy said.

"No," he said. "She's not suffering, and that's the only reason I'd ever put down an animal. But everyone is different. Some people find it too difficult to bear the decline. Has she eaten anything?"

"Some kibble this morning, but in an hour she threw it up," Roger said.

The vet crouched down and petted Snaps's black and tan head. He ran his fingers down her fur. When his hand came near her grayed muzzle, she poked out her tongue for a tentative lick. "Just be with her," he said. "She's here now."

As soon as Dr. Gordon left, Judy wished they had put her down. She knew it was wrong to feel this way, which made her feel even worse. She thought back to her mother's death, how she'd pushed that awful task of witnessing her passing onto her brother while she'd stolen away to her bedroom to literally hide underneath the covers. Judy hoped that she would be nowhere near Kevin's dog when Snaps expired and felt no compunction to tell Roger otherwise.

"If you say so," he said, which she knew was his way of telling her that he didn't agree.

"I just don't like it, okay? Dying sucks, and I don't want to see it. I know this makes me a monster, but I don't care."

"You're not a monster," he said. "But you could look at what it might mean."

"It means my father didn't love me, I didn't love myself, my mother abandoned me through her death. Believe me, I've gone over it a godzillion times with therapists and gurus and swamis and transcendental spirit-guides, and it all still points to the fact that when a being goes from here to wherever the hell they go, I don't want to be there."

That evening, they ordered Chinese takeout from Lo Fatt, a place that made healthy versions of staple dishes, which meant everything tasted as though it was missing something.

"It's all sort of horrible, isn't it," Roger said, holding up a brown piece of General Tso's chicken skewered through a chopstick.

"At least we'll live longer to eat more bad food."

Thankfully, there was decent wine to go along with it, and after emptying a bottle of shiraz, they stumbled to the bedroom and crashed. When Judy awoke to a full bladder, it was still pitch black, and as she felt her way to the bathroom, she almost tripped on the figure lying on top of the bearskin rug.

It had been Snaps's favorite place to sleep, so at some point during the night, she must've crawled her way over here. Judy crouched down, terrified that she might be already gone, even more terrified when she realized that the dog was, at this very moment, straddling the mortal line between life and death.

It took every bit of strength in Judy not to run. She bit her lip as she stopped herself from yelling out Roger's name so he would be here and she could disappear, but this was it, it was happening right now, and as she heard the unnatural quickening of canine breath and the sudden shuddering from the dog's body, she knew that turning away would be an unforgivable offense to the spirit of this dog who'd been her brother's companion for her whole life. Kevin should be here comforting Snaps instead of her, but that was the idiot part of Judy's brain talking. She had to be brave, no excuses.

She placed both hands on Snaps's ribs and was surprised at the stiffness of her fur, the coldness of the flesh underneath. Enough moonlight shined from the window to see the dog's amber eyes as they focused on hers. There was an understanding in those pupils, of exactly what, Judy didn't know, but Snaps knew, and Judy wished she spoke dog, or she wished Snaps spoke English, because there was such clarity there, and then, all at once, it was gone. Snaps let out a sigh, her final breath, her release. Judy wept, and when she smelled the emptied bowels of the dog, it seemed appropriate that there was no dignity to this, that in the end, it was all shit, this life, this death, forever and ever.

Forever. What a cruel and impossible concept humans had invented, since nothing in the universe was forever, not even the universe itself. Here was the opposite of forever, this deadness underneath her fingers, and there was nothing to be done.

After her mother passed away, everyone told Judy that with time, she would get over it, that the wound would heal, but it wasn't that simple. If a cut is deep enough, it leaves a scar, and that's what Judy had now instead of her mother: this gash inside that opened up and bled. These tears she shed now went beyond Snaps. She grieved in the darkness for the woman who brought her into this world—but then something unexpected happened. Not only did Judy see her mother in her mind, but she also saw her father next to her, the two of them sitting catty-corner at the dining room table, with Kevin and Judy completing the family square. Those were the good times, together for dinner, the aroma of her mother's Korean cooking smoothing out the bumps and divots of their daily grind. For that hour, the war between Judy and her father came to a begrudging cease-fire as they bit into the falling-off-the-bone *kalbi* shortribs, as they spooned the kimchi stew into their hungry, grateful mouths.

Her father was going to be no different than Snaps here. When she'd imagined his demise with grim satisfaction, she saw him in the coffin, his black suit in stark contrast to the white satin interior, his hair combed neatly against his scalp, a red carnation in the lapel of his jacket, but now she knew she'd jumped several guns, if not the entire armory. This was death in front of her, from being to nothing, from movement to permanent stillness. When she'd taken him to see Dr. Elias last month, she'd glanced at his hands, how bloated his fingers were, nothing like the long, elegant digits they used to be. His hands were her hands, this she knew every time she picked up a pen or a brush, and it had hurt to see their transformation.

Like the good cat that he was, Momo sidled up next to her, rubbing her thigh. The Siamese feline sniffed at Snaps's nose, then laid a momentary paw on it, a gesture that seemed so human that Judy wondered if she'd imagined it. Judy rose and found the beach towel she'd brought from Kevin's house, the one that Snaps used to lie on until she'd fallen in love with the bear rug. With several sheets of wet paper towels, she cleaned the mess as best she could, scrubbed her hands clean, then tucked Snaps in with the beach towel, wishing there was something more she could do.

When Roger awoke in the morning, Judy was already making breakfast.

"Oh," he said, when he saw Snaps. "I'm so sorry, Judy. It must've been awful finding her gone."

She cracked two more eggs into the pan. She'd thought about how she would tell him about what happened last night, but when she tried to form the words, none seemed appropriate, nor entirely necessary. After all, she hadn't actually done anything but just be present for Snaps's passing, but maybe that was the point of it all, to have been conscious and aware as this being had moved from this plane to the next. Everything felt light this morning, the spatula in her hand a mere feather, the pan levitating over the flames as if it were made of clouds. As terrifying as it had been, last night was also a gift, and Judy promised herself she wouldn't squander it.

"I'll join you in five." She slid the eggs, sunny-side up, onto Roger's plate. She found her cell phone in the living room and clicked through her list of outgoing numbers until she found it, Dr. Elias at the University Medical Center of Princeton.

As Judy read the arrival schedule on the giant flat screen at Logan Airport, she thought that once upon a time, she could've met Kevin as he exited the gate. It wasn't that long ago, and yet it seemed like a different world, a bygone era that should be seen through black-and-white footage. She remembered receiving him during his tour days, watching as her brother emerged from the crowd, his enormous tennis bag slung over a slouched shoulder. She'd hug him and pat him on the back, commiserate with him for being good enough to win one or two matches but no more than that. He had to win four or five in a row for the title of his satellite matches, and to her knowledge, he'd done that only once, winning the ATP Challenger event in Tallahassee, receiving a check for six thousand dollars and a gaudy trophy. That was the year he'd almost cracked the US Open, the zenith of his short career.

On the phone yesterday, he'd told her he was coming in at quarter past eleven, and there was one flight that matched. He wasn't expecting her to be here, so it would be a surprise, but she didn't think Kevin would mind. And if he did, tough tarts. He'd have support whether he wanted it or not.

By now, Roger would be halfway back to New Jersey, Momo making his infantile cries as he paced back and forth in the back seat. She missed that dark-faced cat, and she missed Roger even more. She loved him, and that was okay, better than okay, even. The lightness she'd felt in the morning was still with her, and instead of trying to figure out when the good feeling would fade, she decided to just enjoy it.

Judy had half an hour to kill, so she got a cup of coffee and took one of the stools facing the café window and watched the unending stream of people hurrying to their destinations. There were so many of them, young ones and old ones, slim ones and fat ones, and inside every person was their own individual story. Before today, she would've found this notion exhausting, but now, it fortified her. Considering the root pointlessness of human existence, wasn't it an act of courage that people did rise every morning, some even with optimism? It was a miracle that the world simply didn't explode from the collective emotional baggage of its populace.

Sipping her coffee, she thought of her father. Since finding out about Kevin's origins, Judy had mulled over the reasons why he had been so much more critical of her than her brother, a fact she never understood and therefore feared. Perhaps it was pop psychology, but wasn't it possible that it had been a form of compensation, that because Kevin was adopted, her father wanted to make sure never to favor her, and in so doing, ended up taking it to the other extreme? Or maybe it was just the irony that her father found difficult to handle, that the boy they'd adopted was more like him than the girl born from his own seed?

All bullshit, every bit of it. In the end, none of her musings mattered, because they were all just stories anyway. Life was one big story, comprised of littler stories that people told themselves to get through the day, and each day lived consciously was a victory in itself.

Judy laughed, and the woman who was sitting next to her, a tiny, shrunken granny nibbling on her coffee cake like a squirrel, said, "I like your laughter, young lady."

"Thank you," Judy said. "I was just thinking that every day is a victory."

"As someone who's been around for eighty-eight years," she said, "I can assure you that you're absolutely correct."

A heavier rush of people pushed through the hall, and Judy looked at her watch.

"Have a great day," she told the old lady as she rose. "I'm here to meet my brother."

"Me too!" she said. "He turns ninety tomorrow."

Ninety. It seemed like an impossible age, but Kevin was now forty and that still didn't seem right. In her mind, he'd always be frozen in his early twenties, the professional tennis player in his most vibrant mode, his muscular thighs like trunks of oak, the racquet singing in his hand as it swooshed through the air. The old lady and her ancient brother were two years apart, just like she and Kevin were. Judy leaned against the wall and scanned the waves of people for his face. She tried to see herself and her brother at their respective ancient ages. That would be a sight, wouldn't it? If they were lucky, they'd both be healthy enough to enjoy whatever life offered them. Maybe Kevin would still be playing the game he loved, exchanging forehands in the back court and volleys at the net, and she could be sitting with her brush poised in front of an empty canvas, ready to fill it with whatever she imagined.

They saw each other at the same time. Even from here, a good twenty people between them, Judy could feel the melancholy seeping out from him.

"Thank you," he said. He took her deep into his embrace, and she squeezed back equally hard, wishing to transfer any positivity in her through this physical transaction. She had more bad news for him, but she also had good news. Judy hoped they'd balance each other out.

28

Was this what it was like to experience a panic attack? Kevin didn't know because he'd never suffered through one, but belted into the passenger seat of Judy's car, his mind wouldn't sit still, jumping from thing to thing. The woman he loved was dying. His dog was dead. And his sister was scheduled to go into surgery next week to donate a kidney to their father.

What?

He didn't know what to do with his legs. They were twitching all on their own, in revolt, wanting to run away from the rest of his body, and really, he couldn't blame them. If he could get the fuck away from himself, he'd do it, too, gladly.

The night before he had left for San Francisco, two months ago, he had Snaps sit, then snapped his fingers above her head so she'd pay attention to his face.

"I'll be gone, but I'll be back, girl. Fourteen days at most."

From puppyhood, Alice had insisted that they do this before they left Snaps in someone else's care. Kevin had felt it a silly thing to do, since it was obvious Snaps did not comprehend his words, but Alice disagreed. She assured him his intentions, his feelings, were absolutely conveyed, and even though he remained skeptical, he'd kept up the tradition.

If Alice had been right, then did he lie to Snaps? Because he'd been gone for way longer than a fortnight, and the thought that his dog had been holding on for his promised return, waiting day after day for him to step through the door—it was too much to bear. When she needed him most, he'd failed her.

"Snaps," Judy said. He hadn't meant to tune her out, but her words had turned into noise until now. "I know it sounds crazy, but your dog saved my life."

It wasn't crazy, just insensitive. Judy was turning his beloved canine into some kind of martyr, and that wasn't fair. Snaps was an old dog, a good dog, and there were no ulterior motives to her death, as there were no hidden agendas to her life.

"From what it sounds like, Snaps is gonna save Dad's life, not yours."

Judy nodded, slowly then quickly. "Both lives," she said. "Mine and his. I know you're angry and sad, Kevin, and you'll just have to feel it until you don't, but I do hope you'll find solace in what I've told you. There is meaning in every death. I'm certain of it."

They were on the Longfellow Bridge, crossing the Charles River, a barge floating on the water, the Boston skyline to the left. The people on the bridge were bundled up and hunched against the wind. Kevin tried to appreciate what Judy was doing for him, but she wasn't making it easy with her platitudes and psychobabble.

"So when Alice dies, what's the meaning in that, sis? Please enlighten me."

"I don't know," she said. "But you will know, and that's what matters."

"Jesus Christ, will you stop?" he said. "It's very kind of you to be here for me, but please, just let it go, let *me* go. You can't make this better. Nothing can make this better."

He regretted his outburst as soon as he'd said it, because he knew it would lead to Judy getting ornery, defensive, make her twice as annoying as she attempted to sway him to her point of view—except none of that happened. To his surprise, she reached out to pat his hand.

"You got it," she said. "Let's just get you to Alice."

They continued on Cambridge Street, passed by houses and shops and parts of Harvard, an imposing redbrick church to the right that took up a block.

"I feel like I'm in some alternate world," Kevin said. "You've hated Dad for so long, and now you don't? It just seems, I don't know, it doesn't seem real."

"I still don't like him, Kevin. I'll probably never like him. But death is final, it's tragic, and he doesn't deserve it, not now, not when I can prevent it."

He watched her as she kept her eyes on the road, negotiating the busy Cambridge traffic. They were on Garden Street, and according to the readout on the GPS, Alice was less than two miles away. Judy was a changed woman, of that there was no question. He'd never heard his sister speak with such conviction, and he knew he should feel proud, but instead, he resented her. He didn't know this woman, and right now, what he needed was stability when so much of his life was crumbling down.

"I don't know what to make of you," he said.

"I don't know what to make of myself, so we're even. I'm still your sister, Kevin. Always will be."

Words meant for comfort, but to Kevin, they felt like a threat. He was on edge, and waiting in this awful traffic was just making it worse. It was early Wednesday afternoon, nowhere near rush hour, but the street was like an extended parking lot, discordant honks both near and far polluting the air. Every building here seemed to be built of the same red bricks, even the short wall that wrapped around the next block, the Radcliffe Quadrangle. They were driving by some of the smartest people on the planet, and Kevin wished to absorb their collective intelligence and make it his own. Maybe then he could figure out what he was supposed to do. Was there a single thing worth living for at this point? He had no job and no desire for one. His blood father made a movie of himself in the nude and had fabricated a sister, whom Kevin had made out with. He had stayed with a famous painter who redefined the concept of selfishness. His dog of twelve years that he raised from puppyhood had passed on without his presence or his knowledge, and now the woman he loved would be gone for good. If this had been someone else's life, he would've felt sorry for this sap, washed up at forty with misery in the rearview mirror and nothing worth looking at through the windshield of his existence.

"My life sucks," he said. "I suck."

"No argument there. It sucks and you suck . . ."

"Thanks, sis."

"You didn't let me finish. For the time being, is what I meant. We Americans have this notion that we should always be happy. It's even in the Declaration of Independence, right? Life, liberty, and the pursuit of happiness. It sounds so optimistic. I've always considered happiness like a brief visit from old friends—a great time that's over before you know it and leaves you feeling empty after they depart."

The female voice on the GPS told them to turn right, so they did.

Judy parked in front of a brownstone that stood five stories high. Alice was on the fourth floor, a number Kevin had never liked because in Korean culture, it was bad luck.

"You're sure you want to do this alone?" Judy asked.

"I don't want to do this at all."

"You don't have to."

"Of course I do."

"No," Judy said. "You actually don't. She's not your wife. We both know she cut you out so you wouldn't have to see her like this. Her dad called you, she didn't, so for all you know, this isn't even something she desires. In fact, knowing Alice as well as you do, you know this to be true. You have a choice, Kevin. We always have a choice."

"But this is ridiculous. I'm right here. I flew from the other side of the fucking country to see her."

"She doesn't love you," Judy said, and the words sliced him in half. "She did at one point, but not anymore. You know this, too."

Kevin placed a hand on the door handle. "I can't believe you're the one who's telling me this. You of all people."

"What does that mean?"

"Have you already forgotten what you were like before you met Roger? You were more married to Brian after your divorce than before. You were broken, sis, and I'm glad your new man has put you together again, but if you haven't noticed, I don't have a Roger, okay? All I have is Alice."

"But you don't," Judy said.

Kevin closed his eyes, wishing everything around him would just go away and leave him alone. "I've tried, Judy. I've tried to put her out of my mind, but she's still here, inside me. What if I can't? What if I want her for the rest of my life?"

"Now," she said. "You start right now by walking away from here."

How could his sister be so cruel? Alice was dying up there. If he didn't see her now, he'd never see her.

"I don't see how I can do that. It's not human."

"Then let me do it," Judy said, and she cranked the car's engine. The car started crawling forward. "All you have to do is just sit there."

"Judy . . ."

"Start counting, whatever you see. It'll help."

One tree, two trees. One house, two houses. One block, two blocks. He was letting go of her, of his old life—but no.

"Stop the car," he said.

Judy sighed and pulled over.

"Well," she said. "It's a start."

She offered to take him back to the front of the brownstone, but Kevin told her to stay. He could use the walk. The day was cold and gusty, a clammy thickness in the air portending autumn rain. He zipped up his windbreaker as far as it could go and tied the hood tight around his head. On the street and on the sidewalks in front of each house were piles of leaves, brown mounds wet from the previous night's storm, looking like miniature Korean graves. He'd never seen one himself, because in the two times he'd been to Korea, he'd spent them in the concrete city of Seoul, but he'd seen pictures, giant grassy hummocks that contained the body of some long-dead royal. Would Alice opt to be buried or cremated? They'd never talked about it, but that wasn't a surprise. People often called communication the cornerstone of a good marriage, but Kevin thought that was wrong. It was the keystone, and once it broke down, the whole structure fell apart. It was remarkable, really, how long they'd stayed together without saying much to each other. It used to be enough that she was there next to him, and he was certain she'd felt the same way. But her body had failed her. Was that really the reason why she'd wanted to leave him? Alice had always had a rigid sense of fairness in everything they did, whether it was paying for a vacation getaway or buying a new bed, always insisting that they go dutch from their separate bank accounts. Here was the ultimate going dutch, going her separate way when she could no longer hold up the healthy half of her bargain.

But it wasn't fair to place the blame entirely on her dependence on independence. He was guilty, too. He would've wanted to dissect the treatment plan, create charts for her pills and shots, take on more than what he was capable of handling—in short, he would've driven her mad. Still, she should've given him a chance. In San Francisco, he'd done all right letting loose the leash of his life. If she could've seen him, if she had been there with him, if she were still his wife—all of them wishes, none of them true.

He approached the brownstone, loving her and loathing her. He wanted to tell her how much she'd hurt him and how he would never be right without her. The last words he'd spoken to her were whatever stupid things he'd blurted out as the elevator doors were closing at her office.

Fifteen steps to the door, five white buttons to the left of the handle: Judy was right, counting did help. His right index finger shook as he pressed the button for the fourth floor: COOPER. There was a speaker next to the list of names, but it remained silent. Instead, there was a mechanical buzz and the electronic unlocking of the latch. Kevin grabbed the doorknob and pulled it open, the rush of warm air failing to thaw him.

Alice was not well. After the initial awkward handshakes and half hugs at the foyer, that's what her mother had told Kevin. All he knew of Creutzfeldt-Jakob disease was what he'd briefly read on a website, that it was similar to mad cow disease, the brain disintegrating, loss of memory and mobility, death occurring sometimes as fast as a few weeks.

"The doctors can't tell us exactly how it'll progress," Mrs. Cooper said. "But it's happening. Sometimes she forgets who we are. Sometimes she doesn't know how to use a fork. But then for an hour she's perfectly normal . . ."

She turned away. Kevin had always imagined Alice would grow to look like her mother, but now that thought was meaningless. Mr. Cooper placed his hand on his wife's shoulder, and she leaned into him. He motioned Kevin to follow them. Kevin looked around as he walked down the hallway and paused when he noticed a book on a side table. The man on the cover was the same man Alice had posed with on the computer desktop wallpaper. *The Present Path*, by Pali.

"He's a spiritual teacher," Mrs. Cooper said. "She went to see him, after she got the diagnosis. I think he gave her some comfort."

Kevin picked up the book and stared at the author, who sat Indian-style atop a mountain peak. All this time, he'd thought this guy was some sort of a boyfriend, a rival. Pali had kind eyes, a friendly round face. He looked like someone who could help people in need.

Mr. Cooper stopped in front of a half-open door. Alice was in bed, but she wasn't asleep. She stared straight up at the ceiling, as if she could see through the off-white paint.

"Honey?" Mr. Cooper said.

They waited. She didn't move.

"Well," Mr. Cooper said. "Here you are, Kevin. You made it this far, so you might as well spend some time with her."

Kevin nodded and sat in the chair next to the bed. When the Coopers turned to leave, he felt foolish for wanting to tell them to stay. It was just a gut fear reaction, nothing more.

"I see you," Alice said.

"Okay," he said. "Do you know who I am?"

"Kevin," she said, and he let out a sigh of relief that soon segued into a sigh of disappointment. "That's what Dad just said."

"Right."

The strangest thing was that she didn't look different. Thinner than the last time he saw her, but she'd been at this weight before, years ago, when they'd just started dating. It was almost as if time were going backward, but only for her, not for him. For him there would be no easy way to forget this woman he loved. He'd have to wrestle with his memories of her for the rest of his life, and for a moment, Kevin felt such a spike of bitterness that he almost got up to leave—until he realized that he would live while she would die. The cruelty of life was on glorious display here. He took in a breath, and then another, then let it out slowly. He waited for his throat to open up, for his voice to be functional.

"How are you today?" he asked her.

"I have a little headache," she said. "But it's a good day, I think."

She was still Alice. So many mornings, he woke up and saw her face, and it'd made him so happy.

"I love you."

She met his eyes for the first time. They were so clear, so blue. How could eyes like that ever dim?

"I just wanted to say that, more for me than for you," he added.

Her slight frown lifted. "That's good."

"Is it okay if I hold your hand?" he asked.

She paused, weighing his request.

"I'll do you one better," she said, and she took his hand in her hand.

Outside, rain started falling, quarter-size drops plopping against the windshield. Kevin was back in Judy's car, having told her of his encounter.

"You're angry," his sister said.

"What?"

She pointed at his hand, the hand that Alice had been holding, now a fist.

"I had things to tell her," he said.

"I know."

"No you don't."

"You're right," Judy said. "So tell me. Say what you were going to say to her to me."

"This isn't some therapy session, Judy. This is real."

"I know, but maybe it'll help. Would it hurt to try?"

Kevin thought it might, but Judy insisted. The drive back to Jersey was five hours, and halfway through the trip, as they were crossing the state of Connecticut, the rain tapered down to cloudy skies and he hadn't stopped talking. He apologized, he accused, he took responsibility, he blamed. He started from the beginning, when they met at the chiropractor's office. Alice was waiting to get her back worked on, while he waited for treatment to his left knee, the one that took the brunt of his serves. Neither had believed in love at first sight, but they did believe in its lewder incarnation, sex at fifth date. He couldn't remember the last time they'd made love, and this shamed him. It was awful to think that he would continue to bed other women while she would be—

"Gone," Judy said. "I'm so sorry, Kevin. I don't know why we humans have this unquenchable desire to live when we're all going to die. It's just a rotten deal."

"Maybe you should talk now." He wiped his eyes with the sleeve of his shirt.

So she did. Judy told him about her and Roger's disastrous first date, the dragon tattoo that traversed his back, and about the anhedonia, too, his inability to enjoy life. As Kevin listened to his sister, he thought of that phrase she often quoted about being kind to others, because everyone is fighting his or her own battle. Inside every passing vehicle, there was at least one person who was suffering a private war of his or her own making. Why did it have to be this way? Why was it that when the world was created, when gravity and time and our planet and its primordial soup came into existence, there also had to be pain and sorrow? It was no wonder so many people found comfort in religion. Kevin wished he did, too, but it never seemed right to him, that some great being was in charge.

"Do you believe in God?" he asked.

"Yes," Judy said. "You don't?"

"No."

"I have to tell you, I'm surprised. I mean I know you go to church as often as I do, which is less than never, but I always took you to be a believer."

"Why is that?"

"I don't know. I just never thought you paid much mind to stuff like this, that you believe what most people believe."

"Because I'm a dumb jock."

"Because you're not that complicated, which is a compliment, by the way. What *do* you believe in, then?"

"Nothing."

"Dude," Judy said. "Really?"

Was that true? No, not entirely.

"I believe in us, you and me. That we're brother and sister, if not by blood, then by habit."

Judy laughed. "I am pretty used to you being my brother. We're a routine."

"And that we'll see each other through, to whatever's out there."

"Always." She licked her pinky and offered it.

"Pinky swear." Kevin licked and linked his with hers. "Now it's official."

After being away for the better part of two months, the sound of his gravel driveway crunching underneath the car's tires was like the voice of a dependable friend. When he opened the front door, even though he knew full well that Snaps would never greet him again, he heard the silence of her soundless bark, felt the barrenness of her missing furry body. Absence was as substantive as its opposite, perhaps even more so. He leaned against the door jamb as a morbid thought crossed his mind: I'm the last one left. This was no longer his home, it was just a house of sad memories, one he couldn't continue to pay for anyway, not without a job.

Judy followed him in with an armful of mail, envelopes falling to the floor as she brought it in. "Two pieces from California."

One was what looked like a card envelope, addressed from Claudia. The other was a puffy mailer, about the size of a DVD case.

"Oh no," Kevin said, seeing the name on the return address, Norman Kwon. "Not again."

"Relax," Judy said. "Maybe it's a copy of *Brian's Song.*"

"I'll bet you a million dollars it's not *Brian's Song.*"

He opened Claudia's first. Inside the beige envelope was indeed a card, and on the front was a painting of hers he recognized, the one of her as a shipwrecked alien. Inside, she'd hand-written a note in cursive so perfect that it looked like a font.

Dear Kevin,

I know you think, like most people, that the way I live seems immature, childish. But I assure you that it is exactly the opposite. To go with your true intentions no matter what—that is, in my opinion, the most grown-up thing that anyone can do. Even though I've been living this way for a number of years now, it still isn't easy. Denying your sister's works at the opening was not only difficult, it took a great amount of courage, because I knew it meant I'd lose you. But I cannot compromise my way of life, not at this point, when it is the only reason I exist. Every decision counts, however small, because it is the accrual of those very decisions that determines our fate, our tiny place in this vast, indifferent universe.

I enjoyed our time together, and it would bring me great pleasure to see you again. I do miss you, more than I thought I would. I doubt you miss me as much, but that's all right. What matters to me is the way I feel about you, since that's all that I can control. You're welcome in my house, so consider this an open invitation. If I were to come home and see you there at the entrance, well, that would be a very good day.

Claudia

He showed the note to Judy.

"She's still a bitch," she said.

"Well, yeah."

"But don't let me stop you from your budding romance. At least with her, you know what you're getting."

He hadn't thought of Claudia much since the incident at the gallery, but reading the letter reminded him of her strange and uncompromising ways. And her hair, the gloss and thickness of her locks, how she hadn't bothered to keep the gray at bay. She was right; he hadn't missed her. But now that she was on his mind, he sort of did.

"Are you going to open it, or shall I?" Judy asked, pointing at Norman's envelope.

He let her have the honor, and sure enough, it was a black plastic case with a disc pinned inside. There was no note, nothing at all but the media. It was déjà vu all over again.

"Just be glad you have one father and not two," Kevin said.

Judy blew off a layer of dust on the remote while Kevin placed the disc into the tray. The couch was full of dust, too, and a fine mist rose up when they sat on it. The side table with the New York Mets coasters, the rug with its red wine stain, the TV stand with the uneven gap between the doors—these signatures were at once familiar and distancing, as if this were all taking place in the future and that he was visiting his house that'd been boarded up.

Kevin picked up the remote. "I don't know, sis, if you should see this."

"Because it might have naked people in it? Kevin, I've probably seen more porn than you have. Do you remember that guy I dated, Barry?"

"No."

"That's because all he ever did was watch porn. We never left the house."

"This is different. It's my father."

"Don't be a pussy," she said, and she yanked the remote back. "He's just a man, like you."

She pressed Play, but the screen did not change from the blank black screen.

Hello, my son, said the voiceover, Norman. *After you left, Denise told me everything. I know I shouldn't have done that, pretending she was my daughter, your sister. You'd think that as a mental health professional, I'd know better. But I'm a human being, and when it comes to you, my son, I'm afraid I do things like this, and I convince myself that they are the right moves to make. I wish I could take it back, but of course, I can't. We can never undo the things we do. I'm sorry. I shouldn't have lied to you.*

Everything else I've said, I've meant. I want us to be closer. I have trouble elaborating my true feelings to you in person, but not here, not to this microphone. Is it strange that talking to you like this seems more real to me than if you were in front of me? I can answer that question myself. It is strange. I am a strange man. But I'm not a stranger to you. I am your father, and I'm very glad.

I was going to give this to you as a birthday gift, but I don't see any reason for waiting. I suppose it could still be your present, just many months early. So happy birthday, Kevin. I look forward to hearing from you soon, my son.

What followed was a grainy video of an outdoor park, a pink blanket on the ground. There were readouts on the bottom part of the screen: The date, 4/2/1971, and a counter that started from 1:00:00 and increased a second at a time.

"It's a rough cut," Judy said. "When I interned at the video studio way back when, I saw films like this. It's how it looks before it's mastered."

Two men carrying cables looped around their shoulders walked by, then men holding standing lights. A large camera rolled by. Then there were people dressed like pirates, men with their three-point hats and swords hanging off their belts, a trio of topless women. There were shouts, then suddenly, the light went out.

They waited two minutes, then three.

"That's it?" Judy asked.

"Maybe we should fast-forward."

But they didn't have to, because the lights came back on, and a female voice cut the silence.

Norman?

Right here, love, Norman said.

The camera shook, then zoomed to the blanket until it filled the frame. Two naked figures jumped on it, and even though the picture wasn't perfect, the woman was instantly recognizable.

"That's my mother," Kevin said.

"How do you know?"

"Looks just like her," he said.

Judy paused the video and examined the centerfold picture on the table. She looked back and forth, comparing the two. "Yup," she said.

"It has to be her, because that's him, Norman, forty years ago." Frozen with his arms extended like a touchdown pose, he was in his physical prime, lean and muscular.

Judy pressed Play, and it was obvious where this was going.

"Oh God, no," Kevin said.

His mother lay down on her back, and Norman mounted her missionary-style.

Are we rolling? she asked.

Oh, it's rolling, baby, it's rolling, Norman said.

They went at it like the kids they were, thumping away amid unrestrained laughter that soon turned into a steady pair of moans.

"Look at the date, Judy," Kevin said. "That's around nine months before I was born. He saved this video for my birthday. Like a present? Jesus."

Judy looked at the centerfold picture once again, then stepped away from the couch to get a closer look. Now the two on the screen were doing it doggy-style, the woman facing the camera as the man thrust from the rear, disheveling her wild hair.

"Please just turn it off," Kevin said. "I can't believe he thinks this is—well, no, I guess maybe I shouldn't be surprised."

Judy paused the screen again, then advanced the frame one at a time, the frozen expression of Kevin's young mother in ecstasy fractionally progressing, her mouth opening and closing and opening again.

"It's not as if he's earned your trust," she said.

"What—you don't think that's her?"

"It's perfect, don't you think? The date on screen, the way she's facing the camera so you can really see her. Fool me once, shame on you . . ."

Fool me twice, shame on me. Sad to admit, it hadn't even occurred to Kevin that Norman could've made this up. How naïve of him.

Judy pressed Play again, and the two people on screen were on the edge of their impending orgasms. The man let out a blissful scream, the woman did likewise, and the screen cut to black.

"I don't know," Judy said. "But you know what? Who gives a fuck. If it's true, then you just saw something almost no one sees, your own conception. Which is kinda cool and gross at the same time. If the video was fabricated, then Norman spent a lot of time and probably some money making that for you. Either way, he must care for you an awful lot. And isn't that what matters in the end?"

Kevin stared at her. "Is it?"

Judy went into the kitchen and found two tumblers and a bottle of scotch. She poured a double in each.

"I haven't a clue, Kevin. But I do know this."

She clinked her tumbler to his and raised her glass.

"Happy early birthday, dear brother. And many more."

SATURDAY

•

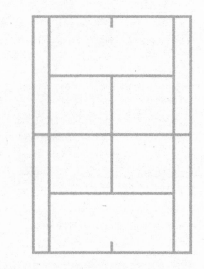

It was a beautiful day, in the high sixties and deep blue skies, an unusually warm afternoon for November, so much so that the tennis match was moved from indoors to out. The courts at this swanky tennis club were nicer than most of the satellite tournaments Kevin had played at, even featuring a concessions stand with a full bar. Alexa would be on the show court, with four ball boys and a complete set of line judges, because her opponent was the first seed.

"I don't like it," Alexa had said when the official informed them of the change in venue, spinning her racquet with so much torque that it was making Kevin nervous. He snatched it away from her before it could helicopter into a bystander's head.

That was an hour and a half ago, before the match began. Alexa's opponent was taller, bigger, and stronger than she was. She jumped lightly on her feet as they'd called heads or tails at the net. It wasn't exactly David versus Goliath, but their physical disparity was significant enough for concern. Alexa lost the toss, and it hadn't gone well since.

Many professional athletes are known to be superstitious, but Kevin never thought that was the right label. It was that they were people of habit, and it was important for them to keep everything the same, because in that way, they were in control of at least some of the variables. Winning a match required a lot of things to swing your way, especially if your opponent was as tough as this girl was. Her name was Vera, and she had a crushing forehand, one of which she hit so hard that the racquet flew out of Alexa's grip upon the ball's impact.

With the wind at times gusting at twenty miles an hour, Alexa couldn't always let loose with her backhand down the line, and it was hurting her. Last-minute court changes weren't uncommon on the tour, especially at the lower levels, so this was a good learning experience for her. And for him, too. He was enjoying this one-on-one coaching far more than he'd imagined. It was different than at the tennis club, because the game was on now, and whatever he could convey to Alexa had immediate results. Nothing quite like instant gratification.

The first set went quickly, 6–2 in Vera's favor, and Alexa was already down a break in the second set, 2–3. Because on-court coaching was now allowed by the WTA at non–Grand Slam events, it was allowed in junior tournaments as well.

After taking a long drink from her water bottle, Alexa walked over to where Kevin was sitting, in the front row of the bleachers. There were perhaps two dozen people in the stands, mostly family and friends.

"Can I blame this on you?" She adjusted the strings on her racquet.

"You can, but you're the one out there, not me."

"Really? Can you impart some more brilliant nuggets while I'm getting my ass handed to me?"

"I'll tell you a secret. You don't have to be perfect. Not every shot you hit has to be a winner, and that's what you're doing right now. All you have to be is better than the person across the net. Not always, even—just today, for the next ninety minutes, enough to win."

She heard him, every word, and understood. Whether she would be able to execute would determine the outcome of this match, but he could see he got through to her, and that was no small thing. A lot of players in her situation would be stuck in panic mode, but she wasn't at all. She was still trying to figure out Vera's game.

"Okay, coach," she said, and she put on her business face.

The game was close. Alexa pushed Vera to two deuces and a break point, but she couldn't find a way to break Vera's serve. Alexa almost rammed her racquet into the ground but managed to stop herself, which was good because she'd done it earlier and this would've been a second violation, a loss of a point.

As expected, she played horribly on her own serve, unable to pull herself out of the disappointment of not being able to win the previous game. At love–30, she looked at him, on the verge of tears, and all he could do was clap for her as hard as he could. Seeing her go through this was like experiencing his own life all over again. How many times had he fallen into the same dark, frustrating hole?

On Monday at six in the morning, he would pick up his father and drive him and Soo to the University Medical Center of Princeton. Roger would already be there with Judy, and then the transplant would take place. When he'd asked his father about it, Kevin could see his old man was still baffled. He was thankful for sure, but no matter how many times Kevin had explained it to him, he didn't get it.

"Your dog? It die, so I live?"

"That's what Judy told me."

His father leaned back into his armchair, eyes closed.

"Life is funny," he said.

Alexa battled back to 30–40, but then she committed the worst possible sin: She double faulted to give Vera a commanding 5–2 lead.

"I'm sorry your first coaching gig has been so miserable," she said, back at his corner. She ripped off her hat and retightened its strap.

"You're still playing, right?" He pointed up at the score. "It's not over yet."

"Yes, this is true, the torture will continue for one more game."

On the other side of the court, Vera sat with two towels, one draped over her legs and the other pitched over her head, looking like a ghost.

"Maybe it's not too late for me to slip her a mickey," Kevin said.

"What's sad is that she'd probably still beat me, half conscious."

"Maybe this would be a good time to tell you how I won my only Challenger tournament."

"You've been holding out on me?"

"It's not pleasant, what I'm about to tell you. Kinda shameful, really. It took a lot out of me. Too much. I could never do it again."

"We have sixty seconds, so out with it."

"In my final match, I learned to hate my opponent enough to want to kill him. I'm not talking about having some killer instinct bullshit. I mean really kill. Murder. With every stroke, I envisioned hurting him. Blood, bones, all of it."

Alexa looked at Vera, then back to him.

"Interesting," she said, and something both controlled and animal flashed behind her eyes. She was about to walk back but stopped.

"I'm sorry about Snaps, by the way. I never got a chance to tell you."

Just the mention of her name poked the wound inside him.

"Thanks. I wish you could've met her."

Alexa took her racquet and tapped his head lightly with it. "You're too young to have a senior moment. You brought her to the club before one of our US Open bus trips."

And just like that, he did remember, and it was so clear in his mind that it felt as if Snaps were right here. He'd brought her in because his pet sitter had canceled at the last minute and one of the women who manned the desk said she'd take care of her for the day.

"You threw two tennis balls to Snaps at the same time, and she just froze, not knowing which one to go for," Kevin said. "It was years ago, seven or eight? You were just a little girl, and Snaps was a big dog, but you weren't afraid of her at all."

"No," she said. "She was your dog, so I figured she was all right."

Time was called, and Alexa headed back to the baseline.

"Kill," she said, and she meant it.

Jesus, did he just create a monster? Or perhaps a future Wimbledon champion?

On Tuesday, he was to meet with a real estate agent to put the house up. Next month, he promised to travel to San Diego with Alexa for her first USTA match, the sixteen-year-old division tournament that would feature some of the top players in the country. It was possible he'd see Claudia again, and the prospect of that reunion filled him with not exactly a pleasant sensation, but not an unpleasant one, either. What he felt was anticipation, the possible, the unknown future. He'd purchased an open-jawed plane ticket. His family was here in Jersey, but it would be okay if he were to leave for a while. They were in good hands. They were in each other's hands.

A cheer roared through the sparse crowd. From the south entrance of the court, Judy saw her brother rise up and clap, then raise his fist in the air.

"Fifteen–forty, double break point for Alexa," she whispered to Roger. "If she wins the next point, then she's a step closer to being back in the match."

Judy was late, but this time it didn't matter, because Kevin didn't know she was coming.

"What are we waiting for?" Roger asked. They were standing by the steps leading to the seats.

"It's customary to wait until the game is finished to sit. Can't disturb the players' concentration with noise and such."

"But that other girl—she's grunting like she's having a bowel movement every time she hits the ball."

"It's a strange sport," Judy said.

The next point was a blur, Alexa's opponent firing a serve to her backhand and Alexa drilling it down the line for a winner. This time, Kevin had company as many others stood up.

"Let's sit over here," Judy said, pointing to the empty row in the back. "Just for a bit."

Kevin was on the other side of the court, and Judy watched him as he studied the game in progress. Sometimes his right arm jerked, his body still trained to respond to the ball. For as long as she'd watched the game, she saw her brother from afar. It was strange to be at a tennis match and not have him down there, twirling his racquet twice in his hand before receiving a serve, springing to the net like a coiled panther. But that was years ago, when their father was healthy and their mother was alive. Judy let the nostalgia run through her like water.

Another burst of applause, and the score was tied 5–5.

"One more and she wins?"

"You have to win by two when the score goes to five. Or if it goes to six–all, then they'll play a tiebreaker to win seven–six." Roger didn't know much about tennis, but he was learning.

She was learning, too. Learning to love this oddball of a man, learning to accept her father, learning to become an artist in her own time. Yesterday, she'd called Cody, the gallery owner in New York who wanted to show her works after Claudia's rejection.

"I think you're nuts," Cody had said. "You know my gallery is hot, right? You've Googled me, girlfriend?"

Judy laughed. "I have, and I know, and I really do thank you for the offer. I have every intention for you to see my stuff when it has nothing to do with Claudia X or anybody else. I want to do this right. I want to do it on my own merit."

"The road not taken," Cody said. "I get it, I get it. I still think you're wrong, that this business, like any other business, is about timing and who you know. But I respect your wishes, Judy Yoon Lee. And I fully expect to hear from you again."

And he would, when she was ready. But for her to get there, it would take more than a few weeks, or even a few months of work. For the first time in a long time, she felt hopeful about what lay ahead of her. Maybe none of it would work out. Maybe she'd end up going nowhere, but she was going to try.

"Yeah!"

It was her brother, jumping out of his seat again, raising both hands in the air. Alexa had stormed back to win the set 7–5.

"Okay." Judy patted Roger's leg. "Let's go."

Kevin was talking so intently to Alexa that he didn't even notice Judy and Roger approaching. Judy liked seeing this side of him, the mentor, a notepad in hand, a pencil stuck behind an ear. With the baseball cap, he looked like an athletic scholar, and it fit him nicely. It looked like a life he could grow into.

"Judy!" Alexa said, looking up from the court.

"Great set, Alexa."

"Hey, what are you guys doing here?" Kevin asked.

"Came to see the match," Judy said.

"I'm good, Kevin," Alexa said. She slapped the strings on her racquet and walked away.

"Serve into her body," he said after her. "It'll throw off her timing."

Judy sat next to Kevin, and Roger sat next to her. Flanked by the two most important men in her life, there was no other place she wanted to be.

"I'm surprised to see you here, sis," Kevin said.

"That was my intention. You don't mind?"

"Of course not. Did you catch the last set? Alexa's been pretty fierce. She has a real chance."

"All tied up, one set a piece. It's a brand-new game."

Kevin and Judy watched the ball boy offer two balls to Alexa. She considered both, dropping one back to him and keeping one to serve. She positioned her feet against the baseline, bounced the ball three times, then tossed it to the sky.

ACKNOWLEDGMENTS

Thank you, my readers: E. A. Durden, Paul Gacioch, Arun John, Ava Sloane, Dawn S. White, and Jessica D. White. A special thanks to Stewart O'Nan for his friendship, his guidance, and for making me want to be a better writer.

Thank you, my bosses: Tiphanie Combre and Sterling Norcross.

Thank you, my agent: Anna Ghosh.

Thank you, my editor and publisher: Rolph Blythe and the rest of the fabulous Counterpoint team.

Thank you, my copyeditor: Mikayla Butchart.

Thanks to the authors Legs McNeil and Jennifer Osborne, who put together *The Other Hollywood: The Uncensored Oral History of the Porn Film Industry*, Timothy Greenfield-Sanders's *XXX: 30 Porn-Star Portraits*, and John Bowe, Marisa Bowe, and Sabin Streeter, who edited *Gig: Americans Talk About Their Jobs*. Their books were invaluable during the research phase of this novel.

Thank you, John Greenwood, for creating *The Dream*, and Gaela Erwin, for your disarming self-portraits. If some of Claudia X's works resemble yours, that's because they do.

And finally, thanks to my family and friends, near and far, who've always supported me.

ABOUT THE AUTHOR

SUNG J. WOO's short stories and essays have appeared in *The New York Times, Guernica/PEN,* and *KoreAm Journal.* His debut novel *Everything Asian* won the Asian Pacific American Librarians Association Literature Award. A graduate of Cornell University with an MFA from NYU, he lives in Washington, New Jersey.